A WAVE OF LIONS

A WAVE OF LIONS

THE COMPLETE SALT SONGS TRILOGY

JAY REQUARD

Charlotte, NC

FALSTAFF
BOOKS
WWW.FALSTAFFBOOKS.COM

THE ILLUSTRIOUS CONTINENT OF JUUT

500 Miles

The Hyader

Pearl Coast

Edena

Aranth

Zelo,
the Slave City

Gypus

BRYNTHIA

Reina

Hom

LAGLOS GAHULLAH
UNIFACTION

GRAND
EMPIRE OF
GYPUS

Shem

BELIT

Tolia

Cortith

Kus

Tolivius
the Dead City

Panther Tri

ETERNAL
EMPIRE
OF LATIA

THE
DEADLANDS

Anlako

Thessalo

TERRITORY
OF GYPUS

Laconia

Cyrus

Lower Sava

The
Eschan
Ocean

Bricto

TERRITORY
OF LATIA

Herkus

Gorgo

Kwant

Calia

Lethe

Hyser

The

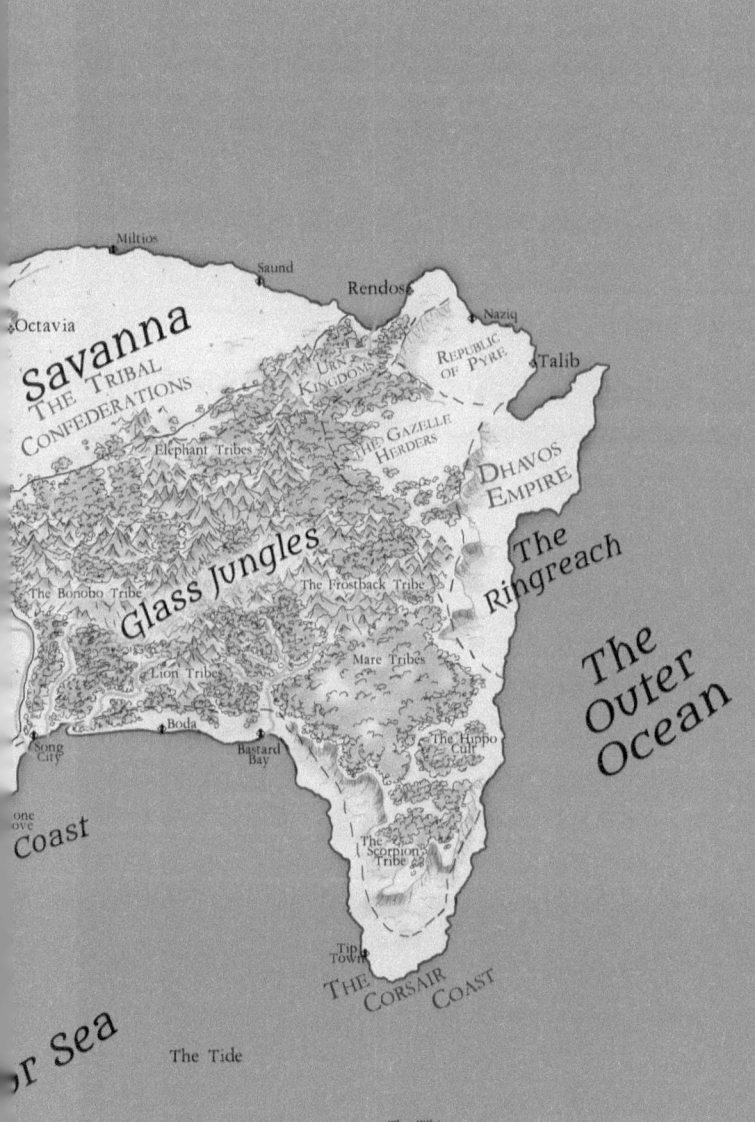

Miltios

Saund

Rendos

Octavia

Naziq

Savanna
THE TRIBAL
CONFEDERATIONS

URN
KINGDOMS

REPUBLIC
OF PYRE

Talib

THE GAZELLE
HERDERS

Elephant Tribes

DHAVOS
EMPIRE

Glass Jungles

The
Ringreach

The Bonobo Tribe

The Frostback Tribe

Mare Tribes

The
Outer
Ocean

Lion Tribe

Boda

The Hippo
Cult

Song
City

Bastard
Bay

one
ove

Coast

The
Scorpion
Tribe

Tip
Town

THE
CORSAIR
COAST

r Sea

The Tide

The White
Rovers

For Charles R. Saunders, author of Imaro and so much more
1946-2020

PART ONE
THE CURSE OF SHALLOW BAY

CHAPTER I

GODS OF WAR ARISE

Ngala stared hard into the darkness of the ship's hold, his men on the benches as they stroked the oars in time, dark faces set to their dire task. Taken by a madman's grin, not even the ache in his knees dimmed his satisfaction, their desires unified for the grim work ahead.

The ocean answered to each pull they made, roaring as it rushed beneath the ship's keel. He got the attention of the timekeeper standing on the wide platform a few feet from the stern-side steps, who turned in perfect time with his drumming, eyes bright in the gloom.

"Hail, Captain," said Nkuku, his beater rapping the goatskin. "Ready to drop sail?"

Ngala gave the man a firm nod as he watched the rowers, their display hypnotic. Everything came down to timing on the Mirror Sea, her shining surface an illusion for those who did not know how to keep seconds by the sun, stars, and waves—unfortunate sods who often ended up dead for such ignorance.

"Strike the benches the moment we wedge the sand. Only release the second and third banks when the last of the raiders clear the deck."

"Bring me some coin, and I'll have the deck swept by the time you get back," Nkuku said.

Grinning, Ngala nodded to the timekeeper's blessing before he ascended back to the top deck, his raiders already arranged in their arrowhead formation on the boat's flat boards. They shouted prayers to the starry sky above, to gods old and beyond, begging attention to the glories and treasures they would claim this night.

At the point of their two slanted columns knelt a tall and sinewy youth painted in streaks of green and white, calling louder than the rest. His grim face revealed by heavens' small lights, he bashed the iron head of his short spear against his hide shield, leading the call-and-response.

Satisfied with Tausi's management of his troop, Ngala looked on ahead as he backed to the steering oar.

Over the bow rose a misshaped line of starlit sand. Not far beyond lay the sprawling piers of Boda, a busy port despite a populace of no more than a few hundred with a garrison too paltry to worry about if the word was right. Ruddy light slit open the roofs of the nighttime markets, bonfires and torch-lanes so bright he knew no watcher would see *The Gamka* coming. The trireme cut through the water, driven onward by the rowers toiling beneath Ngala's feet and the mud-green sail filled by the night wind.

A lone figure manned the lifeline of the ship's steerage, the long wooden handle controlling her tilt and turn. A tall and striking image, the broad-faced Zaki set course ahead at the target, a fierce smile carving her smooth face apart in a lioness's snarl.

Confident in Zaki's poise, Ngala returned focus to his destination in dark satisfaction. The salt in the air on his scarred black body clung blessings upon him, fueling the bloodlust hunching him forward. He squeezed the shaft of his spear. A sword hung heavy at his side, begging to be seized.

He glanced to Tausi. The boy laughed like a hyena descending on prey.

The Gamka drove toward the midnight beach, the sail billowing in the last few moments before a pair of raiders struck the cloth, leaving the rowers beneath to power the trireme's charge. Supported by the tide propelling them landward, the extra push created by their collective strength nearly doubled their speed. Knowing the might of his ship's bronze rostrum, her lion-faced ram, he watched the faded line of pale coast inch closer, growing larger and larger and larger...

The trireme furrowed the earth before the sand stopped her with a booming thud.

Ngala leapt overboard with his forty raiders and landed on the beach, sprinting hard for the outlying line of tents, their striped fabrics bright waypoints for plunder. Eighty of the rowers followed next, armed with javelins, slings, and sacks. The corsairs, each a veteran of Ngala's raids, ran headlong into the stalls, carving their way past whoever rose to stop them. Most vendors fled at the appearance of their painted attackers.

The Latian guards, many young sellswords unprepared for sudden battle, stood in shock as the first bodies struck the pavestones. Ngala went at one of these armored men, piercing his throat. He withdrew his bloody spear in a quick jerk, darting to the side for the nearest table, letting his nose lead him to the heady musk of a wine stall. Bottles lined a long bench, neatly laid out for the picking.

He called high and loud for a rower, knowing one would appear and fill his personal loot sack. Ngala visited the herbalists next, opening the belly of the man that had stayed behind to protect his wares. He quickly studied some of the more potent mixes when his daughter appeared.

"Faster than the last raid," Zaki said, hardly out of breath from her dead sprint to him. Tucking away opium, cannabis, and some gentler things for pain, she took her place beside Ngala as she filled his bag. Solid and upright, her ebony hands moved with perfect grace. "Either I'm getting faster or you're slower."

Her hair shaved close to the scalp, he noticed she had done nothing to distinguish herself from the other crewmen, deep in their rapine. Ngala grunted at her handsome smirk. "I'll keep up."

The corsairs clawed into Boda, robbing until a horn sounded from the beach when Nkuku called the return. The rowers who stayed behind with the boat had pulled the ship back into the surf and turned her about in the water, doing the work usually required by men twice their number. Elongated gangplanks laid to the stern, double-layered and double-nailed, allowed Zaki's rowers on first while the raiders set fire to Boda's outlying tents.

Their bare bodies lit darkly by the smoking infernos, they danced and killed on the way back. Ngala raced alongside Tausi, cleaner than the powerful youth, who ran like a wildcat for the ship. The sight of his youngest, almost a mirror of bloody yesteryears, spurred a panic within him. His heart thundered in his chest.

Feet rattled the planks, and, after leaping over the portside rail, Ngala took his place at the steering oar and set his gore-crusted spear aside. The last few raiders pushed the trireme into the sea, clamoring aboard the moment the keel freed from the sand beneath.

"Row," Ngala shouted above the noise.

Zaki, his bosun, clambered forward just as the oars dipped into the drink. "Row before the devils catch us, Nkuku! Row!"

The wind lashed, and seeing his true foe foaming before him in the night, Ngala settled beside his oar, ready to fight the currents on his way to freedom.

Dawn peaked at Ngala's back when *The Gamka's* sail, secured to its lone arm, finally gathered the wind. Locking the steering for a westerly course, he plopped down beside Zaki after a long stay through the night. "Quiet the song," he relayed to her. She crawled away, slipping beneath deck after a series of yawns. The oars drew into the boat a few seconds later.

The world warmed when the golden sun came, and the surface of the Mirror transformed to smoke. Moving quietly over the water, the trireme sliced the lapping swells. Ngala watched the firmament shift purple-orange, the stars fading slowly to a fresh day's molten sky. The breeze's whisper dried the sweat on his bare chest.

"Did you get a count?" he asked Zaki when she came out of the hold.

"All hands aboard. We didn't lose anyone."

He glanced to her, the profile of her masculine features sharp in the strengthening light.

"We ran it perfectly, Father," Zaki said, her voice light. "I'd bet on my numbers before I bet on Tausi's."

"Fine, fine," he said. "Tell Nkuku to break out the mess. I'll bring your brother down."

His daughter disappeared into the ship for a second time, leaving him alone. He stood and unlocked the steering oar, letting the trireme come alive in his hand. Guiding his joy, he angled her slight to starboard, back toward the unseen coasts. Although he was able to travel for forty-eight hours at a time, he preferred a piece of beach somewhere, space to cook better food, and time to rest in hiding after their bloodletting, watching for patrols while regathering their strength. His eyes strayed to the water a second time.

Warm, shining diamonds.

For a corsair like Ngala, the sea's treasure was itself—a freedom rarer than gold, silk, or saffron. At sea, he was unbound, tethered only to the horizon and whatever lay in its direction.

Wakened by the sunshine, the raiders rose as one from their unrolled blankets. They stretched their shoulders and arms, bending at the knees before they marched on the hold where the first meal of the day was being made for them. Those who risked danger received the best food and two coins for each one that a rower made, and the best food, unless that rower traded with his raider-ally for a bauble or portion.

Tausi led the pack, his fierce expression searching. He kept his sword slung on his shoulder in its baldric, an unneeded thing to carry among friends. Ngala noticed the deference other raiders paid his youngest son, as they had not long ago with Zaki, before...

Before she became his daughter.

"What are you thinking, old man?" Tausi asked his father when they met. "You're staring at me again."

"I think upon things I'm proud of."

The young man smirked. "It is what you do that feeds us, Father, not your thoughts. And I'm hungry."

"Nothing wrong with that," said Ngala, holding his oar steady with his bare thigh as he worked to lock it. "I was the same, once."

"You will be again soon. Once you become Old Bones, we'll make real money—have real power."

"We're making money now."

His son's eyes, hardened by violence, met his. "Isn't there more?"

Leaving the steerage secured and the probing question unanswered, Ngala slinked into the hold. He earned a nod from Nkuku when he landed on the timekeeper's platform. "What's from the pot?"

"A few fish, cumin, salt, and a few vegetables," Nkuku reported. "I mixed some pepper and coconut milk in. Lots of pepper."

"We stole a lot of spice last night," Ngala noted as he approached his small three-man table, just out of the way of the steps to the deck. The rest of the crew, raider and rower alike, ate clustered in the hold, drinking their stews from earthenware bowls. Those on the higher benches reclined as they sought comfort after hours of work. Zaki and Tausi sat on both sides of their father's stool at his small counter, picking at their food with knives.

Ngala slipped in between them, splitting them apart. "How's the stew today?"

"Over salted," said Tausi.

"The raiders caught some tasteless fish, Captain," Zaki replied in an off-handed manner, waiting for her father to eat before she continued. "We made up for it in vegetables and spice."

"Did you tuck away my winnings, daughter?" Ngala asked.

"I did, Father," Zaki said. She raised her carved spoon and sipped, turning her eyes to Tausi in wait. She tensed, prepared to fight as they both were. "What did you think of the crew that came along last night?"

"They did well." Ngala looked to his son. "How far did you get?"

"I sighted the governor's wall." Tausi's eyes flicked between his father and Zaki, on the hunt for some unseen threat, always ready to respond with violence. "We might have grabbed more loot if the rowers had kept up with us."

"Aren't we supposed to work as a group?" Zaki shot back, eyes firm on her brother.

"I thought it a fine raid," Ngala said, patting a weathered hand on the table between them. He watched the rowers and raiders mingle in *The Gamka's* well, eating earnestly together like a family should. Children bicker, more so after a great change, but the peace eased the coarseness of the conversation. Tausi ate quickly, devouring his meal.

"I'm setting course to Stone Cove," Ngala said, spearing a chunk of fish in his bowl. "I say we sail out and turn for home past Shallow Bay. We can beach tonight, run through The Glass Belt, and make it by week's end."

"There are more places to raid nearby," Tausi reminded. "Rich ones at that."

"And yet we have more than enough treasure to count," he replied, mouth full of delicious meat. "I'd rather go home."

"For how long?" Tausi asked.

"Until our father says otherwise," Zaki answered before Ngala could reply. "It's his ship, brother."

Ngala almost stepped in to nip the growing argument when a rower on the high benches shouted, pointing out his oar hole. "Latian Navy off stern-to-starboard, Captain!"

CHAPTER 2

SHALLOW BAY

The sun had freed itself from the horizon by the time Ngala scrambled to the top deck. Its light flamed over the Mirror Sea until the waves shimmered like heated silver. His boat's course still set westward, and he spotted three orange sails in the opposite direction, their color clear in the morning.

"Get the rowers set," Ngala told Zaki, who stayed with him at *The Gamka's* rail on the trireme's starboard-stern. "Set shifts for the half-hour until the next dawn. I'll try to keep the sail on your side for most of it."

"I'll keep Nkuku playing a steady beat," she said before retreating below deck.

He looked to his youngest son standing on the portside. Tausi stared, dead-eyed in the face of their oncoming enemy. "Order the raiders to get their bows ready," Ngala told him. "I'll let you decide when to volley."

Tausi glanced to his father. "Are you planning to slow down?"

Unlocking the steering oar, Ngala searched for Juut's coast to the north, trying to place where they were. "Not if I have to." He leaned to the left, beginning the trireme's gentle correction northward. Wind caught in the mainsail, stretching the green cloth at the corners of its rigging. *The Gamka* hurried, the sea calm for the first few miles, its rhythm easy as the ship's bronze rostrum parted the waters like a knife.

The Latians turned in chase.

Zaki popped her head out of the hold, face beaded in sweat. "Banks are set if you cut sail. I had them put their clubs on their benches."

"We're not cutting the damn sail!" Ngala wrestled the steering oar. He had set *The Gamka* at an angle that would bring her close to the coast, which meant they would soon contend with the sea's morning chop. The hull had soaked in enough water to worry about sluggishness. "Get the map. I need to know where I am."

Zaki's head disappeared under the deck when the prow struck new tides, bumping the water hard. Sea spray, cold and crisp, wetted Ngala's face, chest, and hands as it washed him. He grinned when the oar in his hands started to fight again, pressured to turn west by forces only Oyla, goddess of the seas, knew the secrets of. Bare feet on the wet boards, he balanced himself to the rocking surface of his boat, knowing he had spilled more of his own blood on her than any other. This boat was his, and she would give him everything—Ngala had to show her the same.

Miles passed by, and the Latian's orange sails closed.

The wind held for Ngala, his experience easing *The Gamka* through rough tides as his raiders had belted on their quivers and strung their bows in the center of the deck. Tausi split the forty troops into three groups: one for the shield wall to protect his battery of archers, and the second and third groupings lined the rails of the boat, knelt down in preparation to face boarders if the Latians found some way to grapple onto their ship.

"Ready," shouted Tausi, pulling an arrow from his quiver. His archers obeyed, setting shafts to bowstrings. They stared eastward, squinting against the bright orb in the sky.

Zaki rose from the hold for the second time, bringing along a stack of wooden slats wrapped in a tanned cowhide. "We're dead to west."

Ngala fought to keep the boat straight. "Where's Nkuku at?"

"Ready to beat down the day if you tell him to." Zaki unrolled the bundle in her sinewy arms, laying out the ten wooden slats on the deck near where her father stood. Each slat, painted in a series of black hashes, came together to form an image of the southern continent of Juut. A long coastline built upon by thousands of years of civilization—

human or otherwise— stretched far to the east and west. A recently applied red splotch on the map marked the port of Boda.

Zaki knelt over the map, doing her best to keep the slats together. "We hit Boda at midnight."

"It's been nine hours since we left," Ngala said, the sun on the back of his shaven head.

Zaki's voice was lost as the wind shifted direction, its force buffeting against the portside bow. Ngala locked the rudder under his armpit to keep them headed north. "Where are we, Zaki?" he grunted through the effort.

"Shallow Bay," Zaki shouted back at him. "We're close to Shallow Bay!"

Ngala cursed under his breath. "Is that the closest beach?"

"It's the only one where we won't be arrested if we land!"

The wind clapped the green sail, leaving it slack as the wind failed to gather. Teeth gritted, Zaki bounded forward like a cat, halfway into the hole down to the hold. "Stroke! Stroke! Stroke!"

From the dim maw came the stirring heart of the rowers. The first double-strike pushed the oars out the trireme's flanks, the second dipped into the water, dragging against the sea current.

The third strike drove *The Gamka* with more strength than it held.

Nkuku's four-on-four drumbeat rumbled the boards, echoing beneath the deck in typhoon-song. The oars answered in refrain, their blades cutting into the Mirror Sea's surface like lightning bolts. The three Latian triremes, now a few miles off stern, began to shrink slightly, flagging on the sprint toward Juut's coast.

Ngala ordered a few of Tausi's raiders to strike the sail before it dragged against their momentum, which drew the wrathful youth back to the steering oar. "We cannot outrun them," he shouted, stopping beside his kneeling sister as she disassembled the map. "Cut to three beats. My archers will slow them."

"Go back to your men," Zaki chided her brother. "We've not the blood to spare."

"Where are we going, Captain?" Tausi asked his father, ignoring her.

Ngala looked at his son, speechless for a moment. The sun was behind them, the Latians in sight, and the chance of turning west plotted a course to a death the westerners would gladly chase them toward. "Get your men back in formation, boy," Ngala ordered. "Keep the raiders low so their bodies do not break the wind. Have a team ready to raise the sail when I find it."

"Where are we going?" Tausi asked again, a deeper note edging his voice.

"We're going to Shallow Bay," Ngala answered. The weight of those words bent his posture. "We'll lose them in the Avarice Reefs."

Nyam's orb had crested the sky's apex when Ngala let Nkuku's beat rattle the oars as *The Gamka* rode the outlying edges of Avarice Reef, shards of yellow shining like dull gold beneath the crystal blue waters of Shallow Bay. The beating sun, white and blazing in a cloudless sky, lingered hot upon the black shoulders of the deck crew, who hid in the shadows of their hide shields held above their heads. Bows and arrows rested by their crossed legs, ready for the moment they were needed.

"They turning yet?" Zaki asked, seated beside her father as she hid in the shadow of the starboard rail. Sipping from a small water gourd, she watched from afar as the raiders sat in their loose zig-zag formation, perfectly still against the assault of the sea, salt, and wind.

After hours at the rudder, Ngala's ankles creaked as he pivoted, checking over the stern. The Latian triremes had drifted into a single file in order to follow them into the reefs. Orange sails struck, they rowed after the corsairs with clean white oars. "Not yet. They're in single file, though."

"Still have to lose the first one."

He glanced to Zaki. "What's wrong?"

She flicked her strong chin in the Tausi's direction. "You know he's crazy, right?"

Ngala looked ahead to the ship's bow, where Tausi sat alone. Fixing his shield into a slanting roof to protect him from the sun, he stared out from his shadow, watching the entire deck like a sea eagle would watch the water for prey. He swept the world in expectation of a cruelty he found more than happy to return.

Father studied son for long, long moments. "No more than I was."

"But you didn't terrify the rowers," Zaki quickly replied. "Not like Tausi."

"Does Tausi really terrify the rowers?" he asked, annoyed at the accusation made toward his youngest, no matter if it came from the same blood.

"Tausi terrifies everyone." Zaki brought her focus back to her father, looking up at him with her bright brown eyes. "Nkuku even mentioned it to me."

Age settled Ngala's eyelids, closing his vision as he shook his head. "Why has no one mentioned it to me?"

"Because everyone loves you too much—we cannot wait for you to be Old Bones." Zaki's face opened in a sorry grin. "But I feel he's not the only child people are concerned with."

"Now that I do not hear."

The daughter returned to her watch of the raiders—hard, taciturn men with hard views and harder thoughts. "Wait until we get back. They will have had time to think."

Ngala sighed at his daughter's pessimism, a recent shift that had come along with so many changes. Checking the stern again, a brief chance to think on what to say, his effort petered when he noticed the Latians had shifted drastically westward, back toward the waters where they claimed sovereignty. Not far to the north, he could see the shores of Shallow Bay. The white sand beaches vanished into the immediate walls of green, the towering border of the infamous Glass Jungle.

Relief ebbed to panic.

"Halt the oars," Ngala shouted, searching for the peg needed to lock the steering oar. "Ready sail! Raiders, at time!"

Zaki dashed under the deck, shouting for Nkuku. Finally jamming the peg in its correct slot, Ngala let his hand pull away on the oar's handle, confident when it jerked out of his grip with a knock. He ducked under rising ropes as they were pulled taut, lengthening lines raised by the raiders as they prepped the sail for a light breeze from the southwest. The oars retracted into the boat, and from below came Zaki, flanked with ten rowers carrying the long poles used to navigate reefs and shallow inlets.

Both Tausi and Zaki met their father on his way to *The Gamka's* bow, the younger speaking first. "Why did they turn?" Tausi demanded to know, looking far to the south at the diminishing points of orange.

"Latians don't break off a chase unless they have to," Ngala said as he glanced over the portside bow, catching a glimpse of the rostrum cutting the water. "They know something we don't."

"Then we should turn," said Zaki.

"Or perhaps they grew tired of chasing us and decided to make for home." Tausi roared in his hyena laugh, the muscles in his face creating cruel lines. "They realized they were simply too slow and—"

The corsair ship slammed to a stop in the water, a cracking boom that deafened Ngala as he flung forward, crashing hard into the trireme's bow-post.

He grabbed enough of the sharp wood to halt the pitch overboard. Out of the corner of his eye, he saw Tausi tumble through the air, colliding with the surface of the water before flopping into the clear blue. The boy reemerged seconds later, vomiting seawater as he struggled to stay afloat.

"Check the hull," Ngala screamed to whoever listened.

Zaki darted by, leaping beautifully into the air and piercing the water in a perfect dive. Kicking to Tausi, she dragged her flailing brother to the portside. Raiders and rowers rushed to meet her, arms outstretched. Tausi fought those that hauled him from the water, thrashing as he cursed at them. Set on the deck, he slapped away all further attempts to help.

"Down sail, you fucking idiots!" Tausi reeled in rage before he settled on Ngala, who still busied helping Zaki up the portside of the prow. "What happened?"

"We're dead in the water, Captain," one of the raiders called. He pointed with his short spear over the side. "Look at the water."

Certain of Zaki's place back on deck, Ngala studied the rolling sea, noting how the trireme no longer produced a wake in the water. Thinking *The Gamka* moored on a sandbar whipped by the summer's many coastal storms, he searched and saw nothing—only endless emptiness.

Then he heard singing.

CHAPTER 3
SOUTH OF HEAVEN

O men, hear the air I sing,
 Coupled in dread and harmony..."
  Ngala did not know the song, but the voice latched onto his soul, singing of pleasures he never thought his to have—another day with his wife, a gallant rogue who had passed away giving birth to Tausi. He missed her. The rush of the wind, sweeter and cooler in memory than the summer stale breathed upon him, harkened him back to *The Gamka's* maiden voyage.

He could have it all again.

The spell spread through the crew. Weird, stupid smiles crossed their faces like jagged tears as they seized in the throes of some malady. Struggling to control their limbs, the raiders threw themselves to the deck, kicking and shouting at the glories they saw.

The voice wove in the air, each delicate note a pull on a heartstring. Ngala gripped the starboard rail hard, unsure of how he got there. Hand over hand, he pulled himself for the stern before a raider slammed hard into his back. The man rolled over the side and into the water, floundering in the salt bath before he regained the sense to swim away from the trireme, northward toward Shallow Bay's far shore.

"...come below to the green,
Forever trapped with the beast of Agony..."

Fighting the urge to leap in after the first raider, Ngala screamed helplessly from lust-ache as more corsairs cast themselves overboard. He fixed his eyes on the sea's surface, searching for the origin of this curse. Allowing his wail to deafen him for a brief second, he spotted a flash of white in the waves.

As beautiful as her song, the otherworldly maiden seemed to float on the water, as if she stood on the swells. The hot sun glistened off the tight, bare curves of her long legs and arms, the latter she held up to gather her seafoam hair. Eyes darker than ink, she looked right at Ngala. Her perfect body bared, she danced for his gaze, the words louder in his ears now.

"A curse upon Hy's brightened dreams,
The day will come to pay for lives..."

"Bbbbrrr...brrri...brine-singer." Ngala blinked a few times, wondering if she really did resemble his wife between the points when his eyes closed and reopened, unable to believe her presence. He bent forward, across the rail, and screamed a second time to get the song out of his head.

"Bow," he forced out, voice raspy. "Bow..." He had to climb over the rail. He had to be with her. He had to find this place where his failures began...

Raiders piled over the side, swimming toward their caller.

An arrow zipped over Ngala's shoulder, arching in the distance before it dropped a few feet from the brine-singer. The small splash jerked the world still as she dove beneath the water. Realizing how far he had tipped himself over the side, he threw his entire weight backward and smacked the deck hard, driving the air out of his lungs.

Zaki appeared over him. "Father! Are you hurt?"

Ngala took his daughter's hand when she offered it and let her set him right. On his feet, he leaned on the rail again, coughing for the lack of air in his lungs. The water below frothed, agitated by his raiders, who began their unexpected swim back to *The Gamka*.

He looked at Zaki. "What happened? How did you break her song?"

"I grabbed Tausi before he ran to jump off the boat. We crawled the deck to his bow. He made the shot."

Looking from his daughter to his son, Ngala focused on the intense boy standing in the middle of the deck, barking orders at his fellow warriors to secure the gear that had been knocked aside during the crash. Tausi leaned his corded body on his longbow, allowing its length to carry his exhausted weight.

"Go check on Nkuku," Ngala said to Zaki. "I'll find why we're moored."

"I'll bring up some rowers and shovels if it's a sandbar."

"Aye," he said, marching to task. "Raiders!"

His warriors, some of them veterans of over a decade, lined the deck in columns of five by eight. Those who had gone overboard remained still, unflinching as the water dropped off dark brows and noses. Tausi took his place beside Ngala, his hard eyes fixed on their men.

"I want six archers on guard at all times until we've cleared Shallow Bay," Ngala said. "The rowers will come dig us out, and we'll beach immediately to let the hull dry. Tausi will be with me."

Pressing the back of their hands flat to their foreheads in salute, the raiders hopped to the order. Their possessions were quickly repacked, and taking up their stout bows, they assumed their posts on the port-side and starboard.

"You did well with your sister," Ngala said to his son, hushed so none heard him. "A fine shot."

"I didn't take the time to aim," Tausi answered in wicked amusement. "I just pointed at the sound."

Ngala tried to match his son's grin but failed to find the venom he'd had in his own youth, when celebrating such recklessness had been natural. He reached forward, almost slowly, and patted his boy's strong shoulder. "Either way, a brave display. I shall be looking to you more after today."

Tausi left for the stern, his back to Ngala. "I shall not fail."

Paused by the earnestness of Tausi's reply, Ngala followed after a few seconds of contemplation, his responsibility to *The Gamka* next in mind. He checked the sun directly above him, certain the day had drifted past noon. The heat had built with the standstill, the scent of brine high with sweat, a dangerous smell when he knew thirst might make the men seek more water than they could spare. Moored in the middle of a bay, and with the trireme's hull soaking in more seawater like a sponge left in a basin...

He had time. Ngala placed this notion before everything else—a corsair's life was built on what they made of it.

He and Tausi met Zaki and Nkuku at the top of the steps to the ship's hold, the pair accompanied by four muscular rowers carrying ropes, wedges, and pitted shovels crusted in old sand. The ship's time-keeper fought to still the tremor in his face, full cheeks and forehead coated in rivulets of sweat. "Two men broke fingers, and one twisted his ankle during the jar, Captain. Minimal injuries, though—"

"What?" Tausi asked before Nkuku could find his words. "What happened?"

"The bar cracked one of the planks near the prow, on the portside of the keel," Zaki said, annoyed at her brother's rudeness. "The men were able to seal it with soft tar, but we need to make for the beach so I can pull the pegs and see how bad it really is. I don't know how long we can keep patching it before we have to start bailing out of the oar-ports."

"Any water get in?" Ngala asked. He kept his dread stuffed beneath the bass in his voice.

"Not even an inch fell before the boys were on it," Nkuku crossed his arms, restraining the last of his shakes. "I'll have the Rat boys check on our stores."

"Make sure they move the grains up onto the rower seats," Ngala said. "Tell them I said so if any make a fuss."

"Get us on a beach, and they won't make no noise," Nkuku said.

"Then I need to get to work." Zaki signaled for the rowers she had chosen to fall in behind her. Tools passed between the four rowers leapt over the side, dropping beneath the waves. They broke the surface seconds later, doggy-paddling to both sides of the boat. Climbing up the starboard at the bow, Zaki tied off a rope she had coiled around her torso to the corner of the rail.

Ngala and Tausi joined her at *The Gamka's* bow. "How deep?"

"Didn't touch the bottom. We must have cut through the top of the dune before the keel caught it." Hanging off the side of the trireme, calloused feet on the wood, Zaki ordered the rowers to dive down to find the bank near the dune's apex.

The first two men had submerged when a watcher shouted, "Off portside!"

A flash of green-black shot beneath the Mirror's surface, the wake of its passing manifested in an exploding string of bubbles and foam. One of the divers burst from the water. He flailed his arms, screaming before what lay beneath dragged him back down. A flower of red blossomed in the azure depths.

"Raiders to port," shouted Tausi, whipping an arrow from the hide quiver on his hip. Setting the shaft on the string he rose to full height, set his shoulders on the draw—

Ngala tackled his son into the mainmast. "Get the rowers on deck! Raiders, hold fire until you see your enemy!"

Another rower screamed from below, a short yelp choked by a gurgle. More blood dirtied the water, a new point floating beside the first as the current ripped shreds from the congealed mass. Startled by the second immediate death, the archers that reached the rail loosed their volley at the dark shape zipping toward the bow. Its shadow grew near where Zaki hung on the trireme's side, still working to assist the last two rowers out of the water.

"Fire! Fire at will," shouted Ngala. "Fire a—"

The monster broke the Mirror, its bulk emerging like a nightmare torn from mortal men's minds. A green mottled claw, giant in proportion, stretched for the leg of the man Zaki had raised onto the rostrum. Scissoring open his thigh, the weird thing dragged the rower from his grip, a fan of pulsing blood behind him. Arrows bounced off the armor carapace of its broad, brown back. The central ridge the monster's fin sliced the water as both killer and its prey disappeared. A few yards ahead, a severed leg popped out of the water, the femur snapped above the knee.

"Zaki," Ngala cried for his daughter, his voice ragged in terror. "Get in the boat!"

The spot appeared again, snapping through the water at jagged angles. He saw the monster's chittering, sharp face as it rose, tearing claws at the front. The tail, flat-fans of sharp obsidian, extended at the ends of a propelling spasm. Inhuman eyes on the side of its head glared out on a world it despised.

Several of the raiders volleyed arrows that pierced the water behind the monster's flight. A few others, discarding their bows, charged for the rail and reached over. All three grabbed Zaki by her neck and hands, ready to lift together when the nearest claw slashed opened their bosun's broad back, a jagged wound that made her screech as the flesh split apart. Flayed, she collapsed on her knees and face when she reached the deck's bleached wood, unable to contain a wretched wail. Blood splashed the boards.

Stunned for a moment by the unexpected sight, Ngala shook awake when Tausi dodged past him, nearly knocking him into the mainmast. Watching as the raiders converged on Zaki's body, both of his legs turned to honey, soft and formless. He barely felt his ass thud the floor when he caught himself, splinters in both palms.

"Get her down to the hold! Get Nkuku," Tausi shouted. "Out of the way!"

His son emerged from the mass fighting with each other to take her to the stern. The rage on the boy's face startled Ngala, who froze for a second time when their eyes met. For a moment he thought he saw Tausi's eyes flare in response. Like some bodiless ghost, Ngala wandered to the trail of blood that had leaked from his daughter as she was carried past him, the smear of where her body lay against the scrubbed wood an indelible splotch. Entranced by the gore, he looked back out at the Mirror.

The calm, undisturbed Mirror—save for the severed leg and plums of blood caught in its prism—was as it had ever been.

Tausi came up beside Ngala. "That was an Ulmo, Father." The break in his voice revealed his fear.

He glanced to his son, unable to answer. To the north, the wall of green forests burned a line of swaying emeralds tied by the smaller white line of the sand. That coast seemed so close, yet so far. To the north resided heaven and he, *The Gamka*, and his crew—his family—lay to the south of it.

"Oh, no..." he finally got out.

"What?" Tausi asked.

"We're running out of time."

CHAPTER 4
UNDER THE KNIFE

Massed at the back of the boat, the raiders watched as Ngala and Tausi approached their eyes wide with shock. The trail of red, spotted and streaked, led a path down the stairs to the timekeeper's landing, its outcropping a station for Nkuku's drum and table. The rowers who lived in the hold sat like tombstones in the gathering darkness. Their shapes were revealed by the piercing gaps of sunlight coming from the deck above them.

They sat silent, on guard as the ship's timekeeper took on the grisly role fate had cursed him with. Zaki lay face down on his table, the long, jagged gash on her back oozing a foul color. Sweat and fetid breath pervaded beneath the deck, a sickening smell that made the wound seem ghastlier. The few lamps they had, wicks in lightning glass, burned above her to light the gore-valley the monster had made of her flesh.

Nkuku worked at the ripped layers of flesh, drizzling honey into the gullies before packing them full of the healing herbs Ngala had raided from Boda. His surgeon's tools lay ready by Zaki's feet, dull and dark in the ruddy light.

Ngala stifled the shudder in his chest.

Nkuku came to him, fingers reddened. "I fed her opium and cannabis. One of them will put her out soon." The timekeeper noticed his fingers and hid them behind his back. "I can stitch her up, Captain, but I will have to tie her down. It will be painful, bloody, and I cannot be sure she will survive. Zaki is strong, but we are not on a beach, and salt air is not good for wounds. If I could gather some maggots, perhaps I could better prepare the flesh, but..."

Ngala clapped his old friend's shoulder. "What must we do?"

"We must rescue the crew," Tausi said loudly.

A gasp stabbed through every man in the crew. Ngala glared at his son. He quickly calmed his expression into the detachment required of a captain. "He's right to say so," he said. "Raiders, maintain watch with your archers. Tausi, go lead them on deck until I arrive. Alert me the moment anything occurs."

Tausi slunk up the steps, growling for the soldiers to follow him to their posts.

"We still have that leak near the keel, and we've been at sea for too long," Nkuku spat out when he and Ngala were alone. "We've three days of food if we can beach, but it will be cut if we stay moored on whatever we're stuck on."

Ngala nodded, fighting the listlessness in his voice. "The bar we're on will shift with the tide soon. It might let us go with the current."

"You better hope, Ngala," said Nkuku. "Because we've never moored on any bar like this one. These waters are infested with demons."

"Please, Nkuku," he begged, "Let's leave the gods out of this until we need them. Give me time."

"You'll always have it with me," the timekeeper replied. "But what about Zaki?"

The deeper matter assumed the forefront of his thoughts again. Ngala's panic refreshed as his eyes went to his daughter. Seeing Zaki breathe, shudder, breathe, shudder, as her drained body shivered on the surgeon's slab—he placed a hand on his quivering mouth. "Close her up, Nkuku. I'll get us to the beach by morning."

"Aye, Captain, but you'll want to go up-deck. This will be bad."

Ngala marched out of *The Gamka's* hold, his despair resigned to a hard, stony anger washed by the hot sun. Much to his ire, Tausi waited at the top of the steps, carrying both his sword and his father's. Sure he did not fall within earshot of the raiders patrolling the trireme's long deck, he snatched the offered blade from his grasp. "Don't ever challenge me in front of the crew like that again. You will wait for my word and my word alone. You will heel when I say and work when I order. Do you understand, Commander?"

Tausi stared ahead, his fierce eyes onyx. "Aye, fath—"

"Captain, boy."

The two looked at each other.

"Captain," Tausi said, the word bitter in his mouth. "Your orders?"

Antagonized by his son's tone, Ngala swallowed the daring words he wished to utter. "Have you set patrols?"

"Aye, and our fishing lines." Tausi stood a bit straighter, proud of his forethought. "I'd rather us die of thirst before starvation."

The boy's bravado forced a grunt from Ngala.

"How is Zaki?" Tausi quietly asked once they reached the mid-deck. The raiders held watch at the rails, their backs to their leaders as they searched the glistening voids around them for signs of threat. Small fishing lines hung over the sides, their corks bobbing with the rhythm of the sea.

Ngala held his hand above his eyes to block the blazing sun. "We'll give Nkuku room. Thankfully the boat is not rocking."

"It is the most amazing sandbar, then," Tausi said, changing the subject. "Perhaps we struck a part of the reef none have ever seen. They can feel like striking stone if rooted well enough."

"Shallow Bay is known on many charts all along Juut's coastal lands, and more so the Avarice Reefs, which our kind has used to lose the enforcers for ages," Ngala said, recalling old tales and bits he had traded with his corsair-lords at Stone Cove, where he would sit at the top step of Black Lizard's empire of nautical crime—The Old Bones and his Lion. He checked where the sun sat in the pale blue sky. "I'd say we have six hours of sun left."

"We need to go back in the water." Tausi steeled, his shoulders set. "I'll lead this time."

"No, I'll do it. I need you to be there for Zaki."

"The captain—"

"Has his orders followed."

Tausi gave his father a hard look. "What do we do about the brine-singer?"

"Keep a weathered eye near." Ngala continued on, exasperated by Tausi's mien. "And the other on your sister."

Exhaustion nailed spikes into his left shoulder as Ngala leaned over the starboard. His head felt like a weight on his entire body, the clear sign of thirst. The cool water below beckoned with tricks of movement and light, its transparency an illusion for a corsair's poison. Mouth dry, he worked some moisture into his throat. "Ready, boys?"

Three young raiders, one to his right and two to the left, joined their captain at the rail. Each carried their long fighting knives in their left hand, iron hooks in their right. Behind them and on their flanks clustered the rest of their troop, bows drawn toward the water.

"We're with you, Captain," the raider to his right said.

Ngala addressed everyone. "We'll dive right for the keel. First one to hit the dune, retreat back and mark the rail. The rest of us will climb up the port side. Archers, keep your eyes open. Fire at will if the brine-singer appears."

"And the monster?" asked one of the young men to his left. All three corsairs froze in the quiet, waiting on their captain for something he could not give.

He clutched the wedge in his right hand tightly. It had been a long time since he had keel-crawled the trireme's bottom, and the last time had not been kind—his shins still hurt from where the seams of planks had broken them. The sun burned his black shoulders as he threw a leg over the rail. "Pray it's not down there."

The three sat on the rail with him, their knees bent. The archers behind them lowered their bows while the others crowded in, sights set afar.

"On three," said Ngala.

"Three," the raiders intoned on the next beat, falling forward with hard dives. Their bodies shot through the membrane between sea and sky, entering a realm of hazy blue. Salt stung Ngala's eyes as he kicked, twisting in the cold currents. He forced himself below, expecting to meet the dune immediately. He panicked when the chill of *The Gamka's* shadow swallowed him. The light of the sun shone on the other side in strands of gold.

Black warmth enveloped his vision. Ngala kicked through a cloud of oily crimson, its mass a gross silk on his body. Eyes shut to keep the red out, he nearly sputtered when the rich taste of iron seeped into the corners of his mouth. When he opened his eyes again, he saw the surface of the water approaching, the silver sky beyond blocked by large, weeping chunks of dead flesh.

He emerged from the water, gasping among the body parts frothing on the waves.

The brine-singer popped from the red waters in front of him. Alien eyes looked into Ngala's, the silver flecks of her irises expanding and contracting. Blue hair framing a milk-white face, her purple lips parted.

"Oh man, hear the air I sing..."

The winds caught in *The Gamka's* sail, full and flowing as the trireme glided across Shallow Bay's widest point, with him at the steering oar, at last lord of the sea, the sun, and his time—

Ngala slashed his wedge. "Away," he screamed, at her and the images she put in his head.

The brine-singer dodged the swipe, whining a human sound as she swam away. She held her hands out to Ngala, a pleading gesture. The sorrow of the sound she made stopped him.

"There's the captain! There's the—"

"Fire!"

Arrows rained the water between them, a rare miss for corsairs trained in nautical combat. The brine-singer dipped below, disappearing amid the gore-dyed waters Ngala stewed in.

Ngala lay against *The Gamka's* mainmast, a blanket around his shoulders. The warmth of the sunset bathed his uncovered face, the first bit of relief he had felt since the raiders hauled him out hours beforehand. The archers patrolled the boat's perimeter; grim faces to the coming death the sunset seemed to promise. Nyam layered the western sky in pinks, purples, and whites, all atop a burning line that fought to survive night's descending gloom.

The stars had emerged from hiding when Tausi lumbered from the hold. His cheeks, blanched a few shades lighter, were hollow like the expression he bore. He retrieved his own blanket and plopped down beside Ngala and the steering oar, making no noise other than his breath.

"How did the closing go?" Ngala asked.

Tausi's dark eyes seemed so much darker in the waning sunlight. "She woke once. I had to tie her down so Nkuku could re-stitch her wounds after they had reopened. She kept breaking them every time she convulsed..." He let out a wounded sigh. "Her skin turned to the color of ash. She stopped breathing at one point."

Ngala reached out from the confines of his blanket and grabbed his son's bare shoulder. No words passed between them, or any real affection in a moment where a father wanted more than terror. His raiders had told him how quickly the monster had appeared, slaughtering the young men whom he had ordered to their deaths. The body parts he had arisen among had been torn from their bodies only a few moments before he had broken the surface to find the brine-singer.

A shudder passed through him. Ngala retracted his hand. "But she will live?"

Tausi remained expressionless. "We need to make for a beach."

"I know."

"There will be no sleep tonight," he said, a declaration he voiced with surprising authority. "Have you thought on what we should do about the brine-singer?"

"We took a load of beeswax from Boda," said Ngala. "I'll have Nkuku and the rowers melt some down and fit everyone for earplugs. It might help."

"I want the raiders to have theirs made first."

"Each man will be equipped when they are equipped," Ngala replied. "No man is above any other."

"Save the ones who hear her song before the rest."

His throat too dry to swallow the harsh rebuke he would have paid his son, Ngala instead rose to his feet and walked away. The plod to the stairs down to the hold felt like a lifetime to traverse. Met by the flicking lights hung above the timekeeper's table, he saw the shape of his daughter's body under a clean blanket Nkuku had placed over her. The rowers beyond watched Ngala enter their cramped world, posted on their three tiers of benches. Small red lamps guttered, gleaming dully in exhausted, terrified eyes. Many nodded to him.

The Gamka's timekeeper squatted on his stool beside his butcher's bench, still washing his bloodstained hands in a small bowl of seawater.

Wreathed in his blanket, Ngala drew close. "How is she?"

Nkuku blinked his deep eyes. Fingers dripping from his bowl, he shrugged his round shoulders. "Zaki is strong. She will make her way through this if we can reach the coast. Until then, she cannot be moved. She will need to remain tied down so she does not hurt herself when the pain comes."

Solemn against the hard news, Ngala gave no reply. He stood there in the creeping dark of his hold.

"Did you find the dune?" Nkuku asked.

"There's no dune." Resignation slouched his posture. "There never was."

CHAPTER 5
THE DAYS PASSED

Heat. Hard, biting heat.

Ngala searched the deck of his trireme while the heat bit at the edges of his mind, a headache always at the front of his skull. He squeezed his hand a few times on the steering oar's handle, unable to budge it against the stout pegs locking it in place. Across *The Gamka's* top sprawled the raiders, laid under their shields and small, converted lean-tos, safe from the sun—but not thirst.

His tongue swollen in his mouth, he climbed to his feet with huge effort, groaning as his dry joints creaked in pain.

Then the trireme groaned.

He made a dry-throated sound of derision. Every move a slow, slapping plod on the sunbaked wood, he eased down the steps at an uneven gait. On the border where the sun's reach failed to pass into the hold's stinking murk, Tausi sat, staring into the humid darkness. Their lamps snuffed, the rowers went about their business of waiting, the constant discomfort of their lot. Some played dice with their fellows, gambling small bits of what they had won in Boda while others traded stories, their bodies slicked by their collected body heat.

"You look like you're glaring at them," Ngala said.

The young corsair kept his hard eyes ahead. "We get our next water ration in an hour. I'll wait for it."

Ngala spied the timekeeper's station. Zaki's comatose form lay face down on the slab, the knots of her stitches sprouting like spiders tearing free of the ghastly wounds. The edges, smeared with dried honey, flaked black and bloody crust. "Where's Nkuku?"

"Somewhere in there with the carpenter and shipwright's assistant."

"Kangana." Ngala sighed at the news. The shipwright and he had been friends for long years, their mutual love for *The Gamka* blessed in blood, sweat, and salt through their many adventures. He had been among those who'd followed his daughter into death so willingly, never once hesitating to offer life and limb on the order—and the price was exact. There would be no goodbye, he knew, but that did nothing to assuage the twinge in his heart. "I'm sure his man will do."

"We need to build a raft that we can use to get to shore and back. Something that can withstand the monster's..." Tausi's thoughts carried him away.

Ngala licked his broken lips, his sandpaper tongue rough on the raw flesh. "We will make it, son. There's not a man on this boat that has not experienced the worst of storm, rain, and iron. They are brave."

"They are men. We are men." Tausi straightened and turned, side-eyeing Ngala. "You hear the boat. We're soaking in too much water. Time is running fast, Captain. What do we do if we have to abandon ship?"

Pain flared in his temples, the ache of a body gone too long without water. Ngala mustered some power to his voice. "Why would we do that, Commander?"

"I'm simply serving my captain," Tausi replied, haughty. "It is my place to remind the captain of all possibilities that must be considered in preserving his crew."

"Of course, you are," Ngala replied with sarcasm. "Because you care so deeply for the crew."

Tausi gaped at his father's response.

"Be clear, boy," he continued, delirious as thoughts he had held so long spilled forth. "Don't mock me with your tantrums. Everyone here is ready and willing to do their absolute best to save your ungrateful ass. Stop being a petulant child."

His youngest struggled to find his words, embarrassment and anger crinkling his nose, forehead, and mouth. "Ungrateful?" Tausi's words wavered. "You think me ungrateful?"

"I think you walk around angry and mean because you think that makes you a commander," Ngala shot at him, unconscious of his volume.

"I'm angry because I'm angry at the both of you." Tausi spoke low and tight, the words squeezed out, as if held behind his tightened lips. "We all are."

"What did you say?"

"I said *we*, Father." Tausi rose like a cobra from the step. Facing his father, the sun passing through the hold's entrance revealed his ebon flesh in full clarity, as well as the fury of his wrathful gaze. He stood against that daylight, unhindered by the lack of water, sleep, or peace. The specter of Ngala's violent youth, personified in his own blood, glared back in harsh disrespect.

He did not bow to Tausi's fierceness or pay attention to the eyes upon them. "You will remember yourself, boy."

His son did not.

Ngala towered on the edge of the step above his, relying on his tone for effect. "Now."

The younger man averted his eyes first, stalking up the steps to the deck.

"He's not you, Ngala. Not yet."

Ngala turned to the timekeeper's station in time to see Nkuku rise from the hold's shadows, his dry eyes tired and mouth drawn to a grimace. He motioned him over with a small wave to the great drum that served as a second table, the goatskin stained dark from half a decade of beatings. His hand trembling from hunger and thirst, Nkuku brought a lamp up from the floor of his platform along with a peculiar roll of hide and a small bottle.

"Not the time for joy," Ngala said when he spotted the dzan, the corsair's heady black liquor.

"Well, I need one." Nkuku popped off the cork and took a heavy slug. His face cast in a knowing expression he offered the dzan to his captain.

After a moment of reluctance, Ngala took the bottle from his hand. "You're going to have to be bosun again until Zaki is on her feet."

"Old times, hard times," the timekeeper responded in his sing-song way. "We've re-tarred the crack near the prow twice, but water keeps leaking. Coins down I bet there are broken pegs too. I'm having the men break up the loot and hold it on their benches, but it if keeps getting cramped in here..."

"I have time."

"Not much."

Ngala took a few sips of dzan, the cinnamon burning his tongue. He coughed heat and sugar. "What's my new shipwright's name?"

"Amare, and he is as sharp as Kangana." Nkuku stared at the roll of hide in his hand before unveiling it on his drum. Setting a small lamp on a corner of the illustration, he sparked a match off the furred side of his drum. Lighting the small wick, the flame washed the skin orange, the black lines of the drawing revealed.

Ngala leaned back in surprise. "It looks flimsy."

"It is flimsy. We might have to pull pieces from *The Gamka* if you want it otherwise."

He lifted the bottle back to his lips, his focus on the outline of the raft. "How many days you think we have, Nkuku?"

"I've heard the ship groan twice. If we keep rationing, we'll run out of water in three, and then the food will be lost in five days when the seals rupture." He waved off the severity. "Ah, but the monsters will get us first."

Ngala offered the timekeeper back his bottle. "Let me know what you need."

Nkuku took it with a dark laugh and a swig. "I'll have them bring you an extra water ration."

Ngala lay on his poor pallet of blankets, trying to find a comfortable position so he could watch the stars in peace. A cloudless night, its map of years and experience etched into his soul, punctured the indigo fabric to form a shining, shimmering path homeward. Constellations wove the currents back to Stone Cove.

He turned his face away from the sky to earthbound things.

Ngala's raiders continued their shifts on the deck, the main body sitting in their rows around the mainmast while fewer of their number, armed with bows, patrolled *The Gamka's* railings. This main grouping busied themselves at the base of the trireme's strongest point, continuing to roll dice to gamble rations on their way. They built small fires to read the hash marks on their cubes; the tiny trails of smoke from those controlled, muted flames carried a crackling odor.

"Nkuku told me to bring you dinner."

Tausi stood at his father's feet, eyes cast askance at the Mirror around them. In one hand, he carried his father's tin plate, spotted with a chunk of bread, a few pieces of softened salt pork, and a pepper-vinegar sauce Ngala could smell from where he lay. In the other, he carried two horn cups, one larger than the other.

Ngala sat up on his blankets, jostling the ache Nkuku's liquor had left behind. He took the plate and cup handed to him but was surprised when Tausi spun away, back for the hold with not a word said.

"Tausi," Ngala called.

His son stopped but did not face him.

"You and I should speak."

Silent, Tausi returned minutes later bearing his own ration of food. He lowered down a few feet from Ngala, close enough that they could hear each other even in quiet tones, but far enough that his son's gist was obvious. Ngala paid more attention to his meal, drinking half of the extra water Nkuku had promised. The cool liquid rolled down his stomach like soft wine, upsetting it while at the same time easing the constant gurgle. The pepper sauce on the salt pork, harsh in his nostrils, cleared sinuses. Thanks to the vinegar's tang drawing out small bits of saliva, he swallowed down the meat bit by bit. Tausi mimicked his father, eating his meal in total silence.

Ngala put his tin plate on the corner of his blanket when he finished. "We need to speak about earlier."

"Will you dare to see what is happening around you?"

Taken aback by the blatant disrespect, Ngala steadied the urge to smack his son. "You will mind yourself."

Tausi rolled his eyes at the warning. "Have I failed you in these last days? Have I ever caused ill times upon your beloved boat?"

"What does that matter?"

"It—" Tausi fought in a startling moment of self-control, his visage twisting in a torrent of dark emotions. "It matters, Father. Captain. *The*

Gamka has run the Mirror's waters for more than fifteen years. She has never faltered in battle, never sunk, never stayed in one place other than the beaches we rested her on. Until now."

"We have not sunk, nor has this crew given—"

"Nobody is worried about the crew's courage or ability, Father," Tausi said dismissively. "Don't insult us. This has nothing to do with our loyalty to you."

The answer caught Ngala. "Then what?"

"Do not be a fool, Father—a brine-singer? an Ulmo? *The Gamka* marooned *on water*? If the gods could speak, I doubt their words could be any clearer."

"Oh, the gods—" Ngala grunted at his fool of a son. For the many long years he had lived, Ngala never put great stock into heavens or hells, least of all those that peopled them. The wind in the sail was as real as the wind against his skin, or the color of the sky when the sun gilded for dusk. He knew blood, and iron, and anger—he knew all his failures, yet they were his.

"What has been different since we left Stone Cove? What has changed?" Tausi asked. "Who has changed?"

"We're not talking about this again. Just because your sister—"

"Zaki will die in that hold and be blamed for what happened."

"Not by any choice she made."

"None made the choices she did, and they are a superstitious lot," Tausi replied, indignant. "Oyla and Bas, who wrote the first salt law, deem that we are born, we grow, and we die as we are intended, as how our vodunis tell us. What is given is what is spent, nothing more. Many of the men, including those among the raiders, thinks she goes against this nature."

"Or perhaps some foul sorcery of man is afoot instead of some faceless gods being angry at my child," Ngala said, hard enough to stifle any more interruptions. "Blaming a crew member won't help matters."

"And denying something larger than us won't either. At least not to them."

Neither flinched from the resolve they set to their faces. Impassive against the angst he remembered from his own youth, Ngala bore old stoniness into his youngest child, pushing out the heartbreak over what chance had brought between them. "Nkuku has produced plans to build a raft we'll take to shore," he said, slow and to the point. "We will launch it when it is ready, and we will save this crew and your sister. We have—"

"No, you don—"

"Do not interrupt me again," Ngala told Tausi, each word punctuated in warning.

A distinct lack of respect settled within Tausi's blank, black eyes, a beast enticed by the challenge. Hands on his knees, his tapered torso gleamed with sweat in the half-moon light, a bloody past renewed in a more haunting vision of the present.

Yet Ngala did not deter. "You will follow my orders to the word. Do you understand, Commander?"

"Yes, Father."

"Try again."

A dangerous light flickered in the young man's gaze. "Yes, Captain."

CHAPTER 6
WHERE THE LAST WAVE BROKE

Morning lifted night from the world's edge, burning away the darkness until bolts of warmth fanned on the sea, setting the breeze alive.

Ngala squinted at dawn with weary eyes, his mouth parched and dry. The thirst and a gnawing in his stomach that food did not soothe had kept him awake. Long into the night he and the raiders had worked alongside the rowers to construct, piece by piece, the great raft a contingent would use to journey to Shallow Bay's pale shore. Stars faded on the silvered Mirror, her unmarred, unyielding surface daring the corsairs to try their hand at escape.

He and Tausi had not spoken for two days after their spiteful meal, other than the affirmations and answers a commander had to provide for his captain—and each time, new developments soured any attempt the other made to lighten their mutual ire. While *The Gamka's* rail became the raft's small frame, the tar seal in the hold had sprung a slow, seeping leak not even the new shipwright could seal. Adding to the creaking groan of the trireme's sea-swollen hull, each meeting heaped disunity upon the whole crew. Rowers eyed Tausi while the raiders, cliquish as they were, treated the mistrust with a terseness of their own.

"I'd like to make a request, Captain," Tausi asked in one of these latter instances, when the rowers lashed the last emptied barrels to the raft's frame. Tacked tight into a square, an old hide held the footboards together. Floating alongside the trireme's starboard, it bobbed as supplies, weapons, and a make-shift sail were loaded aboard.

"What?" Ngala asked, sharp in his address.

"I'd like to lead the party to the shore," Tausi said, lacking his usual acid. "It would do well if a senior officer led this jaunt, and I am as good a sailor as any."

"That you are," Ngala said. A hand over his eyes to shield them from the sun, he watched the archers mass on the right side of the boat, putting knees on the bare edge of the trireme's wall. Arrows at rest, they scanned the low tide shoals between them and the beach, their wax-cloth plugs stuffed in their ears.

"So may I depart, Captain?"

He lowered his hand. "No. You will pick a raider, and Nkuku will pick a rower in Zaki's absence."

"But the men need—"

"The men need to follow orders." Ngala faced his son. "We already have our bosun injured, and to lose either the commander or captain at this venture would leave Nkuku alone to handle things in chaos. I cannot allow it."

Tausi flared his nostrils. A snort he barely concealed escaped him as he departed toward center deck, away from the steering oar where Ngala always stood. Lacking the energy to reprimand his child, he simply leaned on the stern-wall he often used as a bench for rest.

Not long after, his son brought Nkuku, a rower, and a raider to the back of the ship, ambushing Ngala with a sudden council. "What is this?" he asked Tausi when his son massed their fellow crewmen before him.

"I chose my man to captain the raft," Tausi replied, speaking at a harsh pace. "Nkuku has chosen his. We need to cross the bay before the tide rises."

"Is this truly your man, Nkuku?" Ngala asked his timekeeper.

Nkuku glanced at Tausi with a hardness to his eyes, the gentle kindness in his voice absent. "If there is one to choose, then Abeeku will serve you well. He's a strong back at the oar and can carry a beat or two. He'll get them to shore."

Ngala appraised the rower, mustering his best smile and nod possible.

Brave even after days on meager rations, Abeeku's fist came to his chest. "I'm ready, Captain."

"I believe in you both." Ngala clapped the raider and rower on the shoulders as he eyed Tausi. "Go about your business. I will see you all off when you depart."

Ngala forced his wads of waxed cloth in his ears, nodding to Nkuku to cut away the moorings holding the raft to *The Gamka*. The raiders crowded the bare starboard, on the watch for an unexpected shadow or flash of color out of place on the shifting peaks of the water. Eight men —four rowers and four raiders—embarked northward for the beach. The raft drifted on the currents, swept up by a spiced wind.

On guard at his place near starboard, Ngala watched the scene unfold before him while shadows flagged the wave-swept span of his mind. Hope swelled against the pervading worries Shallow Bay had brought, and the chance that the crew could reach the shore, find water, locate a place for Zaki to rest lifted his spirits.

He scanned the deck of his ship. Tausi's broad back faced him, his son's focus fixed on their expedition as much as his own. Ngala's living ghost, flesh of his flesh and his damnation, looked out at the world much like he had.

He stared off in terror of it.

"Oh..." whispered Ngala, the sound low in his chest.

He had forgotten those days, when every squall harbingered a storm and the slightest speck of color on the blue horizon drew him to arms. A raider and commander under the infamous Black Lizard, it had taken time for the ruling Old Bones to teach his heir how to trust the worth of a good rower and treasure a great one, the usefulness of seeing eye-to-eye with your bosun and timekeeper, and to trust the wood beneath the corsair's feet. Ngala worshiped the boards he stood on, a place where time was his to own and make the best with. This trireme was his kingdom.

Was it so for his son and daughter?

The raiders, expert archers to the man, patrolled the top deck, eyes afar for a shred of something small and out of place, or worse, the Ulmo's shadow. The raft had entered the Avarice Reefs when Ngala made his round of the stern, portside, and then back to the bow along the starboard, his attention always on the craft. Every man on the ship soaked the sweltering air with their fear.

Tausi shouted, his voice booming past Ngala's earplugs. "Off starboard, to the northwest! She's there! Fire!"

Ngala shouted. "Cease fire!"

The raiders raised their bows in unison, the iron heads of their arrows glinting bright. The shafts arched high into the blue vault, falling in a wide, ineffectual line of wasted fletching.

"Cease fire," Ngala repeated, hoarse with anger as he pulled down the nearest bow he could reach. He glared at the raider who held it, a young boy who shrank under his ferocity. "Damn you salt-dogs!"

Turning without thought, he stalked upon Tausi, who pointed in the direction he had called.

"She's there," he yelled at Ngala before his father could question him. He yanked him over by the arm where the rail had once been. He pointed again to the northwest. "There!"

Wrenching free of Tausi's grasp, Ngala spotted the speck of gray upon the far-off waves, the small shape of the brine-singer a flare of bleached shale. He held his hand high and flat, a silent order to hold all fire when he saw the raft had not deviated from its course to the beach.

"She's there," Tausi screamed at him when his hand did not lower. "She's attacking."

A trio of raiders jostled together at the starboard, near to the bow, loosening their arrows as they shouted warning to their fellow crewmen. A dark splotch darted from beneath *The Gamka*, the Ulmo racing through the depths at jerky angles toward the reefs.

"Fire," Ngala shouted. "Stay ahead! Stay ahead of it!"

The archers sent volleys, trying to shower the Ulmo. His black bulk murky in the clear waters, every single turn, every dodge forward, brought him closer to the raft while the archers wasted more and more arrows.

"No," Tausi cried, almost launching himself over the side. Ngala grabbed him before he toppled into the water and dragged them back onto the deck. Son rolled atop his father, a hand smashing the latter's face until the youth's well-muscled weight lifted off his head.

Ngala launched to his feet, his sword suddenly freed of its scabbard. He laid the iron blade to Tausi's shoulder. "Hold fire!"

The raiders sputtered to a stop, a few arrows flying from fingers unready to catch them.

The Ulmo tore into the raft. Chaos broke between the men aboard, the four raiders hurtling into the water with their knives and swords, finding death in short, brutal instances of wasted glory. The rowers for their part held course to the beach, their oars pulling hard while the mottled-shelled beast cracked open skulls, gorging on brain matter.

Ngala, his son at the point of his sword, checked the northwest again, only to find the brine-singer had vanished. He lifted the blade from Tausi's shoulder when it met with his neck, and he slid it back into its leather scabbard. Many removed the wads of wax cloth in their ears, only to shove them back when the cries of the rowers sounded in the far-off distance, small noises followed by the crashing, cracking sound of splintering wood. The cacophony silenced, leaving the crew of *The Gamka* to the horrors of their deafness.

Ngala pulled out his wads of waxed cloth when his son turned on him. Tausi had drawn his sword, his sullen eyes meeting his father's.

"You disobeyed my orders," Ngala said, not reaching for his own weapon.

"We are under attack." Tausi's grip did not relax on his hilt. His expression devoid of emotion, he set his left shoulder forward slightly, a subtle set-up for attack. "Our crewmen were under attack. You let them die."

Ngala felt the sudden weight of a hundred eyes on him, and he unconsciously knew every man on the trireme's deck had stopped. The cold gleam of his son's sword, the lap of the waves on the trireme's wet wood, set a sloshing dirge for what lay next.

"You ordered them to pay your foolishness with their lives." Tausi edged closer, the point of his sword set at his father's face. "I relive you of command, Father. You're out of time."

Ngala stepped back, whipping his sword out in a fluid movement that batted away Tausi's point. "Then have at it."

CHAPTER 7

HE WHO BREEDS PESTILENCE

T ausi roared into his cut, a heavy chop Ngala sidestepped. Batting down the blade, he followed through with a hard smack of the flat on the back of his son's neck, a rasping blow that made the boy yelp. Pleased by his quick move, he did not expect Tausi to come back. Iron bit iron as edges bound together.

Father and son wrestled, the younger powering his elder into the main mast. Their bodies smacked the wooden pole, breaking them away from each other long enough for Tausi to step back. The two faced off, blades clashing in the morning light.

Ngala thrust at his son's chest, who countered for his face. He brought his sword up by his cheek to block the quick cut, the power behind it knocking him to the right a step. Tausi battered Ngala's defense, who struggled to regain his base after his son's stinging blow sprained his wrist.

Holding firm against the hot pain in his sword hand, he deflected one of his son's slashes and shoved Tausi headfirst to the ground, making him roll on the wood. Ngala bared the point of his blade. "Stay down!"

His son reared on his legs like a gorilla, chest puffed and sword ready. The tip of his father's sword a few inches from his face, Tausi scowled, unflinching in the face of cruel metal.

"You can't save us," he said. "I won't sit here and wait to die."

"You're relieved of your rank, boy." Ngala lowered his sword and looked away, the sudden exhaustion of battle aching in his dehydrated limbs. "And nobody is waiting for anything," he shouted for the crewmen to hear. He did not lift his eyes to gauge their reactions. "We will build another raft."

"With what?"

Ngala brought his gaze up, searching for the voice that had called the question. "Who said that?"

One of the raiders, a man of middle years, stepped forward from his place near the starboard bow. "I did, Captain."

"Do you have something to say, Mtumbwe?" Ngala asked. "You've never been one to countermand me."

"And I do not, Captain," said the raider, holding his bow in his hands uncomfortably. The eyes of Ngala, Tausi, and his fellow corsairs fell on him, putting a wheeze in his throat. "But we built a raft and more men died. Why would we build another?"

A grumble of agreement spread throughout the top deck.

"We cannot give up," Ngala said to them, sword low by his side.

"No one said give up," Tausi cried, grabbing onto the spoken doubt. "But your ways are not saving us! We are miring here, waiting desperately for what? To escape? There is no escape!"

"And what would you offer?" asked one of the rowers on the deck. A slight young man, he weathered Tausi's glare.

Tausi averted his gaze. "I would offer the only means of deciding our fates—we hunt the Ulmo. We hunt the brine-singer."

Another rumble of agreement arose, more from the raiders than the rowers.

Ngala recognized the fervor on their faces, the desperation of men like Mtumbwe, who had been raised for war. He slammed his sword back in its scabbard. "How? Will we dare to swim for the keel, where it waits?"

"We will draw it out!" Tausi charged for the starboard with his weapon still bared, pointing overboard. "We will set a trap, and like a lobster, we will capture the beast and pith it." He flashed a hungry, enthralled smile, the grimace of dehydration and madness. "We'll cook it on the beach!"

The rumble of agreement turned into cheers. The raiders banged their bows on the wooden deck, their backs to the north, opposite the dark red ghosts that were drawn away by the flow of the sea.

Ngala shook his head, not forgetting so quickly those lost souls. "You'll only go to your deaths," he told them, awed by the living's stupidity. "You'll never get the brine-singer close enough to slay her with arrows, and if you do, you shall hear her song and be ensorcelled."

"A corsair relishes a chance to grin in death's face," Tausi said, his confidence blooming with the crew's enthusiasm. "Or has the great Lion forgotten how to roar in the face of danger?"

Ngala noticed the hesitation on the faces of a few men, more of them rowers than not. Seeking more hints of doubt, he seized on it. "So, who will go in first? Who will take their knife, or their sword, and dare the darkness beneath the ship? There's no dune. Only the cold."

"The cold is rushing in, Father," Tausi replied in sardonic amusement. "How wide is the crack down in the hold? Perhaps you and old Nkuku are not telling us on deck the entire truth. How long will it really be until our food runs out?"

"I have never kept anything from a single man on this ship."

"Except your freak son," called another of the raiders, known as Kwalik the Braggart, one of the younger raiders known for his short temper that outmatched his intelligence—a dangerous man, nonetheless. "I wonder how long you knew about that."

Ngala looked to Tausi immediately, expecting his youngest son to defend his older sister. Instead, the impenitent youth, flushed by the flames he had stoked in every fighting man he led, gazed back in smug defiance. Shock snuffed any sense of argument Ngala wanted to make. He yearned to speak, but the silence carried until the sky rumbled. Off to the west, a long line of gray clouds haunted the horizon. Thunder drummed in the distance.

The portents for rain made themselves known.

The sick-shit stench of the hold misted in a foul cloud that was revealed by the sputtering flames of the rowers' lamps on their benches, which browned the rank air. Their lights, meager and lacking, shed their illumination on the gathered point by point until all things were seen in the gross haze.

In the center of *The Gamka's* belly, the men toiled around their small frame-fires, the iron squares smoking hot as they fanned the sour tendrils toward the ports on the ship's flanks and stern. They cooked a thin rice-mush steeped with soft onions and spiced heavily in cloves and peppers before they tossed in days-old bits of dried meat and fish. The aroma failed to hide the brine that spread throughout. No one missed the trio of men near the prow working to seal the crack with gummy tar while their third bailed small buckets of seawater. Rain pelted the deck above them, rattling the roof of their cramped space. Lightning flashed through the dripping cracks, scorching the roaring skies.

The raiders crowded the steps up to their level, and the men in the back mantled in old blankets to keep dry. They watched the rowers with dispassionate interest as the evening meal was prepared, content to handle their weapons as if displaying them. On the timekeeper's platform, the captain's table had been set, its small circle in isolation.

Ngala sat on the other side of Nkuku and Tausi, facing the raiders who sat behind them.

"The crew usually eats together," he said.

"Circumstances have changed." Tausi leaned toward Nkuku. "What are our stores?"

The timekeeper glanced to Ngala, waiting for the order. He nodded to his old friend. "After this meal, we will have two days' worth of food left if rationed correctly."

"I will make sure that happens accordingly," said Tausi. "We need a portion of it for bait. The men are still fishing the waters, but in case it comes to it, I want it ready."

"And where will this portion come from, child?" Nkuku asked incredulously. "Last time I checked a man's spoils are his spoils, not something you can order away from him for your convenience."

"What is more convenient, old man—the rowers keeping their spoils or their lives?"

Laughter grumbled from the raiders on the steps.

Nkuku bolted off his stool. "How dare you try to steal from your men!"

The rowers stopped their toil at the raising of the timekeeper's voice. Each man reached for the cudgel they kept by their sides.

Ngala did not miss their reaction. "Let any man who would volunteer his portion do so at their own will. You will not like what happens if you don't, son."

"We fight just as well as they row," Tausi said, still seated. "And nobody has anywhere to row unless they follow my plan."

Ngala leaned back on his stool, hands on his knees. "All I hear is a plan to take from others. What will you do if you draw the beast or the brine-singer? Someone will have to get into the water."

"Or these beasts will come out it." Tausi set forward against the table. "We will build nets from the extra rigging, thick ones made from rope soaked in seawater and then oil to make them harder for his claws to cut."

"What happens if the nets fail when we get the beast into the ship?" asked a skeptical Nkuku, lowering down on his three-legged stool. He brushed his hand on his scarred chest, the animal designs pale on his dark flesh. "I've no doubt the strength of any man, above or below deck, but this monster is a thing of sorcery. And I fail to see what this does to free *The Gamka*."

"Damn *The Gamka*," Tausi dared to utter.

Nkuku, older in years than even Ngala, launched himself across the table, clawing to get to the youth. The rowers flowed from their benches to ascend for the platform, their cudgels raised when the raiders came down to defend their commander. The two sides shouted calls for a mortal match.

Ngala threw Nkuku off the table and into the rowers, who caught their man in their waiting arms. Tausi came up with his blade drawn, only to be grounded by a hard, looping right cross by his father. Taking his son's sword in his left hand, he drew his own with his right before he leapt up onto the table. Blades pointed in both directions, and he dared rower and raider alike. "The first man to move will die on my iron!"

Tausi popped to his feet. Blood leaked from a broken nose; long strands of sticky red ran over his hands. His eyes tearing, the expression he made at Ngala fell somewhere terrible—somewhere between pain and betrayal, rage and sorrow.

The young corsair lowered his hands and spat a red glob on the floor. "Put your weapons down."

"You mutinous cur," Nkuku shouted from the hold's well. Someone had handed him his great wooden beater, a solid club made of ebony. He bared it like an angry spirit come from the night. "You'd dare raise against your captain? Against your crew?"

"Better mutiny than death," Tausi screamed back. "Put down your swords, Father. Now."

"Don't you speak to him that way."

The sudden voice, deep femininity edged by dark notes, startled the hold into silence.

Rain beat the boards above them, and the storm outside groaned out the swelling hull of the trireme. Unless *The Gamka* could dry on a beach soon, she would fail before she carried them home.

Zaki winced as she grunted herself off of Nkuku's table. Landing on her feet, the bosun collapsed to her knees. Ngala dropped his weapons and came to her. "Don't crowd me," she chided her father as she lifted herself up, taking care to not aggravate the crusty wound lining her back. She winced when he moved her to a stool at the captain's table. He stopped afterward to retrieve his fallen swords.

"Leave them." She pointed at the stool next to hers. "Sit down. Nkuku, serve dinner."

Nkuku held his beater, unsure of what to do. "Zaki?"

"Serve the damn food, Nkuku," she shouted. "And serve the raiders first—at least everyone that lays down arms to accept his meal. Extra water rations as well."

The rowers roared in protest but were silenced by her raised hand. "They spent all day on deck," Zaki reminded them. "Let them have some damn water."

Dinner arrived minutes later, a tense service. The raiders, having gone the entire day without a scrap of food or drink, laid down their swords and spears to accept their plates of steaming fried rice, the color darkened by too much jerk. They ate the food in silence while the rowers were served next, taking a larger portion of the rice to make up for one less cup of water.

The captain's table took their food last, four plates laid on the round surface. The sufficient layer of rice, chunked with bits of old fish and specks of dried meat, let its appealing smell mingle into the stench of the hold.

"Timekeeper," Zaki called, and then looked to her younger brother. "Commander."

Ngala allowed Nkuku to sit before he took his seat next to Zaki, across from the stool where Tausi would sit if he accepted the invitation. Hunger grumbled in his stomach, and he yearned to take his meal. Pride waited on his obstinate son.

Tausi finally took his seat.

The crew's meal carried on in silence.

CHAPTER 8
LAST IN LINE

Ngala ate fair bites of his rice-mush, the unbalanced mix of savory palatable enough for his hunger. Bits of fish, salted past the point of taste, added the texture needed to make him chew it more. Spoon in one hand, he committed to one bite at a time—anything to forestall what came next.

The storm-song outside buffeted the silence of *The Gamka's* hold. Rower and raider stared at each other in the lamp-lit dimness as the waves battered the trireme's flanks, the harsh booms underscoring their conflicts.

Nkuku sat to Ngala's left, neither speaking nor touching his food. Like the rest of his rowers, he rested a thick beater across his loin-swaddled lap, a natural club. Tausi loomed across the table from his father, doing whatever he did. Ngala went out of his way to not notice, but the knock of his son's spoon against the bottom of his plate spoke enough.

His anxiety spiked when he considered his daughter.

Zaki braced her long arms against the table; her head leaned over the steaming pile of food. Sweat pasted her chalky, drained flesh, and her lips swelled from dehydration. Eyes shut, she shivered in the cooling night air.

Ngala slowly reached for her hand, only to be rebuffed by a small slap.

"Let me eat my food, Captain," she said, husked by thirst. Her right hand swung for the small horn cup set out for her, knocking it over. Crystal water flowed upon the wood. Nkuku clucked like a sorrowful hen, trying his best to catch the liquid in his trembling hands while Ngala reset her cup. Grunting at the kindness, Zaki shooed both of them.

The steady trickle broke their chatter.

Tausi poured half the water in his cup into Zaki's, watching it closely with no regard to the attention on him. He lifted the same cup toward Nkuku. "She used to be a raider. That's her extra ration. I'm still owed one more."

The timekeeper's face rankled, but he called for a rower anyway. Their cups somewhat evened, they resumed the tense meal. Lightning crackled outside, its blue light shooting through the cracks where water didn't drizzle in.

Her masculine features soft in the lamplight, Zaki managed a sip from her cup. After a few small spoonfuls of food, more water, and she cleared her throat. "I've been sleeping, but I haven't been sleeping all the time. Fair use of your drugs, Nkuku."

Some of the crew chuckled, which drew a natural smile from the timekeeper.

"There isn't much of the deck left." Ngala's seriousness severed the levity. "We tried a raft. It didn't work."

"And yet you want to try another..." Tausi muttered. "There is no escape from this boat. Our only choice is to fight."

"I agree," said Zaki.

Ngala grunted his annoyance. "Really?"

"Yes, Father." Zaki mustered the strength for another spoonful of rice. "Even if we make it past the Avarice Reefs, we still have to cross the bay," she said through bouts of chewing. "That is more than a few leagues, even with a sail."

"This monster almost killed you," Ngala said.

"Oh, but it would be fine if it killed me?" asked Tausi.

"You know that is not what he meant," Nkuku snapped. "Stop being a bloody ass and think outside yourself for a moment."

"Think on who is your superior, you old bugger," Tausi replied.

"You little fucking brat! I was swaddling your shit-ass in cloth when you were pissing and puking all over the goddamn place. Don't tell us about your superiority when you have none, boy," the timekeeper said, dropping his beater on the table. An amused cheer lifted from both sides with every knock it made. Tausi glowered.

"Stop it," said Zaki, shouting down the noise. "This ship doesn't run on your egos or mine, but it's supposed to run. Maybe we should consider things we haven't done."

"Like what?" Tausi brusquely asked in return.

"Listen," she said.

Quieted, they sat there, listening to the sounds of the Mirror Sea come to claim them. Beyond the battering of the waves, the sputter and rattle of rain on the hull, they heard the churn of the water, the wail of the wind against the groaning mast. The storm raged onward toward whatever horrible conclusion it would bring, and the smallness, the helplessness of that, settled on every person there.

"What do you hear?" she asked.

Tausi answered first. "Death."

"A storm," said Nkuku.

"Movement," Ngala said at last. His brow furrowed when he looked to his daughter, who nodded in appreciation of his deduction.

"The world is still moving around this ship," she said. "The winds are changing, the currents are flowing, and yet we are not moving. Why?"

"There's no dune beneath us," Ngala reminded.

"Then it's sorcery," Tausi said, slouched on his stool in boredom. He had cleaned his plate. "And it's either the brine-singer or the Ulmo. Either way, both of them need to die."

"We need to get free of this curse," Ngala said, loud enough for all to hear. "That is what matters most."

"Then we should do battle," Tausi said, matching his volume. "If these beasts entrapped us, then it is their slaying that will allow us to make our way ashore."

"Maybe, maybe." Zaki shuddered herself more upright. "But even if we slay both monsters, we will still need to get free. We must find a way to free the ship."

"But there is no dune," Tausi repeated.

"Then maybe it is not a dune," Zaki said. "Maybe it is something else."

"We cannot know that without going into the water," said Tausi.

Zaki forced her tortured expression into a weak smile. "So, who is going to be the bait?"

The fourth day dawned gray and cool, the remains of the previous night's clouds strung across the brightening sky like scraps from the cloak of night. His throat dry, the smooth surface of the water was an appetizing sight, like liquid mercury to end his suffering. Ngala coughed at the stupid thought. A soft breeze carried the smell of the ship's heady stink.

A small team of rowers worked on the top deck while the raiders busied at their own part of the ship, the three buoys between them slowly pinned together with what scraps of meat they could cobble from the hold after the seal had ruptured again, ruining a quarter of their food stores. The shared meal had blunted the tension residing between the two sides of the ship, allowing a rare calm.

Past them, the last pieces of the green sail were torn into long shreds, each twisted length woven into the next strand of their heavy net. Pieces already constructed lay in large pots of acrid oil weighed down by stolen loot, soaking until the fibers swelled.

Zaki leaned against the wall buffering the steering oar, wrapped in two blankets that failed to ease her shivering. Ashen, she watched the coming sun with grim satisfaction, as if eagerly awaiting the heat to wash her into death.

"Go back down in the hold," Ngala whispered when he reached her. "I can handle Tausi."

"No, you can't," she said, mustering a stronger posture. "I'm not dumb about him being mad at me."

"You knew?"

"Of course. He won't say it, and he's taking the stress of all this out on you because I went too fast for him. On everything." Hooded by her blankets, she let her head fall back and bathed her wide face in sunshine, her smile pretty if not for the bloody, receding gums. "And I'm not surprised that he's not the only one."

"You did reveal yourself suddenly. Goddess' breath, Zaki, you and that sorcerer almost carried out your marriage right there on his feast table."

"The Old Bones laughed."

So did her father, though painfully. "But—"

"But what? Corsairs are supposed to be free folk, weighed only by what we take and what we lived, as Oyla and Bas said in the old stories. I'm still in that same body I've always been in, but I am not this body—and the gods knew. The difference now is that I've put everyone else in a place where they've never been—am I a woman? We don't let salt-wives on this boat for a reason—we never talk about her because it hurts. But I'm now too famed to simply be a manly raider, and more so as a rower. But a woman? And salt-wife to a sorcerer everyone hates?" Her smile turned rueful. "What did you think when it happened?"

"That you were my bosun," said Ngala, "and my child, and whomever you choose to be. Those weren't choices, in my mind."

"And who I am isn't a choice. Do you understand that? Does Tausi?" she asked. "He's going to be captain of his own ship one day sooner than he'll be ready for, but I won't be. I'm your bosun until my bones rest or you get rid of me. He now bears the responsibility I would have taken on if I had not chosen the truth."

"No person is ever free of fate," Ngala said. "It doesn't excuse his mutiny."

She offered a sly smile. "Don't lie, old man. Black Lizard has told me many stories, including a few you'd like to forget."

"Once or twice," Ngala said, unhappy at the admission. "All over good intentions to save the crew or keep things even between the rowers and raiders. But I had Nkuku for shipwright. Helped he's a decent drummer."

"Tausi has no Nkuku yet, and none of your wisdom. Not yet."

"Shut up with your sense-talking, Zaki. One of us has to go into the water soon," said Ngala. "And it isn't going to be you."

"You're both strong swimmers."

He grumbled on his way to the middle of the deck where Tausi and his raiders rolled dice to decide which two would dive. Ngala shouldered his way into the circle, two fingers up for the dice. The din died a bit, muffled more by thirst and hunger, but the two ivory cubes made their way to him.

"What are you doing, Captain?" Tausi asked. "This game might be too much for you."

"Twelve three times makes me the Hand of Glory," Ngala juggled the dice in his closed hand and let them roll. The faces turned up, six apiece. A surprised noise passed through the raiders. Turning away from the circle, he returned to his place beside Zaki.

"You got lucky?" she asked.

"Oh, yes," Ngala chuckled at his numbed face and hands, so surprised by his fruitful toss. "But Tausi would need to roll perfect hands to beat me, and I just need two more good rolls. I'll pick someone else."

"So we're screwing family with old salt laws now?"

"From one criminal to another."

Zaki hacked out a laugh, followed by a series of whooping coughs that put her on both knees. Ngala helped her to the floor, where he repositioned the blankets across her balled-up body. A small crust of blood at the corner of her mouth fanned red and gross, like raspberry jelly fallen from a biscuit. He pressed his thumb to it and smeared it on her sweaty cheek, cradling her limp head in his hand.

"I need to get to shore," Zaki said, her voice small. "I need my wound redressed, and rest, and ground that doesn't shift every moment."

"I'll get you there." Ngala struggled against the tears in his eyes. "Were you listening the entire time?"

"Most of it."

A raider appeared, standing behind Ngala. "It is your roll again, Captain."

Ngala did not remove his eyes from his daughter as the warrior walked back to where his fellows gambled with their lives. "Do you know what I don't understand?"

She grunted at the question.

"You can be captain of this ship when I take Black Lizard's place," said Ngala. "Why can't things change?"

"My choice was simple, Father," Zaki whispered, nodding off to sleep. "I chose myself, which all corsairs are taught to do. I knew what the consequences would be. What will you choose for yourself?"

Ngala wondered as he walked away from his sleeping girl. In the center of the deck, he rolled the ivories again on bleached wood. By some miraculous turn of fate, he rolled double sixes a second and third time, leaving Tausi to fight out the odds against five other men in the field.

"I do think of the consequences," he said when he rejoined Zaki, not knowing if she heard him or not. He spoke anyway, privileged by an ear and no son to talk back. "Tausi has to grow up sooner. I had to. We all do. Maybe that is my problem." Ngala unconsciously touched the steering oar of his trireme—his first kingdom—ruminating on the blood the boards had soaked, and so much of it his. "I thought a boat would make my sins more acceptable. My responsibility and love to this crew covers the fact that we are thieves and murderers. And every time I look at Tausi I see who I am—not who I am now, but who I will always be. And I do not wish that for him."

Zaki snorted, making a wheezing noise. "Then why aren't you working with him on it?"

"Because I don't understand who I am."

A raider came for Ngala. "Captain. We are down to the last roll. It is between Tausi and Mtumbwe."

"Of course it is," said Ngala, exasperated. "Of course it bloody well is."

CHAPTER 9

DISASTERPIECE

Standing before Ngala, Tausi and Mtumbwe flipped a gold coin between them, deciding who would roll first. The latter called heads before it struck the boards.

The fan of a phoenix gleamed up at them.

Tausi pumped his fist. "Yes!"

"But I am the Hand of Glory," Ngala said, a quick reminder that dampened the young man's mood. He glanced to Mtumbwe. A shorter man, he made up for his lack of height with great muscle and skill. A veteran of many raids both at sea and land, ugly scars streaked and snarled across his left shoulder and chest, the healed wounds of a foe hacking beyond the meat.

How he lifted his sword arm, Ngala never knew. "Tell me, old hand —who would you rather serve?"

The veteran gave a heavy shrug. "I'm with whatever man gets me out of here alive."

"A fair answer." Ngala turned his attention to his son, who stared sullenly in wait. "You think you can get these men out of here alive? And your sister?"

The question surprised Tausi, who stood a bit straighter. "I do."

Ngala fought more bitter words behind pursed lips, chewing them.

"No need to roll, then. Tausi and I will go down. Mtumbwe, you are in command of the net and buoy crew. Can you catch me a lobster?"

"Get me to shore, and I'll butter him too," said the corsair with a smile.

Ngala nodded for Mtumbwe to go on, who left them without any fuss. He stepped closer to his son. "You'll be captain one day. Captains should always be willing to take risks to themselves before their crew. Will you do that?"

Lacking his usual rage, Tausi nodded thoughtfully. "I'm the one who wanted to fight the Ulmo."

"Fighting first doesn't make you ready to lead," Ngala said. "That makes you stupid."

Tausi froze, his mouth set to a frown while his eyes widened.

Hesitating for a moment, Ngala clapped his son on the shoulder. "I was the same way until I learned better. Do you want the stern or the ram?"

"Longer climb back up the end of the boat," said Tausi. "Your old bones can take the ram."

"You sparing me now, boy?"

Tausi responded with a strained smile as he left for the trireme's rear. Pleased by how they parted, Ngala made his way to the prow, giving a few more orders to Mtumbwe along the way before they began their dare. He climbed atop the prow's fencing, or what was left of it, and stared down into the depths.

The sun, long freed of its moorings to the earth, barreled for its noontime apex behind a sheet of hazy white. The sea turned from silver to unpolished jade, clear for a few feet before the tide diffused the light.

Ngala had left his sword in the hold, taking instead a small, sharp wedge strong enough to chop wood and crush chitin. Stuck in his belt, he felt the flat's cool iron against his stomach. The wooden edge of *The Gamka's* side bit into the naked soles of his feet, the last barrier between him and death. He carried a fish knife in his left hand.

"Are you down there?" he whispered at the water. He checked terror with defiance. It was a spark of youth he clung to while spurning it in his youngest son, a contradiction he left to roam the darker corners of his raider-heart. He sneered at his beloved sea, silently daring anything below to take his black soul.

"First buoy," Mtumbwe shouted, his words followed by a loud splash.

Ngala bent down, shaking head to toe with anticipation—or cowardice.

"Second buoy!"

Another splash. He lurched, shamed by his eagerness. He held his breath, the knuckles of his knife hand aching.

"Third buoy!"

"I see the Ulmo," cried an archer. "North, northeast! It is going for the first buoy!"

"Dive," cried Ngala, hoping his son failed to hear the order as he pitched forward, plank-straight. Plunging into the cold wash, he opened stinging eyes to a green realm, muddled yet bright. He expected an Ulmo before him, scissoring him open with those great claws.

Instead, he found a spire.

The spike of marble pressed against the broken face of *The Gamka's* shattered ram, the shards bonded to the rock by glowing blue veins that pulsed.

Shocked by the sudden realization of what had happened to his boat, his breath caught in his chest, the lack of air burning his throat and nose. Kicking to the surface, Ngala broke the water to find the sky slashed apart by unexpected lightning. Storm clouds smothered the hazy daylight he had started with, leaving the sea around him in deep shadow.

On instinct, Ngala grabbed his ship's rostrum to steady his place in the sloshing waves, letting it serve as his anchor. Rain drenched his vision, and through splotches of clarity, he watched in sheer awe as Tausi dove through the air. His son landed on a green, gray mass, stabbing his sword into the holes of the net. The Ulmo writhed beneath the weight of the soaked knots, clipping at the oiled lengths in a desperate attempt to get at his attacker.

A wave smacked Ngala forward, cracking his forehead on the rostrum. Sinking back into the cold water, he drifted in the throbbing mire, unable to grab onto anything. He watched the boiling surface of an ocean assailed by uncountable raindrops. Finding it almost beautiful, he felt his breath roll up his chest.

Bubbles escaped his mouth as water flooded in.

He woke above a blaze of pulsing blue.

His burning eyes opened for the last time...or the first time—all Ngala knew was he floated above the ocean floor, his shadow crossing a dome of white marble inset with clear glass. Behind the translucent shards, he could make out the foggy details of a stone altar before the darkness recaptured him.

He awoke a second time when the brine-singer dragged his body to the surface. She flung Ngala on his back to float him on the water, allowing the seawater to gurgle out his mouth and nose. Choking in agony, he groaned as his vision cleared and he realized who held him in her arms.

Ngala kicked, screaming in panic until he sank again.

Below in the gray-light depths, Ngala shut his mouth in time to stop his air from bubbling out from his lungs again. Suspended in the ether of the dead, bodies torn and gashed went by in gory shrouds as they hung like discarded puppets, trailing on the threshold of light and darkness. A shape moved in the water.

Ngala curled his body into a ball, unwilling to be ripped limb from limb without giving the monster some sort of resistance.

A sudden force latched onto his loincloth and yanked him skyward. He came out of the water, flailing until the same power pressed two hands to his chest and slammed him against the trireme. The brine-singer's inky black eyes, speckled in silver and pearl, dilated to an impossible width. Her expression frantic, she opened her ash-purple lips.

"Come below the green," she sang. "Help me."

Ngala reeled when a vision flashed in his mind's eye.

Twelve priestesses knelt at the edges of a segmented pyramid, forced on all fours by chains binding their wrists and knees. Proportioned blocks at the apex met in the capstone that served as their altar, where a sorcerer dug his knife deeper in the torso of his victim. Bile spilled from the rents in sludgy viscera. Electricity crackled up the pillars supporting the marble and glass dome above the sorcerer.

The man screamed, his beaded robes shimmering as magic twisted his cheeks into hard, mottled patches. Twitching antennae sprouted from his mouth, which oozed red when his human teeth popped out.

A scream woke Ngala from the dark dream. Panting, he hung against the ship, the spray whipping his face before his senses recovered. The Ulmo's horrid screeches rose above the searing thunder and mixed with the blood-curdling screams of dying men.

The brine-singer looked at him pleadingly, the pressure of her hands softened on his chest. She dipped beneath the water, vanishing beneath the tides.

Ngala twisted against the wet wood, fingers searching for a hand-hold, which he found. His entire body burned while he climbed, dragging his weight hand over hand until he reached the top of the portside. Hauling himself over the edge, he lay there, face pressed into the swollen plank, one arm still over the side.

When he turned his head, he nearly let himself roll back into the torrential sea.

Swinging battering claws to and fro, the Ulmo knocked over raider and rower alike when they attacked in concert, brave souls throwing themselves to instant death. Latched onto the Ulmo's wide, shelled back, Tausi hacked the damaged stalk that had once been the beast's eye. The wound spurted glowing, yellow blood.

The Ulmo twisted twice and dislodged Tausi, who rolled away among the corsairs rushing to the fight. Summoning one last reserve, Ngala rose to his feet, swaying as *The Gamka* creaked beneath his feet. He struggled for his balance, teetering forward into a headlong stumble before landing hard onto his knees.

A sword lay near the body of its dead raider. Ngala snatched it up.

Picking at the armored chest with their short spears and iron swords, a tight-packed formation of raiders forced the monster to the starboard side the ship, battering at the Ulmo constantly as he reached out in response, snuffing out a life in his sharp claws every time. Gore drenched the wooden deck of the trireme, mixing slick blood with the sloshing seawater.

Ngala roared deep in his gut as he dashed into the small space he found between two of his raiders, his head down and sword held like a bar. He collided with the Ulmo, the force of his blow driving the beast back over the starboard, its glossy tail twitching in jerky spasms. He did not look to see if his enemy tried to fight its way back up the side.

"Wedges," shouted Ngala, searching for a handhold again. "Hack off the rostrum! Hack it off!"

The crew fumbled in the disarray of the halted battle: some scrambled to save men too wounded to save or gather together what will they had after surviving—simply surviving—the onslaught of the primeval horror. A pair of short axes were produced. Discarding the dead man's sword he found, Ngala took up one of them and dragged a raider with him to the prow.

"What if it's down there?" the corsair asked, the battle-hardened man hesitant after his close brush with mortality.

Ngala glared into the whites of his eyes and saw the terror in them. Exhaustion had filled his arms, legs, and face like heavy, sluggish lead, but the fear renewed his will. He dragged forth his courage as he laid a hand on the raider's battle-scarred shoulder. "I don't think I know you."

"Kaholo, sir." The young man said, his sword hand trembling.

"Tabor's son. Your father serves on Black Lizard's *Wingu*."

"Yes, sir."

He patted the raider's shoulder a second time. "Go find Tausi. Or Mtumbwe. Or whomever is in charge."

"Captain?" Kaholo gaped at him. "I can't leave you."

"Sure you can, boy," said Ngala. "Just do it before the monster leaps out of the water and slays you too."

The raider escaped without another word of protest. Crawling past the prow, Ngala straddled the wooden frame securing *The Gamka's* rostrum, clinging to it in desperation whilst the chaotic waters beat at him. Blinded by gusts of sea spray, he braced his free hand on the most solid surface he could grip and raised the wedge in his right. He brought it down with a clang, the iron edge dinging bronze. He brought it up and down a second time, biting wood on the next blow.

A weird, triumphant howl issued from deep within, and hacking savagely, Ngala assaulted his own ship until consciousness crumbled one last time.

CHAPTER 10

RIDERS OF THE STORM

W e need to row," Zaki screamed, each word strained. Men shouted their voices in support of her while others made ruder responses.

"This crew will never make it past the Avarice Reefs with those monsters on our backs," Tausi's voice cracked over the din. "Look! I have the Ulmo's eye! We can beat this monster."

"At what cost? We've lost so many already," Nkuku said aloud, cutting past the rabble.

The noise broke in Ngala's ears, forcing out the cold comfort of pained sleep and spears of light. His entire body aching, he opened and shut his hands, pleased to know he still had all his fingers and, after a small wiggle, toes too. He sat up on Nkuku's surgeon table, the red blanket they had laid over him falling away.

A sense of solidity confirmed his survival before a better discovery dawned. He sensed the water pressuring the hull at his side, pushing it along the currents.

The Gamka floated free.

Overjoyed, the scene around him could not have offered greater contrast.

The entire crew was packed into the hold, their reduced numbers noticeable when he compared how many had left Boda alive and rich. A pool of water gathered in the center of the ship where a team of rowers bucketed. They dumped it out the nearest oar-holes, sliding past whatever goods and loot they had rescued from the bottom and stacked. It reached the tops of their ankles.

"The ship needs to be washed—we all need to be—or we'll be dealing with disease in no time," Zaki called. "And not a man here has had more than a mouthful of water since we rationed it, and the breach dirtied the last barrel. We need to get to shore, or we will all die."

"We might die in the attempt," Nkuku said. Squatted on his stool at the captain's table, his flabby back faced where Ngala sat. "The rupture along the keel isn't going to be sealed out here, and I don't know if rowing even at a half-beat will open it further with the hull already saturated."

"She'll float," Ngala said from Nkuku's surgeon table. "*The Gamka* always floats."

The crew cheered at Ngala's arrival, the exultation resounding in the tightly packed compartment. The corsairs before him made room for him to limp to the table; he forced a smile to cover his wince as dozens of hands slapped and patted their thanks. The chatter died as he took his stool.

"What happened?" he asked.

"I found you hanging off the prow, face down in the Mirror," Tausi replied, speaking with an almost uncharacteristic calm. "I thought you dead."

Ngala searched for disappointment in the eyes of his youngest and discovered nothing, only the same grinding exhaustion he had arisen from. His attention turned to order. "Zaki is right. We have to row."

Nkuku touched his captain's arm, a subtle acknowledgment of his return. "We might sink if we do."

Ngala shrugged his scarred shoulders, already sweating from the sweltering heat of stale breaths. "And if we don't?"

Zaki coughed herself wheezy, her mother's bright brown eyes staring from beneath the natural hood her blankets made for her. When she ceased, she wiped spittle with the back of an ashy hand, a slight trail of red left behind. "We sink. If we stay and fight, we sink. Whatever we were connected to held us by our rostrum. We broke our anchor point so the pressure on the crack is unstable. Go or stay, we're going to be swimming to shore if we don't move."

"If we can get anywhere," Tausi said, his tightly muscled body rising and falling in a frustrated sigh.

"You never know," said Ngala. "I don't think there is a man here that's not a strong swimmer."

Laughter arose from the crew, no matter the faction.

"If we go half-beats and pilot our way through Avarice Reefs without having to stop or correct because we get caught, then we can make it," Zaki said. "And we can pail the water, Nkuku. Give me five men, and I'll make sure we stay balanced."

"How?" asked Tausi among the murmurs. "You're barely alive."

"You can have six," said Ngala.

"I still need to fill the benches, Ngala." Nkuku dabbed at the corner of his eye, rubbing away a tear of exhaustion. "Especially if Zaki must fight the sea."

The obvious question was held behind the mouths of every man, all of which had survived days without water, a real meal, and sleep. Mutiny's spirit tried to summon itself from these battered corsairs, many of whom simply laid a tired hand on what weapons they possessed. Those without knew they would go without.

The stare between Ngala and Tausi chained the two into mirrored positions on their stools, natural predators hunched forward. The older one did so without bravado, the years settled in his bones. He did not know what his youngest felt staring into those black irises of sparking oil.

Ngala broke his silence. "Will you spare me your men?"

Tausi snorted back. "Who says they're mine?"

"There are those here who will fight for you, son," Ngala said without bitterness. "A captain needs men that devoted."

"And you think I'm not?" Tausi's wounded smile revealed his clean, crooked teeth as he gazed out at the audience. "The crew comes first."

Ngala bowed his head in agreement. "To the benches."

He pulled on the wooden bolt that locked the steering oar in place, the handle coming alive in Ngala's left hand as the Mirror's current caught its flat fin. Life flowed up his arm while he forced his ship steady, correcting her drifting into an actual course. *The Gamka* rocked side to side until she calmed, passing northward again under a starry midnight.

"So, I'm your bosun," Tausi said, dry as the flaking boards under their naked feet.

"No." Letting the oar guide him, Ngala motioned with his free hand for his son to take it.

Tausi started at the offer. "Are you sure?"

"You think you can be captain?"

"I do."

"Then you'll need a bosun." Ngala stepped away from the steering oar and allowed Tausi to assume command. He took in their surroundings—the calm night, the lapping waves—and laughed aloud.

Tausi kept the oar steady, his poise perfect as he spied his father. "What's so funny?"

"We have plenty of time, son."

Ngala set off for *The Gamka's* bow. Recovering a bow and enough unbroken arrows to fill a discarded quiver he belted to his waist, he assumed his guard at the trireme's most-forward point. The wooden oars slid out, against the edges of their ports, and dipped into the water.

The ship crawled toward Shallow Bay. Each stroke of the oars, far apart and brief, were followed by the splash of buckets emptying out the unused ports. She ran slow, sluggish. Hard to sea, the sound of the prow shearing the currents carried the song of the rower's grunts for hours.

Ngala made rounds sometime before dawn, walking the perimeter like any raider would. The steps on those boards brought a smile he suppressed before he passed Tausi, who slipped them along currents and with waves, easing their way to the Avarice Reefs with a skill belying his youth. Undeterred, inexhaustible, the first-time commander cut a kinder image to his father—one of resolute endurance.

"Do you need rest?" Ngala asked when he came to the steering oar.

His gaze eastward to the warming line, Tausi shook his head, steady as he guided them. The pair waited in silence for a long while afterward, watching the stars wander by before sunlight cleaned the sky of their beauty.

"I was never against having this when it was my time," his son said. "You're always talking about time, Father—how much we have, how to use it. But I had mine taken. She was supposed to be captain first. Not me."

"So you don't think she's cursed?"

"We both said things we wished we didn't. At least I did."

Ngala set the butt-end of his bow on the deck and sat against the stern on the starboard side. "Have any of the veterans told you stories of how Black Lizard made me captain?"

Tausi loosed a sad sigh. "I'm their commander now, so no."

Ngala pressed his lips in a hard, flat line, both hands on the bow as he balanced it against the boards. "That is the curse of my name, son. They will open to you if you endear yourself to them."

"And how do I endear myself when I might send them to their deaths when I'm younger than most of them?" Tausi trimmed the trireme slightly to port, its broken keel aligned with the rolling waves, allowing the ship to surf atop the current. "You've had years to be captain, and Zaki has years of exploit. She was expected to—"

"And sometimes I run a boat into a temple," Ngala replied. "Now let me finish my story—

A massive impact struck the starboard near the bow, jerking *The Gamka* a few degrees off course. The boat groaned in response. Heavy and hard, the blow rocked the trireme left before the point of balance swung the ship down, smacking the water in the middle of a wave-trough.

Ngala whipped an arrow from his quiver as his son fought to right the steering oar. "Does it have a mouth?"

"One full of hell," Tausi shouted through his fight to calm the thrashing vessel.

"Head on to the reefs!"

Ngala dashed to the right side of the deck, one foot on the side as he aimed down at the black water. A speckled brown fin drew across the surface of the sea before the Ulmo submerged. He eased on the bowstring.

The crew beneath the deck grunted in unison as they maintained their sluggish pace, the chop of the sea batting the sides.

The Ulmo rammed *The Gamka's* starboard a second time, rattling the hull. Seawater flooded the rowers' ports when the trireme rocked on its side for a second, drawing horrified screams before she righted. Ngala, balanced well after years of heavy storms and battle, drew his arrow on the Ulmo when he spotted the beast, who glared back at him with a blighted eye.

The first arrow zipped the water above the Ulmo's shoulder as the ship dove deep.

Tausi called for his father. "The prow is dipping!"

Ngala sprinted from mid-ship to stern, turned hard at the steps, and almost tumbled into the hold.

He found Nkuku struggling to right his surgeon's table while three rowers wrestled one of their mates to keep still. Zaki had taken the old sailor's place at his drum, the young bosun drenched in water as she beat the goatskin. Half a dozen raiders scrambled in the bottom of the ship's well, bailing as many buckets as they could before the water reached their knees.

"We need to keep the prow up," Ngala shouted.

"We need to go full beat." Zaki gripped one side of the drum and struck the hide. "Faster, my dogs!"

"You'll kill us all!" Nkuku stood between the captain and his daughter, having reset his table. He looked back and forth, setting his worried expression on Ngala when their eyes met.

Ngala shrugged to his oldest friend.

Nkuku thought for a moment before breaking into a hysterical laugh. Fishing his bottle of dzan from a box beneath his restored table, he pulled out the cork and took a hard, long draw.

"I'm at least going to hell drunk," he replied, wiping his mouth.

CHAPTER II
VANISHING LIGHT

Men bucketed the broth welling around their knees, tossing it back out the same portholes it entered. Their loud shouts at each other of "keep moving," or "more water," reduced to grunts when the strain inhibited words and fell in time with the groans of the rowers.

Benched in their staggered tiers, those of the bottom level pushed and pulled the long length of wood while sitting to their waists in water, the collective fear held back by sheer determination. Two men to an oar, they made their noises in unison as they moved as one, dragging *The Gamka* through the Mirror.

Nkuku struck the goatskin drum, now teetered on the edge of his platform, his beater raising again for the next blow as he called out. "Full beat!"

The rowers groaned their rotation.

He struck again. "Full beat!"

Standing to the timekeeper's left, Ngala held his daughter in his arms, her lithe body heavy after her turn at the station. Her back dripped, small cuts of the great gash opened by her movement.

"Leave me," she whispered in gasps to her father. "Tausi... Tausi..."

"Keep us floating," Ngala shouted to Nkuku, who answered back with the high laughter of a dead man that knew time neared. He lifted his daughter in his arms, unsteady, and carried her to the steps. The trireme's constant rocking, interspersed with rises when the ship crashed through the waves, tested every step of their ascent to the top deck.

"What are you doing?" Tausi cried at Ngala when the latter laid Zaki on the other side of his son's place by the steering oar.

"Keep us toward Shallow Bay," Ngala shouted in his face before he ran for the middle of the deck. The sun edged over the horizon, turning the sea to gold save for the waters near the ship. As the navy-black illuminated to aqua, he spotted the Ulmo barreling beneath the waves on the portside, his wake a rapid column of bubbles and foam.

Drawing an arrow and setting it to his recovered bow, Ngala loosed, striking the Ulmo's mass. The monster deviated from his course, retreating westward.

Ngala brought another shaft out, waiting for the next shred of shifting shadow, for the next movement of light and liquid out of place. *The Gamka* powered northward, the wind whistling around the naked mast as the rowers hauled them to the edge of Avarice Reef.

The treacherous collection of gnarled, twisted coral networks were named not for the droves of sunken treasure left from the many shipwrecks that littered its overreaching limbs, but for the luster of the coral itself. Under the sun they shone with the satin gleam of unpolished gold. Empty and silent as the trireme entered, no schools of fish or other life emerged from their natural shelters in the crystal waters.

Ngala stalked the edge of his boat, eyes wide to the threat of what lay in those maze-like growths. The discovery of the underwater temple, a thought shoved away in the face of constant danger, crawled from shadow to pluck dark tunes on his heartstrings.

"Sorcery," he said to himself, a word spoken with hatred.

Sorcerers had ruined the face of his continental homeland, from the still-smoking ruins of Tolivius in the central savannah to the west, and the Gypians' continued "Moonlight Wars," smiling and trading in the daylight world while their mystics and seers designed devastations at night.

Plague, possessions, even the talk of centaurs—nothing good came when humankind sunk into the labyrinths of the arcane.

Steady on the boards as Tausi steered through switch-currents and hidden riptides—sincere dangers that would do worse than maroon them at sea—Ngala watched the shifting waters he had revered only days ago, wondering at how he had missed its ancient dread. The sun obscured the ocean surface, the glare setting his hairs on end.

The Gamka rode the gentle waves of Shallow Bay as they cleared the shimmering reefs. The clean sand, once only a wisp of a thought at the edge of the world, smiled pale with welcome. Ngala scanned the inlet, on the hunt for any sign of trouble. He doubled back to the stern where his children waited.

Zaki lay on her side in the wrenched position, stark spots of red wetting the dirty blankets she hid within. Her eyes glossy, she gazed up at the sky in whatever daze death gifted toward the end.

"Right for the shore, Captain," Ngala told Tausi. "I want that beach."

Enlivened by the fresh wind, his son snarled in harsh laughter, bearing down on the steering oar so it did not deter or stray. "Right to the beach!"

Ngala left his children again, darting into the hold.

Raiders and rowers worked side by side in the ship's well, hauling buckets of water back to sea as the sea pushed back. The timekeeper had kept his rhythm solid, save for a few off-strikes here and there, unnoticeable enough that the crew knew to carry on. Nkuku emptied the last few drops of dzan into his open mouth and tossed the glass over his shoulder, spotting Ngala as he did so.

"Hello, Patros! Time to die?"

"Run me aground!"

The timekeeper's smile took on a mad, leering quality. He nodded and dropped his beater. Hand after hand smacked wet goatskin, fast and sharp, banging out thunder shots that rattled every oarsman. Stuttered by the order, they halted their revolutions, unsure of what to do.

Nkuku sneered at them. "At it, you salt-dogs! Life or death! Choose!" He pounded the drum, unrelenting with its tempo.

The rowers let up a macabre cheer. Heaving themselves back, they whipped the oars ahead in a time unnatural for starving, depleted men, and in unison dug into the calm waters that threatened to choke them in a death worse than most—drowned, trapped, and without hope. They carved their blades into the sea and pushed.

The hull cracked in reply, the fissure of the keel sounding doom as water sprayed through, soaking everything and everyone within the hold.

"Row! Row!" Nkuku lashed his arms on the hide. "Row! Row!"

The men screamed back every time they pulled.

"Go tend to your children, Captain," he cried. "Let death earn it!"

Ngala roared up the stairs, nearly hopping onto deck in time to see Tausi point far ahead. Turning on the spot, he spied the bright green leaves, soft sand, and the lapping white breakers running to shore.

And the Ulmo.

Standing at the edge of the water, the primordial monster dripped yellow mucus where Tausi had torn an eye from the blighted, alien head as waves pounded his stout legs. Heavy claws low to the sides, he stood hunched, black tail extended fully into the sand beneath the rushing tide to bolster a wide stance.

Ngala made contact with the fallen priest's remaining eye, not letting his own leave until a long, intentional moment vanished between them, one foe to another.

"The beast is mad," Tausi shouted. "We have to turn!"

"No," Ngala said. "Run him down!"

"Father?"

He turned on the steering oar, rage inhabiting every line of his face. "Run him down, boy."

Tausi slipped the locking peg from the band of his loincloth. Securing steerage for dead-ahead, he crouched down and slid underneath it, covering his injured sister's body with his own.

Pleased with his son's action, Ngala faced the enemy who had taken so many.

Hunger, thirst, the ache of the flesh—these hindrances tapped the last wells of strength, of resolution, he had. Charging from his place by the steering oar, he ran in a broken, tired gait, unwilling to let this moment pass without satisfaction. Along his route, he retrieved another of the raiders' fallen bows, and counting the final five arrows in his quiver, he reached the front of the ship in time to see the Ulmo hunker down, ready to accept the onslaught.

Their gazes met again, man and monster.

Ngala growled while he extracted an arrow, the bowstring tight on the pads of his fingers when he set the shaft. He aimed for the center of the Ulmo's dark mass.

The Gamka, driving hard as the prow dipped beneath the blue water, struck the bottom, the keel cutting hard into the earth. Ngala loosed his first arrow, which deflected off the Ulmo's broad shoulder. The trireme creaked, groaned, and screams followed a splintering. The ship continued its death race, forward unto ruin.

Ngala pulled his next arrow when the shock calmed, then aimed and fired. The shaft broke on the Ulmo's wide chest, who barely moved save for the soft twitch of his antennae, the slow motion of his unbound claws.

He screamed at his unassailable target.

The Ulmo stared his baleful stare, one-eyed and implacable.

The third arrow came out, and without taking time to place his shot, Ngala raised the bow and loosed.

The trireme shifted again, riding high as her keel skipped on unseen rocks beneath the sand, forcing her up and to the right. Unable to see whether his arrow flew true to target, Ngala rolled hard to the side, across shoulder and neck, ending up on his feet at the trireme's swinging portside. He heard the steerage snap in two with a thundering crack.

He rose to find his enemy again.

The Ulmo had fallen to one knee, the white fletching a flag he had taken to his leg.

Showing no emotion, no hint of actual pain, he struggled to support his injured limb. A claw came around and snapped the wooden shaft before he yanked the rest out, leaving a gross hole behind where the iron head had done its work.

Ngala cackled like a hyena in his yesteryears, no longer an echo of Tausi's fiery rage. The fourth arrow appeared on his bowstring, barely a thought before it too left, zipping into the Ulmo's leg again.

Deflecting off the chitin, the arrow caught in the space between the groin and main carapace, an intrusion that made the beast's tail spasm. The Ulmo wailed, thrashing in the waves as his legs gave out. *The*

Gamka's prow closed, the meters between force and sorcery meeting in a shot no arrow could match.

"I see you, you infernal bastard!" Ngala threw his bow up, celebrating his feat. "I see you, you son of a—"

The trireme's prow ground its way into the beach, the hard-packed sand ending its drive with a crunch and *thunk*, a low sound Ngala might have found peculiar if the air rushing past his ears had not been so loud. Existence disappeared in a spinning, flashing mess of sand, trees, and sky.

Ngala's body crashing in the hard earth ended in immediate, unforgiving blackness.

CHAPTER 12

DARKNESS

"He can't die. Not now."

Tausi's broken voice woke Ngala, yet he could not open his eyes. A pinion of darkness, sharp and searing, radiated through his skull. He felt the sun on his face, an easy and gentle wind—but his body did not respond, mired beneath the weight of the spear affixing him to the sightless earth.

"He's still breathing," said Zaki. "We just need to let him alone. Let time decide things."

Breathing. He could feel that.

The expanding of his chest, his lungs taking in sweet, cool air. Cooking fires flavored its wonderful scent. Focused on the joyous sensation, he refused to let go of any gain, centering every thought on his breath, then his lungs, and finally that sweet savor. A clue of his body's existence flared somewhere in the pitch of his concussed mind, a beacon he ran toward.

Ngala wiggled his big toes.

"What is it with our brood and time? Time, time, time! You both speak about time when we are here, now," said Tausi.

Nkuku joined in, his delivery flat. "Your father hit his head. It's not the first time I've seen him do it, or the hardest. There was this one time—"

73

Zaki grumbled at the timekeeper. "Nkuku..."

Ngala forced open his swollen eyes. Pulsing white light threaded agony in his nose, cheeks, and forehead. It took effort to work his jaw loose. "It's still not good for you."

The light ceased its heartbeat attack, ebbing until shapes, shades, and color reasserted in hues of blue, green, and finally the rich chestnut of Tausi's wide, relieved expression.

The boy's smile, from ear to ear, spurred Ngala's heart. Zaki came into view, followed by Nkuku, and then a rower, then a raider. Soon every man crowded around the pallet he laid upon, a hundred smiles beaming. Tall shadows fell over him, yet the darkness of their looming was a warm welcome to the mind's aimless splinter.

Tausi touched his father's forearm.

Ngala formed his lips in a small, sheepish grin. "Were you worried?"

The crew broke out in laughter, even Tausi, who roared as loudly as the rest.

When the men settled, Nkuku shooed them off, sending rower and raider alike back to work at the camp they had formed beyond the line of trees. In the gaps between the straight trunks of emerald and purple canopies, the blue sea called beyond, its slight waves crashing on Shallow Bay's white, smooth shores.

Moored on the beach lay *The Gamka*, or what remained of it.

Zaki noticed his study of it from her place at his side, resting upright on a pallet much like his own. A full flush had returned to her cheeks, and the sweat of her brow did not run thin or clammy. "Do you want to get up, Captain?"

Ngala stuck his hands out for assistance, nodding. He kept his sorrowful gaze on his wounded trireme, her shape becoming more uneven the longer he looked at her.

Tausi helped him up with both hands, earning a thankful nod from Nkuku when they were both up on their feet. Supporting his father's full weight on his powerful frame, the young man carried him forward.

Zaki called after them. "Tausi."

"I know, sister," her brother said. "I'll keep him under control."

"Like hell," said Ngala. The warm earth, sandy and brown, cushioned his feet as he rocked onto his legs. He tensed for a long, frightful second before blood rushed down his shins to set the nerves in his lower body on fire. The first few steps uneasy, he soon plodded ahead, each motion smoother than the last.

He cleared the jungle trees with his commander and timekeeper in tow, his gait soon turning into a march.

"Slow down, Captain," said Nkuku. "Captain!"

"Did I get him?" Ngala asked, arriving at the sands. A tropic wind brushed every crevice of his body, emboldening his trek. "Did I get him?

Tausi kept up. "We destroyed everything in our path."

"Did you see him?"

"Captain."

"Did you see him?" he asked again.

The beach ebbed slowly with the coast's natural descent, the low tide having drawn the sea back to expose the scoured battlefield the trireme stripped in passing. The giant rut the trireme had made still formed itself in cement-like sand, closer to where the waves painted the edge of earth brown and black, an indelible mark. Pieces of the hull too heavy for the pull of the ocean lay like butchered meat, bits of a body ripped apart.

Nothing.

No bits of chitin, no broken claws. Ngala stalked around his boat, seeking any sign of the monster's deserved end. "What happened?" he asked after the first circuit.

"The prow collapsed when we struck the shelf, but something bumped us up onto the keel," Tausi said, his feet sunken in the small waves. "She tilted to port when the front quarter sheered half the planks."

"We lost six benches of rowers," Nkuku added. Even in the fresh day's sun, the circles around his big eyes were as dark as night. "We haven't found their bodies."

"Did the Ulmo take them?" Ngala asked, stunned by the horrid revelation.

"No, Father," said Tausi with a broken smile, somewhere between the elation of being alive and the despair over those that were not there to say the same. "Nobody has seen the Ulmo since we arrived on land. We're on land, Father."

"We made it to land, Ngala," Nkuku echoed, forcing a grin past his tortured exhaustion. "We did it."

The reality of their words was underscored by the wind on his back, the rustle of the green fronds in the coconut trees. Ngala looked to *The Gamka* on her side. A quick smile crossed his face—the starboard had remained relatively intact save for a few cracks along the keel, but a quick check of the forest behind them promised enough timber to do the job.

"How much of the loot did we give away to Oyla?" Ngala asked.

"Just a third," Nkuku said. "The rowers held onto most of it, and those that didn't...well, they were paid well."

"Aye," said Tausi.

Satisfied, Ngala returned his gaze back out to sea. Whatever waited out there could not get him, his children, or his crew—not without a different sort of fight. Contented by this change in fortunes, he shut his eyes and breathed in the sea salt, its notes sweet and pure.

He allowed himself all the time in the world.

The cooking fires smelled sweeter in the cool night air. The smoke trailed off into a perfect sky strung with stars. Beneath those pinholes of heaven, the corsairs sang their old shanties, swigging a rough dzan one of them had concocted from "their old ma's spell at the pot," a rude saying for the sugar-swill that burned instead of bled, sickened instead of healed.

After so many days at sea without fresh meat, the weakened men pleased themselves with a rougher fare like sand snakes and beetles, and a few hunted down small dust hares that liked to clean their silver coats in the dunes. A small stream filled with fresh water subsisted their heavier thirsts.

Ngala sat by his own fire, a tiny pile of burning leaves and sticks. The small trails of smoke disappeared beyond its red smolder, but the heat offered more than enough warmth to keep him for the chilly night ahead. Wrapped in a dry blanket, his eyes blinked heavy as he dreamed in the distance, his thoughts somewhere near where the real world faded away.

"Are you awake?" Zaki asked.

He coughed on some unexpected spit, which startled him awake. "Of course. What do you need?"

He spied his daughter's form under the tree next to his, swaddled in extra layers to keep the cold from her frail body. Her color had returned fully, but the days at sea left behind a toll she would pay in bedrest.

"Nothing," she said. "I was just watching you doze off."

The observation discomforted Ngala—he almost heard Zaki's mother in her voice. "An odd thing to watch."

"Sorry. You're so intent."

Ngala searched the ground beside him, spotting his short iron sword. Tausi had recovered it from the hold, a surprising gesture he had not expected after their enmity. Being on land had changed every man in the crew who valued their piece of beach as much, if not more, than the trireme they had called home. Peace settled as if it had never left before they struck this cursed bay.

"Things are never so simple. And we...I almost lost the crew because I did not contend well with sorcery."

Zaki hummed back. "Well, it was sorcery. Some things do not come down to simple muscle and brawn."

Ngala reached from within his blanket and grabbed his sword's hilt, secured by the iron's natural chill he felt every time he touched the weapon. He squeezed the bone handle again, tighter to make sure he felt the carved ridges dig his palm. "It was more than brawn and muscle. We had something more, something I wish I had seen when I was younger."

"When your father fled Tolivius."

He met his daughter's quiet gaze, nodding gently after vexing on bad, bad memories. "I watched sorcery tear down an entire city, and I never thought we could defeat that sort of power."

"You led us," Zaki said.

"And you led me," he replied without missing a beat. "And you did it half-dead. If there isn't someone more qualified to be a captain of her own ship—"

"You say too much," she chided in good humor. "That's a lot of tradition to take on."

"It is also tradition to recognize merit, no matter who it comes from," said Ngala, refusing to see doubts—not when he sat by his small fire, in a warm blanket, with a belly full of food in a place where both his children were safe. *The Gamka* would be seaworthy soon after the crew regained their strength and plied a jungle rife with potential planks. "And it is also tradition for a father to fight for his daughter." He mused with a chuckle. "We could even call your boat *The Ulmo*."

A warm smile crinkled Zaki's tired face. "Goodnight, Father."

❀

The strong sugar-drink burned hard in Ngala's chest, a reflux that tormented his sleep.

His dreams did not help matters, for in the depths of night's fog, a hulking shape crept into the small, lighted places where it sullied goodness with foul spells. The screams of dying men, many of them his own, wailed and echoed in a chorus of ghosts, their faces bright and fading as they stood in their multitude. These dead, some of them decades gone, fixed their pale lifeless eyes on him, ready to see vengeance realized.

Screams, real and close, punctured this underworld. Caught in the lucidity of his fugue state, Ngala started as his nightmares appeared before him, alive in lime colors only vodunis conjured in their spirit-chants. Dancing bodies, black against the scattered fires of the camp, pounded the dirt around them as the same shape emerged from the shadows.

Screeching as he flailed his claws, the Ulmo flayed corsairs alive.

From beneath his blanket, peering through the crack of its broken seal with the sand, the screech woke Ngala when his foe disappeared back into the shadows, only to appear again from a different direction, cutting down a fifth man before he arose with sword drawn. A cloud of hot blood and smoky fires hazed the way before him. His blade up by his side, he toed forward.

Men ran from shadow to shadow, on the hunt or in complete terror, searching for hiding places before the brutal beast found them.

He held his sword's hilt in both hands, ready to swing the moment the hulking shape tore out of the murky night. There were more screams, and, pausing every time something moved before him, Ngala heard three more corsairs shriek before they were sharply silenced. "Tausi," he called. "Nkuku?"

"Captain!" The timekeeper appeared out of a cloud of smoke, his heavy beater in one hand and a sword in the other. Swaying on his feet, the rotund corsair teetered, belching a foul smell born of their foul liquor. "The beast has fled, sir. The raiders chased it off to sea...Patros, I—"

"After the bastard!" Ngala moved to pass his old friend only to have Nkuku stop him with a hand to his chest.

"Your crew needs you," he said. "So does your daughter."

"Why? What happened?"

In the starlight breaking past the trees, Ngala watched Nkuku's expression shift from sincerity to dread before real, pure helplessness broke it to pieces. "The Ulmo took Zaki, Ngala. She's gone."

CHAPTER 13
HOLY DIVER

For too many a time Ngala had seen the sun edge the horizon, dawn scattering stars and seabirds alike as another doomed day started much like the last one.

The leftovers of his crew, only enough to row out of Shallow Bay when the time came, tended to the bloodied remains left strewn across the beach. Many had been snapped apart, their hands left far behind when they had fallen to bleed out. The monster mutilated many of them, battering them into pulpy, bruised heaps before finishing them off with a skull-crushing blow or a jagged gash made at their throats. Dozens of arrows had flown, more than a few swords broken. The fifteen men who died gave their lives for the most peculiar prize taken from them.

"The Ulmo kidnapped her," Tausi whispered through swollen lips, the corners raw and bloody.

His left eye, swollen shut and purpled darker than his umber skin, made his good right eye starker in its contained shock. The sharp defiance they had taken on while aboard *The Gamka's* hell-ride had eased during their momentary peace on the beach, but now fate had sharpened them—this time in absolute doubt of whether or not they would be safe again. Ngala recognized the real trauma beyond the horrid cuts and abrasions afflicting his son's worn body, the bruising spread across his back, shoulder, and chest where the beast had injured the limb to the point that his son could no longer lift his sword arm.

Left helpless, lame, and exhausted, Tausi groaned through his ruined lips. "I tried," he said, words slurring. His clean eye brimmed tears. "The monster appeared out of the shadows, standing over her. I didn't even think of what to do when I realized I had my sword in my hand and I stabbed it in the back. My blade went in..."

Ngala shushed him. "It's all right."

"It's not all right," cried Tausi through the pain. "He dragged her away on her back. She could be dead. She could be dead, and I never got to tell her how sorry I was."

"You'll still get to tell her," he said, gently holding his son's bruised shoulders as he positioned Tausi into a more comfortable pose on the ground. The strong body quivered from the deep shame of a brother, a son, failing his family in the moment they needed him most. Ngala sat there, cradling Tausi until he ceased to murmur regrets about his sister and fell into a stupor.

Leaving his son beneath the palms as they fanned in the gentle wind, he regathered with Nkuku near one of the smoldering bonfires while the last of their dead were buried in shallow graves, given little more than a few salt-chants and old charms to see them off to whatever waited them in the world below.

"We can't go looking for her," the timekeeper said, staring hard into the embers at their feet.

"I don't expect anyone to come with me," Ngala said. "Do you remember when Black Lizard disappeared?"

"This isn't the same thing."

"She's my daughter, Nkuku." He locked eyes with the man beside him, who turned his gaze away in defeat. His final reservoir of hope sang for him to carry on. "I'm not leaving her to that damned creature."

"I know, Patros," said Nkuku. He offered him a scarred arm. "But they are the crew. I'll keep them here for two days and no more. After that, I might have to march them through the jungles." The weight of those words made the timekeeper swallow hard. "If you don't find her by tomorrow morning, you should come back."

"I won't."

"I know that too."

Ngala took his friend's forearm. "Two days."

"Godspeed, my captain." A broken smile dimpled the timekeeper's cheeks. Tears flooded his eyes. "Know that I love you."

The beach went onward, forever to the horizon, where the sun neared after another noon, another failed day. Ngala dropped his first canteen of water in the sand as he plodded, wiping his mouth with the offending hand.

Even with the green scrap of sail one of the rowers had given him when the crew saw him off, the headscarf offered little protection from Nyam's constant study of this lonely, weakening fool. His sword, the only tool or weapon he had brought with him, hung like a stone in its baldric. Thankful that years of sea, sweat, and blood had softened the strap so it did not cut his shoulder, he marched forward, eyes always to the sea for a clue—for something.

The rush and retreat of the waves, boundless but eternal in its steadfast rhythm, cast a hypnotic spell.

The roar of the charge, the whispers of the retreat, the way the fading sunlight played on the Mirror before the stars embedded bits of heaven in its formless surface embedded those same diamonds in his heart. Shades of peach and plum spread across the darkening vault, and slowly, each little lonely soul that had gotten trapped in the sky's tapestry arrived. His bare feet crushed shells, shifting sand. The drone of the march carried him forward, step after step, until the beat came like the oars.

He nodded to the brine-singer when he marched past her. "Good evening."

She watched him go on by, her smooth brow furrowed.

Ngala stopped in his tracks. He looked back over his right shoulder, main hand too far from his sword and he too far from her to pull the blade in time. At a standstill, they stared, two souls trapped on the shores of Shallow Bay.

"I figured it out," he blurted when the silence grew too long.

The brine-singer tilted her head to the side, her hematite-eyes curious like her posture—slightly forward and waiting.

"You were probably one of the priestesses around that altar, weren't you?"

The question froze the brine-singer. After a second she nodded, shaking her light blue mane.

"I hate magic," he said, a tired smile on his face while he rubbed the scruff on it. "I've always hated magic, and sorcerers, and whatever goddamn reasons your lot uses to excuse what they do. And I don't feel bad for you, if you're wondering." His grin ebbed at her wounded expression. "I've lost a lot of men in your bay, brine-singer. And that damned Ulmo has taken my daughter."

The words lost their freshness, and the brine-singer stepped forward in a small, hopeful gesture, her hands out in peace to match her grateful smile. *"Azinza."*

He saw a young girl's smile, heard her laugh, and the smell of fresh flowers surged through Ngala's senses, weakening his knees. A maiden no older than sixteen ran across the stone in a bright corridor, chased by a cadre of younger adherents not yet grown into their robes. She scooped up one of the smaller ones in her toned arms, the hem of her simple himation blossoming outward as she spun the child around, laughing as the rest cried for their turn.

The vision ended as quick as it came, leaving Ngala blinking hard in search of his bearings. He was unsurprised when he rose from the murk to find he had turned completely and walked to the brine-singer.

Now separated by half a foot, the proximity tore at Ngala. He should have yanked his sword free. "I am Captain Ngala," he said, forcing himself to remain poised. "Do you know where the Ulmo took my daughter, Azinza?"

The brine-singer nodded. She offered her hand.

Moments passed before Ngala accepted.

She led them to the edge of the Mirror, its darkening tide gentle and calm.

Hesitating where the last wave broke, Ngala put up a meager resistance as Azinza pulled them into the shallows. The wet, sucking sand rooted him to reality until her preternatural quickness yanked him forward. Bobbing for a few moments, he took in deep, heavy breaths before she dragged him beneath the water. For long moments he flailed, knowing nothing but the warmth of her touch and the movement of the cold against his bare flesh.

Azinza kicked. Her gray form, almost luminescent with speckles of blue, red, and purple, streaked like an eel through the water, twisting and turning past stone and small reefs.

Saved from striking any of these hard surfaces, Ngala struggled to keep the air in his lungs when the brine-singer banked hard, shearing him in the unseen currents as she darted left. Only her powerful grip on his forearm kept him tethered to her, though the strain in his sword arm stretched beyond imagination. The sear arrived, departed, and arrived before it settled. They entered an earthen tunnel far beneath the waves.

His lungs ached.

Caught in the perfect darkness of a realm where sunlight had long not touched it, Ngala merged into the surrounding fugue.

Air bubbled from his nose and mouth, the smoke of his soul aflame like the city beyond. He remembered watching, crying, as his father reached with a charred, oozing hand to stop his son, a silent plea to be left behind. Tolivius burned gray columns of ash, and for days afterward, he marched southward with the rest of the refugees beaten out of house and home.

Triremes charged the coast, corsair flags unfurled. Black Lizard shouted havoc, waving his sword in the air above his head as Ngala led the raiders in their battle chants, smacking the flat of his blade against his hide shield.

The Mirror Sea glittered, greater than any jewel, bauble, or coin he could pilfer.

His wife laughed in his ears when he fell asleep.

CHAPTER 14

THE THING THAT SHOULD NOT BE

N gala awoke when Azinza dragged him from the water, setting him on a hard stone floor. Cold air bit his wet skin, pricking it in a thousand points of gooseflesh. Using his sword's scabbard as a crutch, which had somehow migrated from its baldric to his hand, he drew in great breaths to feed his air-starved body.

Stale water dripped from the glowing points of the stalactites on the limestone ceiling above him, their pale light soft and constant.

"Where are we?" he asked between gasps.

Azinza remained beside him, her reflective eyes gleaming. She said nothing as she looked down the passage, bringing a finger up to her full lips. Feeling a fool for his noise, Ngala shut his mouth and struggled for the rest of his air by nose alone.

When she could help him to his feet, they crept forward in silence.

The soft pat of his bare feet and the smooth brush of hers soon became a solitary beat, each echo a dread call to whatever lay in the dark. Azinza led Ngala down a long passage lit by the glowing rock as he recovered from the drowner's sickness. The narrow path eventually widened, its rough walls smoothing in a polished luster.

A doorway opened to a grand chamber, its outline cut from the tunnel's gloom with azure-emerald light. Broken columns of twisted blue and purple marble lay in chunks across the flagstones, their light color almost whitened by the dome rising from the low, circular wall. Made of translucent pieces of pearl-white glass, the sea waited beyond that roof, a filter for the night sky above the water.

At the center of the floor lay a wide step pyramid cut from limestone. Blood and bits of gore stained its faces, and around it rested many corpses—some burnt, most of them rotted. A few among them were unwitting corsairs Azinza had lured when she first appeared, though the rest were victims of the Ulmo's attack. Yet among the bodies around the base of the sacrificial table were drier, more feminine shapes. Beneath their crust shined bits of purple and gray scale.

Able to walk on his own power, Ngala pointed to them. "Those were your sisters."

Azinza stiffened at the observation, enough to confirm his recollection.

"Is the Ulmo here?"

The brine-singer shook her head "no."

Weaving their way around the crooked path formed by the broken columns, they reached the sacrificial block. Close to the bodies of the slain brine-singers, Ngala noticed how their bodies were arranged around the pyramid, one at each point and the others strewn evenly at the sides—save for one space where a body should have lain.

Ngala nodded at it. "You?"

A nearby clatter broke the quiet before Azinza answered.

Ngala drew his sword and stepped in front of the brine-singer. "Run if I order you."

A hand shot up from behind the altar, bloody fingers digging into the spaces between the flagstones. Zaki pulled herself up to the edge, grunting red spittle as she clawed to complete her monumental effort.

Ngala leapt, bounding to the top of the pyramid, all thoughts of the monster and the brine-singer set aside. "Zaki! Zaki" He gathered his daughter in his arms.

Zaki wept, her tears leaving lines in the blood and grime caked on her face. "I never thought I'd see you again. I thought I'd never be able..."

Ngala quieted her, his thumb across her broken lips as he held her face. "Where are you hurt?"

She coughed a second time, wincing with each breath. "My ribs are broken. I think my ankle as well."

"All right, I'm going to get you up slowly." Ngala lifted Zaki onto the elevated slab and laid her upon it. He examined her ankle first, gently touching the swollen joint. He felt the shallow cut where the Ulmo's claw had torn the flesh. "How long have you been down here?"

Holding her ribs, Zaki squirmed, hissing while her father's fingers touched the wound.

"Sorry," Ngala whispered, his fingers coming away sticky.

Azinza touched his shoulder. He glanced to her, noticing how she stared back at the tunnel where they had entered.

"Did you see where the Ulmo went?" Ngala whispered to Zaki.

"It left me here. It kept trying to make sure I stayed on the slab. Even lamed me for it."

"We have to hurry." Ngala motioned for the brine-singer to help him.

"No." Zaki pushed their hands away. "We have to clean this block."

"Why?"

"I don't know, but the beast has been bleeding the crew on it. It sparks when the blood touches it. I think..." Zaki groaned in pain as she forced herself up. "I think this altar is what kept *The Gamka* trapped."

"Do you have a bucket? A bowl?" Ngala asked Azinza.

The brine-singer disappeared into a darkened corner of the temple. She reemerged with an accomplished grin and an old bowl of hammered brass.

"Stay with her," said Ngala, taking the vessel.

He had only made it halfway to the passage back to the sea when a heavy thud echoed out of the tunnel. Hard shell scraped the walls.

The Ulmo emerged, the width of his body barring the entrance. His single brown antenna twitched while the remaining eye simply bored, its violent luster obscured by a thick membrane. Across the whole front of his carapace, a gooey, yellow substance had seeped between the endless cracks and fractures *The Gamka's* prow had made of it, drying to a hard clay consistency.

The two foes paused when each realized the other's presence.

Sword in his right, the brass bowl in his left, Ngala marched out to die. He wished he had said better goodbyes, smoked a bit of cannabis, and drank a strong glass of dzan, yet for some reason, the challenge chiseled a cruel smile on his face. The young corsair, that black wraith of the past, flickered alive in his heart. His sword's hilt had never felt so at home in his hand, or the blade a better part of himself.

No matter their disagreements, he never misunderstood his son. Time had taught him the value of accuracy over speed, precision over power, and the worthiness of not rushing in.

Not now. Not after all these sorcerers had taken from him.

The Ulmo had not left the tunnel's opening, almost frozen in an ugly statue's pose, claws at his side.

Ngala banged the flat of his blade on the bottom of the brass. He barked in dark laughter. "Look at that chest. You'd think even with that kind of wound, you'd have just slunk off somewhere, like all you damned sorcerers do."

The Ulmo clicked from its writhing, inhuman mouth, which almost sounded like a rebuttal. (This is not your world, worm-of-the-coast. You and all your kind entered my lands, no matter how you came. My power here is absolute, not yours. You dared me.)

A sneer like a lion's transformed Ngala's face, a mask of snarling rage that ran heat from his jaw down to his hands, which gripped his weapons tighter and tighter. "And you probably thought you'd seen the last of me."

Chittering.

Ngala swung the bowl around, sending it flying.

The bronze vessel struck the monster in the face with a loud clang as he charged from the threshold, undeterred by the missile.

Ngala met his enemy in the middle of the floor, leaping over one of the fallen columns and landing in a crouch. Both hands on the hilt of his sword, he stabbed forward with a hard lunge, the iron point piercing the broken chiton.

The Ulmo looked down at the barb with his alien stalk. Bringing a claw up, he batted Ngala in the head.

Thrown like a rag doll, the corsair landed hard on the floor and rolled. Rising on hands and knees, Ngala spat red onto the stone, frothy drops joining the smeared puddle formed by the blood leaking from his broken nose. The Ulmo battered him with an underhand swing, rolling him on the round flagstones until he ended on his back. Grunting through the pain, Ngala rose on his knees, somehow aware he had kept his sword in his hand. He slashed, screaming as gory iron skipped across the wide, broken chitin.

The monster answered the blow with his own. The world swirled in painful stars. The Ulmo clubbed him again, putting Ngala again on his back. The sharp saw-like edges of a claw slid around his neck, narrowed enough to rasp his skin.

"Oh, beast."

Torn away, Ngala saw the original face of the Ulmo—a dark, handsome man cursed by wild, frantic eyes. The Ulmo paused, claw open.

"I have a song which holds a promise."

Explosion of light. The eleven priestesses knelt on all fours, screaming pleas for the sorcerer to stop. The Ulmo pulled away, tearing skin from both sides of Ngala's neck. He marched upon the altar.

Ngala pawed the ground beside him as his vision restored, and his hand fell on his blade. He rose, lancing every nerve in his body as he crawled atop a broken column. He leapt with all his might, wrapping himself across the Ulmo's back.

Clinging as the monster twisted to throw him off, Ngala brought his sword over the Ulmo's head and stabbed downward. The point plunged into the speckled shell, forcing the tip past the hard plate. He yanked it out and drove it in again, this time finding the yellow brain beneath.

The Ulmo screeched, hurtling them backward into a standing column.

Wind stolen by the crushing impact, Ngala stabbed once more, breaking through the tough exoskeleton. Yellow slime and gelatinous rank leaked from the fissure. He forced the blade deeper.

The Ulmo shuddered. His remaining antenna ceased to twitch. The carcass teetered forward and crashed into the stone floor, never moving once it landed.

Rolling off the back of his slain enemy, Ngala crawled, fueled by the odd, concussed hope he would end up at the altar.

Consciousness ebbed and pulsed before his swollen eyes, the rough, broken floor below spotting crimson. Heartbeats throbbed in his ears. The world rang, rang and rang, until he shut his eyes again, contented with cutting his palms on shattered marble and scraping his knees.

The chamber thundered, stone cracking while glass warbled. Hands

—strong, delicate hands—gently guided him onto his back. Ngala stared up at Azinza, not recognizing her. She shouted at his deafness, and unable to focus on her features, he wailed when she took him up in her slight arms.

When the pain paused, he looked up at the dome of the temple. Gaping fissures raced across the stone, unleashing jets of seawater through the cracked pearl glass supported by its compromised lattice.

Somewhere in the mess, Zaki appeared, hobbling beside Ngala as Azinza carried him into the tunnel. The roar of the world split his ears open to a crackling, thundering noise.

He mired in perfect, ineffable darkness.

CHAPTER 15

SAIL

Waves crashed cold foam against his face as he sputtered alive. Coughing the seawater from his lungs, Ngala turned over on his hands and knees in the swirling surf. He retched out salt and saliva until his lips burned.

The brightness of a blue morning blinded him, and the sun shone silver across the endless sky. When he finally swallowed enough air past the knots in his chest, he crawled, reaching the dry sand where he collapsed for a moment.

Grit pasted against the side of his face, the coolness of the fleeing night threatened to lull his exhausted body into unwanted sleep. He could not sleep, he knew—to sleep, without fresh water, would mean death.

Death meant he would not see his children again.

"Zaki," he mouthed with his raw mouth. He summoned his voice, or what he could of it. "Zaki!"

He dug his hands in, set his knees, and raised up. On his knees, he braced both arms against the slant of his lap, heaving before a calm breath found him. Nausea threatened to buckle his focus. The sun glared off the white sand.

When he could muster the will, he opened his eyes to take in his surroundings. Alone on the shore, he scanned immediately to the water, and without fail, spotted an obvious change to the Shallow Bay.

Connected to the land by a sandstone bridge that had risen with its mass, the broken roof of the underwater temple shaped a jagged crown where the stone and glass had fallen away. Gulls circled above in a long, swirling cone. Many dived, feasting on the dead that lay out of sight.

Exposed to the sunlight, the rainbow murals of the leftover walls glistened. Tamed leviathans, attached to objects he could not recognize for his own sanity, ushered droves of travelers in a golden sky above the still-blue, still-shifting waves. Below them, sorcerers raised great metropolises of green and yellow, the earth red beneath their naked feet. Thousands lived happily in scenes of commerce, dance, performance, and magic.

Somewhere in the clouds, etched in almost-invisible relief, peered the gods from their celestial hiding places.

Awed by the sight, Ngala could not tear his gaze away.

And then he remembered what had happened there.

He shouted past the exhaustion. "Zaki! Zaki!"

Heaving when his breath left him, Ngala stumbled to his feet. Able to walk a few yards to the first low dunes of Shallow Bay's crescent coast, the shade of the first beckoned from a distance he hoped was closer than he imagined.

Fighting its temptation, he turned where he stood, thirst driving his panic. "Zaki!"

"Captain Ngala."

The voice froze him. Soft and melodious, it possessed a familiar power. The immediate instinct to reach for his sword stalled, and he half-slumped to his hip to find the source behind him.

Though by look and sight, the young woman on the sunny beach could not have been older than fourteen, maybe fifteen, the age in her silver eyes, which had specks of shale—spoke of one who had seen centuries pass. She had appeared as if from nowhere. Long umber hair framed an unblemished face, the locks glowing at their ends in a blue-purple light.

The garment wrapped around her, strands of silk and a blue weedy-like material shimmered against the orange cloth.

When she spoke, her voice sounded like sunset, caught fresh before its coming.

"Do you recognize me?" she asked, calm and assured.

Ngala gulped at the salt in his throat, too parched to speak for the moment. He nodded.

Azinza, now transformed to her original form—at least what he guessed she had reverted to—nodded back in grim agreement. "Good. That will save us much time."

He licked his lips. "You can speak."

"You're already daring."

"My kind come that way," said the corsair captain, confused by the response.

He almost seized when this girl, an impossible, centuries-old maiden, shot her gaze at him with a weight behind it. She held him there, letting Ngala heave a bit while he tried to find some moisture in his mouth.

"You, as a man, do not," she said, empty of any real bitterness. "You are not like the others of your kind."

"Don't flatter me—" The pain of his thirst knotted his stomach. Ngala tasted the blood on his cracked lips as he doubled over.

The priestess came forward in silence, the sand muffling her bare footfalls. Her soft, strong hand lay on his drying back. A coolness spread beneath his skin, and his gut slackened. Able to find his breath again, Ngala rested his forehead against the warm, shifting ground.

"I swam Zaki to the shore where your men were still camping," she said. "She was delivered into safe hands."

"My son?"

"He greeted me...coolly," she said, her voice suddenly mortal for a moment. "Hopefully, that will change. He and Mr. Nkuku are now on the way with men to collect you."

Restored by her powerful touch, Ngala rested back on his knees. Wiping the sand from his forehead, he did not take his eyes off her. Azinza stood there, her checking him as much as he guarded her, until she turned away.

The hem of her wrap, golden and shimmering, whipped in the coastal winds. Her silver stare rested on the temple at the bay's center, where she watched it for a while before she continued southward, away from the land.

Away from the rest of the known world.

He arose, quicker this time, though the pain in his legs slowed him. "You're human."

"One may say so. I hope as much."

"You hope?"

She gave no response to that. Azinza stopped a few yards from where she had found him, arms crossed before her stomach, like she felt a chill instead of the warm breeze that enveloped them. Much to his surprise, a shiver took her on the sand.

Reduced to his mortal, unknowing role, he waited a long time before she calmed.

"I never thought I would be free of him," she said aloud. "I thought that he would find me. That I would be the last..."

"I'll not harm you, nor will anyone else." He scoffed at his own answer.

"Why do you do that?" Azinza turned his way a second time.

"Do what?"

"Scoff at what fate gives you?" She spoke almost with pity, but of a sort mixed in disbelief at Ngala's cynicism.

"I don't know what fate will give me anymore," he said. "Why did any of this happen? Why were we drawn, out of many? How did any of this get this way? How can I promise anything?"

"Oh, Captain," she replied like they had been friends for years.

To Ngala's apprehension, it felt like they had. "What? What did I do now?"

She scoffed this time, then loudly as any strange young woman was wont to do. "Captain, for the first time in centuries, someone listens. You listen, as I knew you would."

She sat up on her pallet of blankets and beddings as tall as she could, trying to reach up with one arm so she could scratch the itch on the back of her head. Zaki winced against the bandages binding her, the half-tear, half-sear of healing flesh pulling against itself. She brought down her firm arms when the effort became too much for her breath to bear.

"You could have simply waited."

Tense from the neck down to the bottom of the back, she slowly turned her head toward the balcony door of her bedchambers.

He stood there, tall and striking in the half-light of the moon. The front of his face was dappled in silver piercings that set his sharp face ablaze in the mask of a sea horse, and his ebon eyes shined from the night. In the shadow beyond her doorway, he watched with curiosity as he muddled something in a small clay bowl he carried in his long-fingered hands.

"And you can stop doing that and just come in. They know we're in here now," Zaki said at half-volume, some of her stamina regained. "I imagine things might be easier."

"Yes. Imagine." Agwe entered her corsair's den nestled beneath Stone Cove's high north-facing cliffs, which protected the long piers and float-towns from the rain and most of the harsher winds.

The light of her small oil lamp on the table across the room flickered dimly before he looked to it. Without a thought or word said, it blazed back to life, its flame growing vibrant.

"It's only cute the first dozen times."

A hoarse chuckle rose from his broad chest. He made it to the side of the bed and lowered the bowl in his hands. Crushed seaweed and honey mixed with salt and specks of many other things was rolled and watered into a green-brown slurry.

"I need to put this on you, my love," he said, presenting his salve.

She nodded, scooting forward among her blankets. He plopped down behind her, and a moment later, the pads of his fingers, cold with the chunky mix, traced at the top edge of the great mark the Ulmo had left. The salt, save for the honey's sweet warmth, ate painfully before it settled. A dullness flooded to the back her head.

"Did you talk to my father?" Zaki asked, her words mushing together a bit.

"Enough that he understands my usefulness," he replied. His fingers left near the first quarter and returned a second later with a larger scoop of cold salve.

The herbs taking hold quickly thanks to her lover's magic, Zaki grunted in passive, accepting displeasure. "So, is she safe?"

"She's a victim," Agwe said with no happiness. "The few times we have spoken, she has revealed much...more than anything you all witnessed."

"I'm sure."

"Zaki?"

His fingers worked down to the middle of her back. Her head swirling, she blinked with sleep in her heavy eyes. "Yes?"

"What happens next? What do you want?"

Her lover's question broke her lethargy, long enough the events of the last few days were taken, in measure, against all the days of her life. The raids, her mother and aunt, the first kill, the last one, Agwe's shining face...

And the Ulmo. The hulking, speeding, terrifying Ulmo.

She wondered then, in a dark, quiet moment, if she had lost her brother and her father, would any of these people have adopted her as she was? Where would she have fallen with Black Lizard? What if fate had been far harsher? What if she had lost Ngala, who only now she felt kinship toward? What if it had been Tausi, lost but desperate to prove himself? Or Nkuku, her compass? What if she had been the only one left?

What if they had all died?

"Zaki," called Agwe. "You're staring."

"I don't want to go back there. Both my father and Tausi will want to, but I don't," she answered in a hollow voice.

Finished smearing the paste down and across her stitched backside, Agwe readjusted his position and wrapped his arms around Zaki. Safe and warm in the solace of the sorcerer's embrace, she gave in to the numbness of the medicine.

His words echoed in her ears. "Your father will give you his ship when he can. Don't you want that?"

"No," she said, too dazed to lie. If anything had been learned in the last weeks of her life, she'd gained knowledge of how feeble lies were next to the wonders of the world. "I don't want that boat. We barely got back on that boat, even with enough crew."

Agwe's curious response, another sound that vibrated in his chest and against her bare back, reached her heart. That safety, the sense of being where she should, deepened with every word he spoke.

And the sorcerer whispered playfully in her ear before she succumbed to healing sleep.

"So, what kind of boat would you like?"

THE END

PART TWO
AT THE MIRROR'S EDGE

CHAPTER I

THE MIRROR SEA

His sandaled feet slapping the top of the stone wall, Tausi sprinted hard for the western tower, his sword out. "Archers on the wall! Prepare for volley!"

Ten men on the tower's high platform lifted their bows in unison and pulled back, waiting for their order.

Tausi batted the wall of the base with the flat of his iron sword, his eye on the targets floating on the sea southward of their position. On the unspoken command, the raiders loosed, shafts arching in a clear blue sky before they fell upon the small ship far to port.

"At distance! Volley, volley," he screamed, booming over men shouting above and below. The beating sun on his bare face and shoulders, his attention turned to the dock in the center of his fortress-city, nearly growling when he observed the portcullis crew raising the Sea Gate off-beat from everyone else. "Speed, you salt-dogs! Get that gate up!"

He stormed the wooden stairs and platforms scaffolding the inner walls of the city down to his trireme, ready to launch from the small bay. The crew aboard had already set their places, the raiders on the top deck arrayed in their arrowhead formation with bows at the ready. As Tausi passed the last few rowers struggling to board with their gear, he leapt from the warped gangplank to the wide starboard rail, avoiding the congestion.

"Pull free! Fly out," Tausi shouted to Nana, a wiry man by the steering oar who answered his captain by dashing down into the ship's hold. *The Ube's* crew pushed out the oars while he rushed over and unlocked the great rudder. The long handle came alive in his hands when the last pin freed.

Rowing forward, the boat sliced the still waters approaching the Sea Gate and was quick to pass into the currents of Shallow Bay.

The Ube struck the tide. Braced against the force of the world's oldest primordial, Tausi grunted as he held firm, feet, hips, and shoulders straining to keep the steering oar straight. Spray bathed his face slick, the salt high in his nostrils.

Nana, Tausi's full-faced bosun, bounded from the hold. "Amare is carrying the beat, Captain! Full on ahead!"

He spotted the three targets and aligned his boat in their direction. A harsh smile creased his tight face, his eyes almost tearful. His sword hung heavy in its holder, eager to be drawn again. "Find the wind. I'll—"

Nana followed Tausi's gaze out in time to see another trireme dash from the west, its weathered green sail billowed with a zephyr's breath. Hard to starboard, the legendary *Gamka* did not deter her course to ram *The Ube*.

"That fool," cried Nana. "He's insane!"

"He's my father," Tausi cried, roaring laughter. "Let's show him something, then."

Nana joined in his captain's laughter and scuttled back into the hold.

"Fix the arm," Tausi ordered the raiders before him on deck. Most of them lowered their bows and crouched at the rails on both sides of the ship, arms snaked around sweat-polished wood while a few remained on the move, leaping high from the boards to pull at hanging knots in the rigging. A clean sail unfurled, a shade of seafoam emblazoned in the black profile of a singing woman.

Tausi pulled hard to starboard when the raiders fixed the cloth, the handle of his steerage groaning in protest as the wood fin chopped through the currents. *The Ube* rushed against the northward surges passing through the golden Avarice Reefs. Her sail fluttered.

"Please," he begged the trireme, hoping that he had bled enough into her that she might bleed back for him.

A breeze caught in *The Ube's* sail, and she banked right. Relieved by his luck, Tausi stayed in his torturous, lean position, the exertion pooling blood into every muscle until they ached.

The trireme completed its turn, aligned with *The Gamka* for a head-on collision.

"She has to turn," Nana said above the rasp of the salt-spray in their faces. "She has to!"

Inflamed by the challenge closing upon him, Tausi half-sneered. "Let her come."

"Captain!"

"I said let her, damn you," he replied, laughing at his bosun's earnestness.

Tausi could feel every soul aboard brace, even the grain beneath his feet. For a moment he wondered—could *The Ube* stand it? Would she bear him through this after he had taxed the hull so many times before?

Every heartbeat, every yard taken, the two triremes closed until they were near enough that Tausi spotted the top deck crew, the raiders arrayed at their rail as he had arrayed his own.

Close enough for a bow shot...then a spear's toss...and then they were too close.

Tausi held to the steering oar. "Impact," he shouted before *The Gamka* veered to her port, taking the last possible moment to avoid their rostrum's fatal kiss. The green sail dropped, and on the starboard side, the raiders stood, launching iron grappling hooks.

The prongs caught on *The Ube's* portside rail, tethering the two boats together.

"Man the portside," Tausi shouted as he locked the steerage. "Nana, get the rowers ready. I want them up here before *The Gamka's* crew hits our rail!"

"Aye, Captain!"

Captain and bosun parting from the stern, Tausi leapt down the stairs to the hold and landed on the other side, drawing his sword as his raiders built their shield wall before the portside. Fastened to each other, the weight of the two ships had slowed the speed dramatically. *The Gamka's* weight tugged both of them to a stop in the water, setting them slightly parallel to each other. The raiders started to reel them together.

Tausi stopped at the end of his raider's formation. "Show these bastards what the men of Shallow Bay are made of!"

His men banged their short spears on the sides of their shields. Instead of chants for war and wrath to their stone and wood gods, they sang welcoming songs, bright choruses they had rehearsed for weeks until every note harmonized, and not one fell flat. His sword still on the last man in line's hide shield, Tausi joined them, not missing a single word of verse.

> *Hail, high the winds they roam,*
> *Endless on the silvered sea,*
> *Where brine-singers dance,*
> *Hail, high with the waves they roam,*
> *For plunder and gold...*

The crew of *The Ube* resounded on the second verse, raising their voices louder when the rowers emerged from below, three teams of two carrying large barrels from the darkness. They scurried along their trireme's starboard. Two more came behind them, carrying small, x-shaped stands.

Close enough that the crew of *The Gamka's* black faces were bared under the mid-day sun, Tausi's grin grew when they lifted a gangplank up like a great monolith before dropping it over the side of their boat, forming a bridge with *The Ube*. Three more rose and fell with loud slams on the boat's rail, until there was absolutely no way either side could stop the other from boarding.

From the cheering men clustered on *The Gamka*, two figures rose.

The man on the left, upright with the help of a walking stick, stood almost as a mirror for Tausi's future. Old Bones Ngala, his woolen hair cut close to his umber scalp to better highlight the gleam of his decorative gold teeth, flashed a wide smile when he caught eyes with his son. His scarred body draped in a length of tawny leopard-skin, worn by only the wealthiest of seafaring warlords. The sword of old iron hung from the baldric on his shoulder.

Tausi matched his father's grin, which grew when the second figure started forward.

She was clad in a gown of bright blue silk that ended at her knees. Two twin swords hung from the belt tightened at her lithe waist, which made her strong shoulders broad and fuller by comparison to her powerful, narrow hips and small breasts—all of which were illusions, he knew, but he wouldn't take those dreams for his sister Zaki, the famed heroine.

She almost danced on the wooden plank as she sauntered over, the cheers growing louder the more flamboyant the poses she struck. Every raider, every rower, and even the ship's two bosuns celebrated—none hid behind one moment of defense, not greed nor violence, for even among bloody men, the notion of family reigned in all hearts.

Gladdened he had done well enough to bring this together, Tausi met his father and sister as they hopped onto his deck. They drew their swords in unison and turned over the handles to each other, the common respect among captains.

Ngala clapped his son's shoulder. "A roaring welcome!"

"We did not expect you for another hour," Tausi replied, at ease under his father's touch. He looked to Zaki, who waved to the last of his men that still cat-called and praised her great beauty. She took his hand when he offered it, their fingers intertwined.

"At least you did not open your archers on us, little brother," Zaki said, still peering at the men around her. "Considering the disregard you paid that poor raft."

Tausi turned his gaze westward, back to the original target of his breakneck launch onto Shallow Bay's azure face.

A small raft floated upon gentle swells, a single layer of wood lashed to a few old wine barrels completed with a grass sail. Hundreds of arrows sprouted from it like an overused pincushion. "*The Mbe* sinks for no foe, sister. But speaking of ships, where is yours? I hear from the messengers you've built one."

"She's working on it," Ngala said in a rehearsed, wry tone.

"And it won't sail until it is ready," she said while they laughed. "It just would not do."

"And it won't do to go without a proper meal before the day carries on." Ngala cleared his throat, as he always did before a new order, when Tausi interrupted.

"Avast, Old Bones!" Tausi signaled to his men.

The Ube's raiders broke their shield wall, revealing four barrels and platters of dried fish, cheese, and bread set out on benches by the starboard that sent a roar through the joined crews. From the rowers marched a drumline led by Amare, the handsome young timekeeper who, wide in his gyrating hips, started up the first thunderous beat on his talking drum. He was soon joined in the next movement by a pair of bone flute players and the youngest crew member armed with a rattling shekere.

"A roaring welcome, indeed." Ngala raised his hand and waved everyone to get started.

The Gamka's crew skittered across the gangplanks, and after some friendly pushing and shoving, the favors were divided so none went without.

The seals on the barrels of dzan, the corsair's powerful liquor, were cracked so the dark brown concoction flowed forth into cups of wood, horn, and clay until more songs rang on the peaceful ocean winds.

In the middle of cracking open the second barrel of fiery dzan, a crewman approached and whispered into the Old Bones' ear.

"Tell her she can come out whenever she likes," Tausi heard Ngala relay to the man. His face flushed immediately and not from drink.

Searching the deck of his ship, Tausi spotted Zaki by the barrels, cradling wooden cups in her hands while a giddy raider filled them. Slipping through the men and few women-raiders *The Gamka* had brought with them, he reached her before she tottered off for more drunken fun.

"Is she here?" Tausi asked her the moment he drew close enough to whisper.

"Why are you whispering?" she asked, deep and loud.

He grabbed her by the arm. "Is she here?"

"Would Father go anywhere without her?"

"Why didn't you tell me?"

Zaki handed him one of her full cups. "Drink, Tausi. She's not here yet."

He took the clay cup and gulped, the sugar burning his throat while its smooth warmth rolled down his chest. Wiping his bearded chin of the sweet dribbles, he scanned the deck of his father's ship, worried beyond words.

His sister made a low, amused sound. "You know if you don't talk to her someone else might one day. And it'll be too late."

"Shush. Don't put that on me."

"Don't put it on yourself," Zaki replied before her gaze shifted ahead, nodding to someone in the distance. "Here she comes, Tausi. Don't freeze."

He turned and leaned against *The Ube's* mast at mid-deck, facing the two inter-joined ships, and spotted her.

The clamor ebbed when the striking young woman ascended from the hold of his father's ship. Every person's eye, no matter their focus, whipped around to watch a black goddess dressed in the finest blue-purple silk to be found along the long coasts of Juut. Her long seafoam hair fell down in waterfall locks that caught Tausi's breath in his chest. Silver eyes, cooler than the moon itself, looked upon every man and woman there with gladness.

Then Azinza glanced Tausi's way, and he averted his gaze.

"Tausi," Zaki chided quietly.

He sipped another mouthful of liquor, numbing his embarrassment. "Leave me alone, sister."

Ngala, his walking stick tapping the boards, padded to his children. "Zaki, go give Azinza a drink and eat some food with her. I need to talk to your brother."

"Aye, Old Bones," she said, off to collect his nursemaid. Left alone together, father and son settled next to each other.

"This was very good of you to do," Ngala said.

Tausi found an abandoned cup lying on the deck nearby. Dumping out its wash, he poured half of his dzan into it and presented it to his father. "Times are good in Shallow Bay."

"How good?"

He stayed a sip. "You gave me four years since its rise to turn it into something of my own. Why do you want to know now?"

Ngala's amusement rankled him, as did the soft, weathered hand on his shoulder. "Humor me, Commander."

"Captain," Tausi said with an edged smile. "You made me so."

His father dipped his head in agreement. "And I'm Old Bones."

"The city holds—"

"City?"

Tausi pressed forward. "The city can hold ten triremes, and we have a barricade ready to extend a new wall if we need more, and there are enough supplies from the citadel to the tunnel to keep us fed for five days of siege—if the attacking boats get past the secret route through Avarice Reefs."

Ngala turned his gaze to the pearl shores of Shallow Bay.

Following, Tausi noted the slight apprehension in his sire's brow, a sight he had not seen in many years, though he understood. This gentle body and its city had not always been a haven for the sons and daughters of plunder—its past was far, far more terrible than that.

"Father," he said, "tell me what is going on."

Ngala looked at his son, and the tension between them disappeared, replaced by a calm, cool peace both had forged as Tausi approached his twenties—a place they both preferred over the strife of Tausi's younger days. He nodded his head at the city, the rebuilt and repurposed temple of the monster they had survived before taking it for their own gains. "Is she ready?"

"Answer me."

One of the corsairs on *The Gamka's* side cried out. "To the north!"

Tausi broke away from his father "Crews to their—"

Ngala grabbed his son's arm. "Crews to their boats! *The Ube* will depart back to the city to prepare for our guests."

"Guests?" Tausi asked aloud.

That old glare his father used to give settled on him. "*The Gamka* will remain to lead them in. Tausi, you will take Azinza and Zaki with you so they can help you prepare rooms."

Tausi interrupted, the dzan cloying his mouth. "Rooms?"

"Go, Captain. You've little time."

The two crews ceased merriment and divided themselves to their native decks, the rowers disappearing by the droves into their holds. The raiders on *The Ube's* side rushed to put away their party favors, though more than a few snuck a few draws from the barrels.

"Well," Zaki said after *The Gamka* lifted their last gangplank and broke away to paddle out to the oncoming fleet. "This was magical."

Tausi held his place at the stern. He recognized the sails among the fleet of triremes headed for his home—the corsairs of Tip Town, Bastards Bay, The Face-Slashers, and even the White Rovers, who lay far to the east past Juut upon a floating city of wood, rope, sail, and iron had come.

He also recognized the bright orange sail of the Land Dogs, Latian bastards and outlaws who had come south when their homeland found them too bloodthirsty, too wild. Captained by the nefarious Illus the Gelded, the thought of letting Stone Cove's longtime rival into his city made Tausi's skin crawl. "Turn about, Nana. Full beat."

Nana, brooding at the oncoming fleet, lugged down into the hold to let Amare know.

Zaki cleared her throat. "Azinza's coming!"

Frozen momentarily by the mere mention of the former brine-singer, Tausi straightened and turned on his heels too quickly, almost tripping forward. Zaki caught him by the arm, laughing as she righted him.

Azinza still stood mid-deck, pleasantly dealing with the intoxicated raiders who awed at her beauty. None of them made any crude moves toward her or uttered something rawer than what they whispered to their salt-wives. Instead, many asked quiet things about their children, their futures, and their fates. They led her on her way, even when she didn't answer them with more than a kind denial.

"Oh, fuck you," Tausi whispered at his sister, who covered her mouth to muffle her chuckling.

The blue-haired goddess approached, her hands laced together in front of her as she locked eyes with Tausi. Azinza made the most beautiful smile he had ever seen. "Captain Tausi. Thank you for letting me aboard your ship."

Zaki nudged him in the arm.

"Welcome aboard *The Ube*," Tausi said in his captain's tone. He bowed slightly, unsure of what to do. "I hope your journey from Stone Cove was uneventful."

"As I like them to be," Azinza said. The wind rustled her blue hair gently, making it seem like a mane of wonders.

He nodded, wordless for a better reply.

"So, what did you call the city?" Zaki asked, breaking the awkward silence.

Tausi awoke from his stupor at the question. Searching for words, *The Ube's* sail caught his attention. The color not too far off from the hue of Azinza's hair, the canvas had been fixed to the main arm and pulled tight to reveal the black singer's face emblazoned upon it. Sweet and soft, the breeze welled in the cloth to push the trireme onward. The youthful pride in the city he had spent the last four years of his life building, re-building, and making his own, disappeared in quiet embarrassment.

He looked to Zaki, who nodded for him to answer, and then to Azinza, who simply smiled.

"Song City," he revealed. "I named it Song City."

CHAPTER 2
AN UNWANTED PARTY

M en stamped across wood ramparts, knocking dust from the beams as they emptied rooms cut from the inner wall of the stone city. Taking out loot stored away from some previous raids to the east, they busied as quickly as they could, setting up fitting but sparse bedrooms and cells for their oncoming guests. Corsairs argued while they dumped stinking urine and shit from chamber pots into the bay in the center of Song City, where *The Ube* lay tied to the dock.

One of these shit-showers splattered right by Tausi's feet as he led Zaki and Azinza along the lower catwalks set against the converted temple's base. He halted, hand on his sword, and glared up. A young girl froze when she saw who had caught her clumsiness.

"Sorry, Captain," she blurted, drawing snickers from Nana and Amare, *The Ube's* respective bosun and timekeeper. They brought up the rear, and their mirth spread to Zaki, who tried to hold it back when Tausi's glare shifted to her. It immediately died when he noticed Azinza curiously staring at him, waiting to see what he'd do.

"Get back to work," he barked up at Song City's rat, one of a collection of orphan boys and girls left behind by dead corsairs who never came home. She scurried off.

"The Gamka approaches!" cried a lookout on the top of the walls.

"Open the gate," Tausi shouted to whomever listened, and the order repeated along the walls. He looked past Zaki to Nana. "Would you please take my sister and Lady Azinza to their chambers in the tunnel?"

"Where's that?" Azinza asked.

"Follow me ladies, and I'll happily show you," Nana said, striding between them like a rooster there for the hens. He hooked his arms out, his grin revealing white teeth.

"Never let it be said I turn down the offer of a handsome man," Zaki declared, threading her arm through the bosun's. "Nana, did I ever tell you about the time Tausi threw himself at the Ulmo? He made the screechiest sound anyone ever heard. Even women say—"

"I don't like that story." Azinza grabbed Nana's arm and pulled the three of them forward, setting ahead at an impatient pace.

"Captain Tausi."

Tausi's gaze lingered when Amare cleared his throat.

"So, when are you going to put a baby in her?"

"Could you not?"

"No." His dark timekeeper chuckled, hands held to his broad, scarred belly. "Orders?"

"Nana will talk to the men in the tunnel and set watchers at the Far Gate. We need to get this place ready for a meal." Tausi darted off, his trusted friend following behind them. Unwinding the leather strap of his sword's baldric, he slipped it over his shoulder on the way back to the docks. "And make sure everyone knows that Illus is coming."

"Aye, Captain. I'll make sure the rowers have their clubs, the salt-wives their cutters, and the Rats get rooms."

"Put them in the tunnel," Tausi added. "They will like to hear Azinza sing."

"Should I invite her to come sing in your chamber?"

"I'll cut you open if you don't stop."

"Then who's going to ask her to come to your room and sing for you?"

Tausi laughed, loud and brief, before he resettled his focus on his father's trireme rowing into port beneath the Sea Gate. The trail of their wake dissipated into the placid blue waters, the day already hot and heavy with humidity. He spotted the five figures beside Ngala, and among them, a shorter figure caught his attention. Pale-skinned, even from a distance, he knew Illus when he saw him. A tremor woke in his sword hand.

"I want him kept away from the salt-wives. And Amare, do your damnedest to keep me away from him, too," Tausi instructed his time-keeper as they descended to the dock.

The gangplanks banged on the end of the small pier, and Ngala ascended first, no longer bearing his cane—only his leopard wrap and his sword, which he carried in his hand while sweat dripped from every pore of his body. Blood oozed from his nostrils.

Tausi ripped his blade from its holder while Amare called for the raiders still at work preparing rooms. "Father!" For the second time that day, he leaped off the stairs, arcing through the air to land hard on the platform beside Ngala. His men followed, thundering down to the stairs to join him.

His father held his hands up. "It's all right! It's all right!"

Tausi straightened, confused. "Are you drunk?"

Ngala slurred some words in answer before the next captain crested The Gamka's starboard, a heavy man with a bushy black hair and a beard that went down to his chest in segmented, braided dreadlocks. Dzan dribbling like brown syrup from his mane, he laughed loudly and thrust his sword in the air. A shallow cut, angry red, lanced his shoulder.

"Good blow, Ngala! We're even now and on," cried Captain Dra, the corsair-lord of the Face-Slashers. He lifted his bottle of drink in his other hand and tilted it over his mouth, spilling more liquor down his gullet.

Tausi lowered his weapon and addressed his father. "What blow?"

"Captain Dra brought a bottle of his own dzan," Ngala said, recovering his breath. He wiped his brow with the back of his black hand. "And would only open it if I bested him to blood."

"Aye," Captain Dra said, waddling his solid girth down the gang-plank that groaned beneath the weight. He offered his bottle to Tausi. "You must be the young cub."

"Captain Tausi of The Ube," Tausi replied, taking the bottle with respect. He brought the green-glass mouth to his and sipped a small mouthful that tasted of hard licorice. "Welcome to Song City, Captain Dra."

The bearish man laughed, low and deep, his arm bleeding as he looked about the inner walls. "Bah! Hahahaha..." He sauntered into the mass of raiders arrayed behind Tausi, who nodded to them to take their first guest to his chamber with the additional order for dressings to be brought afterward.

Three more corsairs crossed *The Gamka's* rail, led by Captain Cleona of Tip Town, a sinewy old woman wrinkled like a prune, though her hearty smile beamed above the dozens and dozens of tiny, feathered darts sewn to the front of her leather jerkin, tinkling with every slight move she made. Shaved bald, she studied Song City with great intent.

Tausi stepped forward. "Captain Cleona, welcome to Song—"

She groused, loud and quick, something that sounded like an empty thanks as she broke between Tausi and Ngala, through the raiders, and, like before, a few of Tausi's own tailed her up the stone steps to the city's lowest proper.

Another woman came, dressed in a short tunic of bright blue trimmed in cloth-of-gold. Her braids coiled around the crown of her beautifully formed head in the shape of a conch shell, Captain Oya of Bastards Bay laid eyes on Ngala, her gaze feverish and hungry.

"Captain Oya, welcome to Song City," Tausi started before she wrapped her arms around his father's neck to plant a long, lingering kiss on his mouth.

"Oh, shit," Amare whispered.

Tausi almost gagged when Oya withdrew her tongue from Ngala's mouth with the sound of a wet seal breaking. She turned and went off, and again more raiders broke away.

"What the fuck?" Tausi asked Ngala.

"She likes violence," Ngala said in a half-mumble, his grin wide when he raised his head to acknowledge Captain Popobawa. The corsair-lord of The White Rovers ambled down the gangplank, hiking the hem of his long wrap of undyed cotton. His wrists, neck, and head gleamed in polished copper set and precious stones that clashed and jangled. The long sword on his hip was single-edged and curved, suspended from a holder on his wide belt.

"Captain Popobawa," Tausi said before anything could interrupt him again. "Welcome to Song City."

The tall corsair offered him a restrained smile. "Thank you, Captain Tausi, but I must be the bearer of bad news—it seems Captain Illus refuses to depart *The Gamka* unless you personally escort him off of it."

Tausi tightened on his weapon's hilt. "Gladly."

"Please let my son's men take you to where you and your men will rest, Captain Popobawa." Ngala stepped in front of his son. "I'll follow you soon. I would like to continue our conversations, if you'd be so kind."

Popobawa's smile remained tight. "Of course."

Tausi ordered the rest of his raiders to take their guest to his quarters, leaving him and his father on the pier. "He's leaving rowers stuck down there. They haven't been called to break."

"Then go clear Illus from the deck," said Ngala, making to leave. "Without killing him."

Abandoned to his pier, Tausi summoned the will to remove his sword from his hand and ascended the gangplank of his father's trireme. The raiders, still aligned in their formation for presentation, rose and presented their spears when their commander called them to attention. The man who gave the order, Mtumbwe, nodded respectfully to his old crewman.

"Hello again, old dog," he said when he greeted Tausi. He looked behind his shoulder as his men disembarked. "Do you want him removed?"

"I'll handle it," said Tausi. "Go get your timekeeper to free your rowers. No need for them to wait."

"Aye, Captain."

Tausi remained until *The Gamka's* crew emptied the boat, his gaze focused on the lone straggler.

Illus stood at the portside rail near the bow, his back to Tausi as he studied Song City's year-old ramparts, a new level Tausi had built from the glass remnants that had once been part of a great white dome. A man of short height but possessing a strong, athletic build, the disgraced Latian soldier garbed himself in the mish-mash of any land-born bandit, strapped with harnesses, war sandals, and the small accouterments of an infantryman. A gross skin flayed from sand hounds —the feral dogs that roamed Juut's southern beaches—stitched together in a belt he wrapped around his barrel waist.

"I'm surprised at the size of this place," he called in clear, barking Juutan.

Even his words in Tausi's language grated in his ears. "People assume many things. Say many things."

"I didn't lie about you, boy."

"Don't call me boy," warned Tausi. "You don't get to call me that."

"Why not? They call me what they do because of your lack of spine. Boy."

Tausi gritted his teeth when Illus turned on him, his muddy eyes feral and wide. His old foe's hand clutched the handle of his Latian broad sword. "They call me 'The Gelded.' Because of you, Tausi," he said with a snarl. "And as far as I'm concerned, you can get fucked if you expect me to say other than what I think about you."

"I was on the walls of Doba, fighting to finish what we started that day. It was not my fault you did not hold the bay."

"And finish it you did," said Illus. "At the cost of two triremes and their crews. At the cost of my own body."

They stared death at each other, *The Gamka* shifting gently beneath their feet. Both men clutched their blades, wordless as they waited for the other to attack—or be the first to surrender.

Illus let go of his hilt. "I came here at your father's invitation. Even a foreigner like me knows how to honor things."

"And remember that while you're here, Illus—you're a foreigner," Tausi said before he spat on the ground between them. "Now get off my father's boat."

After a brief, dead look to the ramparts of Song City one last time, Illus marched for the gangplank. Off the ship, across the pier, and up the stone staircase to the city proper, the Latian lord of the Land Dogs said nothing when he passed by Ngala, who perched on the uppermost landing to watch what transpired on the deck of his ship.

He met Tausi when his son reached the step below his. "Thank you, Captain. I know such a thing is not easy."

Without hesitation, Tausi stepped onto the same level as his father, eye to eye with his mentor, his best friend, and at times his greatest adversary. "I hate that man. He's a traitor to his own people."

"Who are our enemies," Ngala replied, a stern note in his deep voice. "And there's value in making men who would be our enemies into friends."

"That man lost a nut because he couldn't hold the bay in Doba. He'll never be my friend."

"Says the man who has carved a grand city from the bones of evil."

Tausi met his father's proud smile with a frown. "Why are the corsair-lords here, Father? You keep trying to sneak away from it, but I can't let you."

His mirth waned, Ngala turned for the rest of their climb up the stairs. "We're about to hold congress."

The first stars peeked when the raiders and rowers of *The Ube* rejoined their captain on the deck of their ship, bringing along fresh planks, nails, and enough mismatched chairs and stools that the long table they built for the occasion would hold more than two dozen if needed. Tausi and Nana took their time placing torches along the rail of her wooden sides, leaving the top of her deck awash in warm light. Some of the Rats, dressed in their hand-me-down loinclothes, stuck little sticks of incenses in the cracks of the deck, lighting them to perfume the air with sweet herbal scents.

Amare lit a cannabis cigar and blew into the hold, an old salt-spell to purify the food heaped upon the table. As they'd had earlier that day, barrels of dzan were stacked and tapped, each one ready to be emptied. *The Ube's* three cooks started on the meal, constructing small fires at the bow and aft for their wide iron pots.

The crew of *The Gamka* arrived by the time the sun was fully set, with Ngala leading their march from the higher rooms carved into the city's inner walls. Both Zaki and Azinza flanked him as he stepped gingerly down the steps, playing up the use of a cane to the deepest effect.

Tausi nudged Nana when he noticed his bosun struggling to contain his knowing smile. "Shhh."

"Azinza's looking at you."

Tausi restrained a grunt, doing his best to hide his annoyance. His father's nursemaid, older in years by whole centuries but with a beauty belying a girl on the cusp of her late teens, wore a shimmering gown of flowing white silk that darkened her skin and made her hair look like blue fire, a sight so enchanting only a cough from his father brought back his attention.

"A fine stage," Ngala said as he stepped past his son and ascended the gangplank.

Tausi glanced to Zaki, who responded with a pleading nod that communicated an old need for patience. "Thank you, Captain," he said as he followed behind.

Once on deck, Ngala did away with his cane, setting it at stern-side of the table. The cooks had overtaken the incense and sage scents, replacing it with the heady smell of boiling crabs and roasting fish in the pots that bubbled and hissed not too far from the gathering place. He went by and made an inspection, requesting tastes of everything, which he responded to by giving brief, accepting nods and pats on the back.

Tausi followed him completely around the deck, saying little.

Ngala turned to face him after he had tasted from the last pot. He licked his lips of the last bit of fish stew. "I need you to do something for me, Captain."

Tausi sighed but nodded. "At your order."

"Give me command of Song City."

Tausi hesitated for more than a few breaths. "It's yours."

"Thank you, son. Make it official."

Tausi stepped to the prow of his ship and called out. "Let every man and woman of this city know that Old Bones Ngala is now in command, as my word is now his word!"

Zaki called out without a moment of pause. "Crews to your hold!

The Gamka's men broke from the pier, many of them leaping the sides of the world-weathered trireme, scrambling to throw down the gangplanks so the rest could surge into the hold. Minutes later, they returned in droves, carrying their own barrels of dzan, and without even an order, their cooks built fires in what seemed like mere seconds, getting their ironware hot for the oils.

"Get that bloody gate up," Ngala cried to the raiders stationed at the Sea Gate's winch.

"What are you doing?" Tausi asked, set on edge as the chains rattled.

"Just watch," said Ngala with a coy expression. "Send the signal, Azinza."

Azinza rose up the gangplank, helped by none. Tausi hurried to meet her before she reached the top, his hand held out.

She took it even after she had hopped down to the wood. "Thank you, Captain Tausi."

He bowed his head with a sheepish smile and escorted her to his father.

"So, what notes do you want tonight, old man?" she asked with a weary smile.

"Just lead them here," Ngala said, retrieving his staff. "And get on with it. I'm going to be thirsty soon."

Tilting her face up, Azinza drew a soft, subtle breath through her nose before her mouth opened and out came the purest note Tausi had ever heard a human voice produce. Clear, clean, it pervaded his entire body, setting hairs on end and stirring something in his chest close to joy. It was as if this note was bringing him home—even for all its bits of sadness, which inflected it with a wonder beyond the understanding. He stood there, near to this goddess, and did not flinch when she moved, her gaze following the tops of Song City's walls before she spun completely to face him, her back to Ngala.

Azinza stared right in Tausi's eyes while she ended her note, and, trapped, he froze for the second-longest moment of his life before one of the raiders on the lookout towers called.

"Captain! Bottom-Boats at sea!"

"Let them in," Ngala called back.

A sudden commotion woke behind them, and at the lowest proper, the corsair-lords had appeared, bedecked in their fineries and their waists girded in swords and knives. They marched down the steps before stopping midway, posed in unusually placid manners given their natures. All smiles and grins—save for Illus—they watched in anticipation as the first bottom-boat glided through Song City's entrance.

Arriving in the handmade canoes carved from trees lumbered from the coastal jungles, three riders manned each of the five boats that paddled their way through the Sea Gate, legs hanging over the sides. The corsair-lords came down to meet these new guests who were revealed to be the bosuns, timekeepers, and commanders of their respective ships.

Ngala jumped on *The Ube's* new table and spread his scarred arms wide. "Salt-Dogs, Shell-Stealers, and Devil-Ghosts—welcome all to Song City. The feast before you is yours, without debt or duty, and the dzan flows until it stops. Dine! Dine and sing your way to hell, for tomorrow you may be dead!"

A cheer went up, cups passed around, and the first trickle of muddy brown liquid filled a flagon. From the rabble of feasting, men raised a song when the corsair-lords took their chairs around the table alongside their chosen hands.

Salt swell to see
Beneath skies of gray
Forward to plunder and
a bloody day!
Ride! Ride! Ride!
With the salt swells we ride!
Ride! Ride! Ride!

Somewhere between his fourth and fifth cup of dzan, Tausi let his fears go. All men joined in play and pride. The local salt-wives, free women that through fate or fortune had fallen in with corsairs, snuck down from the city to revel in the flesh and fervor.

Everywhere he looked he thought he saw Azinza looking at him, but none of that mattered when Zaki started up the next verse and handed him that fifth drink of many.

CHAPTER 3
LATIA

L ong after the songs echoed into the night and a few of the
barrels had been tipped over to float in the middle of Song City's
bay, men snuck away to sleep off their intoxications or bed the
salt-wives that invited them back to their small hovels.

One by one, each and every person left, until only the captains and
their commands remained—all except Azinza, who sat next to a weary
Ngala in a struggle to get him to drink a cup of clean water. Illus arm
wrestled with Captain Dra while Oya watched, muttering threats under
her breath while grasping the edge of the table, the veins in her arms
swollen with excitement. In the seat next to her, Cleona watched nothing, her gaze far away.

At the bow, Captain Popobawa nursed his small clay cup, watching
the proceedings with detached interest.

Tausi sat by Zaki beside *The Ube's* locked steerage, splitting the last
cup of dzan they would drink that night between them. His free hand on
his gurgling stomach, a mistake created by too much liquor and too
little food, his brain felt swollen in his skull. The dryness in his throat
did nothing to help the cloying sourness the alcohol had left behind.

"What are we doing here?" he whispered to his sister.

Hunched forward and with her legs crossed at the ankles, Zaki
rubbed her eyes, smearing the streaks of makeup down the sides of her

sharp nose and cheeks. "Holding a corsair congress...didn't you hear Father make that speech?"

"He makes a lot of speeches."

"Just wait," Zaki whispered, slurring her words. She tried for another sip from their cup, making a face and hissing like a cat at the taste.

Tausi took the cup from her and finished what was left, the dzan's harsh sweetness having been stolen by the long hours it was left exposed to the air. The smell of the cold cooking pots, burnt rice, and over-fried fish stuck in his nose until the knot in his stomach seemed to loosen. He grasped Zaki's strong shoulder when the liquor struck. "I need to get up."

It was at that moment Ngala wrenched out of his seat, leaning hard and heavy on the table before him. "My lords! My lords...let's get down to business."

"Curse him," Tausi whispered, grabbing the rail by him to assist himself to his feet.

Much like their father, Zaki popped to her feet first. "Keep your guts about you."

The five lords of the Mirror Sea took their seats by the time Tausi and Zaki plopped down on the right side of the great table. The commanders, timekeepers, and bosuns that had survived the debaucheries slunk onto stools near their captains. Only Amare had appeared to represent *The Ube,* sliding onto the seat beside Tausi when the court convened.

"Ha, got you!" Dra turned Illus' arm onto the table's surface. He raised both hands and howled before snatching his cup of wine.

"Calm, Captain Dra, if for a moment." Ngala almost slouched on his seat, his muscular body bent in a way that made it seem broken and weak. He forced himself straight, playing each strained movement for full effect. He brushed away the cup of water Azinza pressed at him, instead reaching for a glass bottle's throat. Brown-black liquor sloshed in its green well, and he took a quick swing that drew affirming nods and grunts from his fellow captains. He slammed the bottle on the wood with a loud bang. "We've done our feasts and fiending. I'm ready to be honest if all men are."

Dra grabbed his cup and searched its abandoned brothers. Finding leftover grogs and wash, he refilled his drink before sitting down. "Aye, Ngala. I'm ready."

"Ready for what?" Illus asked, terse as he rubbed the pads of his fingers with his thumb.

"I did not call every lord here to simply drink and eat my and my son's food." Ngala swallowed to gather the needed moisture. "It is well known that the last few years have been good to those of us that plunder the coasts of our spoiled homelands. Every single one of us has grown wealthy."

"And fat," cried Cleona, nodding in Dra's direction, drawing an amused grunt from Illus. Blades would have lifted if the barb's target did not guffaw at it, raising his cup to his mouth to drown out the noise of his barking.

"Either way," Ngala said when they calmed, "we have done well against the kingdoms of the west, enough so that our navies now rival many of their smaller-city states, and not a single man here doubts that we are better stewards of the Mirror Sea than they."

Ayes rounded the table. Even Illus' quieted, his usual ire shifting to curiosity.

"Many of you were not born to the sea, though," Ngala said, letting his finger point at all of them. "We all came from the land at some point, and now we are the coast's natives—not the Latians, or the Gypians, who try to tame the untamable. And like the waves, they have not tamed us."

"Get to your point," Oya said, leering at Ngala suggestively. Her hand slid between her legs.

Ngala grimaced along with Azinza. "We are strong like the sea itself, and our fortunes have grown beyond the dreams of those that enslaved our parents and ancestors, who would not know our world if they were here now. And yet..." A sneer took his face, the result of a silent thought born of the silent sufferings all corsairs carried in their hearts.

Tausi waited, shocked at how much that seething reminded him of his own.

"They call us corsairs," Ngala continued. "Pirates. Bandits. Yet I look around this table, and I see Captain Oya, who held Bastards Bay against a land army sent by the petty lords of the Glass Coast."

Oya's smile tightened with pleasured anticipation as she gripped the edge of the table. "Don't sweeten your tongue too much, Ngala! I might bite it out."

"And Captain Dra!" Ngala forced a pleasant expression to cover the unease Oya instilled. "The Face-Slashers now control coasts far to the east of Boda, and does any man dare to challenge your fleet?"

"No man dares," cawed Captain Dra.

"From my hold from Stone Cove in the west to the Floating City of the White Rovers, corsairs have ruled our territories for more than a century. And yet they still call us pirates." Ngala left his chair, walking around the long table to be nearer to the captains, patting Zaki and Tausi on the shoulder as he passed. A silent signal to follow him, they traded glances and quiet nods to the crews, who clustered closer together.

Ngala knelt down beside Cleona, who shifted her faraway gaze earthward, settling her old eyes on Ngala. Reaching past her plate of half-eaten food, he topped off her neglected cup of dzan before setting the bottle on the chair arm between them.

A small smile creased her flat, wrinkled face.

"Tip Town is a city," Ngala said. "So is Bastards Bay. Even the Land Dogs have built a town and defenses worthy of their homeland." Ngala looked right at Illus, along with Tausi, who viewed the disgraced Latian soldier with far less appreciation. The bastard did not even raise his eyes from the table to acknowledge the Old Bones, intent to study the dagger he held, spinning its point in the wood.

Cleona reached for her cup with a calloused hand. She took a small sip and cleared her throat. "You ask for alliances...binding ones."

"I ask for kingdoms," said Ngala. "The politics of the West are false —they think rule comes from the sanctity of their beliefs and beliefs alone, but they violate their own laws for the sake of wealth and wantonness while demeaning us for doing the very same! I'd rather die on this stool than live in a world where these imperialists let our people suffer like they did in Tolivius. Or in The Moonlight Wars. Or in slavery, which they would put each and every one us in if they had the chance."

Tausi felt the words weigh down every person at the table. The worst of western sins upon Juut's chaotic face, each corsair could claim at some point they had been a slave, or their parents, or their parent's parents. A stain on the soul of any person not born "a citizen" but a thrall.

He admitted foreignness at the feelings displayed by the older ones. He and Zaki had been born with no such knowledge, free to the salt and sand.

"Where would you go with this, Captain?" he called out.

Ngala turned his head and looked down the table at his son, pleased by the question. "We no longer need to scuttle and hide. There are patrols that avoid Stone Cove's waters, and we are closest to the west than any of you. They avoid us! This is a moment to seize an opportunity that some of us have only dreamed of in the dark nights on our cots or freezing in the wind while outrunning those that have done nothing throughout history but run us down."

"You'd turn you into me." Swarthy from the sun, Illus leaned an arm on a knee as he searched his empty cup for another drop. Seeing no full bottles on the table, his glower deepened. "You'd have territories on water instead of land, but it would still be territory. You'll end up no better than my people, or the Gypians, or whatever bedeviled thing you don't think yourself to be."

"We are not you," Tausi said, sharp.

"And you're not honest, boy," said the Latian. He jabbed his empty cup at Ngala. "Neither is your father."

Ngala remained composed. "How do you see that, Captain Illus?"

The bronze-skinned marauder laughed aloud. "As clear as anyone with half a brain. You said it yourself—there are patrols that avoid you. But not all of them."

"I must echo Captain Illus," said Popobawa. "The Floating City does not fear Latians or Gypians—because they are too far for us to worry about. We are free upon the sea itself, living and breathing with it as it feeds us, and we in turn feed it. Who is to say we White Rovers are not already a kingdom?"

"Then why do you raid?" Ngala asked aloud, and not only to Popobawa.

The captains and their crews had nothing—no arguments could be made against the point Ngala had made, for none of them could truly say they had established the needed trading routes that separated them from larceny.

Ngala bent down and picked up a half-full bottle of dzan, which he stared at for a bit. "I'd raid for this," he said, holding it up for display before he reached across the table and dumped it into Illus' cup. The Latian's face turned in a broad, sated smile as he immediately swallowed a mouthful, coughing with his chuckle.

"You said 'kingdoms,' Ngala," Dra said, his mania halved by an intense focus. "Would you be a king?"

"No," Ngala said with a forgiving smile. "I would ask no man or woman to give me their boats or their souls. No, I would only remain Old Bones, in Stone Cove, growing and letting it become what fate gives me to make it. My corsairs would still raid the west and the east, but things would change—no longer would corsairs war and feud with each other when our pettiness overtakes us. No longer would we leave burning ships there to burn, or her crews to die. We would trade, and seek to trade with others, and—"

"And there would be peace among us," Cleona interrupted. The old woman, her face aged by wind and battle, craned her head up so she looked directly at Ngala. "But what would we have to do for that peace?"

Ngala shrugged his shoulders. "We would raid Latia."

The commotion that arose from each captain save Tausi and Zaki sent the meeting reeling into disorder. Illus spoke without pause, reiterating his point about corsairs becoming imperialists, while Dra surprised most with an impassioned defense of the idea. Oya simply stood at her place near the table, her mouth gaping as her eyes rolled back at the conflict, her whispered words lewd and arousing. Cleona stared at Ngala still, waiting for him to speak aloud. Popobawa sat at his far end of the table, watching with deep interest at the argument between Illus and Dra.

"Gods," Zaki whispered, leaning toward Tausi. "Oya's crazy."

"He's crazy," Tausi replied, keeping his eyes on Illus while nodding in Ngala's direction. "This won't work."

"He'd have to tell secrets," his timekeeper Amare added, seated behind Tausi's right shoulder. "Secrets no man tells."

"Then on cue," Zaki said before rising. "My lords, hear me."

The sudden intrusion quieted the arguments, yanking everyone's attention to Ngala's daughter. Dra and Illus held their peace, both of them observing her with foreign interests, not sure what to make of a man who had made herself a woman speaking to them as equals. Even Oya had silenced.

"I understand why so many of you would hesitate to dream dreams unheard," she said, laying her long, strong hands on the wooden table lightly. "The very idea of going into the heart of our foe's great stronghold, to plunder them like they have plundered us through the ages... when Captain Ngala first told me, I did not believe."

"And you do now, my little one?" Cleona asked, her voice ragged.

"I believe in my father's will, my bigger one. The fact that my brother and I stand here, in this city he has built, is proof of it. Can we take Latia's coastal cities? There was a time when the very idea of corsairs raiding cities like Boda seemed ludicrous, or the towns of the Sixteen Teeth, and yet we did. And you're right, Illus, not all the patrols avoid Stone Cove—but how many do you hear of leaving victorious?"

Dra grunted in his chest. "What say you now, Latian?"

"So I would be king of what I held, and you'd give Stone Cove over to your insane daughter or your idiot son," Illus rebuked to Ngala, ignoring Dra. "What makes us play well together? You all think me a traitor to my people, you who would easily gut me and make yourself like your former slaveholders, and what would a kingdom do but make that worse? So one day we can war again to gut each other? We're already doing that, and let's not forget the captains not here at the table, or how we took their lives."

"How many triremes does the smallest city in Latia have?" Ngala asked, undeterred.

"None," said Illus.

"And the next city?"

"No more than three, usually," Illus answered, exasperated. "Get to the point."

"I have sixty-five triremes," said Ngala.

Tausi rose this time. "Father!"

"Please, Captain," Ngala quickly said, withholding the scolding tone Tausi expected. "Please. The only way we trust each other is by the truth, and no greater truth holds us to defense than the true number of boats we have. The more boats, the more men, and the more men the more lives we waste when we fight each other. I have sixty-five boats. I'd rather point them toward the west. Toward Latia."

Captain Dra laughed his mad cackle. "Latia! Grand old Latia." He tugged on the thick tuft of his salt-and-peppered beard. "I have thirty triremes full of men that would see Laconia if the chance was right."

"Forty-five," said Oya, placid in her answer. She shook her head in surprise. "That was easier than I thought."

"You're all fools," said Illus. "Why don't you tell Ngala where you each keep your hordes of loot while you're at it!"

"I keep mine in my bedroom," said Ngala. "But I don't want what's in my bedroom, or your bedroom, Illus. I want what the Latian Lion has in his den."

"I have twenty-nine triremes," said Popobawa, his expression blank.

"And I have forty-three." Cleona finally broke her stare on Ngala, settling inward to resolve within what she had done. "Though I don't think I will see the walls of Laconia."

"Zaki will carry you," Ngala replied gently to the old woman. "But before you say anything, Illus, you all must know that before any agreement can be made, we first bind ourselves to something new and different. Where are we to hold our courts when we have disagreements? Where are we to convene to discuss the future of our kingdoms?"

"We must have a place where we can all be equals," said Captain Dra.

Ngala lifted his hands to the fort surrounding them. "What if it was a city?"

"What?" Tausi asked. "Wait a moment!"

"Your son's city," said Illus.

"Perhaps not for long," Ngala replied. "I would move, with your agreements, to make Song City independent of Stone Cove."

Tausi could not remain silent. "On whose damned authority?" he asked, standing.

Zaki tried to block him, a hand on his chest. "Captain Tausi..."

"Exactly." Tausi turned his glare from her to the entire table. "I am captain of the ship you're all resting your asses on—in the city my crew and I built. You'd decide the fate of every person here for all your glories."

"There is not a discussion about taking things away, Tausi," Ngala said, his face hard. "It is about building a coalition. What I suggest is that we vote."

"Vote?" Illus grasped the handle of his knife hard, holding the point to the wood. "Gypians vote. Latians vote. Kings don't vote for other kings, Ngala."

"Well perhaps we will be better kings, Illus," Ngala said, caught between Tausi and the cutthroat. "To prove my sincerity to that, I am giving my son ten of Stone Cove's triremes for his own use. I ask you all to commit ships to this city, whether we vote for him to rule it or not."

Unable to respond to yet another swing in fortunes, Tausi gaped, glancing around the table for someone to match his confusion when one of the lookouts on the walls shouted.

"Latian fleet to the south! Sails sighted!"

CHAPTER 4

SIEGE

Tausi climbed the wooden steps to the top parapet, ascending them by twos and threes. Zaki kept pace behind him, her twin swords already out as the raiders on the walls drew their arrows. "Close the Sea Gate! Send runners to the beaches! Archers assemble! Assemble!"

"How did they get past Avarice Reefs?" Amare called from a flight below Tausi's.

"Live to worry about it tomorrow." Tausi surged past a cluster of corsairs working to line themselves along the wall, heading for the southwestern tower. He nearly leapt upon its ladder when he neared, climbing hand over hand with no regard for anything else save reaching the top. He heard Zaki grunt behind him, the second up the rungs as a third man came after her.

At the top, he met a raider who shouted the warning.

"More than two dozen sails sighted so far, Captain. They're hard to hit us in minutes," the raider said, offering a hand.

"Thank you, Bo." Tausi let the young raider pull him up to the tower's platform. Parting the line of five archers at the ready, he stopped at the thin rail and looked out to sea.

Beneath a starry night without moon or clouds, the flares of bright orange caught in the silvery light, almost blood-dull upon the sparkling surface of Shallow Bay. Ten, twenty...and more, Tausi realized.

Too many.

"Get a messenger to the beach parties," he shouted over his shoulder, trying to count in the rest in the dark. "Raise the breachers! Get the Rats inside and make sure the coves disembark!"

"I already sent them along."

He whipped around to find his father standing beside Zaki, his walking stick forgotten. Ngala had strapped his old iron sword around his panther-girded waist, his drunkenness yet another act done away with. Tausi nodded both of them over.

"There's at least forty triremes out there," he said when they joined him at the rail. "It's a fleet."

"How did they get past the Avarice Reefs? Only Azinza can transform them, and nobody but us know the route through," said Zaki.

"You have your command back," Ngala told Tausi. "My crews are yours."

Hesitation caused him to stare, but Tausi broke it with a nod. He led his hand to the hilt of his sword. "I need raiders. More raiders. They are going to bring ladders. I need someone to figure out how they got in here."

"I'll go scour the tunnels and the Far Gate," said Ngala, darting for the ladder. He turned and slid down with the grace of a man many decades younger, disappearing before Tausi could utter a word of reaction.

"Because it's my command," he said to the empty space.

Zaki smiled in the gloom of the grass roof above them. "I need to borrow a few people."

"You can have Nana."

"Oh, the flirty one," she said. "I want Azinza."

"Why wouldn't you have Azinza?" Tausi asked. "This is not the time for games."

Zaki scoffed on her way to the ladder. "Do hurry up and repel this invading force."

"Thank you!" Tausi nodded to the archers standing by, who took their place at the rail when he stepped back. Setting gray-fletched arrows on their strings, they waited for the order, their flesh made even darker by the nocturne world. Again, he hesitated, staring at the massing specks of orange. Looking down at his side, he suddenly realized he had pulled his sword from its holder.

One of the raiders whispered to him. "Captain?"

"Hold fire until I give the order," Tausi said as he went for the ladder. At the bottom of the tower, he was met by Amare and a trio of raiders, one of which carried a spare bow and quiver of arrows.

"Spread the word to keep the towers quiet until the Latian's ships are in a stone's throw," Tausi ordered his timekeeper while he looped the quiver around his body, setting it on his hip. "Do we still have those barrels of oil we won in the last raid?"

"Maybe half of them," said Amare as he silently signaled their men to follow the first direction. "If we set their boats on fire, the Latians will make a bridge on their own corpses."

"Better their corpses than ours," said Tausi, turning away with his mate in tow. "We need to hold them until they hit the anchor yard."

"It's not finished on the western side."

He clenched his jaw as he marched the stone path to the next battlement. "Then my father better be quick."

They charged through the silently writhing lines along Song City's southern walls, checking their stone towers and wooden parapets for any weaknesses in the masonry, hoping quietly that the Latians had only brought ladders instead of mounting their triremes with things far worse.

Amare's runner found them near the eastern tower. "We're bringing up the barrels, Captain, but the tunnel is still open. Captain Ngala left to see it shut."

Tausi stifled a growl, hissing his question through his teeth. "Where is my sister?"

"She's gone to fetch your father," said Captain Oya, who ascended the ramp up to Tausi's platform. Hunched beside Captain Dra, she balanced the torch behind a piece of cloth he used to shield its light from onlookers. "Where are you dropping your first barrel?"

"Captain Oya, you are not needed—"

"Shut it, boy." Teeth bared, Dra struggled to keep the light covered while keeping his prodigious belly from the flame's reach. "Just get us moving so we can burn a few before manning the lines."

Grunting, Tausi silently pointed the way with his sword as he and Amare led their new companions back along the path they had already taken. Casks of oil stolen from outposts of the nation attacking them now were distributed by the strong-backed. They carried the containers on their shoulders two by two until every battlement had at least one for their use.

Along the way, Tausi located more torches for Oya. The she-devil of Bastards Bay snickered every time Dra whined at a fresh source of heat, wine-sweat dripping from his face.

Song City lay in bustling quiet, the nighttime breeze covering the sounds of arguing warriors cajoling each other while it eddied through the passages and alcoves of their fortress. Every moment allowed to raise one's head and look out upon the sea offered the proper motivation to set their lines tight and check their swords as the orange sails grew into a fleet of fifty ships rowing toward their walls.

Tausi, Amare, and the two captains took up position at the city's most southern point, a wide balcony overlooking Shallow Bay's waters and behind, at its horse-shoe shaped coast. They joined the raiders already massed there, many of them crewmen of *The Gamka*.

Captain Dra knelt down with Captain Oya, waiting to dump the three barrels of oil allotted to their platform. Tacked hides, leather layered two inches thick, provided fair shields from any arrows the Latians launched.

"Wait for the first ladder," Tausi whispered to Amare. His time-keeper nodded, digging his knife into the barrel's cork before he yanked it out with a pop, the substance within wafting an earthy stink.

The bustle ended, and in the stillness, the wind batted against sails, a common mistake made by infantrymen who thought their knowledge of how to sail made them sailors, not the cunning navigators that all corsairs were raised to be. The chop of their shaky strokes, untrained at cutting the water instead of beating it, sloshed breakers against the wall.

Bronze rostrums, the fixed ram at the prow of every trireme, scrapped against the city, the walls of a former temple bearing an ancient mural emblazoned in the figures of its arcane past, human and monstrous sorcerers clad in bright robes and flocked by their minions.

Men shouted in their rough western tongue. Wood knocked against wood, and more men grunted in unison.

A ladder arched up and banged against the wall's lip.

Tausi grabbed its top rung. "First load overboard!"

Raising it over his head, Amare threw the barrel over the edge, shouting with might to speed its fall. Oya came right after him when Dra whipped away the cloth to expose her torchlight. Crying in joy, she launched the burning brand down like an ax. Dozens of barrels shattered on the decks of the Latian trireme, lit by torches that struck fresh slicks half a second later.

Watching from the edge of his city, Tausi saw men scream and dance amongst the flames. The smell of roasted flesh—like burnt liver —blossomed in columns of black, curling smoke. Hoplites in bronze and leather breastplates pitched away from the ladders they now wrestled to stand upright, many of them breaking the ranks in frantic attempts to find the water. For every smoldered body that pitched into the sea, three more took his place, bringing forth buckets of seawater to douse the blaze.

"Fire at will," Tausi shouted, and the archers responded in a volley of shafts that flickered in the light of the burning trireme, which had spread its ruinous heat to the next boat behind it.

More corpses fell atop those unfortunate enough to meet their deaths in the fire, adding to the haze ripped high by the breeze. The heat of burning wood and rent flesh bathed Tausi's face as he stared down in a mix of ecstasy and horror. The raiders on the towers, coordinated in their rate of fire, made easy work of the ships closest to them, felling dozens with each rain of arrows.

The next wave of triremes crowded behind the fire-line, their deck crews already set in shield walls to guard themselves under the torrent of arrows and stone. Some of the Rats had joined the batteries on the towers, bearing small slings. The annoyance provided an off-beat to the rhythmic volleys, allowing a few shafts to punish the slightest carelessness.

Zaki rejoined Tausi at the back of his overlook, who readied to step forward in a line of fresh archers. She drew close to his side.

"Ngala is holding the Far Gate," she said in his ear.

"Get the next barrel ready," Tausi shouted. The archer ahead of him loosed his second to last arrow, and on the next draw, he'd step in, bared to whatever came back up in answer. "Did the anchor yard work?"

"Three ships sank and another was moored, but the crews are escaping. Ngala pelted them with arrows while he evacuated the eastern beachhead of our guests' crews, which will join the defense as soon as they are in. The Latians took the western beach. Illus and Popobawa now support him in the defense."

"Get him back here," he said, snarling each word. "The old fool will get himself killed!"

Amare dropped the next barrel while Dra and Oya dropped another pair of torches. The wall of cinders throbbed with flickering light, blood red as the bowmen fired the last arrow in their quivers before stepping back.

"Bring up the hatchets," he shouted to Zaki before he approached the line. His sister disappeared from his side, now replaced by the dark outlines of his compatriots. "Raise!" His shoulders tightened as he pulled back the string, aiming past the rippling wall of suffocating smoke. "Fire!" Mouth opened to exhale past the noxious fumes, Tausi loosed into the thickened air.

Iron arrowheads rattled and cascaded on the bronze walls the Latians formed on their decks, the only sign that the corsair's arrows struck true.

Amare forced his way through the line, the last barrel in his arms. Drenched in sweat, he groaned loudly when he dropped it over the wall, crimson running from the small cuts the bands had sliced into his arms and shoulders. He turned and slumped onto his knees, crawling between a pair of raiders.

Tausi forgot his friend in the constant draw, loose, draw of his volleys, the sting in fingers and thumb of his draw hand settling into a burn he managed through rage and focus. *Fire into hell*, he thought, again and again until the demons emerged, crazed enough to fight. He gritted his teeth through the image of a gray specked Ulmo, his mottled claws shining in the ruined light.

"Fire," he shouted, answered each time by a cloud of rocks and arrows. The stench of death seeped into the pores of his body. "Fire!"

The beat of battle echoed in his chest, his head, until the crackle of flames became the only sound he heard. Sweat dripped in Tausi's eyes, and at some point, he simply closed them, letting the heat dry the last bit of sweat and salt from his flesh, daring his heart to fail.

Seconds, minutes—nothing mattered but drawing his arrow, setting it on the string, pulling back, and letting go. Many times, he wondered how he breathed through the ash in his lungs, or survived the mortal furnace he had created, spurned by hatred alone.

Latians marched forward from the third and fourth line of their armada, bringing their lines to the burning husks of their lost ships. Holding their shields above their heads, they snaked the ladder through their mass. Coordinating their efforts in the small pauses between draws, the ladder came up, smacking at the edge of Tausi's parapet.

Zaki burst past his line, bearing hatchets in one hand, hide shields in the other. Dra and Oya flanked her, hacking into the rungs of the ladders that lurched up from the smoking darkness. Giving way after a few whacks, the splintered pieces forced the climbers to drop their shields and spears to find new handholds at the top or risk the fall back onto the splintered heaps grinding the walls below.

"Halt arrows," Tausi tried to shout, his throat parched. Amare repeated the order, then another. Satisfied, he licked his lips with a sandpaper tongue. "To the death, my red waves! To the death of the Latia!"

The sound of men tearing iron from scabbards, ebony clubs knocking against hide shields, soared above the clamor in war-sung chaos. Raiders and rowers shouted the names of *The Ube* and *The Gamka*, and a few hearkened the names of other ships from other clans. Joined together against their age-old foes, they stamped the wooden boards and struck out at the smoke, ready to slay when the pale ghosts were made real.

Song City readied for war.

Zaki fell into line with Tausi, discarding her hatchet for her second sword. "Ngala turned them back at the Far Gate. He'll be on his way soon."

"He can shovel them over," Tausi cried, banging the flat of his sword on the frame of his shield. "Death to Latia!"

"Death to Latia!"

The first crested head popped over the parapet wall, both hands clutched on the stone edge. Tausi looked him dead in the eyes when the

Latian tried to haul his armored weight up, and the latter paused a second too long.

Cackling, Tausi dashed forward and stabbed the hoplite through his face.

The Latian shivered on the point of his brand for a moment, gasping before his destroyed head slid off the blade. The body tumbled backward, ripping two men from the ladder on its way down. Tausi cried victory and kicked the ladder back to the water.

Corsairs surged Song City's endless wall, abandoning their towers to join the growing battle. New ladders rose, half a dozen at a time. Carrying buckets of seawater, the Latians doused the burning triremes, leaving them uneven platforms to build a foundation for their climbers. Song City's ax-wielders did their best to hack at the highest rungs, breaking them to hamper even the most ardent attacks, but time and patience were an attribute known to these western warriors who braved the falling bodies of their brothers.

Comprised of the crews of ten different ships, the hoplites' numbers swelled, their constantly moving formations clinging to the city's walls like bees to a hive. Beyond this frantic line, the rest of the enemy fleet dropped anchor, lined up in a two-by-two formation spread upon Shallow Bay's face in staggered rows. Under the stars, hundreds of arrowheads gleamed against the dying fires.

"Shield wall," a corsair shouted over the din.

Stepping back to kneel behind his shield, Tausi braced for the errant shafts that flew up in a great arch and failed to reach the top on the city's walls. The few that did reach high enough to clear the parapet shot overhead or scattered on the wood where the heads did not dig the boards.

These showers lasted for three bursts, each one creeping higher and higher as the Latians learned their distance.

"Hold," Zaki screamed above the constant rattling. "Hold on!"

When the shower ended the Latians roared in challenge, climbing at a faster pace than before. Some clustered in the shield walls had reversed their ladders, restoring that needed rung that allowed their troops to ascend with weapons in hand, their shields strapped to their backs.

"Keep them off," cried Tausi from the other side of the parapet when the first hoplite cleared the wall. They clashed swords, banging their shields against the other before he found a gap in the Latian's defense. Slicing open the side of the man's throat, right under his helmet, he shoved the body to the side in time to stab the next man before he completed his climb.

Zaki reappeared in from the smoking haze, cutting away at foes. Enemies kept on, always climbing the ladders to spring forth and die by corsair hands, until the wood beneath their feet ran slick with gore.

How long he fought, Tausi forgot, as the drone of battle muted all thoughts, all emotions. Men fought and died in flashing instances when the fires below the walls flared in the wind, growing high with the death stench of broken bones and scorched fat. He cut, hacked, and howled, screaming as the armored terrors ascended from that throbbing red pit of hell.

Each and every one of them became an Ulmo.

Hours of sheer horror ended when the sky brightened beyond the low-hanging clouds, turning them to a smoky shale. Thunder rumbled on the far-off southern horizon, promising rain, and more wind. A horn sounded in the distance, the Latian call for withdrawal—but not retreat.

The corsairs, racked beyond the limits of exhaustion, shuffled along the walls, set about tasks they mustered the last bit of their will to complete. Some crawled on their hands and knees in search of unbroken arrows needed for the next battle. Others poured buckets of seawater into the stairs, washing them of the blood until the inner stone walls, once pale and bright, streaked pink and runny.

Tausi and Zaki found their father on the deck of *The Ube*, seated at the table where the echo of a dream now lay buried beneath the number of unreported deaths.

His brow cut by an errant blow, Ngala rested his pitted iron sword across his ashen knees, the dried blood as dark as his skin. He nodded to them both when they marched the gangplank, then signaled for them to take seats.

"How high counts our dead?" he asked.

"Nana is doing it now. We'll know by sunrise," said Tausi, plopping down in the chair next to his father. "But I don't think we lost that many. We were lucky they tried for the ladders first."

"Aye," said Zaki, shaking the random dzan cups left behind from the feast in hopes one still had some liquid. "But they won't again."

"Not for a while. They will come in from the western beach," Ngala said. He slouched on the wooden stool, his hands hanging at his sides. "We'll have to defend the Far Gate."

"Then they'll try the walls and the gate at once, until we break." Zaki breathed through her nose, flaring her wide nostrils in thought. Her makeup had ran through the night, leaving her face covered in a layer of grime made deeper by the constant smoke that had billowed into their faces. Beyond exhaustion or fear, she finally found some liquor. Wide-eyed, she paused for long moments before she finally sipped.

Tausi watched his father and sister. He was in awe at their calm, and at the same time, in spite of it, marveling at how broken they seemed. No words came, just the sinking, endless cold he felt inside. He looked up to the walls, expecting to see Latians invading its heights already.

"We can hold this city for a week. I stored enough fresh water and food in the tunnel," he said when he found the will for words. "That's not the problem."

Ngala grunted. "What is, then?"

"Someone let them in, Father." Tausi locked eyes with Ngala when the two glanced at each other. "And they are still within my walls."

CHAPTER 5
ANTS AND SAND

Near the main level of the city, a great opening at the northern point of the ring ushered Tausi's company of Zaki, Amare, and Nana into brief darkness before they found the torch-lights, which shone along a stone passage streaked in glittering blues and bright ruby reds.

Stretching his neck to loosen a crick in the back, Tausi stared into the glowing gloom with tired eyes, already spotting the congestion gathering in the lanes. Song City's underground buzzed in movement as raiders, rowers, Rats, and salt-wives ran to and fro to recover from a night of terrors.

When Tausi had first settled the ancient temple that rose out of Shallow Bay's depths, the result of one of his family's many misadventures, he had kidnapped and bribed masons and engineers into becoming corsairs. Plying them with wine and voracious salt-wives, he encouraged them to design and carve a network of stone apartments and storage spaces with skylights that allowed fresh air to rush down and cool the tunnel, leaving it a cozy nexus where much of Stone Cove's loot was kept for transfer between raids.

Now he hoped they had made it well enough to withstand a siege.

"Nana, go check with the quartermaster in the larders," he ordered his bosun who walked beside him. "Tell Baako she needs to find five men to guard them with her, and to expect little sleep. She can have more Rats, too, if she wants."

"Aye, Captain." Nana broke off, down one of the many subterranean paths into the city's depths.

"Wait," he called after his friend. Tausi stopped his group in the middle of the hall as a team of four corsairs ran by carrying baskets of blankets and bandages toward daylight. He signaled them to the nearest wall. Zaki and Amare drew close as Nana rejoined them.

"From here on, death or victory, we three report the truth and only the whole truth to each other," Tausi said, glancing to each of them to register their reaction, pleased when they all nodded to his order. He glanced to Zaki and frowned. "You can tell Ngala the bad news."

His mates smiled darkly while his sister scoffed. "You better have a good reason, little brother," she said, emphasizing the last two words more than the rest.

"Because we need to keep our eyes and ears open. Whoever led the Latians through Avarice Reefs had to have sailed upon a corsair-lord's triremes—if it isn't one of the captains themselves." Tausi waited for their response a second time, almost predicting to the corsair their answers.

"I'll make sure the men keep their eyes on our guests," said Nana.

Amare hummed, nodding in support. "We might gather the Rats and put teams of them on each captain, bosun, commander, and timekeeper."

"What if it wasn't the captains?" Zaki asked, placing her hand in their circle they had formed to pause them. "What if the Latians have a sorcerer who divined their way here? This city is built on what used to be a center for magic."

"The only way we are going to know that is if we ask a Latian," said Tausi. "And I have a good idea who we should ask."

"Why would Illus betray his own people and leave himself vulnerable to being betrayed again?" Zaki asked, quick to her brother's conclusion. "These are the same people that cut off his nuts. I don't think they would work with him."

"He's a Latian," said Amare.

"They may have cut off his balls, Zaki," Tausi added, "but he thinks I was the cause of his capture. I can think of him doing many things."

"Fine," said Zaki, breaking off from the group. "Let's watch them all."

Picking their way through the knots of traffic, they followed the main hall north until they came to a wider intersection, the last junction before the Far Gate. From the clusters of people going to and fro, a small girl emerged from the crowd. Hair braided close to the scalp, she wore a red sack dress and shells around her neck.

"Captain Tausi?" she asked when she approached, her voice light and high.

Tausi knelt, his crewmates and sister stopping beside him in easy stances. "What's the word, Speck?"

The little Rat-girl, no older than eight, came close. "I was told to come get you and Lady Zaki by Lady Azinza. She has opened the ward."

"The ward?" Amare asked, her slight brow furrowed. "We don't have a ward."

"Go on ahead," Tausi told the timekeeper and Nana. "We'll meet you at the Far Gate."

The four separated with Tausi and Zaki, following young Speck down the forking hallways.

In one of the older chambers the stone carvers had made large, high, and wide, they found Azinza and a contingent of salt-wives hard at work constructing small cots stretched with hides. Her shimmering blue dress was ripped off at the knees; she had used fabric to wrap her iridescent blue mane up in a headdress that highlighted her perfect cheeks.

Tausi's heart skipped a beat when he saw her. For even in the scant light the skylight above provided the chamber, her mere aura enraptured him.

"You're all alive," she said happily, crossing the room to the entryway of the great chamber.

"I brought them, Lady Azinza," said Speck, pulling out the skirts of her sack dress for a curtsy.

"Thank you, Miss Speck," she said, bending down before the child. "Will you go and get me Asha? Tell her we'll need forty more oil lamps if they are there to spare."

"Yes, Lady Azinza," she said with another curtsy before she left, walking between Tausi and Zaki like they were the posts of a door.

Tausi spoke first, surveying the completed cots lined along the walls. "What's this?"

"You have wounded and will have more by the time you get your counts," she said, her bright expression dimmed. "So, you will need beds."

"We might need many beds." Tausi stepped past Azinza, walking down the aisle she and the salt-wives had made aligning the cots—no more than old, soft sail stretched over a wicker frame—into rows and quadrants that allowed those attending to enter and exit beside each one with little worry of space. Turning on the spot, the bottom of his sandals scrapped the stone floor when he moved.

"This is more than I could have asked," he said to Azinza as he tried to muster his kindest expression. "Thank you."

"This was my home once too, Captain Tausi," Azinza replied, her hands folded in front of her lap. "And it is yours."

They stared at each other, neither one saying any more, before Tausi broke the awkward tension by clearing his throat. "Aye, my lady," he said, returning to stand beside his sister. "We must be off. Anything you need is yours to ask for."

Azinza hesitated, her lips slightly pursed before she replaced that perfect smile. "Thank you, Captain."

He left the chamber with Zaki in tow.

She reached out and stopped her brother in his tracks. "What are you doing?" she asked, holding his left arm.

He glanced down at her strong, masculine hands on the corded limb. "What are you doing?"

"Go back in there and tell her how thankful you are."

"I said thank you," Tausi replied, shrugging free of his sister's firm grip. "And we need to get to the Far Gate."

"You want to go off and die without telling the woman you love something nice?" she asked, stunned.

"I'm not walking off to die," Tausi said, miffed by the thought. "What would you have me do? Go spill my soul out to her and leave before embarrassment forces her to say something?"

She sighed and rubbed her eyes with her hand. "Listen closely, little brother—girls like it when you tell them how much you appreciate what they do, and she didn't do a little thing. She clearly did it because she thinks well of this place, and therefore well of you, and—"

"How could she?" he asked.

Zaki straightened, squaring her shoulders. "Want to say that again?"

"I said 'how could she?'" Tausi mimicked his sister's stance, jutting his head forward like a bull. "Do you need it repeated?"

"Calm down," Zaki said, raising her tattooed hands in a gesture of peace. "I'm not trying to pick a fight. I just want to know what you mean by that."

"She's a centuries-old sorceress, and I'm barely twenty. She is beautiful, and I am not. She is grace and peace, and I'm not, Zaki. I'm not the next Old Bones, and I'm not even lord of my own city. I'm just a boy with a boat and enough murder in his heart to..." He shuddered on the end of that sentence. The brief sorrow passed, replaced by ready acceptance. "I'm just me, and she is Azinza. Nothing matches Azinza—especially not me."

Open-mouthed, Zaki tried what he knew she would try. "But you're not just that, Tausi. And look at this place—you're the father of Song City."

He laughed aloud before turning away for the main tunnel. "If I can hold it."

They strapped pieces of leather armor scavenged from their battles over the years, taken from the victims of the many excursions where they had been the aggressors, ferocious in the burning nights.

Now, as he strapped on a leather harness that covered his shoulder and most of his abdomen, Tausi did not revel in those passionate nights of murder and greed. He thought on how he had killed in the many Latian and Gypian settlements that dotted Juut's southern coasts, thousands upon thousands of miles of beach every power in the west sought to conquer for their ends alone. He killed his first man at thirteen when his father finally let him off the rower's bench and placed a sword in his hand. Since then, he had lost count, as did every corsair if they lived long enough.

He wondered if one of his victims' family members were out there, coming to claim vengeance.

"Tausi," Zaki called from his left.

She stood by the iron portal known to those that belonged to Song City as The Far Gate—two tall, wide slabs of iron bolted to the tunnel's frame by great iron screws. Cut in the center of each slab were equally spaced doors, locked shut by a dozen individual sliding bars and latches. Large enough to let two men out at a time shoulder to shoulder, a guard stood between each, ready to wrench open the hinged metal when commanded.

Zaki wore a long sleeve of polished bronze scale on her arm, each triangular plate shimmering in the sunlight stabbing through the viewing holes in the gate. "We're ready."

Checking one last time to confirm his sword and a long, wide dagger on his hip, he signaled her to go on. "Get them in line."

"Get in line, you dogs! We go to die," Zaki shouted at the two dozen raiders they had gathered at Song City's landward entrance, men who garbed themselves from the same crates of mismatched gear Tausi and his sister had dressed from. They broke off and formed columns at the doors on the eastern side of the Far Gate, lined up two by two.

"Right for the tree line, lads," Tausi said to his men. "Don't stop to look until you hit the shade. You stop and you're dead."

"Ayes" around, the troop buzzed as Zaki pressed her hand to the door before her and Tausi, as did the pair leading the column to their right. The guards assigned to those doors stepped to them and undid all the locks.

Tausi put a hand on his sister's sturdy back. "Race you."

She snickered. "You're on."

Zaki shoved the door open and took off. Tausi was on her heels as he leapt forward, clearing the Far Gate.

They ran headlong across the natural stone bridge that connected the temple to Shallow Bay's main coastline, a wide swath of sandstone littered with the dead from the morning's battle. Gulls dug long yellow beaks into bloated eyes, ripping free the meat before the charging corsairs trampled them.

Tausi ran so hard his feet stung, but the pain fueled him. He chopped his hands with every step he took, willing himself forward and faster as his sandals dug into the beach's white sand, dragging enough he almost stumbled.

Zaki caught Tausi by the elbow and righted him when she sprinted by, dragging him along a little until he found his foot in the shifting field between them and the jungle's leafy edge. Onward, they and the twenty-four warriors behind them kicked up sand and shell, leaping and dodging past bodies left to bleach in the sun.

The cool shadows of the trees neared. Tausi and Zaki ran headlong into the first grove, tied when they came to the stop at the front of their troops, who in unison, knelt down and turned toward the direction they had come in expectation that the Latians had spotted them.

Heaving, Tausi fought to quiet his breath, shutting his mouth and forcing humid air through his nose. He watched the wind shift the palms, making the giants sway until their trunks creaked from the slightest movement. Fronds rustled like rainstorms. With the sun reaching toward noon, the darkness of the clearing was soft, making the bodies of the corsairs gleam like oil.

A few minutes passed before Tausi whispered. "Clear!"

Her fist balled, Zaki pulled her arm down, a silent signal to gather. Still kneeling, they clustered in, forty-eight eyes on the siblings.

"You four," Tausi said, pointing to whom he wanted. "Go scout the eastern beach. Our barricade protected us during the night, and there might be wreckage. If they're clear and you can recover any intelligence, do so, but do not be sighted—and that goes for all of you. I need every man on the walls tonight." He looked to each of them, not letting a single one go without making eye-contact. "The rest will go to the western shore, where the Latians are beached. We'll take counts and return in an hour."

The corsairs agreed silently and parted, falling deeper into the green depths of the elusive Glass Jungles.

Tausi and Zaki set a fast pace for their large troop, slipping through the trees. The canopies above crashed with the sound of animals disturbed by their charge, monkeys chittering while rainbow birds glided from boughs to find nests, sheltering down to hide from the predators beneath.

The scent of the earth, old, brown, and rotted, covered Tausi's entire body as he trailed his sister through the small showers that plagued the coasts during the mid-fall. Instead of being washed clean by the rain, the soil clung harder, until it crusted his eyes and beard.

At the edge of the jungle, they stopped, half a mile westward of the Far Gate. Creeping to where the trees thinned to the sandier soil, the smell of the cooking fires confirmed their foe's presence.

The corsairs broke off on their own paths, sneaking behind thickets to find their vantage points. Tausi and Zaki parted last, with him letting her go ahead to seek out her own glories.

He waited for the wind to blow through the sand forest before he went, bent low and toward the light, breaking through the trees. Stopping behind older vatke trees, he spied past the bush to the beach beyond.

Washed in the bright sunlight, the tanned Latians were at work digging a control ditch beside the well-oiled hull of their trireme. Their bronze armor cast aside to relieve the heat, their chestnut manes hung loosely around their shoulders, combed and oiled for battle, as to their native custom. They wore swords.

Already they had pulled their boat far enough up the beach to set it on its side and transform it into a small barracks for the crews, while the deck mates set their tents at the base of the overturned vessel.

Then Tausi spotted another trireme, next to the first, then another, and then another, before he had stepped to the border between the jungle and the sand, squatted where the soft earth shifted black to gray. The Latians lined the beach off to Shallow Bay's western spur, more than forty ships packed by soldiers trained to sail, row, and fight.

They outnumbered Song City's forces seven to one.

A commotion rose in the west. Horns sounded in succession, and from the middle of the Latian's line of ships marched a square formation of Latians in their breastplates and helms, armed with spears and shields. Behind them came a squad of men who were more lightly armored and carrying bows and arrows—a unit of archers Tausi did not expect his old enemies to include in their infantry. The mass swelled as they passed by each trireme on the march eastward.

Leaves in the soil shifted behind Tausi.

Pivoting, he drew his knife, cocking it back to throw.

Zaki stood off at a distance between two trees, waving for her brother to come close. Behind her, corsairs ran eastward.

His weapon lowered, Tausi scampered back into the jungle.

"They're marching on the Far Gate," Zaki said before he asked what happened. "Run!"

He followed without question, once again on the chase. Over the sound of his feet snapping twigs, the Latian horn blasts echoed, nearing moment by moment until it sounded as if elephants marched after him.

The corsairs reached the Far Gate, breaking out of the jungle to sprint the sands for Song City's stone bridge. A horn sounded, closer than before, and one of the corsairs stopped a few meters in front of Tausi and Zaki. His sister dodged the fool like a cat, gracefully stepping around him while Tausi, enraged by the man's sheer stupidity, barreled in to shove him from behind.

"Keep moving, you damned—"

The Latian horn blasted double, and without regard for the corsair he tried to hurry, Tausi slipped past and forgot him. The sun briefly darkened, and behind him, he heard the clatter of arrows thudding in the sand as multiple men cried out in terror before they were silenced. He refused to look back, too driven by fear that he covered the distance of the bridge faster than he ever had before. Another cloud of shafts clattered on the limestone following a second double blast.

The doors of the Far Gate popped open, the guards holding them wide as Zaki led the first cluster of corsairs through the portals. She turned and waited for the last man, her hand held out in wait for Tausi, who herded his few into proper formation with barking orders on the third double blast. He slipped in the door just as a trio of shafts struck the spot where he had been a second before.

Pitched forward too far, he allowed Zaki to catch him in her arms. The doors clanged shut behind them.

"Fighters to the Far Gate," Tausi shouted when he and his sister recovered their balance. "The Latians swarm!"

CHAPTER 6
FAR GATE RUMBLE

Tausi alone watched from Song City's northeast tower as his archers below blanketed the bridge with arrows, leaving the shielded mass of Latian hoplites frozen in place beneath their tortoise formation.

Beyond, right behind the first line of trees, the enemy set their own line of bowmen who fired feebly in great arcs that fell too short or barely edged the city walls. On the sand between them and the bridge where the hoplites hunkered down, more units hustled in, collections of a hundred men led by one central commander who wore a helm of horizontal yellow feathers.

After giving the order for all north-facing archers to kill these men if they had the shot, Tausi perched for more than an hour and brooded, his thoughts dark like the shadows cut from the midday sun. The bodies of the corsairs that died in the arrow storm had fallen into the surf, a few of them trampled by the hoplites's march or kicked to the side. Pincushions for every archer's failure, their blood dried in weird formations entranced him.

They had been his responsibility.

"Ah, a man should never be so down on his fortunes to not laugh in death's face!"

Grim thoughts broken, Tausi turned toward that barking voice to find Captain Dra climb up the ladder, one hand clutched to a waxed bottle of dzan. Ngala followed behind, offering an apologetic smile to his son when both men got to their feet.

"A fine day for battle," Dra continued in his hard, deep drawl. Yanking a knife hung on one of the many belts he had wrapped around his great belly, he used the small edge to saw at the pale wax on the green bottle's cork. "Fine, fine day indeed!"

"Captains," Tausi said, trying to ease the roughness in his voice. "What may I do for you?"

"You can do what all good captains must do in a moment of crisis." Ngala came to stand beside his son and stared over the tower's rail. He shuddered at the height and stepped back quickly. "Have a drink."

"Father, I am—"

"No, you're not," Ngala whispered under his breath.

"Ah, here we are," Dra said, tossing the cork off the tower and into the world below. He took a hard swig of the sugar liquor before passing it to Tausi. "To your fine defense."

"We should not celebrate until the defense is over," Tausi said, offering a weak smile as he took the bottle. Tilting it back until his mouth filled, he swallowed the bolt of cinnamon-burn, coughing briefly before he handed it to his father.

"There would not be a defense now if you hadn't taken charge," Ngala observed before he took his sip, followed by a light belch that soured his expression.

The bottle rounded back to Dra. "Aye, you're right, Ngala. You're absolutely right. It makes one wonder about the size of that dock down there." A mad laugh escaped his yawning mouth. He slapped his great belly. "It might have to be expanded, Ngala. He might have to move the walls or build new ones."

"Well, he found good men to carve this city from the hell this used to be." Ngala paused on that note, lost for a moment in something terrible, somewhere Tausi often went when the night gained its darkness. "I'm sure he can find ones to move earth."

"Pardon me, Captains, but I don't take well to being spoken of as if I'm not present," Tausi said, doing little to hide his weariness with them.

Dra cackled before taking a bolt of liquor. He grimaced through his grin, then chuckled as he handed the bottle to Tausi. "You can have five if you get me out of here alive."

The mad leader of the Face Slashers departed, his rumbling laugh merging with the clamor of battle until he descended the ladder.

Tausi faced forward, too angered to look at his father. "Well. Did you get what you wanted?"

"I got you five ships that are yours now, and something even more important—Dra's confidence. That will be important on the day we storm Latian shores."

"It seems you are confident that we'll make it out." He flicked his head forward toward the brewing catastrophe below. "How many arrows do Latians carry in their quivers?"

"Seventy-five," said Ngala, "and they usually have four or five sets, lined on their benches and along the deck."

"And near two hundred men per ship—and every Latian is born a soldier, whether they row or raid." Tausi stifled the doubt balling in his chest. "They'll have more than a million arrows."

"And we have Song City."

"Until they deploy their way around that. And you know they will."

His father sighed beside him before reaching for the dzan. "I understand, son."

The awkward pause, heightened by the day's balmy heat, carried too long. "What do you understand?"

Ngala swigged from the bottle, searching the world beyond the Latians, above the emerald jungles. "I know I have heaped much on you, and that I've continued to do so while in the middle of siege to your city —your city. But I do it because I believe in you, and I must believe in you."

Trapped by that old, endless hope his father had plagued him and his sister with throughout life, Tausi tried to keep his face from reflecting the unease he felt about that confidence. He remembered the liquor in his hand and brought the mouth of the bottle to his lips for another burning taste.

"And," Ngala said, "We can agree that Captain Dra is not the one who betrayed us to the Latians."

"That is obvious. I doubt the man knows subtly."

Ngala cocked his head and glanced at his son, his hands on his panther-clad hips. "How so?"

Tausi handed his father the bottle. A thoughtful smile conquered his face. "My answer is a question."

The Gamka's captain laughed, low and merry. "Go on."

"Remember when we were trapped here?"

His father drank more. "Yes."

"You finally got us to the beach after that damned monster had battered and butchered us, and then it came again. When hope was lost, Father, you still went off to rescue Zaki, knowing nothing of why or how you were going to do it. But you did it, and you rescued her. You rescued all of us." Tears threatened Tausi's eyes. Quickly wiping them away with the back of his hand, he forced himself to look ahead, not at his father or his shame. "And why did you do it?"

Ngala reflected. "Because I had to."

"The moment the battle started, Dra and Oya marched for the walls, carrying torches and doing their best to help me. I didn't ask—they simply did. Dra is dangerous, a glutton, and too honest for his own measure—but he is honest. You showed me that I needn't judge a person's salt by its taste, but by what they do with it in their bones."

"Aye."

They traded the dzan a few more times, watching on high as Song City's archers on the three north-facing towers emptied quivers upon the Latians massing on the bridge and on the beach behind them. Foreign shafts tried feebly to respond, breaking on the Far Gate's iron doors.

"Well, if we can push them back, we can go and get some of those arrows," Ngala opined, resting their half-full bottle against his chest. "I bet not all of them are broken."

"Have to push them back first," Tausi replied. He walked to the edge of the tower's platform. The Latian hoplites remained in their shell, well situated to endure a long wait through the arrows skipping off their shields. He licked his lips, tasting the heat of the booze and its sweet-stink on his breath. "But I have an idea for that."

"Captain!" Nana ascended the ladder and stopped at the top rung. When he saw Ngala there as well, he quickly scurried up, wiping his hand back to put his dark, thick braids in order. He saluted, hand to his chest. "Old Bones."

"Have a drink, Nana," Ngala said, holding out the bottle to *The Ube's* bosun.

"Illus and his men are preparing to leave their quarters for the Far Gate," Nana informed Tausi before he took the offer. "And they are bearing their arms."

"Tausi," Ngala called. "Tausi! Stop!"

He ignored his father as he charged down the wooden stairs lining Song City's inner wall, reaching the first level before his father could grab him. His sword already in his hand, Tausi did not deter from his hunt, searching for that one face out of those scurrying about their frantic, simple tasks. Salt-wives carried baskets of fresh arrows and water up the wooden steps, on the march for the city parapets to refresh their fighters.

Some of the children sitting in the doorways looked down when they saw him, his fierce expression enough to cow any sense of safety or protection.

Ngala caught up. "Captain Tausi!"

He turned on his father, eyes flared in rage. "Not now."

"He is my guest," Ngala said, jerking him to a stop by his shoulder. "And a lord of one of the Mirror's largest corsair fleets. We can ill-afford to have war with The Land Dogs, and—"

"He's not one of us," Tausi said, cutting his father's words short. When he realized the Rats had watched their spat, he froze, trying to think of how to banish the scene he had made in front of them. He held his sword flat against his leg, a sign of passivity among raiders. "He's not. He's a Latian, and it is Latians out there. He begged his way out once, why won't he do it again?"

"Because he hates them," Ngala said, calm and assured.

"Not as much as he does me."

Tausi marched on, calmer than before, though his hand ached as he gripped the handle of his sword. When he and his father met the first level, they discovered more Rats and dozens of corsairs packing the entrance of the tunnel to the Far Gate, shouting and making a commotion that ignored the chaos outside the walls. Most that were armed bared their weapons, shaking them every time whatever they watched elicited a response.

"What the bloody hell are all of you doing?" Tausi roared when he approached the rabble.

The corsairs nearly dropped their weapons when they turned in unison, their blades, wedges, and spears laid to their chest. The Rats slipped between the men's wiry legs, reaching with dozens of hands to take Tausi's as he pulled them along.

"Lady Azinza is fighting the Latian-man!" one little boy said, pointing ahead.

"Yeah! The Latian-man!"

Tausi reared for a moment, and the children parted along with the corsairs before him. Out came his sword, and he let it trail behind him like a lion tail.

Ngala shouted. "Tausi!"

He stormed the tunnel's entrance, one man parting a sea of bodies before he broke through. He was stopped dead in his tracks by the scene playing out before him.

Illus stood with his back to Tausi, his sword arm taut as he held its point sword in Azinza's face. Her bright blue hair unleashed, she did not flinch but stared him down with her fierce eyes. She held a knife in her left hand, low at her side like someone who knew how to use it.

His Latian crewmen, dressed in their stout leather cuirasses and helmed in bronze, formed a wall between Zaki's corsairs on Azinza's side. He saw his sister and the point man of the small phalanx jawed at each other, the former doing more to keep back the men of Song City from slaughtering the Latians than the Latians did to calm themselves.

"Sons of whores!" Tausi screamed, his sword flashing toward Illus' head. On instinct, the Latian drew back in time to parry the slash across the flat of his blade before he sallied forth, whipping horizontal cuts.

Tausi blocked the blows aimed at his face and knees, old western military forms his father schooled him on before he had even held a real sword.

Illus thrust forward, too committed to catch Tausi when Tausi stepped to the side and batted down the iron in the lord's hand.

The redirection forced Illus into a stumble, which he rolled through to recover on his feet. Edges bit and wrestled as Tausi pressed his attack, ducking past a heavy slash to nip at Illus' forward knee. The bastard laughed aloud when he shifted but stuttered when Tausi spun to the right, his momentum powering a bashing strike that knocked the Latian off his base.

Careening to the side until he hit the nearest wall, Illus formed his guard and accepted the first blow Tausi hammered at him, which tore his sword from his hand. He stood, waiting.

Tausi coiled his body to lunge at the man's throat.

"Stop," Azinza said.

Frozen on the edge of satisfaction, Tausi grunted like a bull and stalked from his foe.

The entire tunnel had seized, ally and adversary alike dimmed by the flame of what they had witnessed. Tausi paid no attention, but merely looked at the crowd, and he was taken by an instantaneous shame.

Azinza grabbed him by the arm and made him face her. "They're all scared."

"What caused this?" Tausi boomed, fixed by her eyes.

"I want out," Illus exclaimed, already recovered with sword in hand. He held it down, at the side, though the muscles on his pale-olive shoulder stood, tightened in anticipation for the next engagement. "I'm not going to die in this damned tomb, and even if that means I have to get gutted outside. I won't let them take me again!"

"We are rallying against the foe outside," Tausi shouted at him. "You damned fool."

"They've beached to the west, and they've taken that bridge." The Latian captain straightened. "And none of you will break that phalanx, or the ones beyond it."

"I beg to differ," said Tausi, venomous.

"You're a fool," said Illus.

"Bring me a spare sail and three buckets of oil," Tausi called.

Moments later, his corsairs emerged from one of the many store-rooms of the tunnel, bringing with them a length of undyed cloth attached to a long arm of wood. Ordering them to soak corners and edges of the sail until it felt soft and sleek to the touch, he doused the rest of the folds until they stunk like lemons fermented in rotten cabbage.

He directed four strong men to help him carry the oiled sail to the Far Gate, bringing along with him the troops that had crowded for his skirmish with Illus, those who had marched alongside Latians. They transformed, many losing their wonder—though not their curiosity—on the way to battle. Even Illus changed, leaving behind his ire and taking up the load at one of the sail's ends.

"What are we going to do?" Zaki asked Tausi when they stopped at the iron doors of the city.

"I need you to set this sail on fire with an arrow," Tausi said simply to his sister, motioning for the men crowding his way to move so he could set the sail perpendicular to the door, easing its way out when the portal opened. "Who will run with me?"

"Run?" asked a Latian Dog.

"I need five," Tausi said.

He paused when he noticed Azinza had followed as well, her long blue mane the lone spot of brightness in a sea of dark faces. In that moment, he wished he had said more, yet he was glad she had come—at least he would have seen something worthwhile before what came next. "We might not make it back."

To his surprise, Illus raised his hand with three more of Song City's own.

Tausi stared hard at the gelded man—he had been made so because fate had twined the two of them together, and now, what lay outside had come to claim them for their deeds.

Azinza stared deeply into his soul, the one constant, watching and waiting.

Tausi pointed to Illus and four of Song City's corsairs.

The Latian captain stepped forward, skepticism plastered across his hard, stubbled face. Conferring with the volunteers, Tausi instructed three of the larger raiders to hold the sail at its longer bottom, while he and Illus held the yard-arm.

"Cast it like a whaling net, right over their dome," he told them before the guards worked open the Far Gate.

"It's not a net," Illus shouted. "The weight won't fall right!"

"I don't need it to!" Tausi nodded the three men in front of him out the door, carrying the sail in a unified column. "Go! Go!"

The whispering, humid quiet behind the iron doors disappeared in a flash of white that faded in a span of a breath as Tausi stepped onto the hot limestone. He tried to stay beside Illus who had made a whining sound as they dashed forward. Arrows rained to both sides, some of them falling by his feet. He did not look up for fear of what might kill him.

Skidding to a halt, the first three corsairs pitched the rolled sail over the Latian's bronze dome, catching the points of the spears the enemy managed to poke through the gaps. The formation writhed beneath the oily fabric as those three men escaped.

"Pull," Tausi shouted, hoping that his adversary would follow the order. Illus matched him, and they pulled, jerking the sail back. The Latians beneath it reacted, drawing themselves back in response to the tug.

Tausi and Illus let go and turned, sprinting as hard as they could for the doors. Illus outpaced him by a few steps, his focus now drawn to Zaki when she stepped out of a door on the far side of where his troop exited.

The first three corsairs had cleared the entrance when she raised the bow she held, the smoking end of the arrow red and smoldering.

She loosed the shaft, which seared past Tausi, and stepped back.

The sound of flames licking alive, an airy roar, preceded the screams of absolute agony.

Illus entered first, then Tausi, and the guard slammed the door behind them.

Even iron failed to keep the smell out.

Heaving, sweating, the five men lay against the doors, fallen to the ground or bent over to catch their breath. Tausi hauled himself to his feet and waved to the guards to open a viewing hole.

The screams outside doubled, the screeching calls of armored men being boiled alive in their bronze.

Azinza appeared before him, a hand on his chest to stop him from looking out. "Wait," she said. "Just wait, Tausi."

A daze settled on him. Tausi gave a second wave to the guard, who closed the viewing hole.

CHAPTER 7
UNDER ARROWS

After the burning of the phalanx on the bridge, the Latians drew their infantry back to the western beachhead, leaving behind half their archers to batter the Far Gate while under a constant torrent of arrows. An hour later, the rest of their triremes launched from the coast, dried out and able to stay in the bay for more than forty-eight hours, if the westerners took the time.

And, finally finding their range, they took every second to fire on Song City's walls.

Volley after volley descended upon the parapets until the corsairs were called to shelter in their alcoves, in the carved storerooms and galleys where masses huddled in sheer exhaustion. The sun wheeled through the day, almost unseen as shafts blotted out the sky.

Tausi sat in the corner of the tunnel-threshold that led to the Far Gate. Alone at this point between the light of day and clawing darkness, his thoughts ran with the arrows dropping lifelessly into his bay, their momentum stymied by the wind to where they fell like sticks that splashed in the water or clattered on the decks of *The Gamka* and *The Ube*.

"I despair for the poor bastards that will have to sand the boards."

Zaki appeared over his shoulder, walking over to sit beside her brother at the entrance to the tunnel. Caked in the day's grime, all her makeup had washed away in her efforts, leaving her broad face bare. For a moment, Tausi could see the man that had once been his sister—their father's strong, sharp jaw, or the hollowness of his cheeks.

"I'm just worried about how much water they're taking at this point," Tausi replied, sullenly looking back to his ship. "Did you know *The Ube* logged too much once and sat there for a week?"

"Were you just not paying attention?"

"We were drunk and curious, and we had the dock to haul it up the steps and let it drain. Nobody uses the dock to get drunk anymore, but we at least know how long she can stay afloat."

There came a pause, and the two siblings sat there on the stone and waited as the shafts continued to break and batter both triremes. The sky above them, burning colors of gold, orange, and pink, peaked with the withering of the light.

"I wanted to know," said Tausi, abruptly.

He felt Zaki glance his way. "Why?"

"We should have died here."

Zaki sighed, her teeth gritted in search of words. "The gods aren't here to claim us, little brother. At least not the ones we worship. And not because you decided to live in Shallow Bay."

He grunted in non-agreement.

"Are you an atheist like Father now, too?"

"I don't know what I am." Tausi shifted position, tucking his legs under him to take off the pressure the stone had set in his hips. His view of the world shortened to the few feet in front of him. The pocked, rough-hewn stone lay barren like his heart, unstirred by any sense of feeling or thought.

"I thought I could make something different, out here," he continued, his tone low. "I thought I could take this place and turn it into something like Father turned Stone Cove into—his vision, but mine. I wanted mine and what came with it."

Zaki smiled sadly at her brother. "And that was?"

"Adventure." Tausi laughed at the mad notion. "This place would be a place of adventure, where I wouldn't order men into places like Latia."

"So where would you order them?"

"To the farthest ends," he answered with certainty. "We'd build better ships, stronger ships—ships that could go thousands of miles for weeks on end, searching out the corners of the earth for something better than loot and slaves. We'd go and find real treasures. We would find wonders."

Zaki touched her brother's hair when he couldn't hold back the tears. The pounding of the arrows rained on the walls like bolts of thunder, grinding in his chest as it vibrated the stone testament to his dreams.

"We still can go on adventures."

They both turned to find Ngala standing in the shadow of the passage. Eyes to the sky, he fixed on the arrows as well.

Tausi faced forward, banishing his weakness with anger. "What goes on at the Far Gate?"

"Nothing," Ngala said. "The Latians haven't even claimed their dead on the bridge. Their archers paused their fire—probably out of arrows."

"Not on this side," Zaki said.

More wood piled on the decks of the triremes, leaving them in heaps that grew into hills that collapsed under their own weight, overflowing the sides and into the water.

A grim thought came to Tausi—he'd have to order the bay cleaned out if the Rats were to swim again.

They had to swim again.

"Are you sure you want to go to Latia, now?" Tausi asked his father, his back to him.

Ngala made a thinker's noise in the bottom of his throat. "I can only speak for me, son. And the answer in my heart will always be yes."

"Sometimes our hearts play us for fools," Zaki said.

Shocked by an open word of defiance, Tausi glared hard at her sister. "Say what you say?"

"This isn't even a fleet out of Laconia, let alone one of their smaller metropolises. We can go to them, but they will come right back at us, Father." Zaki turned and looked over her shoulder at Ngala, deadpan and tired. "This is the war you wanted—but is this one we can even finish?"

"Against the other outcome?" he asked his daughter.

Tausi rejoined the conversation. "What are you talking about?"

"We don't own these seas—we never will. But that's not what the Latians think, or the Gypians, or any of these westerners." Ngala stepped in the space between his children, forcing them apart. Sitting down, he put an arm over the shoulder of each, loosely laying it about them while pulling with enough pressure to hold them close. "Do either of you ever think about what would happen if you two lived on the mainland?"

Both siblings shook their head at the question.

"Your mother and I were slaves once," Ngala said, his gaze drifting back to the arrow-rent sky. "In Tolivius, you were either poor, a criminal, or a slave if you were black—unless a lord afforded you a true birth name, which most didn't. It's still this way in Latia, in Gypus, and even past The Glass Jungles in places like Shuiryu, where none but the most daring go. To be black in Juut is to be owned or dominated."

"Why are you telling us this?" Tausi asked.

"Because I want you to think about Latia," Ngala answered, turning his head to gently smile at his son. "I want you to think about the Latians outside. I want you, Zaki, to think about how in Latia they would deem you worthy of death for who you are and want to be."

The expression on Zaki's face flattened from curiosity to a minute fear, the unspoken kind one kept to themselves—even when something had to be, should be, said.

Ngala said it, an arm around both his children. "I want you two to have a say in this life. I found freedom the hard way, but you were born into it—and I'm going to Latia so you can keep it. I don't want to raid them forever—I just need them to know what they will deal with if they try to harm my children."

Tausi felt helpless. No words found their way to fight a truth he could not deny his father—he never could argue against his emotion, or his ambitions. Someplace in the heart inflamed at the idea of sailing west, then north to the civilized coasts, where bronze lords dressed in white cotton lounged in chambers full of slave-girls girded in gilt chains while their wives watched on in apathy, their hair piles of dripping, oiled locks.

"We still need to discover who led the Latians here," Zaki said, pivoting away like she often did. She rose and walked into the darkness of the tunnel, leaving Ngala and Tausi beside each other in the chaotic silence.

"It's not Illus," Ngala called aloud.

"We know," Tausi said, annoyed at how loud his father was in his ear. "I can't find fault in a brave man."

The Old Bones smiled. "Very wise."

"They are hampering us for a reason, and it isn't just to wear on us," he said, not grinning in return. "If I was a Latian, I'm building at least three trebuchets."

"And I bet they'll even carve a ram," Ngala said, still amused. "You were not even twelve by the time Stone Cove experienced three sieges."

"But that was at Stone Cove, Captain," Tausi replied. "This is Song City's first—and the first of anything is often painful."

"Why?"

He looked at his father again, this time in confusion. "What do you mean, 'why'? We're under fucking siege."

"And what did Black Lizard used to do when that happened?" Ngala asked with a pleading sigh. "What did I do?"

"You'd tell men that they were going to go die, so they might as well die happy." This time Tausi did smile. "So, I guess we break out the dzan and see if anyone here can carry a tune. Or play games."

"I've one in mind," Ngala said, nodding toward the falling arrows with fresh happiness.

In between the time his order fell on the closest ears to the moment a raider knocked free the cork from the first barrel of dzan, the world Tausi thought he knew so well transformed beyond anything he could have imagined.

He, and those he cared for most, found life in the midst of death.

Night arrived with music, as the corsairs of Song City took to revelries, weapons always in reach while they partied through the constant stream of arrows. The incessant rain of Latian shafts on the walls, once a grating noise that had marred the hours in misery, formed the entertainment for the fighters, who took to macabre games fueled by booze.

Chief among these contests formed the dire challenge Ngala had alluded to, his dare for any man to go out to the dock and return with as many shafts they could recover.

Corsairs and salt-wives alike lined up in the tunnel after some brief arguments between Ngala and Azinza that banned the Rats from play-ing, which devolved into the captain of *The Gamka* stepping up to attempt the run first.

"You're too old," Azinza exclaimed before passing a half-full bottle of liquor to Zaki, who accepted it with a pleased smile and gulped an inch of devilry. A drip of the dark sticky liquid beaded the corner of the priestess' mouth, her lips full, glistening like a star Tausi wished he could reach out—

Ngala jammed the bottle he held into Tausi's chest, interrupting the thought. "You know, I really shouldn't have saved you."

His nurse and Zaki gasped at him in perfect feminine pitch.

Tausi took a step away from his father, which drew a slight grin from the blue-haired goddess he thought he may have imagined. "I'll wait my turn over here."

"Pardon my concern for an old, foolish man," Azinza said, her tone flat. She put a smooth hand to her forehead and smiled. "I merely see your son, and your daughter, and your crew, and all the people at Stone Cove that hope and pray for the safe return of their Old Bones." The hand went to the sky. "Pardon me, Ngala."

"Oh, no," he said, pointing at her as he slurred both words. "You don't get to pull that on me, Miss Thing! Not after everything is going to go to shit, no matter what you see!" He held his hand out. "Boy, have you drank yet?"

"Only every day," Tausi said, passing him back the bottle.

The three of them waited for Ngala to take another draw before he put the bottle in Azinza's hand. "Now, if you excuse me..."

"One arrow," Azinza said.

Ngala stopped on the stone. "Now you demand I lose?"

"You want to ever see yourself back to sleep?" Azinza asked, brows arched in defiance.

"Oh, fine," said the old captain, turning back on his road to the tunnel's mouth. "Listen, you scalawags," he barked to the line formed, marching to the front. "The game's simple—the corsair with the most arrows may demand anything from me on any given day as long as I live. To make this fair to me..." Ngala glared to where Azinza stood with his children, "I shall go first, as to set a respectable lead for you all."

After a brief cheer by those lined up, the hush came—that familiar feeling all people at play felt before the game started where the price might be one's life. Ngala turned his back to all of them, watching the arrows as they flew over Song City's walls and plummeted to the dock at its center.

"I cannot watch this," said Azinza. "Come get me if he's dead."

The asymmetric hem of her coral-blue gown flowering as she departed deeper into the tunnel, a channel clogged with people seeking refuge in fun.

Tausi caught Zaki catching his wandering gaze after her. "What?"

Sighing deep and sharp, Zaki forced the bottle of dzan she held into his free hand, leaving him double-fisting two. "Go on, you dullard."

"She has made no —"

"She made every sign, dummy," she quickly replied, fists on her hips. "I know how girls work."

"And she also mentioned you, and *The Gamka*, and Stone Cove," he said, watching as his father readied to make his run.

"But you came first." Zaki faced toward the tunnel's exit, a sure smile on her face. "Trust me. I've been a woman long enough to know the signs."

A sudden cheer drew Tausi's attention to his father. Ngala broke forward, sprinting with his head down for the steps. He cleared the first flight before he neared the edge of where the arrows fell and stopped a few steps away to recover a single shaft laying on the top step. He meandered his way back to laughter and jeers, calmly ascending the steps with a defeated look on his face.

"I like sleep, and she can argue forever," he said to Zaki, handing her the arrow when he reached them. "One of you go take it to her. I'm going to go get drunk and see what fool asks me for a boat, or an island, or half the treasury..."

"Tausi can do it," Zaki said, excited. "He was about to go have a drink with her anyway."

Ngala loosed a sigh of relief. "Oh, so that's finally happening?"

Tausi escaped before his curiosity found him more trouble. He started into the musty channel, the air a stale stench of sweat and pot-fires. Dozens upon dozens huddled around, some rolling dice as others pursued pleasures of flesh.

Shying away from more than a few offers from the salt-wives, he stopped at one of the byways where some corsairs had built a grill with some bricks and a flat sheet of iron. Spiced fish sizzled next to onions and saffron rice while hot peppers whined from the metal's unforgiving caress. A pot of sauce, its underside blackened by overuse, bubbled in a corner.

His stomach rumbling, Tausi hesitated for a moment when he felt a hand grab his shoulder. He shuttered, gripping tight to the bottles' necks as he turned on Nana.

"Whoa, Captain," said his bosun, eyes reddened from herb-smoke. "Don't drop those!"

"You're a barnacle on my ass," Tausi said with a relieved smile. "You eat yet?"

"That's my fish on the iron now," he said, rubbing his scarred stomach with his hand. "Was going to come to you next. Illus and his mates are gambling somewhere, and it wouldn't surprise me to see them once they hear about Ngala's challenge. Dra is already in line."

At ease, Tausi nodded past a spell of exhaustion. "What about Oya? I haven't seen Popobawa or Cleona in a long time, either."

"Oya hasn't left the Far Gate since the last guard change. I think she is actually standing at her post, hoping for a ram."

"I'll send my father to get her. The others?"

Nana looked back over his shoulder, checking on his meal. "Cleona is sleeping in her quarters after downing some drink earlier—before you gave orders—and I don't know if Popobawa has left his room since the siege started."

He stepped close to his bosun. "But someone has seen him, correct?"

"He and his crew have taken food," said Nana, shrugging his large shoulders. "Should I take some men and go see what's what?"

"Not now," said Tausi. "I'd rather keep him in one place. Dra and Oya are fine, and I doubt Cleona would have time to betray us considering her pickling."

"What about Illus?"

He glanced back the way he came, the smoky din. "Keep an eye on Illus, but I don't think it is him."

"No?" Nana asked.

"Don't take the guard off of him, but no, I do not expect it is Illus."

"This truly is the worst siege ever. Do you want me to get you some food? I bet the cook will put you to the front of the line when he sees you."

"No, I'm off," Tausi said, holding up the bottles and arrow he carried. "Nana, did you happen to see a beautiful blue woman walk this way?"

"Oh-ho, the brine singer!" Nana clapped his hands together. "In fact, I'd been so good with all my eyes I might just know where she went."

Once Nana claimed his board of food, Tausi followed him down one of the forking hallways off the main tunnel, dodging past small groups of men and women who held their own games of dice for prizes better than a few small bits of silver and spices, or couples beginning their dalliances in the shadows where only their bare outlines might be seen. To his surprise, his bosun led him to the ladder of Song City's north-eastern tower.

"What is she doing up there?" he asked Nana.

"No idea," he said, using fingers coated in sticky rice to soak up and grab his cooked fish. "She comes here during the dark hours, between her rounds at the infirmary."

"Thank you," said Tausi, nodding for his crewman to go on. Nana heaped more food into his mouth and headed off, singing loudly an old song chanted by corsairs out to claim their salt-wives.

Sticking the arrow in the band of his loincloth, he held both bottles of dzan by the throat with one hand, using his free one to navigate himself up the rungs slowly. Halfway to the top, the notes reached his ears; her voice carried beyond the sounds of the assault outside. Gentle and soft, they filled Tausi with renewed strength as he hauled himself further.

At the top, he found Azinza sitting at the edge of the tower's platform, the skirts of her gown hiked up around her smooth, brown thighs. Wind moved her cerulean hair like water while she stared off to the south.

Far below, the Latians shifted their blockade into a new formation, allowing crews to rest while fresh lines of hoplites cycled through, lifting their bows with restored arms and renewed focus. The clouds of arrows looked like flocks of strange, small birds that threw themselves to their ends upon the unseen face of the mural-walls.

"Hello, Tausi," she said.

"Hello," he nodded in greeting. "My father made his run and ordered me to bring you the arrow."

"Ordered?" Her silver eyes, like drops of the moon, flashed. "Is that why you brought two bottles of liquor?"

"I brought them..." He bit at the words. "I wondered if you would like to drink with me."

Azinza smiled, her teeth clean and bright. "I would be happy to drink with you. Would you like to sit with me?"

"Thank you." He came over and sat down beside her, his legs hanging over the side of the tower's edge. Linking his ankles together, he watched the arrows fall a hundred feet below, clattering and breaking upon the stone walls of his city. "I'm surprised to find you up here."

"I would rather not be in that tunnel. I remember that tunnel," she said, her stare far off.

"I didn't mean..."

She took one of the bottles and slugged from it. "I like it up here, Tausi. I like how you drowned out the middle, where your father saved me. I liked how it is gone."

"I'm happy to hear that," he said, at a loss for better words. He drank from his bottle of dzan, the burn ruining better words he thought of first. "I was worried that you might not be comfortable in this place."

"This isn't where I lived." Azinza pointed out to sea with her bottle. "I was there."

"What did my father mean when he said you 'saw' things?"

She laughed that the question. "You caught that."

"I'm my father's son."

"You're not Zaki."

"No?"

"That's a good thing," she said. "She catches too much of what goes on."

"So what do you catch?"

Azinza sipped on the fiery drink in her hand, glancing at him with a sly expression. "Time. Destiny."

"You're a seer," Tausi said.

"When I'm shown what to see."

"Have you seen us get out of this?" he asked, bemused. The cinnamon-swill passed his throat in a hot lump.

Azinza caught him again with her metallic eyes, her gaze piercing him to the heart. She seemed to balance on the tower's edge, almost falling forward if the rail had not prevented it. Looking away, she drank, letting the question fade into the starry night.

Tausi remembered the arrow. Picking it up from where he had placed it on the boards, he offered the fletched end to her. "Your prize— you understand my father far better than I ever will."

Confusion tightened her cheeks as she held onto the feathers. "But you're not supposed to hand me this arrow."

"What?"

A thunder-strike, which shook Song City's walls and silenced the corsair's raucous noise, interrupted her answer. The sound of cracked stone falling away into the sea ended when another stone blasted the northwestern corner.

Tausi bolted to his feet, gripping the rail.

"This isn't supposed to be happening," Azinza whispered, almost to herself.

A third stone beat the walls.

"This isn't supposed to be happening."

CHAPTER 8
PARTY UP

D awn came with terror.

Hails of arrows, which had carried on for the entire night, ceased suddenly when the horizon warmed a dull gold. The bay emptied of Latian triremes, the crews berthed at their western beachhead to mass for a great march behind the five siege catapults. The long arms flung black stones dug from beneath the surf at the northwestern walls, between the Far Gate and the tower that overlooked the enemy position.

Hoplites rounded behind their artillery line while the wind blew warm and soft from the south, carrying the salt from the sea inward. Chopping down one of the larger hardwoods, they carved a ram.

Focused on two points of Song City's defense, they hammered the iron doors of the Far Gate while their catapults fractured the ancient stone walls.

Under the constant thunder, Tausi split his forces, sending Nana and Amare with a few hundred to hold the Far Gate. The rest he ordered to the northern and western walls. The city shaking every time a new stone struck the upper half, he divided his corsairs into masses with one hundred and fifty on the other side of where the masonry would fall away when the Latians succeeded at their gambit, and one hundred and fifty on his side. Every bit of armor to spare, every weapon looted from their raids, were deployed from the storerooms and under beds, gathered into great wicker baskets, and marched by the children of Song City to the top, coming in pairs and trios to handle the weight of iron and leather.

The sight of the children carrying spears in the pale morning caught Tausi's building sense of hopelessness.

Latians paid no enemy mercy, no matter their age or surrender.

"Lift up your arm," Ngala told him. Already dressed in a mail-sleeve and a helm, he strapped a boiled leather bracer to his son's strong wrist, his fingers fumbling.

Tausi lifted his hand and held the hardened hide firm, letting his father tie it off. "We can't let them in. The things the Latians will do to the children—"

"Shush," said Ngala, helping his son with the matching bracer on his other wrist. "Azinza will keep them calm in the tunnel. They'll be fine."

"Azinza," said Tausi.

"Yes?"

He met his father's eyes.

Ngala clapped both hands on his son's face, stinging his cheeks. "We don't let them in."

Tausi nodded as he turned away, shaking his head to rid the tingle running through his entire body. He drew his sword, letting its weight find reach and balance at the end of his arm. He checked on the coastal bridge, confirming the hoplites still hammered at the Far Gate.

Archers on the northern towers pelted at them with arrows and stones that slid uselessly off the domes of their raised shields. They rammed at one of the many iron doors with little to show for it, but Tausi understood that they didn't have to. Latians were trained from the age of seven to die in fields farther than his. Those men would hammer all night, if only to keep his corsairs divided while their comrades laddered up into whatever hole they created in the wall.

How much food did they have? What would happen if the wall came down? They couldn't hold off thousands, and not for more than a day.

The floor beneath his feet rumbled when a stone smashed into the wall a few hundred feet from where he stood. Startled back to reality, he banished his doubt the best he could before Zaki stepped in front of his vision.

"I need you right now," she said in a hushed tone.

"What's happening?" he asked, panicked.

"The captains need to see you—the four of them."

Tausi followed his sister to the top of the stairs, finding Ngala, Illus, Dra, and Oya armored and armed for conflict.

"Where is Captain Cleona?" he asked when he came before them, noticing the old woman absent from their number, as well as Popobawa.

"Taken sick," said burly Dra, "She's old and—"

A stone struck the wall with a shattering roar, the pound of the impact lost in the tumble of stone falling away.

"To your posts," Tausi shouted above the din of new shouts.

Corsairs rushed to their stations, leaving behind forgotten pieces of armor and baskets from where they had been moments before. Blades, wedges, and ax heads flashed in the light of another cloudless, perfect blue day about to be reddened.

Another stone fell, then another, each one tumbling down the city's sides before crashing into the sloshing sea below. The wall groaned under the weight of its oncoming collapse, issuing low, loud cracking sounds that filled the salt-air with dust.

Tausi saw the final stone launch from the western beach, rising almost softly from the sand to arc gracefully in the air. He gaped, hypnotized by its flight before it plummeted out of sight with the sound of a thunderbolt.

His home, solid as the roots of the earth, quivered under his feet.

The rampart crumbled, showering in smaller, head-sized pieces before the entire section toppled in great chunks. The gaping hole in the wall grew with each passing second until it ended in a rumble punctuated by a sudden quiet that raised the noise of the corsairs higher in Tausi's ears, words jumbled in the chaos.

From where he stood by the raw edge, he watched ships launch immediately from the shore, five at first, then ten, then dozens, all aimed at Song City.

The sudden shock of the damage, the sight of the boats, woke Tausi from his awe. "Archers on the flanks! Screens!"

Arrows were drawn from hip-quivers as huge wooden frames tacked with thick, oiled hides were fixed on the ramparts on the wound's immediate sides, providing the corsairs cover from the artillery he knew the Latians would bring to harass them while soldiers climbed the ladders.

"They will come, one by one," Tausi shouted to those that could listen. "But they will come! Do not let them take the walls!"

Minutes ran before the triremes reached the pile of rocks rising from the water at the foot of the southwestern wall. A line of black-armored bowmen lined by the Latians's port sides raised their weapons high and loosed, a volley that failed to even reach the top of their target. Those before them rushed to set up their pegged ladders.

Two ladders banged against the rough slope of the hole, an arduous journey for any person to climb under arrow-fire. A pair of initial hoplites launched themselves on the rungs.

"Fire," Tausi said, wiping down with his hand at the enemy.

Bodies piled quickly, transfixed by dozens of shafts until the seawater swelling around the trireme bubbled in a dark red cloud. The Latian archers continued their volley while more infantry charged, stepping atop the grisly hill of dead to reach the ladder.

"More arrows," Tausi ordered one of the corsairs attending his troop, who nodded and gave the order to the Rats. The children had worked out a new route to both sides of the gap as they resupplied the archers with baskets of ammunition.

The Latians formed their triremes in a chain, connecting each boat together with a series of planks until a long flotilla formed on Song City's northwestern quadrant, a line of hoplites growing into an organized behemoth with some solid footing beneath them.

Longer ladders rose, forcing Tausi to employ the captains to lead small divisions of his defenders to knock over each. The thinning of his archers allowed the central point of the Latian assault to push up and in. More than one man reached the bottom of the hole before they were shot dead by an attentive corsair.

The one-sided slaughter carried on for an hour before the Latians called for a halt, drawing their troops back for a reprieve before the next push. Ordering men with long spears to prod and poke the dead men in the hole until their bodies dropped into the ocean, Tausi doled out axes like he had on the first day of the siege.

Ngala met him before the Latians massed for their second assault.

"Oya and I are accounted for on this side, as is your sister. Dra and Illus went to the Far Gate on my order to reinforce your command. They will follow orders."

"What were you all going to tell me?" he asked, listless.

"Cleona is dying," his father said in a plain, tired manner. "We will need to give her rites when we get past this."

"Tremendous," said Tausi, his shoulder slumping deeper at the news. "We need to get past over ten thousand men."

"I know."

"There are things I have said in the past..."

"Tausi." Ngala smiled at his son. "There is no need when one loves another. What matters is that if there are things to say, you say them now before you lose the chance. I don't have anything to say right now, Captain. Do you?"

Steeled by his father's resolve, Tausi shook his head. "No, sir."

Scampering up the ladder, the Latian screamed as he ascended, hand over hand on the rungs. He left his wide bronze shield behind, mirroring what the man before him did to ease the journey upward. His wailing died when an arrow pierced the bridge of his nose; the arrow sprouted from the area his helm did not cover.

Tausi shoved the ladder away from the wall with the broken fork of his pike, watching as the Latian fell back first onto a mound of the dying. Already searching for the next target, he paid little attention to if the bastard rose or not.

War raged upon this section of Song City's damaged wall, and men were slain by the moment as the Latians pushed up and the corsairs cut them down. The hot sun wheeled in a flawless sky on a hot, stagnant day. The breeze blew over stone and current before it snaked through mounds of the bloodied, carrying the stink of their ghosts off to whatever totalitarian afterlife the westerners craved.

After dumping what was left of their oil below, corsairs dropped a pair of torches, setting flesh ablaze. The Latians brought out shovels, hauling smoldering bones into the sea to clear the way for the assault.

Posted atop Song City's parapet, Tausi and Zaki caught their breath as they observed the hoplites massing on the bouncing flotillas, trying to use the smoke to hide their numbers.

"I want twenty archers on the other side to harry them once they reach the burn line," he shouted over the inferno, motioning to the burnt edge of the field their enemies struggled to clear. Some of them added to the count against the Latians, downing a hoplite here and there by a stray arrow shot from on high. "Long spears at the edges."

"They will mass again, Tausi," she said, despondent. Blood caked Zaki's handsome face, a makeup of ash and sweat, giving her a demonic appearance—and an exhausted one. "They aren't just going for the hole anymore."

"Send the ax men to the walls with the captains. Oya will go again."

"Tausi."

"If we can hold for another charge, they'll have to pull back," he said, grabbing his sister's arm and pointing with his sword. "There are only so many hours they can keep this flotilla together before they have to beach the boats. If we can—"

"Tausi, they have the time," Zaki broke in, shrugging free. She grabbed his arm, forcing him to look at her. "We need to be ready to retreat into the tunnel."

He growled at his sister for even suggesting the idea. "Then you go tell the Rats."

The demand staked Zaki where she stood, her set jaw failing to work out a rebuttal.

Drawn close to keep his next words between them, Tausi whispered in her ear, "I need you to live, Zaki. I need you to get Ngala down to *The Gamka*. I need you to take him and Azinza, and as many of the children as you can. I'll send some men to open the Sea Gate and you can try to—"

"I'm not leaving you either," Zaki screamed in his face before she shoved him away. "Don't you ever suggest that again! Don't you dare!"

"The Latians charge," shouted a corsair atop of the walls. "They charge!"

Both siblings rushed to the edge, weapons ready. Joining the throngs of tired warriors, they screamed hoarse curses when the westerners began their march. Their spears waved in time with the bounce of the horsehair crests on their black helms. They moved without words or commands, the pound of their marching feet the herald of their coming.

Song City's archers attacked from their position on the southern side of the hole, slowing the hoplite advance. Pelted with arrows, the Latians formed a shell with their shields and crept forward. Another unit behind them followed, a straight column with shields on both sides, carrying a series of stacked wooden ladders.

"Spearmen at the ready!" Tausi joined the fighters closest to the opening in the wall, taking up one of the nine-foot-long spears. One of a dozen ready to stab at whomever dared to reach them, he weighed the shaft of the spear in his hands like the world. Hundreds of lives stood at its iron tip, fated to perish if he failed.

Two ladders sat up, cracking the rough stone lip of the hole.

Tausi stabbed at the first face he saw, a foolish man who had tried to climb with his shield strapped to his back. Two more cold points pressed through the leather of his cuirass as he slid off the end of Tausi's spear and fell backward and out of sight. Another man tempted fate at the ladder's apex.

Latians died in pairs, skewered in four or five places. Some of them screamed, and some simply died, caught in that frozen moment before animation fled the husk. A third ladder was forced up with the help of a young soldier who held it against the broken wall, even as Tausi stabbed him three times in the back while someone opened his shoulder.

The heroic effort allowed a third man up.

Crowding the hole, the Latians made room for a few more men to crawl up behind them and set a small shield wall, providing a buffer for those that survived the corsairs' arrow volleys. The corsairs held until the Latians swung their mass to the south minutes later, splitting their thousands into two different clusters that attacked the wall with a taller ladder. Unable to focus their fire on a single target, the archers dropped their bows and joined a group of their kind on the way to defend. The groups were led by Oya, Dra, and Ngala.

Tausi lost sight of his father in the smoke after the Latians broke the top of the parapet on the other side of the hole. Panicked, he strove harder to hold back the black-armored horde, stabbing with his long spear at a bronze shield until the shaft broke near the head, leaving only five spearmen on his side to support the six corsairs on the other.

The Latians in the hole broke the spears.

From there on, the world disappeared as the invaders re-lit the bodies of their own at the foot of the wall to cover a final mad push. Tausi breathed poison, his sword in his hand, as he waited for those dark wraiths to part the curtain of cinders.

The crash of arms afterward echoed louder than anything else until he existed in a world of lonesome violence. He remembered cutting into the first man, severing his throat to expose a spraying windpipe. Bodies knocked and shifted together as men tried to get to other men to kill them.

His sword arm burning, Tausi whipped his edge at whoever came at him wearing a crested helm, slaying them on the spot. Gore basted his arms, chest, and face, a coat of warmth.

Somewhere in the cacophony, he heard her singing. Soft but strong, he could hear the ancient words echoing in the endless distance.

Thunder rumbled on high. Cutting down a man until he saw the life leave his eyes, Tausi roared before a single drop of water caught him in the face.

Shocked by cool relief on his agonized, bloody skin, he peered through the smoke to see a sky roiling in dark, heavy clouds. Lightning blinded his eyes and was followed by a loud crack that almost stopped his heart.

Winds whirled, howling low and long before speeding into a keening wail. A sheet of rain stung Tausi's body, the water blinding him. He stood there, defiant to the sudden typhoon while he waited to die.

A horn called in the west for the Latian retreat.

Disbelief froze Tausi in the storm, the men around him exploding in a roar of victory, of shock, before the gale ripped their voices from them. Lightning warped the sky, a dire reminder that they had won nothing.

Battered by the rain again, Tausi ordered the retreat.

The clamber down the stairs cost more than a few lives as men slipped on the slick, dark boards of their bridges and catwalks, some of them crowding the stairs to the point that some were pitched over to their deaths.

Pressing his way through the struggle before him, Tausi rallied those ahead of him into the tunnel where Song City's hundreds packed into the wide passage. Lost in a cacophony of stale, hot air, and the endless shouting of the dying, he brought himself to focus.

"Zaki!" He shouted as loudly as he could. "Amare! Nana!"

"Captain!" Nana appeared at his right, caught behind a cluster of men three deep and struggling to make room for each other.

"Find Ngala! Find the captains," Tausi ordered. Frustrated by the mass tangled before him, he barked loud at them. "Get your bones straight, you tough bastards! You survived!"

The declaration calmed the room. An air of peace infused the corsairs, and looking for a moment at each other, a final great cheer went up before it fizzled in a daze.

CHAPTER 9
REMINDERS

The sea churned throughout the night and into the next morning, thunder and lightning echoing a never-ending argument between Sky Lord Chango and the divine Oya, Queen of Waves, their tempest slamming swells of water into Song City's steadfast walls.

Those raiders, rowers, archers, bosuns, and timekeepers, their salt-wives and salt-husbands, and of course, the Rats sat in quiet awe of the storm, eating small rations while they watched light and dark clash before them.

Camped where the light of the outside world loomed into the tunnel, Tausi sat on a pile of blankets and drank from the first in a row of green bottles. Given space by those also camped in the tunnel with him, he made use of it by building an indoor grill. One of many serving stations set up from his place near the Sea Gate all the way to the Far Gate, he raked hot coals across a slab of stone floor, then heaped dried beach wood, which he built into a thick layer of coals before Nana and Amare laid down a slab of fire-blackened iron.

Setting a large iron pot of rainwater to boil, he studied the deluge as it began to bubble and hiss.

"The Latians abandoned their siege of the Far Gate. Left the ram on the bridge, last time we saw it," said Amare, picking at his teeth. "Can't see shit for all that rain."

Tausi dropped a ladle of oil on the iron, letting it spread and run with the heat. "Someone is going to have to go out there. At least to the top of the wall to see what they're doing."

"What in Chango's name can be they doing in that?" Nana broke the seal he had made with his lips around the dzan bottle's mouth, pointing at a wall of rain so thick it glowed white with the daylight. An orchestra of thunder punctuated the question.

Tausi glanced to his timekeeper and bosun, not sharing their ease. He knew his city would hold fast against the tides, its base deeper and hardier than the sandstone bedrock beneath the sea.

The Latians were stronger than he had been and would have won if the storm had not ended the siege.

Even now, he thought about the numbers lost in the melee. If he looked back, he knew the number of fewer heads in the crowd would sear its mark on his soul. Serving them food would let him see his folk in smaller bits, confirming who he knew survived while readying for the impact of those missing.

Amare fed the boiling pot handfuls of rice until the heady-sweet smell drew a line.

Corsairs brought fish or chickens they had hidden in their cells or their salts. Eggs bubbled and firmed with sunny yellow faces, which were shoveled on bread crusts and devoured. The meat roasted, their juices mixing with the oil to the point that a clean scrape and flip of a knife blade turned the fish to cook on the other side.

Nana and Amare, muttering drunk insults at each other, dumped the pot of cooked rice onto the sizzling poultry and fish, which Tausi chopped up with his sword to make a mash. The line to his grill grew, with more bringing small mollusks or lobsters they dragged out of their traps before the storm took place.

Tausi looked at each and every person in their faces, in their eyes, sharing words with every corsair that came to claim their share of lunch. Many who had served on the walls and survived held little more than smiles and sheer exhaustion, thankful for a hot meal and a kind word from the man that had commanded them through the slaughter.

The salt-wives and salt-husbands came, many of them carrying a

Rat in their arms or at the hip, making sure each child—theirs or not—had a bellyful of food for the day.

For more people than he liked to count, Tausi watched tears run from eyes, some of them falling from faces forced into masks of calmness, or assuredness, or lonesome silence. His heart ached a few times in moments when he shared a laugh or a little joke, trying at words to soothe those that had lost.

Then the wounded came.

Led by Ngala, four of the six corsair-lords lined up before the grill, their plates turned over—a captain's signal to be served after the rest of the crew had been given their due. Nana went over with a few dzan bottles.

"Hey, Captain, did we win?"

That question was repeated from the mouths of every single soul that raised a weapon in Song City's defense, no matter if they had lost an arm, or an eye, or more than that.

The bravery of the maimed to get to their feet and shuffle down the line, only to ask that same question, touched Tausi's heart to the point Nana took over the serving so he could get a plug of dzan in his belly while wiping away tears.

The mound of rice-meat mix, browned by the juices of chicken and fish spiced heavily with salt, pepper, and some bay leaves, was doled out portion by portion until everyone that came to the grill was served.

At the end came the captains, drunk from their bottles.

Oya meandered over first. A bandage pasted to her wounded head with a bit of gauze and honey, she flared her eyes at Tausi with a dangerous smile before looking down at the cuisine for the afternoon.

"You put that tilapia in there with all that mess?" she asked.

"Something like that, Captain," replied Tausi with a restrained smile. "Take what you like."

"How about for every scoop you give me, I give Song City one ship?"

The question stopped him. The next captain in line, his father Ngala, smiled sheepishly when Tausi glanced his way.

"That would be more than this plate of food is worth, Captain Oya," Tausi said. "I would not want my meager meal to sour in your stomach when you consider what you do here later."

An attractive woman nearing her forties, she squared her sword-marked shoulders. A hint of anger tinged her expression but dissipated as quickly as it came. Square with Tausi, she glanced to Ngala. "You know, you do remind me much of him. You were too giving at one point, too."

"How so?" Tausi asked in amused curiosity.

Illus cawed from his place in line. "Some of us are bloody starving."

"Yes," Ngala said, exclaiming. "Get on with the meal!"

Digging his ladle into the food, Tausi plopped a generous helping onto Oya's plate.

Oya's bright tan eyes flashed danger at him, set above a small but wicked smile. "One more."

He added another, leaving half her plate covered in a mix of brown rice and spiced meats.

"One more," she said.

Tausi did not move. "My paltry dish is not worth a trireme."

She put her plate down on the hot iron, the heat sending up a charring, smoky smell. Her hand went to the sword at her hip. "Will you now tell me that my life was not worth your dish?"

"Calm down, Oya," said Ngala, right next to her. "He doesn't mean—"

"Oh, fuck you, Ngala," she said, interrupting her old lover. Oya leaned toward Tausi. "You are going to tell me that my life, which you have defended atop these walls for days, is not worth some wood and iron? If not rice and fish, what of flesh and blood? Is my flesh and my blood not good enough for your meal?"

The tense silence of the other four captains offered Tausi no assistance, so he dug a fourth, smaller helping for Oya. Dumping it on her plate, he put his ladle down and rested his hand on his sword.

Barehanded, Oya snatched her heavy plate off the grill, paying no attention to the blackened bottom of the wood. "Follow me, Ngala. I'll not give you time to do that clever little banter you have with Zaki. I imagine you two would only grunt at each other anyway."

"Yes, Captain," he said in a small voice, not meeting his son's gaze as he shuffled down the line. "Serve me, Tausi."

"Yes, sir," Tausi said, too dumbfounded by what happened to make any more arguments. The odd couple, a pair of captains so far apart in deposition, meandered off toward the mouth of the tunnel, finding a spot near where the rain failed to wet the stone. He thought he saw them share a secret, sneaking smile when Illus cleared his throat.

"I'm still hungry, and I fought on that goddamn wall too," the Latian corsair said, his tired expression hardened. "And don't expect a bloody boat from me."

"I would never dare." Tausi eyed the man hard as he scraped down near the bottom of his diminished rice hill, hoping he sheared off more burnt pieces than tender ones. He turned his ladle over Illus' plate, paying him no more mind than he would anyone else. "Captain."

Dra came last, his face still crusted in splatters like freckles on his dark skin. "I already gave you five boats—I just want to eat."

His jolly chuckle heartened Tausi, who shared a smile with the odd, dangerous man. "By all means. Thank you for fighting on the wall yesterday. I will always remember what the lords of the Mirror did for my city."

"Well, from one lord to another." Dra tossed a wink at Tausi's confusion. "Captain Cleona woke up and is hungry. She told me to tell you to bring her food."

"I'll send Nana along," he replied, scooping Dra two servings, leaving two more. Left was a small serving for him and plenty for an old lady sick in bed.

"She meant you." Dra took his plate and smiled down at his feast, eagerness gleaming in his eyes. "And if you think Oya was bad, wait until you upset Cleona enough that she gets out of bed."

The makeshift infirmary lay quiet when Tausi passed the doorway, and he found the chamber empty save for its two occupants.

Azinza and Cleona chatted by the latter's cot, a plate of half-eaten food on the priestess' lap. They chuckled at something between them before Azinza raised her head in time to see Tausi walk through. A clean, happy smile split her mouth when their eyes met before she studied him from head to toe—a study which made his skin pucker in gooseflesh.

"Here he comes," Azinza whispered to Cleona.

The old captain, closer to her seventies than her sixties, raised her head. "Did that whelp bring me some food?"

"It is still warm," Tausi said, raising the plate of rice and chopped fish in his hand and cup of fresh water in the other. "Where would you like to take your meal, Captain?"

"At least he has his father's politeness," Cleona whispered to Azinza, who covered a different sort of smile with her hand. "Well, go on, girl—give this man your seat. He and I have to get some things clear."

"Yes, ma'am," said Azinza, rising from the wooden chair. "I'll need to go check on the wounded as it is. They just had to march to eat, didn't they?"

"Men," replied Cleona. "For all the good and ills that come with them."

"Oh, hush," Azinza said, her blue dress pulled up in one hand so she could step over discarded weapons and arrows chunked with meat. Her bare feet were somehow graceful among nicked, burred edges. They took not a cut. On her way by, she brushed Tausi's arm with a finger.

"Come see me when you're finished. Zaki suggested I check you over."

He said nothing even after she left the infirmary. The oil lamps in the room, making it warm and comforting against the chill shadows the gloomy skylight failed to defeat, appeared to gutter at her exit.

"You're staring," Cleona croaked. "Girls don't like it when you stare."

Tausi looked back at the old woman in her cot. Without response, he went to the chair beside her bed and sat down. "How would like to eat your meal?"

"Oh, I'm not hungry, or at least I won't be again." The bluntness of her own words paused Cleona for a moment before a single cough was followed by a few more fluttering breaths.

Tausi tensed, unsure of what to do. "I'll go get Azinza."

"So she can do what?" Cleona asked through a tiny wheeze. "Sit with me and wait?"

Tausi set the plate of food on the cot behind him.

The fit passed for the old woman, yet while he watched her shudder, he wondered at how she had gotten to such heights to rule a well-established corsair island like Tip Town, which had two different keeps and a city a hundred times the size of Song City. Even if in the fullness of youth, he guessed she wouldn't have been much more than five feet tall, and in a world where he felt like a giant beside her, a simple consideration of what she could have done to him if she were in her heyday terrified Tausi.

"I hear that Chango came along and started a fight with a greater Oya to save our sorry hides," she said, curled up beneath three blankets. They did little for her shivering. "But you held fast."

Tausi nodded from his seat. "What would the spirits of the dead tell our gods when it came time for my judgment?"

"A good answer in a good question." Her thin, gray lips curved in a smile. "Tell me, what do you think of your father's plans for Latia?"

He cracked a grin. "I have not thought about it for one moment since this siege began, and I hope not to think of it for a long time. I hope he does not either."

"Truly?"

Brow bent in thought, he gave a cautious nod. "He asks much—too much—of us sometimes. He reminds us of our history while demanding we try to chase it down and kill it. But we can't kill it—this is not even a fraction of their fleets. We call ourselves lords, but we feed ourselves on the spoils we take from others, including other Juutans. The Latians grow food to feed soldiers—we steal it to survive. It is asking one man to hunt a panther on his own."

"A fool's gamble," she said in summary.

"Yes."

"Have you told your father this?"

He pressed his lips in a tight line. Bent over in the chair, his elbows rested on his knees. "No."

"And why not?" Cleona whispered.

Thunder boomed above them, vibrating Song City down to its foundation in the water.

"Because nobody says no to Old Bones Ngala," Tausi said when the world calmed. "Least of all his children. We ask for things, and he grants them. That is how it has always been."

"Is that what you want?"

Frustration scrunched Tausi's face. "No, Captain, but it is what he wants."

"Oh, but boy, I see that you want something too." Cleona smirked from behind the edge of one of her blankets. "Maybe someone, too."

"I was staring," he said, conceding the point.

Cleona shuddered, hacking small little noises that Tausi realized, from the way her side shook, was laughter. Feeling like a fish that had gotten picked by the water-snake not to be eaten, the anxiety loosened until he found himself bent over again in his chair, laughing alongside the dying woman.

"I'm giving Song City one ship—*The Immammou*, which carried me to the farthest shores," she said when their mirth ended. "But on a few conditions, young man."

"As many as you like," Tausi said, relieved she did not simply give him ten boats for a plate.

"First, you must give this ship to Zaki."

"Zaki?"

"I have a special fondness for your sister, ever since she was little and boisterous," Cleona said. "And it seems you give her as much rule here as you give yourself."

"She's not like us," Tausi admitted with the same joy her thought brought him. "I sometimes tell my father that he will make her a queen."

"Tell her to study the configuration of the mainmast. It will help whatever she is planning."

"You know about that?"

"She is my little one."

They sat together for a long time after that, speaking on the events of the Latians's siege against Song City, telling old tales of raids and voyages across the Mirror Sea's breadth, before the conversation returned to the topic they hesitated to broach.

"I came to die, you know." Cleona's old eyes, tired and heavy, searched beyond where Tausi sat. She seemed to be part of her blankets, an empty old something lost among other empty old somethings, with only her face to indicate her existence. "I knew the moment I stepped on my ship that I was going to die."

"How?"

"Don't know—I just felt it," she said, her brittle lips widening. "And, split me wide, I knew it was going to be in bed."

"I'm sorry I couldn't have given you a better bedroom," he said, glancing to the red swords and knives strewn on the floor.

She hummed at him. "I think I could be in sunlight and its warmth would still not touch me."

Tausi asked the question all souls dreaded to ask themselves. "Are you afraid?"

"Oh, yes." A tear dripped across the bridge of her small, tight nose. "I'm scared of the dark. But I'm excited as well."

"Excited?"

"I want to look at it, boy. I want to look at the darkness. I might be terrified, but I won't let it see that."

"Maybe you'll have a pleasant dream and wake up somewhere else, or someone else."

"But there is darkness," Cleona stressed the dire word. "There is always darkness in between."

"And you want to face it?" Tausi asked, confused. "I know our fates are sealed, but—"

"They are not! I made my choices. I lived my life every moment as I lived it. And I might live one last day, facing against it, defiant as I had hoped to be in this life."

Life flooded Cleona's small face, and she rose slightly, as if her youth had returned, hungry and vibrant.

"Don't live wondering what you might have done, or didn't do, or shouldn't have done," she said, sinking back into the folds of her coverings. "Hold fast, Captain Tausi. Especially to yourself."

Unable to summon better words, Tausi offered a weak, awkward nod. "Aye, Captain."

CHAPTER 10

EROSION

Cleona passed when the rains ended the next day. Stilled under the grumbling gray skies, Song City seemed weathered clean by the deluge. Even the triremes in the dock had flooded out most of the Latians's arrows that had fallen upon them during the artillery assault, leaving the heightened level of water covered in a thick layer of black shafts. A dense fog fell upon the coast, making it impossible to discover whether or not the enemy remained.

After a careful ascent to the walls, Tausi and Zaki walked along the southwestern parapet until they reached the hole on the northwestern side. Its gully was a stinking grave full of corsair and hoplite corpses, some blued to the pallor of a drowning death. Not even the flies or gulls had come yet to pick at them.

Below, where the sea sloshed against the remains of the wall, nothing of the flotilla or the bodies that the Latians had scorched during the siege were left to block their fall into the water.

"I guess we push them into the sea?" Zaki asked in a weary proposal.

Tausi sighed a deep swell of sadness. He shook his head after a moment's thought. "I don't want to raid Latia. I think it is a fool's errand, and I think the fact these lords are going along with Father shouldn't mean we have to go along with it."

She did not take her eyes off the corpses. "I know, Tausi."

"You do?" he asked, the hint of happiness a ghost on his face.

"Yes, I do." Zaki lifted her eyes to the dark skies above them, scanning the wasted storms as they slowly slid off to the northeast and followed the currents that would take them across Juut's continental face. She looked to Tausi for a moment, her trepidation on full display.

"What?" he asked, knowing his sister well. "What's wrong?"

"I still want to go to Latia."

He stifled a growl of frustration. "Why?"

"Because he might be a fool, but sometimes a fool can be right," she said. "Tausi, they will come back again when this fog lifts, or in a few months, or a few years after this siege. The Latians aren't like Gypians, or Brythians, or any of those other westerners—they stopped conquering the others because they were made to."

The echoes of old arguments, old truths, made Tausi rub his eyes with his finger and thumb.

"He's right, Tausi. We cannot simply have the Mirror—we must take it."

"Must we?" he asked. "Is that what we are? Conquerors? Raiders, fine, but what happens if we go and win? Do we raid Latia? But what if we conquer Latia? Will we go upon Gypus, avenging our ancestors for their enslavement? Will we burn Gypus to the ground like the demon-panther that burnt Tolivius?"

Zaki faced him, fists and jaw clenched.

Tausi pressed, zealous in his anger. "Well?"

"And what do you want?" she asked in cold venom. "To sit here like a little boy, with other little children, and have your own little private clubhouse? Father and these captains are handing you a small fleet of ships—for fuck's sake, you stupid idiot, Father is making you a corsair-lord. He's raising you, and your little fort, to his level. And you're being ungrateful and stupid."

"I never wanted to be a corsair-lord, and—"

"I was born in the body I didn't want," she shouted. "Not everyone gets what they want!"

Cut to a halting silence, Tausi stood there open-mouthed.

Zaki did not once reach for the sword at her side. Her expression still distressed, she stepped closer to him. "We only have so many chances in life, Tausi. Would you rather live with things never changing?"

She motioned to the bodies in the wall's wound.

Someone cleared their throat, coughing not too far away. "May I offer my piece?"

Tausi found Azinza standing a few yards from where he and his sister conspired by the hole in the wall. The moisture in the air dewed her skin, as if she was the goddess of the sea herself, woken by the blood that had poured into her waters.

Not startled at all by Azinza's sudden appearance, Zaki bade her to go on. "Of course, little sister."

Gliding upon the smooth, wet rock beneath her naked and calloused feet, Azinza came to the edge of the hole and looked down at the corpses.

Tausi tried his best to read her mysterious expression—a practiced façade containing a cold acceptance of death still embittered by the taste of it.

"It is simple to think that one can go on living in a world the way it is, hoping that it will stay the way it is—but it never does." Azinza glanced out at the hidden sea, invisible behind the dense walls of fog that swirled and merged anew upon every turn of the fouled breeze. It was then Tausi noticed that she clutched something in her hand: the arrow he had given her before the Latians had breached Song City's walls.

"Yet the world is also unconquerable, untamed, and unyielding," she said, lifting a hand toward the mist. Blinking a few times, she laughed aloud, a mad sound that contained too much happiness for what lay ahead. "And it will always remain so."

"You would have us to go Latia," Zaki concluded, nodding in unspoken agreement.

"No," Azinza said. "I'm not saying that at all."

"Then what should we do?" Tausi asked. "What do we do out in the fog?"

Azinza's gaze fell on him in the midst of wet and wind. "Whatever we're brave enough to go and find ourselves needing to do. But other things matter more than what lies out there."

"How so?" asked Zaki.

"You know what I speak of," Azinza said. "It's time, Zaki."

Stillness came over Zaki, who nodded weakly before she headed for the stairs, hunched in a slow, slow breaking. She sobbed aloud before Tausi could call after her or follow, disappearing down the wooden catwalks back to the city's proper.

Alone on the wall, Tausi looked to Azinza, and she to him.

And he remembered the arrow she held.

The kindness of her words, the grace, moored itself to his mind as he forced an edge to his voice. "Is this how it was meant to be?"

Quiet for a span of thought, she nodded. "Parts of it."

He grunted, saddened by the murky answer. "What parts did you miss?"

Her assuredness was dissolved by the question. "I didn't think I'd summon that storm."

Tausi failed to stop his mouth from falling open.

"To be honest, I thought we were going to die yesterday," she said, then followed the bare avowal with more words, more truths. Gone away went her ethereal beauty, her grace beyond time's mortal measure —for a moment Azinza became like any salt-folk found in any corsair hold, blabbing on about fate and destiny and the day. She made jokes, little comments about Ngala, before he interrupted.

"Pardon," he said, more enthralled with her than ever before. "Did you summon this storm?"

"I didn't make the fog, Tausi," she said with lasting ease.

"But you brought that tempest?"

"Yes?"

Seized, Tausi could only stare at her while she stared back, confused by his reaction.

"What else have you seen?" he asked.

"It doesn't work like that, Tausi," she said. "Some things happen, and some things don't. I can't control it."

"But you brought about a storm that saved the lives of every soul in this city," he said, leaning toward her. "Will the Latians try to take the wall again? Did they leave? Who lives? Who betrayed us?"

She clutched the arrow she held at her side, knuckles tight while panic worked across her features. "I see things, and then I live to see what happens. Or not happen."

"What does that mean?" Tausi rubbed his forehead. "Why are you carrying that arrow around?"

Without thought, she held it up, her focus shifting between the shaft and him. "I...I don't know. Ever since you handed it to me things have not gone how they were supposed to go."

He shook his head.

"Something is here," she said, laying the arrow across her chest like a sword while she examined the fletching. "I don't know what it is, Tausi, but some power is here in Song City—and it feels familiar."

"I don't understand," he said, "if you can see the future, or at least possible ones, can't you flush out whatever troubles you?"

"No, and that is what bothers me. Song City is a temple, and I know its halls and ways better than any that breathe—save the things that were of this place."

"Of this place?" Tausi glanced to his right, toward in the inside of his fort-city.

The ancient stone that had become his home had not always been a place of safety, with its magical golden reefs that Azinza could command to change shape, or the clear, clean waters bursting with enough fish that none went hungry. Before all that, it had been part of an ancient world, a world where humans butchered humans beneath dragon-infested skies, and sorcerer-priests slew untold adherents to please gods far fickler and angrier that the ones Tausi worshiped.

Before Ngala walked in and slew its monsters, Song City had been an ancient den of slavery and demons.

"None have ever seen any ghosts or spirits beyond what vodunis conjure when paid," he said, referring to the shamans and witchdoctors who had migrated from the land and joined the corsairs at sea, bringing with them their rituals. "We covered the ritual space before we flooded it to make the dock."

"It's not that." Azinza leaned in to meet Tausi, nearly face-to-face. "I didn't feel it until the captains arrived. It's one of them."

Tausi's mind carried him to only one possibility. "Nobody has seen Popobawa since the siege began."

"What should we do?"

"Everyone will be gathering to see Cleona off. He may have failed to appear everywhere else, but I doubt he will let that sort of absence be noted by the other corsair-lords, considering what my father has placed before them." Tausi found his hand resting on the hilt of the sword on his belt as he brooded.

"I can find out," Azinza said, tilting her head so her blue hair fell between them.

Drawn back by her attention, Tausi squinted. "How?"

"If I can get close enough to him, I will feel it," she said, sighing after a second of hesitation. "Cleona asked me to sing at her send-off before she passed. It will give me an excuse to get close to Popobawa."

"It might be dangerous."

"After all that has happened here, I doubt it," she said, motioning in the direction of the broken wall.

Unable, or unwilling, to dissuade her, Tausi stood to his full height and took in the iron sky. "Azinza?"

She had joined him in studying the firmament. "Yes?"

Focus descended back to the arrow she held by her heart. "What was supposed to happen before I gave you that arrow? What did you see happening?"

Azinza blushed. "Nothing important."

For corsair captains, funerals were simple affairs—someone carved or made a small boat large enough to lay someone down in, then they piled it with beach wood, small scraps of torn sail, and other little bits that could burn, until a pyre covered them from the sight of those that bared last witness.

Wrapped in the blankets she died in, Ngala set Cleona's little body down in the boat and found more than debris among the things that her bosun and timekeeper piled on her.

Dra donated a pair of his thick dreadlocks while Oya offered up her sword on the whispered promise she would take one from the Latians when the fog lifted. Illus wedged a sack of silver into the dead captain's blankets, grousing about how the others might try to steal it if he did not.

Ngala donated four bottles of dzan, their wax seals unbroken.

Popobawa finally appeared with his bosun and timekeeper,

unarmed and swathed in the white cotton garb of the White Rovers. To the surprise of those who had seen neither him nor heard the man's voice since the almost-forgotten feast, he recited the mourning chant of his people, a poem of matching images that shared the common theme of the sun, the stars, and the sea, but also matched those images to death, loneliness, and loss—his full baritone soared over those gathered in the fog to bid farewell to fierce Cleona.

Once the gifts were given, Ngala came forward again. "As per custom among the people of Stone Cove, we will sing the dead off one final time."

Even the children of Song City knew the songs of Stone Cove. The visiting captains stood aside while Ngala and Tausi lowered her coffin-boat into the arrow-choked dock.

Tausi could not tear his eyes away from the little body. He had seen men die, burnt horribly—yet nothing compared to death's visage than what lay in the boat he held.

Azinza sang the first verse.

"Ride upon the crest, ride it high and far,
Reach the breeze at dawn's light,
Reach far upon,
Ride for sunrise,
For the sunrise never dies..."

Tausi nodded to the men at the Sea Gate's winch, and with a loud creaking, it rose from the water, its iron grate browned by brine.

He let Ngala carry on another foot, giving one last push. Cleona's ship parted the arrows on her way to the world. To his surprise, his father's eyes brimmed with tears.

Tausi turned away at the chorus, wanting to make the words with his mouth.

"High shines the morning,
Upon my gentle days,
No noose or cuff on me,
I reach the breeze today,
For I'm going to the sunrise,
And I am free..."

He spotted Azinza on the dock, walking with a small choir procession that included Zaki, who wept endless tears. They slowly went down the stone stair to the wooden dock, passing by Tausi's guard of Nana and Amare, then the rest of the corsair captains's commands, before reaching the captains themselves who stood at the end.

Azinza did not look away from Tausi the entire time.

Her focus upon him, she led the song down the smooth stone stair. He lowered his gaze, a signal that the game had started. He checked at his belt with his eyes, seeing the hilt of his sword.

The singers redoubled on the chorus after the second verse, Azinza's high voice melting his heart, mixing its beats with both joy and sorrow.

"High shines the morning,
Upon my gentle days,
No noose or cuff on me,
I reach the breeze today,
For I'm going to the sunrise,
And I am free..."

Illus the Gelded leered at her with a lecher's smile when she went by, though she gave him far less attention than he paid her. Oya did not look up to see Azinza when she walked by, nor did Dra, both of whom hung their heads in sadness and contemplation—life's true bosuns and timekeepers.

"Ride upon the crest, right it high and far..."

When Azinza strode before Popobawa, Tausi returned his attention to the man and his two crewmen beside them, somewhat surprised when the three made no reaction whatsoever to her presence. The sun had risen past the morning and into the climbs of the early noon, bringing a heat that thinned the fog, fading it until the first rays of sunlight in days shot over the water.

The clouds rolled away to the northeast, and before long, the sky bared its blue firmament, perfect in its unblemished vastness.

Tausi and Azinza shared a glance.

Frowning as she stood a few feet ahead of the White Rover's captain, she shook her head.

It wasn't Popobawa.

Hiding his disappointment, he gave Cleona one last glance, only to find that her body had floated beyond the Sea Gate, beyond sight.

Like the songs sang for her, the lady of Tip Town had embarked on her last voyage.

Ngala backed out of the water, standing side by side with his son while the crew lowered the gate. "Go be with your sister," he whispered, his voice somehow cutting through the funeral song as it entered its final refrain.

"For I'm going to the sunrise,
And I am free..."

"Why?" Tausi asked, focused ahead on the Sea Gate as it lowered in the water. He had forgotten Zaki, a pit of regret buried in his chest.

Ngala watched beside him, his expression hard. "Because when this is all done, we have to go outside."

CHAPTER 11
AFTER THUNDER

Armored too soon after solemn events, Tausi marched at the head of his warband, leading those who had escaped the siege without injury to the Far Gate. Quiet as they made their way through the tunnel, more joined on for whatever lay outside their iron doors.

Somewhere in the advance, Zaki forced her way to the front beside her brother. "Amare and Nana have posted on the towers, and Nana will have archers on the eastern side of the Far Gate. We'll have cover on the bridge."

"Why would someone keep to themselves something that was part of what was supposed to happen and didn't?" he asked her.

Zaki screwed her face in confusion. "What are you talking about?"

Like the question, he banished the thought for more pressing things when they neared Song City's entrance.

The guards unlocked the iron doors set in the greater iron slab as Tausi's troops built their formations. Lining up at the end of a single file line behind one of the portals cut out of the city walls, Tausi ordered open a viewing hole.

Looking out the gap, the simple stone bridge had dried beneath the scorching sun and was carpeted by the bodies that had bled out on its smooth surface. Blotches of red, green, and black outlined the corpses

196

decaying within their armor. Beyond, the sandy expanse of beach was flowered with thousands of arrows sticking up out of the sand, monuments among the shafts that had broken under the Latian's repeated marches from Shallow Bay's western shore.

Searching as far as he could to the east and west, Tausi paid his keenest attention to the green jungles beyond, the first line of trees silent and still on a windless day. No shadows moved in the depths, and no matter how hard he tried to spot Latians at the ready, nothing gave away the presence of an enemy, let alone wildlife.

"No sign of the Latians," he told Zaki, who was behind him in line as he continued to examine the scene.

She nodded, tying the last lace on one of her leather bracers. "They might still be down at the beach, if they're even down there at all still."

"We'll march for the jungle and see from there. Our archers should be able to cover us." Tausi motioned to the guard who had opened the slot to slide it shut, and he turned to the rest of their fighters. "Everyone across the bridge. Our archers will cover us if the Latian's emerge from the tree line. If it is clear, follow Zaki and me in, and we'll reorganize from there."

"Aye, Captain," echoed the brave eighty.

The iron doors in the Far Gate were flung open, and the corsairs exited in their files, hide shields up on their lefts and their iron swords low at the right. The first fighters that neared the rotting Latians on the bridge kicked them off into the sea below, clearing the way.

They picked their way across the sand, many going cautiously. No archer or hoplite arose from the foliage, and though slowed, the corsairs broke past the initial line of shrubs and trees, sneaking into the chain of clearings where Tausi and Zaki stopped.

The eighty reconvened in the largest of these open floors, knelt in a quiet circle looking outward.

Tausi doled his orders from the center of the formation. "Twenty will go east, all the way to the end of the bay. Come back as soon as you reach it and march for Song City. Do not stop to head west and rejoin the rest of us, who will go to the western shore. We will locate the enemy and decide a course from there."

Dispersing into their two groups, the corsairs ran through the brush and undergrowth of the jungle, dodging past trees and vines for a few miles before they turned south again. The corsairs crept upon the back of the western beach. Tausi gasped at what they beheld.

Strewn along the sandy coast, the waves washed against overturned heaps of broken triremes, their hulls torn apart in pieces that still floated out on the surf. The currents had moved mounds of bodies into staggered, uneven lines in the wet sand. Gulls pecked at them, supping on the dead.

Miles upon miles of the dead preceded every step, and to Tausi's shock, he and his discovered whole ships that survived Azinza's tempest, simply abandoned to absorb rainwater and settle on land, their wooden beams swollen to the point where they sank in the muck, immovable until fair weather let them dry.

This pattern repeated—thousands of bodies washed in lines on the threshold between earth and sea, ships torn or left behind—effigies to fate's fickle whims.

"Are they all dead?" Zaki asked as she walked alongside Tausi. The swords in her hands wavered. The usual expression on her face—an iron mask needed for deadly work—was washed away with a hard swallow.

Tausi covered his nose, the brine mixing with rot too much to withstand. "How many boats do you think we can salvage?"

Corsairs ambled past them, deflated by the lack of expected battle. Some turned and looked back the way they had come. "There's at least six we can sail by the morning if we pull them out of the tide," said Zaki. "And I think we could build a new fleet with the salvage."

"Send a man back to gather rowers healthy enough to start," he ordered his sister. A quick, honest smile split his mouth. "Maybe I'll give each captain a ship to take home."

"Will do," she said, sliding one of her swords back into its scabbard. "I'll also—"

"Latians," cried a corsair, thrusting his sword in the direction further down the beach.

As sighted, the remnants of the Latian navy were clustered near the southwestern end of the bay, their camp spread out in a disheveled pattern. The half-armored guard posted at the meager palisade, a few broken spear-shafts fashioned into stakes to narrow an enemy's approach, ran before Tausi spotted him.

"Formation," Tausi shouted.

The corsairs hurried into a long column, three rows of twenty fighters deep.

Ordering a jog to conserve their energies, Tausi exchanged his sword and shield between his hands, a silent notion that spread among the troops so they would have a unified wall of shark-skin shields toward where they guessed any archer batteries might fire, if their foes had positioned them in the jungle.

A Latian trireme was launched from somewhere beyond his field of vision, the top deck populated by a few hoplites who ran in a struggle to maintain a haphazard rigging. Another boat slipped into the bay, then a third.

Before the corsairs had even reached the cruel line of stakes, nine ships had taken to Shallow Bay, manned by skeleton crews that failed to push every oar eastward.

A small force of hoplites remained behind, half-drowned after the sleepless onslaught by the tidal forces, and many did not even have a shield or spear, or even sandals or clothes to fight. They waited well beyond the defenses Tausi marched his men past, shaped into a phalanx half the size of his own force.

Tausi raised his weapons before Zaki and the man to his right, bringing his column to a halt.

Seagulls cried, loud and high on the sea winds, white wings outstretched as they circled above, waiting for their next meal. Waves crashed and receded, their hypnotic perfection revealing the divine beat that washed in all mortal hearts. The sounds of Latian captains and their voices as they called for their rowers to flee faded.

These Latians were hungry, helpless, possessing little to none of the strength needed to defend to an honorable end.

"Archers," Tausi said aloud.

Arrows knocked against other shafts as they were yanked from hip quivers. Sinew stretched as wooden arms creaked with tension.

The Latians, some of them completely naked, herded together and braced.

Tausi had his archers fire ten volleys before he let the corsairs overrun those unlucky enough not to die the first time.

The march back to Song City slugged upon the beaches as the corsairs retreated west. They met reinforcements led by Ngala and Dra who led a detachment of two dozen men, many among them the bandaged and injured of the siege.

"These the best you have?" Zaki asked when the four captains met at where the two groups passed. A clean piece of beach, they had reached the midpoint between the first dead ships and the corsair-fortress, a peaceful spot one might have thought to sit down, lounge, and drink dzan if no other worry in the world hampered them.

"Best that could come," Ngala said, cradling a bottle of liquor in one hand. He lifted it for whoever took it. "Illus remained behind with Oya and Azinza to help tend the wounded. Apparently in his former life, he had been a battlefield surgeon."

Remembering the bloody sword still in his hand, Tausi licked his chapped lips. "Did you see where the Latians went?"

"Landed into the eastern shore. And I'm not done with that yet, god," Dra said, grabbing the bottle from Ngala. "I'd say that storm beat them for us. They'll probably get out of your waters tomorrow."

Tausi waited, saying nothing on the point. Dra handed the bottle to him and wiped his beard with the back of a thick forearm.

"Decisions for another day," Ngala said in carefree tones not fitting the mood of his children. "You two get home—Dra and I will get the ships pulled to the jungle. I already have Oya watching over the Rats while they fish off the eastern wall. We should be able to eat well tonight."

"We'll see you," Zaki said, expressionless as she stared at the waves rolling onto the beach. Her silence, cold and distant, caused Tausi and Ngala to share a glance of concern before they carried onward.

The walk staggered into clusters of different groups, the crewmen of *The Ube* falling in with their fellow crewman, and *The Gamka* much the same. Breaking off into their little packs, the distance between widened and widened with every step they took.

Before long, Tausi and Zaki marched alone, brother and sister in blood, and in the bloodshed they had committed together yet again.

"I'm sorry," Tausi told his sister.

She looked his way, not disturbing their gait.

"I didn't forget what you've gone through." He continued, "and I know things aren't the way I wish the world would be—but I also know that it is simply the way it is. I wanted to apologize for forgetting that, at least, and for any other insult I paid you without knowing."

Zaki sighed, stopping on the spot. "I wasn't mad at you because you forgot, Tausi—I was mad because you keep wanting for things to stay the same, but you also want the choice to guide the course of your own life despite the fact that life is change and we're all changing around you, too. I don't understand how the man who will go into battle for others without thought is also the man who won't fight for himself."

Unable to summon a rebuttal, Tausi shut his mouth and kept walking. Zaki followed at his side.

Frustration and annoyance ended his quiet. "I..." Tausi stopped himself this time.

Throwing his gory sword in the sand, he plopped down; exhausted to the point that he had forgotten the dzan in his hand. Yanking the cork off with his teeth and spitting it in the sand, he swigged, the burn flushing down his chest. He coughed a few times from the heat.

Zaki stood there, watching him. "What are you doing?"

He offered the bottle to her. "I'm not going back right now. Either sit down and drink with me or carry the fuck on."

After a moment of thought, she stripped her sword-belt, tossing her twin blades on the sand next to Tausi's sword before she sat down beside him.

"Don't hog," she said, her hand out.

Tausi laughed and handed her the bottle. "It's not that strong, anyway."

"I'll be the judge of that." She sipped a small amount, swallowing it smoothly before handing her brother the bottle. "It's not that strong."

The siblings sat there, in the dark sand, the sun baking the earth in the kind of heat perfect for drinking. The currents of the primordial sea worked their cycle, sending cream breakers running hard and fast to flood the earth before they failed another wave in their eternal siege.

They had made it through the siege.

Tausi broke his long draw of dzan. "I don't want to risk her life to live in this place."

"It's her choice," Zaki said. "She's weird, brother—Azinza is hundreds, if not thousands of years old, and yet she started over in the body of a fourteen-year-old lass for us, no less. And she walks around wielding power. Power."

"She is good for Father. What would happen if she left and he had no sorceress? I know what you said on the wall is right—he's giving me so much, but the person I adore most in this world is a far greater treasure than he could ever think to give."

"So what? He'll get a new nursemaid, and I can share Agwe with him when it comes to matters of sorcery." Zaki tipped the bottle back until it stood in her mouth on end, before she brought it back down. Her cheeks full, she gulped the liquid sugar in four hard, painful gulps. The alcohol caused her to hack, shoulders shaking before she let out a long, gross burp. "Maybe it will...get them talking."

Tausi reclaimed the bottle. Lightness crept at the edge of his mind, the first feathering of the dzan. "It's not that I think she is some little woman who can't take care of herself." He laughed aloud at the notion given what he knew. The mirth dimmed, and his thoughts resettled. "This siege showed me how much more she is than me—and Ngala wants us to go to war. She's going to be needed."

"And you won't be?" Zaki shook her head at him while he drank. "You're much bigger now."

"And I can't keep playing in my little fort," Tausi said, not hiding the liquor's bite on his face.

"Well, I'm sorry I said that," replied Zaki. "Happy?"

"Aye," Tausi said. He gave her the dzan and then shook his head in reflection. "I have more than ten ships now, Zaki. That's enough to raid cities on Juut's eastern coast."

"I know."

"I could draw more men from Stone Cove."

"I know," she said, a giggle in her voice.

"I would have to build outside of the fort, probably past the beach."

"More men, more treasure."

"You just fuck everything up," Tausi said. "Could you not have an answer to everything?"

"Fine, then you answer me," she said, sipping sweet fire. "You asked me that question before we walked out the Far Gate, about keeping things that were supposed to happen, but didn't, and blah, bl-blah, blah, blah."

"Oh, can we talk about it?" Tausi held his hand out for the drink, but Zaki put a finger up, supping a third sip this round. "So she sees things?"

Zaki hummed the affirmative.

"That arrow Father grabbed during the game? He had me take it to her, and when I handed it to her, she said I wasn't supposed to do that, and I was supposed to do something else she had seen in some vision," Tausi said, rattling off his memory of the night.

She left the bottle's mouth on her lips, searching the shimmering waters ahead. "She said that she saw you doing something else?"

"Aye."

"She could be lying."

"How can she lie about her visions?" Tausi asked, flabbergasted.

Zaki shed a sneaky smile. "She has spent years in the company of cutthroats and thieves."

Deflated, Tausi grunted at his sister's humor. "What do you think she wanted me to do?"

"Let me ask this," said Zaki. "Was she close to you?"

"Yes, I had handed her the arrow."

"And did she step back when you gave her the arrow?"

"No... we actually held the arrow together. She was close enough I could smell her."

"Then maybe she wanted you to kiss her, you fucking dummy," Zaki said.

He finally got the bottle back from her. "Really?"

"Sounds like it."

"What do I do?"

"Go kiss her." Zaki rose from the sand and dusted off the backside of her tunic. "Gods help me, Tausi, do I have to explain everything to you?"

CHAPTER 12

THE TIDE

On the platform along Song City's southern wall, Tausi hung his legs over the edge, swinging his feet as he waited for the sun to rise.

The Mirror Sea stretched to the black horizon, moving like a sheet of unpolished silver, enlivened by forces undeniable, unstoppable. Even in the dark before the dawn, the white breakers crashed against the unseen murals he knocked his bare heels on. Resting back on his hands, the cool night air clung to his skin like silk.

"One would think after days of siege the last place you would want to be is on these walls."

Captain Popobawa stood a few feet behind, looking in the same direction as Tausi had before the lord of the White Rovers interrupted.

"Captain!" Startled, Tausi sprang to his feet. "My apologies for not noticing you."

"Please, Captain Tausi." The often-absent guest joined him at the rail. In his forties, Popobawa gazed out at the sea with a passive smile containing neither joy nor sadness, but an ethereal quality that caused Tausi to sense this man was not in the world with him. His white-cotton wrap, the common garb of his people, hung on a thin frame dripping with wealth—bracelets set with precious blue stones and necklaces threaded in corals, coins, and shells. He had left his sword in the quarters Tausi had provided him and his command.

"I hope your time here has not been..." Tausi stopped at his clumsiness, surprised at how nervous the man made him.

Popobawa's mysterious grin grew, his eyes wide. "Yes, it has been very interesting, to say the least. I will be glad to come home."

"Don't you mean *go*, Captain?"

"Of course," he said, chuckling light notes. He looked out at the sea again. "Of course. May I join you at your watch, Captain?"

"I would be honored," said Tausi, realizing how much he sounded like his father in that moment.

Popobawa joined him at the railing overlooking the sea, and the two stood there for long, silent minutes, letting the salt on the wind score their faces. Far in the east, light crawled the edges of the world, ready to sneak out and leap for freedom.

"Tell me, Captain," said his guest. "I have heard many things about Song City. Is it true this fort was once a grand temple of some ancient race?"

Tausi turned his attention away from the sea to Popobawa. "Aye, Captain. We accidentally ran into what used to be its spire." He motioned at the stone they stood on. "There is a ring of iron under this platform that served as the brace for a great dome of glass that once capped this place. It fell during Song City's rise from the sea."

Popobawa smiled a confused smile. "Song City rose from the sea?"

"As mad as it sounds."

"Was it empty when you found it?"

Even with the ebbing dark, Tausi felt a shadow fall over him, a hulking shape he only envisioned in his worst nightmares of the past. "No."

Popobawa's confusion sharpened his curious expression. "What did you find?"

"A monster, Captain. The worst monster I had ever seen—a survivor of the last age, a fell sorcerer who had transformed himself into a creature crossing a man and a lobster. He slew many of our crew before my father avenged them."

"And then you took hold of a secret fort in a part of the sea only you know. I believe the gods granted you providence with this place."

Popobawa patted the rail he rested his hand on. "If I may, Captain Tausi...I surmise that your Avarice Reefs are controlled by sorcery as well, yes?"

He hesitated on his guest's question. "After we took Song City from the creature, we discovered that we had the power to change the formation of the reefs."

Popobawa slightly bowed his head. "My manners seemed to have diminished with my self-isolation. Again, I beg pardon for prying so."

"Why do you ask?" Tausi said, dispensing with what his father would do. "Now you must beg my pardon, Captain, but you and your crew have holed themselves up in your quarters, only to reappear near what I hope is the end of this episode with the Latians, asking questions about my home and its history. Why?"

To Tausi's surprise, the lord of the White Rovers did not swell with offense at his words or shrink. Tall and straight, he let out a long breath through his nostrils. "That is fair, Captain. You have defended my life, and the lives of everyone in your city, while I have stayed in hiding, offering neither my arm nor courage in my own defense. It would be right that you know the reason for it." Popobawa drew close enough to speak lower, even though they were alone on the wall.

"I've watched," he said. "While the battles carried on, I watched in wait to see a traitor emerge. These Latians did not get in without help past the Avarice Reefs, and that helper must be here, in Song City. There is a shark in our midst, Captain, and I have been at work searching it out."

"You have?"

"Aye," Popobawa answered, his tawny eyes locked with Tausi's. "But they have yet to rise."

Torn by his vow to his father, his sister, and his command to keep secret their quest to reveal the same traitor Popobawa sought after, Tausi held back any immediate response, focusing again on the man's features. Unless Popobawa was a great actor, no sign of duplicity or falsehood resonated from this odd fellow.

"Lady Azinza has the power to control Avarice Reefs," he said. "She was a creature as well once, a priestess to the sorcerers who had enslaved her people. The horrid ritual that sank this city, created its dreadful host, and transformed her away from her humanity into a brine-singer—she is the last remnant of the ancient powers, and she has yet to detect any sorcery among the ranks of my men or our guests. Including you."

Popobawa arched his carefully shaved brows in surprise. "She was a brine-singer?"

"Aye, until my father freed her from the enchantment her brutish master had placed upon her."

The sun's white rim edged past the earth, inflaming the clouds pink and purple.

Wonder illuminated Popobawa's face. "Amazing, Captain. Simply amazing."

"You would understand if I ask you to keep this in secrecy. My father has been diligent in making the world think she is little more than his young nursemaid."

"Another clever gambit." He bobbed his head in agreement. "Your secret will remain safe with me."

Tausi nodded with him. "My thanks, Captain."

"At least whoever did reveal the way to the Latians failed."

"How do you see that?"

"You held your fort, my friend," said Popobawa. "And like many things in life, I'm sure they did not expect that at all."

Sliding his sword in its scabbard, Tausi let the blade hang from its baldric as he marched down the stairs, Zaki and his father in tow.

He looked up in time to see Amare order the last haul of arrows removed from *The Ube's* deck, each and every shaft yanked from the pocked, bitten wood. The sun towered above the fort at its noon apex, banishing all shadows.

On the other side of the long dock, the crew of *The Gamka* busied themselves about the same task, picking arrows out and tossing them into the choked waters lifting the triremes. On a bridged wooden platform high above the Sea Gate, a third team readied to lift the rusted iron portcullis beneath them.

"The Latians will flee when they see us set out," said Tausi, his sandals protecting his feet from the splintered planks. "Dra, Illus, and

Oya will launch from two of the Latian ships on the western beach and cut them off if they try for the open sea. I shall take *The Ube* and pursue whomever I can catch first."

"Aye, and we shall attack where they landed on the eastern beach," replied Ngala. "If they don't launch all nine first."

"They won't," said Zaki, hands rested on the pommels of her girded swords. "We can only take one or two from them, if we can even do that —we're both running bone crews."

Tausi nodded to his sister, what awaited them heavy on his shoulders.

Turning from his family, Tausi spotted Azinza at the top of the stone stairs to Song City's proper. Gone was the flowing blue dress; it was replaced by war sandals, leather armor, and an ax.

Tausi offered her the lead. "Which ship would you like, my lady?"

The battle-clad priestess smiled, a better sight than the cross sounds of the Sea Gate groaning as the portcullis rose. *"The Ube."*

The gate opened, and Tausi and Azinza ascended the gangplank to his trireme's deck. The bustle of a dozen raiders was endless as they ran to and fro to secure lines and ready quivers of arrows they'd lain on the starboard rails. Beneath where he stood, he felt the vibrations of the rowers, the eighty or so he had taken out to the beaches the day before.

Amare and Nana met them at the steering oar.

"Is one of us being left behind?" Nana asked, the bosun stopping dead in his tracks when he saw war-clad Azinza. "Because I think everyone knows I'm a better drummer than Amare."

"No, you're not," the timekeeper chided. "Stop saying that in front of the crew!"

Ignoring the banter, Tausi pulled the locking pin free, and the steering oar's long handle jumped in his hand, animated by the gentle rock of the cluttered waters beneath them. "Shove off! We have a red day!"

The triremes set out, rowers on both ships pushing their craft toward the Sea Gate with the oars through the portholes, leaving wide tracks of empty water bordered by floating arrows. The moment *The Ube* met Shallow Bay's blue current, she flew from her home, freed again upon destined swells.

Amare disappeared below deck before the rostrum touched the

Mirror, and on Tausi's order, the first full bank of oars extended into the water.

Across the breeze-swept bay, the Latians launched two of their ships from the farthest point of the eastern shore, angled westward.

Even from his place at the back of the boat, Tausi spotted the white lengths of their oars, which dug slowly into the sea and put his enemy at a crawling pace against a headwind from the southwest.

"Raise sail!"

A quartet of raiders did the work required of twice their number, slowing raising the seafoam square emblazoned with their guest's face. Tausi kept his eyes ahead, trying hard not to glance at Azinza for a reaction.

She blew a raspberry, and a sudden wind swelled in the sail, propelling *The Ube* forward.

"You think me far prettier," she commented aloud.

Tausi could not help but laugh aloud as his trireme closed on the Latian crossing his prow. He let this first one past, ready to catch the second chasing them. Off to port, *The Gamka* bounced on the waves, spraying spittle like a snarling lion charging for the kill. She went wide for the coast, directed at the point where the Latians had disembarked.

The second trireme neared in the distance, dragging itself on the sea's surface as the deck crew struggled and failed to raise the sail amongst their own chaos. Archers formed uneven lines, unable to summon a concentrated volley of arrows.

Nana scampered up from the hold, running messages between the captain and the timekeeper below. "Amare has them at a half-beat! Orders, Captain?"

"Tell him to keep it but have the men ready to brace," Tausi commanded.

"Brace?" asked his bosun.

"We're not taking this one," Tausi said, leaned on the steering oar to keep his boat straight ahead. A wicked smile found him.

"Oh, aye," said the bosun, less enthused.

Azinza called out. "Archers on deck!"

The first Latian trireme that had passed *The Ube's* prow to starboard had cobbled together the deck crew into a stable line, and the sheer number of oars working in time to turn the ship back to defend surprised Tausi.

"Raiders, screen the oar!" he shouted.

The raiders, running back and forth to secure the sail's rigging, halted their duties to retrieve their hide shields, charging over in time to form a large screen that shielded everyone behind it, including Tausi and Azinza. The Latians from the forward ship loosed their volley, half their missiles falling short of their target.

"Steady on," Tausi screamed. "Raiders, weigh the beak!"

The raiders, still clutching their shields, broke their screen and sprinted for the front of their trireme, pounding the chipped boards. A sudden shift in weight did not move or budge the ship any noticeable amount, but Tausi knew even a half-inch more depth for the bronze rostrum would mean the difference between damaging the fleeing Latians and sinking them completely.

The enemy ship closed, and to Tausi's confusion, the entire deck was packed with foreign invaders—wounded men were armed with swords, rallying for one desperate, final defense.

"Nana, cut oars! I need poles!" Tausi screamed to his bosun. "Azinza!"

She appeared at his back. "Wind?"

"Wind," he told her, the severity of his request weighting the word.

With a quick glance to the ship's bow, she stared at the oncoming horde of mad Latians before directing her liquid gaze toward the sail. Her cheeks puffing, her tongue poked out of her lips as she blew a harder raspberry.

The surge in the sail made the mast groan.

The Ube hurtled forward in the water like a spear in the air. The peace of the sea broke in a great crash of bronze and wood. Her rostrum shattered the Latian trireme's starboard side at the mid-deck, sending men flying. Water rushed in through the hole.

Rowers from below deck ascended the stairs and joined the raiders at the bow. The warriors fended off the Latians who attempted to board as their broken vessel took on the sea, slowly sinking into the sloshing waves. Those not cut down by the corsairs, or shot by those that took up their bows, were pushed and swatted away with oars as the rowers poked and prodded the dead trireme attached to *The Ube* until they pushed her free.

Latians jumped into the water, swimming for *The Ube's* prow. The raiders with bows stepped forward, drew fresh arrows, and went to work on those poor fools.

Nana, posted at the portside near the steering oar, pointed in the distance to the southeast. "Ship approaching!"

"The Gamka?" Tausi asked, one hand on the oar while he held his sword in the other, waiting and watching for Latian stragglers to climb the sides of the ship.

"No, *The Gamka* has launched again from the eastern shore! She comes to join us! There is a—"

Tausi looked in his bosun's direction, dreading the worst when the man's silence carried. Nana gaped in fear at whatever he pointed at. Turning focus to that far-off direction, he spotted a peculiar shape off his starboard.

A massive conch shell rode on the currents, hurtling toward *The Ube* at an impossible pace for its size and dimensions. Its calcified hull mottled to a white-blue color, its spiraled prow offered no clear sign of a crew or a captain.

"Tausi," Azinza screamed.

He turned in time to see Popobawa wrap his arm around Azinza's throat, the long blade of his sword held at an angle to sever the artery. Wild-eyed, he wrenched her back to the starboard rail. Her ax lay at her feet, its iron head covered in dull, green slime.

Tausi hopped over the steering oar, let go, and came forward with his sword's point leading. "Popobawa!"

"He's not human," she shouted, only to have her breath taken when the White Rover pulled his arm tight.

A trail of the same green goo that coated her ax leaked down the side of Popobawa's husk. The grotesque illusion torn away, Tausi noticed the yellowing of the captain's eyes, the way his brown skin hung off his bones like it no longer adhered to the skeleton.

Those dead eyes locked with his, and wormy, purple lips parted in a dead-toothed smile.

The blue conch shell heading toward them bellowed a drone sound.

It made a sudden, sharp turn toward the remaining Latian ship, its speed reducing slightly to alter its path.

Unable to prevent their own brutal demise, the men clogging the top deck howled in terrified horror as the behemoth of a shell buried the entire boat under its grinding mass.

"Shameful, this world," called the Popobawa-devil, his voice watery. Green slime leaked from a glowing mouth. "Its wonders are still so meaningless."

The blue conch came to a halt in the sea, stopping dead. From the opening—the one where a crab would have snuck in to make the shell its home—came a booming sound, like the marching of a great army.

From the shadow of the conch's entrance emerged a hulking shape, then another, and another, each one setting Tausi to the point of madness when he saw the twitching antennae flicking above bulbous black eyes. Their segmented mouths, dripping the same substance that oozed from Popobawa's orifice, gleamed in the daylight.

Heavy, hard lobster-claws hung low at their sides on spindle arms. The leader at the head of their growing pack raised his blue-shelled appendage, the meat clear through the transparent azure chitin. He made a keening, terrible noise as he pointed at *The Ube*.

Ulmos had returned to Shallow Bay.

CHAPTER 13
DEVILS

When he was barely out of boyhood, Tausi went and raided a large village called Boda with his father and sister back when he was only Ngala's commander, leading the raiders on jaunts of pillaging. Even as a boy, he guessed that no man in the living world could contend with the fury of his sword.

Sorcery cared little for swords or the living.

Song City, Shallow Bay—these names were for places that had not always carried such brightness behind them. Once, Shallow Bay had been yet another piece of beach along the Mirror's great, gleaming surface. It had been home to a mysterious brine-singer, an immortal creature whose song lured men to drowning deaths, desperately in search of help to end the curse that had taken untold days from her.

And the Ulmo, who haunted her every attempt.

The first one Tausi met had murdered many of his early friends, kidnapped his sister for sacrifice, and if not for his father's bravery in the face of the ancient evils of the fallen world, that monster might have murdered him, too.

The knowledge that iron had saved him once emboldened Tausi. His blade still pointed at the thing holding Azinza hostage, he advanced upon the Popobawa-devil. "Nana! Rouse the rowers! Tell them to draw their swords for the reddest day, the blackest day!"

A line of poetry every corsair of Stone Cove and Song City knew roused the bosun. The young man's sword came free, and he stood at the top of the stair down to the hold. "Rowers! Ulmos!" he shouted, pure determination frozen on his face. "Ulmos!"

By now, the raiders had seen a dozen of the blue-crusted devils dive into the sea, but unlike the men Tausi had seen get torn apart by an Ulmo's terrific claws, his men had come with the knowledge that the simple presence of these monsters meant death.

If they were to all die that day, all had agreed none would die cowards in the face of sorcery.

"Startling," said the devil, glancing over his shoulder at a response he had not expected.

"Let her go," Tausi repeated, not halting his approach.

"You truly have no fear of me, do you?" the fiend asked, his peeling face half-hidden behind Azinza's armored shoulder.

"I know that you are a sorcerer," Tausi said, fighting to keep his tone steady. The sun above shined brightly in his eyes, gleaming off the edge of his sword. "I know that this will work as well as your magic does, if I can get to you."

"Defiance," said the devil. Grabbing Azinza's shoulder, he threw her like a rag doll, sending her tumbling into the portside with a bang. He drew his long, slender sword and presented a guard. "I adore it."

Tausi lunged forward, roaring in to cut the devil's throat. His enemy brought his iron sword up with a glancing parry and stepped to the side for a slash, forcing Tausi to break his attack and block, the strength behind the blow knocking him back.

"No," said the devil, whipping his blade in a flourish that ended with being pointed right at Tausi. "No meaning here."

The first blue Ulmo made it to *The Ube* when Azinza regained her balance, pulling herself up with the rail. "Their shells aren't thick," she said, coughing from the choke the devil had had her in moments before. "They're too young!"

"Quiet, you traitorous bitch," the devil screamed in his gasping, bubbling voice.

Tausi used the moment to sally into another exchange. The devil deflected the pair of thrusts, but the rush set the creature back on his false heels. Ready for the counter to his head, Tausi parried the downward attack and pushed hard to the side, trying to extend the devil past the point of balance.

The devil did not fall for the trick, yanking his sword back at inhuman speed to guard against the fierce chop Tausi aimed at his exposed shoulder. With a short, slight heave forward, he knocked Tausi back a second time.

Reeling from the force, Tausi reset his stance. He was at the ready for a third attack when a cry came up from the hold beneath. Rowers rushed out, led by Amare and Nana as they flooded the deck. Assaulted from all sides at once, the devil leapt high into the air, defying gravity itself as he landed on the sail-arm atop *The Ube's* mast.

The blue Ulmos climbed the starboard, their collective weight rocking the trireme hard to the right. Everyone standing found themselves rolling toward the row of snapping, mauling death that rose to meet them.

Corsairs unlucky enough not to grab rigging or rail fell to brutal ends, splashing in the water before one of the twelve Ulmos would turn and dive atop of them, ripping the poor souls apart limb from limb.

The devil balanced upon the point of the mast, at perfect ease above the mortal ruin.

Finding their way to stand on the creaking, groaning slope of their ship, the corsairs crawled backward to the portside and evened the weight of the Ulmo's displacement.

Able to retrieve what bows that failed to slide across the deck, a trio of raiders loaded their arrows and fired at the first crustacean that ambled over the right side of the trireme. They pinned the monster in the chest and face, the shafts piercing the soft, blue shell of his translucent carapace. Green splotches blossomed beneath the shell.

The monster toppled into the sea, floating dead upon his back.

Bolstered by the sight of the dead Ulmo, the corsairs spread their force along *The Ube's* long deck, drawing their swords for close, personal encounters with the screeching giants. Mortal faced off against immoral, jets of red mingling with the slim-green pus leaking from broken chitin.

A loud bang sounded at portside, and Tausi turned to find the crewmen of *The Gamka* tilting gangplanks to his boat, Ngala at the front of the wild raiders.

He and his father shared a cold, hard stare with each other, acceptance of the chance that no final words might pass between them.

Zaki leapt upon the gangplanks when it fell on *The Ube*, her bow drawn. She fired a clean shot off at the devil on the mainmast, scoring a hit that left the fletching sticking out from the side of his broken skull.

The devil reached up and yanked out the arrow, tossing it away with a chunk of gross flesh on the barbed end. Sighing as if bored, he jumped down with impossible agility, landing on the gangplank that lay parallel to Zaki's. She drew her twin swords at her sides and cut at his head and knees. The devil dodged both.

Somewhere in the melee, three men threw themselves at one of the Ulmos, two of them clinging to its snapping claws while the third man, atop its squat, blockish head, reversed the grip on his sword and stabbed at the back of its skull.

In another corner of the ship, two Ulmos separated fighters, decapitating with every swipe they took. Blood wetted the boards as Amare led a cluster of men chopping and cutting at the monsters until one plummeted over the side, the hacked open chest leaking a trail of inhuman guts.

Tausi fought his way to the prow. Pushing and shoving bodies, living or dying, aside, he looked down in surprise and found Azinza on her knees. Her recovered ax was in her hands, yet she had been unable to find space enough to rise. He reached forward and grabbed her by the buckles on her armor, hauling her slight weight to both feet.

She turned, letting the ax lead in a blow he deflected.

"Please don't kill me," he shouted as he shoved her forward, onward toward the Ulmos. To his amazement, she impressed him by not halting a step.

Somewhere in the march, Nana joined Tausi and Azinza, the bosun bleeding from a cut across his nose. Undeterred, the three closed on the nearest of the two Ulmos, Azinza swinging at the joint of the monster's left knee. Brought down by the wicked strike, it swung back with a heavy clawed arm that she ducked and scooted away from as it tried from the other direction.

Another group of corsairs entered from Tausi's right, tackling the Ulmo beyond the one he attacked. One man died quickly, his stomach ripped open while his brethren pounced, digging the points of their swords in the monster's eyes, face, and mouth.

Nana stuck his sword in the back of the Ulmo he and Tausi fought, causing the blue beast to freeze in shock at the pain. Driving low, Tausi stabbed his sword at the Ulmo's right knee, putting the bastard on the floor.

Azinza, on her feet again, raised her ax, shrieking as she brought it down on the shelled head. The Ulmo shuddered in death spasms while she tried to pull the bill free.

Not all the entanglements fared well on the corsair's side—half of Tausi's crew were slain in clashes that claimed more human flesh than it did the spongy innards of the Ulmos. Only the sudden surge of *The Gamka* reinforced across the gangplanks near the stern prevented an immediate rout while Zaki and the devil clashed.

Her two swords flicked at the devil's fluid defense. The devil danced around Zaki's lithe movements, her fast, agile muscles, and the cruelty bred within her from years of plunder. Zaki stabbed under, then over, throwing cuts when she didn't stab and stabbing when not guarding the clever ripostes of her infernal enemy.

The devil laughed louder the more she raged at him, his dead-skin mask hooked upward in a smile.

Azinza ascended the gangplanks and was out of Tausi's reach before he could stop her.

Ngala led a push against the Ulmos crowding *The Ube's* deck, killing by guile alone. Pithing the first when it closed and blinding another when it failed its charge, he left the second monster to die beneath stomping feet and plunging blades of *The Gamka* raiders following him to help Amare cut down the Ulmo looming above a battered Nana, whose leg had been broken. They both stabbed the blue giant through its face, their wide iron blades obliterating his nervous system.

Four Ulmos remained.

A pause in the fray allowed every soul on the scene to take stock before they charged into final darkness. The crews joined together in the chase for this oblivion.

Tausi followed Azinza to the planks in time to see the devil loose one of Zaki's swords from her hands in a deft twist of his blade. She battled with the other, exhausted as the devil batted back, his iron knocking hers aside.

Tausi outpaced Azinza, reaching the devil first in a thrust at the middle of his back. The thing that had been Popobawa spun in a perfect circle, completely out of Tausi's way. He caught Azinza's ax on the flat of his slender sword, tore it from her grasp with his free hand, and kicked her hard in the gut. She toppled backward, unable to summon breath to groan.

"I've grown tired of you, you little thrall," the devil declared, stalking after her.

Zaki recovered her second blade and stumbled to Tausi. They attacked in tandem, their three blades against the devil's razor. Edges burred while flats warped on failed blows and successful deflections until the two siblings had lured away the devil from the downed priestess.

Zaki used one of Tausi's flurries to score a mortal stab, skewering the devil through the heart. Without hesitation she plunged her second blade into the wound as Tausi rushed in for his advantage, cleaving the devil's sword arm off at the elbow.

The devil slapped both of them in the face with his remaining hand, one after the other, sending them sprawling.

"I'm surprised to say I tire of the game," the devil said, showing no real sign of fatigue. "And as much as this has enlightened me, I have gathered what I needed to know."

"And what did you need to know?" Ngala had ascended the gang-planks on *The Ube's* side. Beyond him, the corsairs dumped the last Ulmo over the trireme's side, clearing the deck for their victory. He stared at the devil, contempt and exhaustion intertwining on his focused gaze.

What remained of Popobawa knelt down and retrieved his long blade with his off-hand, twirling it about with his wrist to show there was no difference at all in the switch. He faced Ngala. "You're truly the seed of this world's fresh discontent, Captain Ngala. I'd take my hat off to you, if this vessel had one to wear in the first place."

"I take it you came here for your friend," Ngala said, staked to his spot. "An unfortunate turn, then, for you. I hope you brought more Ulmos."

"Ah, yes, my friends." The devil looked to the north, toward Song City. "I'm afraid I did not wake to that world." The moment of moroseness ended, and he grinned at Ngala. "But what a world to awaken in. In the few thousand years since my kin ruled, your mortals have come quite the distance."

"It would not do to not know my former master's name," called Ngala. "After all, who would I bow to?"

"You're amusing," the devil conceded. "My name is many-fold and varied among the olden peoples that knew their place, but you are not those olden people, my dear captain. I am Clermeil, for those that speak slave tongues."

The corsair-lord of Stone Cove laughed aloud. "I've heard that name before—a little old river spirit to my people, back when they lived on the land."

"Not a moment of your culture matters." Clermeil motioned at the joined triremes. "This. That. You—none of it. But look at you, Captain Ngala. Look at your sons. Even her—," he flicked his blade in Azinza's direction. "None of us ever had that when things were right."

"Then allow me to show you the ways of this new world." Ngala stalked forward, backed by a line of men who had survived the Ulmos.

"I think not." Blue sparks jumped in the air as the devil waved his long edge before him.

Answering his unspoken summons, the giant blue conch shell issued a deep, low note that ripped Tausi's consciousness away, leaving him face down on the planks beside his sister. The massive ship, grinding the bottom of the ocean as it turned about in place, vibrated the sea until unnatural waves broke and sloshed against the triremes.

Grabbing his sister around her waist, Tausi held on for dear life by the strength of his hand alone, trying with all his might to wedge the two of them in the cracks of the gangplanks to save them from rolling off, or worse, under the keels of the boats.

Clermeil spoke, his balance unhindered. "Consider yourselves lucky that I only came out here because I am curious and do not bear the wrath that my former compatriot who ruled these waters let himself suffer, no..."

Tausi heard the devil's footsteps as the creature approached. "Stand up, Tausi," he said.

Zaki grabbed her brother's arm-covering, her fingers hooked in the seams so he would not go. "Stay down," she whispered, on the verge of tears. "Please, gods, Tausi—stay down."

"No, Tausi, stand up," said Clermeil. "Please."

His sword lost in the ruckus of the conch-ships turn, Tausi released his hold of Zaki and shrugged off her hands, getting to his own knees before he rose.

Face to face with Clermeil, he presented no defense and sneered at the devil's milky, bloated visage.

"I like you," said the devil, his blade low at his side. "I like what you did with my people's temple. I like how industrious you are." The point of the devil's blade set on the center of Tausi's chest, the tip biting into his skin. "But such industriousness is only so charming next to my glories."

"Then do it." Tausi grinned like a loon, daring him. "I'm ready."

"But how could I?" asked the devil. "Then the world would be meaningless again!" He lowered his sword and left where they stood, slowly sauntering toward Azinza. The priestess had crawled to an unconscious Ngala. Clermeil stopped out of reach. "Even her. Even in this new world, she found meaning."

"What are you blabbering on about?" Tausi asked, his exhaustion placing him far past his terror. "Why are you even here, if it is all meaningless?"

The devil looked at him once more, his black-toothed grin widening until he showed his blistered gums. "I let the Latians in after telling them of your location. I was bored and curious about how this slave," he said, nodding in Azinza's direction, "could find herself well and free, when that is not her natural state. I wanted to know the measure of the world. And now I have taken it...and I am pleased."

Tausi stood aghast. "Why? Why make so many suffer?"

Clermeil laughed aloud, his yellowed eyes shining like two sick, dimming stars. "Because it is my right to know the world I shall rule."

The conch blew another note, sending Tausi sprawling. The earth ground again under the conch's passing bulk as it started to move back eastward from where it had come.

Fighting to find his senses, Tausi nearly jumped when the destroyed body of Popobawa fell onto the planks, empty of the devil's presence.

The giant blue conch shell sailed away.

Recovering, Tausi heard a dull lowing in his ears, the worrisome effect of what he feared might be a terrible injury to his brain. The muddiness sharpened and focused when the dull lowing became a horn blast. From the west rose two triremes, both of them flying under a red swath of cloth. He sighted Illus at the bow of the closest boat, and much to his surprise, seeing the gelded Latian almost put him off his feet again.

CHAPTER 14
DAWNING LIGHT

W e are all in agreement?" Ngala asked.

Tausi watched each and every captain at the table on *The Ube's* deck nod, one after the other, until it was finally his turn. Looking to his left at Zaki, they shared a quiet agreement in their glance to each other.

She nodded, a frown across her bruised, handsome face.

Tausi refocused on his father. "Agreed."

"Then..." Ngala said as he grunted in an effort to push the cork out of the bottle's mouth with his thumb. Freeing it with a pop, he took a swig before passing it to Dra beside him. "We will go issue a black splotch upon the name of Clermeil. Until the devil is hunted down and slain, he is damned."

"Aye, and the cold cruelty of the Face-Slashers shall see it done," said Dra, who guzzled more than a few mouthfuls before slamming the bottle down on the wooden table and sliding it to Illus, next along their round meeting place.

Leaning back in the high-backed chair his crewmen had dragged out of Song City's tunnels, Tausi lay exhausted in its cradle and waited for the dzan to make it his way. Pausing to view Zaki take more than a few gulps as well, the devil's words haunted his thoughts.

Had any of it meant anything, in the end?

222

So many were lost in the defense of his fort, which had again been shadowed by the memory of what it had been—a hall for devils. And for a devil's sick, minor pleasure they had butchered thousands upon thousands of men who had not needed to come. Had it all been for a devil's minor amusement?

What meaning was there to it all?

"You going to drink, boy, or are you going to share your thoughts with the table?" Oya asked at Tausi's right, her eyes wide with impatience.

"Let my boy alone, Oya," said Ngala. "Enough of your guff for now."

To the surprise of everyone at the table, Oya did not bluster or react. Instead, she accepted the bottle Tausi handed her.

Tausi had not taken a drink. Rising to his feet, he grabbed his sword off the table and nodded to those present. "Excuse me, captains." Leaving on the spot, he strode the gangplank off his ship, marching the length of the dock and up the stone steps to the fortress proper.

On the catwalks above, men scrubbed blood from the stone, smudging them until they stained the surfaces forever gray. The entire interior of the city busied itself—the strongest among those not wounded hauled the last bodies out of the hold in the northwestern section, prepping it for months of repair.

At the mouth of the tunnel to the Far Gate, dozens of corsairs, saltfolk, and Rats moved in and out, carrying what they could to where it was needed.

Tausi threaded the bustle of activity. Women used sand and seawater to buff blood off leather and ring while the children used small rags soaked in oil to polish recently sharpened or straightened swords. The emotion in the channel, tense and tight during the harrowing hours of the siege, had released in quiet, sad ways.

More than once, Tausi broke from the crying eyes of someone now without a parent, or a brother, or sister, or simply their friends. He steeled himself in the presence of men too hurt by what they had seen to raise enough emotion to salute their captain.

He found Azinza in the infirmary, lighting oil lamps while wounded men slept in the cool silence.

She stopped and looked up for Tausi before he even walked in.

Halted, he scanned the room, his eyes going immediately to the corner where Nana slept on a cot, his splinted leg up on a series of grain bags. Amare sat beside the bosun, dozing beside an oil lamp that glistened off his dark face.

Azinza spoke out. "Tausi?"

Tausi broke at the sound of Azinza calling his name, his vexing on his friends lifted. "Come with me. Please."

Checking on the room one last time, she hiked the blue hem of her skirts and exited the infirmary. "What's wrong?"

"Just follow me."

He led her to the ladder leading up to the northeastern tower, dismissing the archers posted at the top. Tausi kept one of their arrows, still unsure of whether or not he wanted to embarrass himself.

"Why are we up here, Tausi?" Azinza asked, confused.

He squeezed the arrow in his hand. "What was I supposed to do?"

"Do?"

He turned on Azinza. "Azinza, what should I have done? What should I have done instead of handing you the arrow?"

She shook her head at the question. "It doesn't matter. It didn't happen."

"It does matter," he said. "Now more than ever before."

"Why?"

"Because all of this has to matter—all of it, even the things that didn't. Something has to come of it, even if it is born of nothing." Tausi fought the trembling he felt in his face, putting on his calmest expression. "I need to know, Azinza."

"Why? Why do you need to know?" she asked. "What if knowing doesn't help?"

"Why wouldn't it?" he asked, offering her the arrow's fletched end. "What if this time is the time you saw, and what if here and now is when I don't give you the arrow? What if I do now what I was supposed to do then?"

"Is this because of Clermeil?" Azinza stepped forward to be close but stepped back when the barb pointed at Tausi's bare flank prevented it. "I don't want you to do this because you're scared."

"I'm not," he said, tossing the arrow into the sea.

She gasped, almost jerking in the direction to chase after it, as if she could dive over and catch it. "Tausi!"

"I haven't given you an arrow," he said, undeterred. "I don't know what that means, or if anything before the siege, or that devil, or afterward will mean anything at all. I want to make this mean something, and to decide my fate without worry. But you're part of that, and my fate isn't mine alone to decide—at least not in this moment."

"I'm a part of your fate?" Apprehension flowed, revealing a slight, mischievous smile she failed to hide. "What would your father say?"

"I don't care, and I don't think he will either."

"Don't you fear what lies on our next horizon?"

"Song City will have hope."

"I'm no goddess."

"Maybe not to you, but that devil thought you were worth the trip—over a slave, no less. I'm willing to contend with him that you've always been more than that. That you're worth more than that."

"Be quiet, Tausi," she said. "You don't know who listens."

"And I don't care in this moment." He dropped his sword next, leaving it by his feet. "I won't care who listens in this moment, be they devils or gods—not until you tell me what happens when I don't hand you that arrow."

Azinza stamped one of her bare feet on the boards. "Oh, you idiot—do I have to spell—"

Tausi kissed her.

She did not let him break away.

In a secret cavern along the corsair-owned beaches of Stone Cove, Zaki slipped into the darkness, going slow to let her eyes adjust.

A long, narrow path of dry sand split the earth, leading deeper into a hidden lagoon where a ship floated in its sunny pool.

Five meters longer than a typical Gypian trireme, the ship sat taller in the water as well, its hull wider at the mid-deck. Made of both the dense oak planks her lover Agwe had procured "beyond the next sea" and common woods like mahogany and Latian cedar collected at great expense, the doweled and layered shell formed walls stronger than iron.

The hull maintained the similar lines and design of the Gypian traditions, with its three banks of oars, but it possessed a uniquely formed keel that would allow it to travel in deeper rivers and tributaries. A long, pointed ram made of bronze capped the prow, lacking any adornments her people usually favored.

Standing on the deck, a man wove his hands in the air and directed the levitating beam carved for the ship's mast into a hole designed for its slanted angle. It would couch itself there as the main locking pin for the keel—something strong and flexing yet replaceable if they had to beach and carve a new one.

Murmuring his incantation, the sunlight from the open ceiling above shimmered off the blue silk shoulders of the man's white-embroidered robe, his bald head, and the dozens of silver piercings that dotted the scarred seahorse pattern on his face and cheeks. In the light, he looked like a god at work on a dream.

Padding her way along the perimeter of the lagoon, Zaki tried her damnedest to make no noise, starting the game she and her lover shared.

Each step careful and soft in the sand, she made the first leg with little trouble, the boat's stern blocking her from sight. Slipping into shadow, she snuck into a small shack at the lagoon's north corner.

Within the one-room shack, she unbuckled the twin swords from her waist and left them on the hay bed of their little hideaway. Across from it lay a workbench littered with sketches of sails and hulls, including a small replica of Cleona's *Immammou*, empty oil lamps, and all measures of rulers, rope, and woodcraft tools cluttered against a windowed wall.

Backing away from the bed and turning for the open doorway, she smiled at her silence, sure she would make it the entire way.

Zaki's glee dimmed when she stepped outside the hut, expecting the ball of her bare foot to strike sand. Instead, she advanced on an invisible ramp that let her march off the earth and into the air.

She stopped a few feet above the sand, seeing the pathway to the steering oar of the ship. "When did you hear me?"

"I felt you when you entered the cave," Agwe called, still out of sight from where he stood on the deck. His clear, light voice echoed off the rounds of the sandstone surrounding them. "I can hear your heart."

Any disappointment she might have felt fluttered away at his words. Walking the rest of the way, the bridge appeared before Zaki like a prism of captured, hazy light, a billion points of dust trapped in a flickering block. The ramp rose higher and higher, and before long, she strode at a height above even the ship's deck.

Agwe came into view, lighting her heart.

He was a tall, dark man. His face and head were completely shaven, and the drape of his blue robes hinted at a firm, handsome body beneath.

His glance came her way, his almond-brown eyes warming. On his forehead and cheeks, across his nose and around his eyes, scars had been etched in the pattern of a seahorse's crown, spiking on his flesh in beautiful, contoured directions that formed at the back of his skull and fed down his back. From each raised dot hung a small piercing of teardrop-shaped silver, layered like the scales of a fish.

The sight of him would have aroused Zaki had the specter of the last month not haunted the corners of her mind. "You were correct. A devil has dominated the White Rovers."

"And now you know why I try to keep so many secrets." Shifting his hands downward, the mainmast slid into its slot with a bang. The entire length of cedar wobbled for a moment, settling as the sorcerer put his calloused hands on his narrow hips.

"Damn," said Agwe. "The grain still isn't aligned."

"You've carved five different masts," Zaki said as she stepped off of the magical path and onto the deck.

"I'll carve a sixth." He stepped back and spun in a fluid motion, going to a small table set by the portside. He took up the bottle of dzan and poured two cups on a wooden plate beside it. "Come drink with me."

She sidled over to the table, reaching for the cup he handed her. After sipping the brown liquid, she snarled at the hot taste.

Agwe slipped behind her, one hand on her flat stomach while the other wrapped around her left shoulder to embrace her. Falling back into him, Zaki let the tension seep with the alcohol's burn while he nuzzled his rippled face against the side of her neck.

"Tell me about the devil," he whispered.

She tensed in his arms, wishing he had asked something else. "Can I just stand here with you for a moment?"

He laughed, deep and musical. "Of course."

Held fast to each other, the corsair captain and the sorcerer basked in the gentle light of the noon-sun, the breeze from the sea winding through the caverns and openings to bathe them in the air's salt-spice. Zaki smiled, her angst breaking when she felt the gentle brush of his lips on her hard, corded neck.

"I'm overjoyed by your return," Agwe whispered. "Did your brother and that little charmer finally find themselves?"

"Maybe too much so. Tausi will stand beside Azinza, though I worry about how well he will deal with what is she now versus what he thought her to be. I worry more about a baby."

"Time will reveal what kind of pair those two will be. Azinza is not without her own ways and wisdom, and true love clarifies."

She twisted in his arm, turning around to face him. Her hand on his face, Zaki ran her thumb across one of his brows, gently touching each bit of metal raised to appear like a droplet of water. "It does, doesn't it?"

Agwe leaned forward and kissed Zaki, his lips there long enough that she gasped when he broke away. Their noses touching, that mysterious smile of his widened. "More than any other power in this world."

"I hope," she said, lost in his gaze.

Her response wilted him. "Zaki."

She pushed off his chest and sat on the portside rail, the wood's edge biting the backs of her bare thighs. Scooting her full weight onto its substantial width, she scratched the back of her scalp. "It was terrifying. I've never been so scared like I was. Being so close to him..."

"What was his name?"

"He said..." Zaki looked up at the blue sky, searching for the moment in her memory. "He said he had many names, but those of the slave tongues could call him Clermeil."

"Clermeil." Agwe's brow hardened. "His name is listed among the five devils of Ge."

"What did he mean?"

Agwe studied Zaki, but beyond her as well, trying to summon something she could not comprehend. The corner of his mouth twitched, a sign of his unease. "There was a world before this one—before Juut was even called Juut, and even before the world bared the name of Dovhain. It was ruled by devils bred of the sorcerer-god, Ge, who remains unseen beneath the earth, though his name changes with every age. It is said that these devils were his sons, but not—they are his bastard children, attempts at making new gods against the true powers."

"What happened?"

"There were great wars across the breadth of the world, for not every land had devils, but in Juut there is an old tale on the land, one of a flood that consumed the greatest kingdoms of the legend." Agwe reached for the bottle of dzan and poured some more. "I often expected that Azinza was part of that lost time, a child spared of an era that would have been much harsher to her than this one."

He did not immediately taste his liquor.

Zaki leaned forward and touched his forearm. "What's wrong, Agwe?"

"If this devil is the spawn of Ge...Sorcery is bound to the purpose of time and balance, and this devil is out of place, out of time, and cares nothing for balance. His power cannot multiply."

"Ngala has pledged to raid the White Rovers, far to the east. Perhaps that is where he keeps his abode."

Agwe downed his drink in a single gulp. "Then we should get this boat in the water."

"Aye," she said. "Agwe?"

"Yes, my love?"

"Are you scared of this devil?"

The sorcerer stepped into the space between them, cupping Zaki's face in his long, worn hands. "Yes. But I won't be forever."

"Why not?"

Agwe's grin refreshed. "Because I have faith in those like your father, no matter what he thinks of me. And I have faith in you, my queen of the silver seas."

He leaned forward so he could peck a kiss on her forehead, and Zaki nodded, at peace with what had to happen. "So, a new mast?"

"A new mast," he said with some playfulness. "Did you bring back *The Immammou* so I can look at it? Maybe it will take my mind of the damned grain."

"Yes. I think we will be making changes to the oar banks and raise the row-deck a foot, as well."

"A foot! Well...we can play with it. Have you figured out a name for her?" he asked, stomping on the board.

"I have." Zaki rose off the portside rail, marching for the gangplank on the starboard.

"Well, are you going to tell me what it is?"

"I'm going to call her *The Ulmo*, my love," said Zaki, determined to get to work. Her hands already ached for her sketchpad. "And I will never be scared of that name again."

THE END

PART THREE
THE QUEEN IN SILVER

CHAPTER I
VOYAGE OF THE ULMO

S tanding upon the clean, flat deck of *The Ulmo*, Zaki fought the urge to turn about, to remember every nook and cranny the eye could see until she knew it to the smallest detail: the feel of the trireme's boards, the sanded grain of the wood against the naked soles of her feet, the buoyancy of the gentle sea lifting the hull against gravity.

"What do you think?"

She found Agwe at his place by the steering platform. The sun in the open blue sky glistened off his dark, shaved head and sparked the silver piercings spread across his face and brow in the design of a seahorse's crown. In the excitement of a long journey completed, a life's goal reached, they had discarded their clothes and stood naked out in the broad daylight.

Full of fresh passion, the release of ecstasy and happiness formed inside her tall, sinewy body flowed into the ship beneath her feet.

Zaki could not—would not—forget the sensation, no matter how hard she tried to focus on the warm wind moaning through the caves of their hidden lagoon, the cry of the gulls outside, the tingle of satisfying sex.

She stood on her boat.

Her boat.

A hard, eager smile cut across her strong features. "Let's take it out."

"Now?" Agwe asked, bending at the waist to rest his hands on his knees. His silver stare fixed her on the spot for a long, quiet moment before he cracked his own happy grin. "But I'm so tired."

Breaking out in laughter, Zaki resisted the urge to rush the sorcerer a second time for the day. She found her sandals where she had discarded them near the portside bow along with the meager hemp shift she often wore while at work. Lacing the high leather war-wraps to the top of her shins, the hobnails clacked on the boards as she turned back for Agwe and the hold.

"Go get ready," she ordered.

"Not only have you exhausted me, but now you'd make me your bosun," cried Agwe, throwing his hands in the air. The day gleamed off his pleasant shape, which Zaki did not fail to notice. Hands on his narrow swimmer's hips, the glittering shake of his head enraptured her. "This will be an impossible situation."

"Impossibility is a mortal thought for mortal minds," Clermiel said from his post at the other side of the steering oar, still locked by its peg. The worms beneath the blanched flesh of his ghoulish visage writhed, bunching and stretching his forehead and cheeks, only for the lines to shrug into the deeper recesses of his skull a breath later before rising again, seeking new crevices. "But this one already knows as much," he gestured at Agwe, "though he acts differently."

Zaki walked when she wanted to bound toward her lover. Along the length of the bright, gray boat, its hull polished to a silvery hue, her saunter ended right before Agwe, so they were face to face. Laughing in complete abandon, she threw her arms around his sturdy neck and kissed his full lips, which were warm like the sun on her shoulders.

Breaking their silent seal, she pulled back. "I did promise half of all my treasures."

"But I've no need for any more now."

Another kiss, another pause of time and space.

"Mortal thoughts for mortal minds," Clermiel repeated in his cold manner. He stepped forward, his footfall rippling the planks. The reality holding them together bubbled. Dead white eyes fixed on Agwe. "But his aren't."

Tossing her shift over her shoulder, she sauntered for the hold. The steps down the wide stair, large enough so a full troop of eighty raiders could maintain its threshold at a bottleneck made for shield walls and courageous hearts, led to a great well of darkness. Her right hand trailing the rail, she stopped where the sunlight ended.

Her fingers brushed over the scalloped end of the runner.

Set in the dark wood, as if grown from the grain, thousands of small blue crystals rose to the glow of the sun outside, bright and golden. Illumination revealed the seats lined along both sides of the hold, almost blossoming from the long keel like flower petals to form three decks for the rowers's benches.

Clermiel stood beyond the timekeeper's station, a slightly raised dais where the great drum to drive the beat rested. He laid his hand on the slanted beam of the "key mast" and glared up at the lights. "So, what are you, vestige of my kin's past? What horrid power will you gift apes so they may better make ruin?" he asked, and not to Zaki.

Zaki went to the drum and laid her hand atop its freshly oiled skin. She tapped a slow beat with the pads of her fingers.

The ends of the oars, fixed in swing arms to keep their strokes smooth and secure while allowing the wielders wide ease of movement, awoke with the same light of the railings. They suddenly rose in unison, as if lifted by invisible men on the benches, and extended outside of the ship.

"A horrid power indeed," whispered Clermiel.

She ascended to the deck and found Agwe fully regaled in his long robe of white silk. Standing beside the steerage, he bent over a box beside the etched oar handle. Lifting the headdress out of the box, its long strands of spun silver fell around it's sewn-in skull cap, which served as the base for the long, straight bangs. A mane comprised of thousands of fine threads of silver draped across the neck and shoulders like any mail headdress, it stayed together in heavy curtains by small, polished rings of obsidian.

"I like that one," said Zaki.

"It's much lighter than the first helm and won't pitch you about." Agwe held it up in presentation and nodded for her to take her place by the steering oar. "But I can't promise it will save you from an arrow. The armor will, though, once I get it fixed."

"The sacrifices we make," said Zaki, who turned and faced away from her lover.

Agwe laid the headdress atop her shaved head like a crown. "Remember to breathe."

A swoon enveloped her. The air around Zaki thickened, almost like it had burnt to molasses. A haze coated her eyes. She steadied herself on the steering oar's long handle.

The ship breathed beneath her feet.

Knuckle-tight, Zaki stood her ground as a new element entered her thoughts. Nothing living or thinking, but a mechanical set of ineffable, fluid ideas, cogent yet beyond the comprehension of her own words. Any words.

The Ulmo's oars, by her simple notion to depart, rose and dipped back into the hidden lagoon on the other side of Stone Cove's jutted peninsula. With the implicit knowledge the anchor was already up, the trireme glided forward. Its dark rostrum, shaped like an upturned lobster-claw, parted the rushing Mirror Sea. The ship lived in Zaki's hands and her mind, and she in it. She set a southerly course for a few minutes, letting the summer winds wrap around her and Agwe while their dreams took flight. The ocean gleamed blue-silver under the noon-time sky, roaring on the tides as the current between the gentle flows of the lagoon where she and Agwe hid from the world and the chaos of the sea met. *The Ulmo* broke into the new resistance with little trouble. Zaki struggled against a shiver running down her spine, wondering if its cold matched the water running the keel.

Gripping tight to the steering oar, she swallowed her will back in her chest. "Raise the sail!"

Agwe brought his hands forth, murmuring words in the breeze. The sail, strung along a line connected from the slanted mainmast to the peg mast at the fore of the boat, unfurled in a smooth waterfall of bright blue cloth. Bearing no sign or emblem, it fluttered limp before its long, sharp triangle swelled.

Zaki trembled as the ship rushed outward, onward, toward destiny.

"This isn't of human hands," said Clermiel. "You should not be able to use these things. I should not let you."

Unable to contain her joy, Zaki whooped as *The Ulmo* sailed gallantly, alive for the first time, and free.

The sky, bare and cloudless, fractured like glass. A growling, rumbling thunder sounded in the distance, but there were no anvil-banks of gray, no sheets of rain or a cold gust to direct the storm's direction. She shuddered when the trireme's keel bumped on the current.

Agwe appeared before her, standing directly within her line of sight.

"Get out of my way," she said. "We hit something!"

"I'm coming, Zaki," Agwe shouted at her, sounding very, very far away. Invisible lightning shattered the firmament. "I'm coming!"

She thought to speak, tried, but a bubbling tightness clung in her chest. Without thought, her hands came to her throat as she choked. Water, hot and salty, spewed the sour stomach acid from between her lips. The world around her, and Agwe, brightened to the point of whiteness before it crashed, deep, dark, and blacker than soot.

A massive claw closed around her face, wrenching her head out of the swirling, sinking seawater. The raw edges of the appendage dug into her cheeks and temples, rasping her skin, cutting it. Warm, red soup drained into the grated coral floor beneath her dripping, numbed feet.

An Ulmo held her head up. Unable to stop her breathing from spiraling into heaving, the inside of the claw took up all the space in her muddy field of vision, a sight which popped in and out of darkness every time she coughed more brine from her windpipe. Arms bound at the wrists by cuffs forged of harder stone and barnacles, she came to when the mottled-shelled monster loosened his grip on her head. The manacles were molded to the walls of her cell, the strain on the heels of her hands made her wince, and her stinging eyes were unable to find needed tears. Hanging there, she groaned and hacked, the fire in her shoulders a match for one in her bruised skull.

"Leave us."

The Ulmo turned on its chitinous feet and shuffled through a hole of light at the edge of Zaki's vision when she brought her gaze down. A deep, red tearing in her shoulder forced ugly heat into the top half of her body. Her neck muscles protested. The green-black block huddled through the bright orifice, there one moment and gone the next.

A new shape took his place, tall and lean. A more humane profile.

"Who is he, Zaki?" Clermiel whispered in her ears. "Do you know?"

She wanted to form the words to curse. Lips raw, she gurgled in an attempt to summon enough spit to hock at the devil.

"I'll find out, either way," he whispered again. "It's only a matter of time."

CHAPTER 2

THE BATTLE OF THE BAR

A drone echoed from the curved horn of a red gazelle. More tones answered in the dawn's gloom, low and long as they returned the call. They came from all directions, a few at first, then responses came by the dozen.

When the edge of day spread revelation upon the great sea's surface, it populated the shifting blue level with dozens upon dozens of triremes, all driving southeastward.

Their destination seemed wayward, a corsair fleet set on the winds toward an empty horizon. It was not until the sun broke free from its hiding place that one of the raiders at *The Ulmo's* long bow sighted the blue speck, its size growing with every second's passing.

"*The Tide* is on the horizon, Captain," the man called loudly over the spraying waves. "Target dead ahead!"

The silver headdress already heavy on her neck and shoulders, Zaki tried to spot the dot in the far distance. The clear line before her was without blemish on the first and second pass of her gaze, and it wasn't until steadying her breath did she see it.

The blue conch shell. A behemoth, even from her faraway vantage, sat upright in the water like a tower sprouted from the sea.

The dauntless target of more than a year's parsing of rumor, its strange orientation bothered her more than anything else. "Set the men on the benches and get Mona at a hard beat. Warn her she's in for it," she ordered Agwe, who waited at her side like any devoted bosun. Hands steady on the steering oar, she willed the handle to lock in place when another nagging thought took her. "Check depth."

"Aye, Captain," said the sorcerer, who had discarded his long, sleek robes for the brown leather and bright mail of a warrior, like any other fighter on the deck of her ship. He made for the hold without pause.

There were eighty men on the deck and more below—she felt their weight and movement at the back of her head, a constant buzz working on her nerves. Steady as she surveyed the rigging, she calmed herself with a series of short breaths.

The bright blue sail came down without an order issued or hands to lower it, save for a few crewmen who bound it away. The raiders before her assembled in their shield formations, iron swords girded to their belts, long-bladed spears gripped in ready hands. The oars from all three banks dug into the water, their strokes slow and steady before, on beat, they leapt free of the water. A constant brushing at her temples, Zaki sought calm in its consistency.

Agwe scampered up the steps, his silver eyes wide in worry. "We're entering shallows!"

"Cut to quarter beat and keep the middle banks lively," she replied, letting him go below a second time before she shouted for her commander. "Mani!"

From the buzzing raiders forming their lines on the deck, a tall, proud youth emerged. The strong angles of his cheeks streaked with bright blue paint matching the retracted canvas sail, he stood at stick-straight attention the second he stopped before her to answer her call. "Captain Zaki!"

"Three blasts for the quarter beat and raise the green banner high." They shared a quiet, knowing stare, the kind that passed on an order the receiver might die for. "Prepare to defend the deck."

"Aye, Captain," he said, no less confidant.

Drawing the painted gazelle horn from his war-girdle, Mani brought it to his lips and sounded three loud blasts. The corsair fleet slowed at the call. At *The Ulmo's* bow, two raiders leaned over the dark-stained rails, waving long pieces of green silk before they withdrew to complete their preparations for the defense.

The triremes at *The Ulmo's* flanks, *The Gamka* and *The Ube*, signaled their acknowledgment with a sharp blast of their horns to warn of an attack. The echoes repeated across leagues of gentle ocean.

The conch, immense in its size and too clean-looking for its evil contents, loomed in the south.

Sweat gathered beneath Zaki's silver headdress and ran down the back of her neck. One hand was on the locked steering oar of her boat while the other danced at the round pommels of twin swords belted to her left side, cinched tight so their ends touched. She perked her ears, trying to hear above the constant batter of sandals on the planks, the thrum of *The Ulmo* in her head.

Agwe reemerged from below. "Rowers have their piths and bucklers on the benches. Mona wants to release the middle bank."

"Tell her to—"

A loud, horrific keening issued from the conch's aperture. A ripple pressed beneath the surface of the water, a line of energy gathering in a wave hurtling toward them. Growing in unnatural speed, the swell shot up in a mound, beginning to peak toward a sharp, hammering collapse.

"Brace," Zaki screamed when the keening ended. "Back on the oars! Full beat!"

No horns needed to be blown for any captain facing down a rogue wave. She grasped the steering oar with both hands and lowered into a fighter's stance as she mentally commanded it to free from its lock. A hard grit took Zaki's jaw when she set herself firm.

Captains also knew sometimes the waves won, no matter what they tried to do. "Full beat ahead! Raiders, rope-in! Brace," she screamed again and again, watching death come with the brightening edge of the growing giant.

Oars stabbed into the waters, frothing the trireme's wake to a turgid gray shade. *The Ulmo*, never tested against an impact, scurried to ready as each raider threw ropes around themselves and secured the binds to what piece of the railing they could find. They hunkered under their shields, each one praying to hold tight to the last. The trireme thrust forward at a hard, driving pace that reverberated down Zaki's spine and bled out her toes, back into the boards where she stood. The cold of the bronze rostrum dividing the sea, like it would divide this wave, numbed her nerves.

Agwe appeared at her side, a lone light in her tunneled vision.

"Everyone is keeping pace!" He searched behind her, checking past the stern and beyond her vision. "I count most of them, but they're crowding, Zaki! They're crowding!"

"They'll have to be ready," she said, trembling as she fretted being unable to look back. *The Ulmo's* steering oar fought against a change in the current, bending against a tidal force. She pressed to starboard to keep her boat pointed where she had last seen the blue conch shell.

The wave formed its white cliff when the corsairs struck its incline. The will of thousands clawed at the water's skin, hoping to find hold by the oar-blade's grace.

Higher, higher, and higher *The Ulmo* climbed the wave. The rest of the world vanished from Zaki's view. The steering oar, wiggling in her hands like a venomous sand-snake, struggled against the shearing current to stay true to course. She watched as the wave crested above the top of her bow, and in the shifting depths, dark shapes moved.

Enthralled by the death brought before her, Zaki contained the urge to scream in its face. "Agwe," she whispered as the lobster-claw rostrum burrowed into the wave. Hard, white spray struck her face, her eyes. A scream, or at least what she thought was a human cry, grew and flew past her left ear as the grinding, grumble of the wet sea blotted out life.

"I'm here," he shouted, somewhere.

"There are Ulmos in the wave," she coughed past the foamy wash invading her mouth, her nose.

"Zaki, get read—"

Her lover's voice was lost as the wave's hard shadow fell over them.

The Ulmo pierced the top of the wave, ascending its apex before plummeting down the other side. The steering oar freed, the sudden shift leaving Zaki hanging by the handle, her feet untethered to any board. Slamming on the slope, the rostrum drove in the waters, every board creaking. Sure to the nail, the ship held as Zaki found luck and the right piece of floor to land on, skidding and scrambling to find balance.

Agwe appeared at her side again, a sword in his hand. He yanked her to both feet roughly by the other and forced her around, facing stern-side. "They're coming!"

She looked up in time to see the blue sky, still clear and perfect.

And filled by dozens of Ulmos leaping from the back of the falling wave.

Shrugging off her lover, Zaki ripped both swords from her belt. "Raiders! At the ready!"

The unified grunt of fighters rising to fight at her back eased the panic in her by the time the first mottled hulks of shell, claw, and evil splashed into the sea beside *The Ulmo.* Any opportunity to check on her father's ship, her brother's, or their friends and allies, fled to the territorial urge to defend her crew.

The first shelled terror climbed over the portside at the middeck, only to be welcomed by clusters of spears in his clicking blue face. The monster fell back into the water, quivering with a pierced nervous system.

Three Ulmos hauled themselves over the side, stealing any chance for celebration. Clustered and frayed, the deck suddenly shrank in its space as the giants charged in all directions, claws snapping for flesh. Raiders fell on them, gallant in the face of their inhuman foes, with more iron welcomes. The trireme's boards were consecrated as blood slicked them.

Zaki cut at the shoulder joint of a blue Ulmo facing away from her as more horrors scattered over the rail. She felt their weight on her head, the silver crown on her head connecting two nervous systems into one. The heat of the blood soaking the wood, the heaviness of the slain, the screams of the dying—she screamed back as she thrust her other sword into the monster's head. Pithed, it convulsed before teetering to the side like a fallen tree. The raiders beyond the dead foe, Mani among them, offered what salutes they could in the heartbeats before the next melee.

"Fall back to the hold," she yelled above the din. She dodged back, striking the starboard rail before the tip of a wayward claw sought to disembowel her. Tearing a strip from her red war-dress, she pushed off those crowding at her sides before the Ulmo turned its attention their way.

The raiders, from the day when one of their corsairs discovered the cursed beasts, had conditioned themselves to fear worse things. Somehow in the ebb and flow of the fleeting, mortal dance, battle-hard veterans pledged to *The Ulmo* from the ranks of Stone Cove and Song City came together to defend each other. They unified in a wedge they used to hurry wounded down shifting aisles. Given reprieve, the brave and bloodied who could rise limped stern-side over the mounded dead, slinking into the ship's arcane underbelly where rowers waited to accept them. Zaki searched the deck among those fighting to hold position while those at the bow knowingly collapsed their corner of the wedge, receding to the hold's stair.

"Agwe!" Running along the back of her fighter's line, she tried to catch every face she could. None of them were the silvered, tattooed beauty of her man. Somewhere near the key mast, she spotted him, yards farther ahead.

They found each other across the distance, sharing a knowing, silent message.

One of her swords lost to the cavity of a slain Ulmo somewhere in the gory mess, Zaki reached up and tore the silver headdress off, exposing her sweating pate to the sun's heat.

"Captain!" Mani appeared in the retreating flow, one of many managing the collapse of the corsair's formations at middeck. No worse for wear and unwounded, he nearly yelped in surprise when a dead Ulmo fell between them, a pair of their shipmates still clinging to the swords sticking out the back of its shattered head.

Zaki yanked him around the heap and shoved the headdress into Mani's hands before pushing him toward the hold. "If you don't see me again, make sure Agwe gets it!"

The man almost hesitated, cradling the shining helm and loose, glittering locks in his hands. "Aye, Captain!" he said as he went, on the verge of tears.

She turned back to find Agwe again and discovered the space had been invaded by a hulking enemy. Without pause, she plucked up a fallen blade. Again, complete with both hands ready to deliver death, she launched into an attack. The Ulmo, contending with two raiders skewering his side with their pikes, jabbed out an open claw to catch her. Ducking, Zaki rose onto her bent knee and raised both swords high. Bringing the first down, the heavy blade opened one of the seams near the creature's horrid, spitting mouth. Wedged there, she kept her wavering handhold and stabbed the second length of steel deep into the wound.

A second keen exploded from the blue conch overlooking the sea battle.

The shock shook the entire sea this time. Several swells struck *The Ulmo's* prow the next instant. The entire ship spun counterclockwise, pitching Zaki and her kill overboard. She smacked the water in a half-ball, stinging her bare legs as she plummeted into the depths. Letting go of the swords embedded in the dead monster, she flailed in the murkiness. Her eyes stung as she kicked for the watery ceiling above. Breaking through, she inhaled a hard gasp of air, trying to stay afloat. She treaded, frantic at first, until she forced her body to calm.

Dozens of ships within her view rowed among the wreckage of the few triremes crushed under the first wave. Shredded bodies lay suspended in the reddening sea, and she watched as dead Ulmos were cast over the sides of other ships to join them. Zaki spotted *The Ulmo*, many yards to her left. She turned in the water to swim for home, one hand in front of the other as she crawled through the slosh.

The blue conch loosed its shrill spell a third time.

Darkness took her without warning.

Seawater drenched her face. She gasped awake, coughing out her lungs until every fiber of her wet body tingled. Her arms and shoulders shook, locked painfully against the blue-yellow coral walls binding her to the tiny room of her cell. Zaki threw her head back in convulsions, clearing her face of the flow falling from the point of light above her head. The jet closed, reducing a waterfall to droplets. They pecked at the top of her aching, hairless skull.

Her face raw and scored, Zaki tried to think past her blinded eyes, until in the darkness she spied a point of light. At an unknowable distance, the fleck of sun shone on a smooth, cream-pink surface, which glowed dull. Zaki swallowed. Her feet free, she padded at the spongy surface beneath her naked soles, too tired to be disturbed by the visceral, slimy solidity.

"Please don't do anything stupid," Zaki whispered at what she hoped could not hear her.

"I'll try to keep that in mind," said a cold, alien voice in the dark.

She knew who spoke to her. Ignoring the rawness of her chapped mouth, subduing the exhaustion at every bloody end of her nerves, Zaki gathered her strength again and stood taller. The pressure of her bonds eased; she glared out in the ether.

"You're not well."

She refused to respond.

"Do you think you're well?"

Zaki blinked a few times and looked to the floor, letting her thoughts amble off to a time she and Agwe went fishing.

"Do you, Zaki?"

"When I free myself from these bonds, I will take your life myself," she answered. "It won't matter then, will it?"

The hole above her head opened again, the brightness beyond too white for the sun.

"Such violence. Such bravado."

Blinded, Zaki tried to lean forward, putting her face back in the dark. She waited.

"Such a conundrum."

A shape moved in the opaque dark. Zaki tensed, unable to control her reaction as it came closer. The blinding light in her tight cell strengthened. The coral, rough against the flesh of her wrist, seemed to burn with her growing dread.

The devil's eyes gleamed, dead white stars in the forever night. "Let me see what end I can put to it."

CHAPTER 3
THE TIDE'S PULL

Zaki felt more like his mama as he fingered the beads of the necklace laid out on blankets on his parent's pallet. Zaki had always found his mama pretty—not in the way some men did, when they were careless enough to speak in such crudeness around children, but pretty in a way that was good. And not good in a way that was only better, but loving, and kind, and gentle.

The rough cylinders of lapis lazuli mixed in polished ebony beads, something taken from someone from someplace else he didn't understand, offered too much temptation. He pulled it from the rippling trough where it sat within the blanket's sea, holding it up like a precious thing.

He carried it to the large, polished sheet of silver set against the corner of the red clay bedroom of his family's apartments. Cut and hammered into a wide oval, Zaki looked into its reflecting, cloudy depths.

The child staring back, holding the same necklace, confused Zaki.

There came confusion every time, like something lost that should have been known but wasn't. Yet hints of things that could not yet be imagined played and doubts roamed, until the cool blue pieces touched the bare skin, the wooden beads mooring them in place. A transformation took place, an idea of joy, goodness.

Truth.

Zaki liked who she saw in the silver mirror.

"The sickness of childhood imaginings," Clermiel whispered.

"Zaki?"

Zaki turned to find his mama standing in the doorway. Her belly swollen to the point she had to hold it with both hands, she walked to the mirror, waddling on her dusty heels.

"I was just playing, Mama," he said, holding up the necklace before he had even tied it on.

The face of a goddess beamed over her rounded stomach. "Oh? What were we playing?"

"I was just playing."

"Well, let me see what I can do to help," she said, taking the beads and draping them back around Zaki's neck. Tying the knot quickly, she straightened, hands pressed to her back. "Let's go sit on the bed."

Zaki took her hand when she offered it, letting himself be pulled along to the pallet against the northern wall of the room. Bright sunlight lit the curves of her gentle face, making them seem more golden the deeper she smiled. "Now," Mama said. "Let me guess who you are...Black Lizard, back from one of his treasure-raids along the Wheat Coast!"

Zaki shook his head.

"No?" She leaned back on the bed and held his chin, studying the round face she loved by every inch she happened upon. "Then maybe you are..." She shut one eye and peered deep within to see what lay in a child's heart. "Are you Cleona the Great?"

Cheeks warmed in a smile preceded a second shake of the head.

"Well, good," she said with a clicking of her tongue. "Your father wouldn't have liked that at all."

They shared in a quiet laugh.

"So," she said, stroking the top of her child's head. "Is it someone I know?"

Zaki nodded.

"Who?"

"Ogbu, the Queen of the High Seas!"

Her heavenly face, the one written on the soul of every child blessed by a mother's smile, warmed like the sparkling sea outside.

"Zaki," she said, leaning to her side on the bed. Their noses touched. "That's me."

"I know, Mama."

There came shouting down the long hallway outside, the grousing of men and the clatter of their arms. They marched into hearing.

Ogbu lifted Zaki up by the arms and waddled them back to her dresser, a grid of baskets built into some fine shelves she had afforded her household through plunder. Standing as comfortably as possible, she pulled out individual bins until she let out a loud, sharp laugh, like the snap of a whip.

"Ogbu could never go to sea without looking absolutely resplendent," she said, playfully serious. "Now, you have a necklace, but I would never ever go out with just one." Reaching into the baskets, she pulled out wads of luxurious black beads strung on threads of silk, chains of drop-casted silver, bangles gemmed in rainbows. She dumped them on the bed by the handful.

"Now pick out something pretty," she instructed Zaki. "I usually pick the thicker ones. Bigger stones have better shine, little one."

She pulled at more baskets full of bits of armor, battle dresses, and long gowns of silk where the hems were ripped to free the legs. Piles and piles of wonder were displayed before Zaki. The edges of old iron swords, spear points broken from the shafts of old enemies, gleamed as bright as the silks and baubles enfolded among them.

"Ah, this one," Mama said, yanking from the pile of clothes a wrap she threw around Zaki's tiny torso. Black-dyed canvas with bright red splotching the fabric in places offered a colorful war gown. Within those red splotches, small crusts flaked like rust.

"Heeled like wolves." Clermiel scoffed from the doorway. "Bloody, repugnant wolves."

Mama drew out the top bin and took her place back on the bedding while Zaki found the right bracelets to fit his little wrists. Finding two that slid between the elbow and base of the hand, the silver bangles caught the light against his deep bronze flesh. His eyes trailed back to the sword tucked in the overturned piles of clothes when shouts echoed a second time from the hall.

Closer than before.

"More bracelets, baby," said Mama as she glanced toward the doorway. She searched the clothes and spotted the hilt of an iron sword. "I'm always wearing more bracelets."

Zaki followed her gaze the entire time. "Mama?"

"Yes, my love?" she asked, her fierce eyes softening for him. She spotted the treasures ringed around Zaki's wrists. "You like the silver, don't you? So do I. It's my favorite."

The clattering from outside arrived in a bustle of men who crowded past the doorway to the first apartment chamber, swords bared and their shields leading the way. One of them, a young man a few inches taller than the rest and broader in his shoulders, pushed his way through the rabble.

Mama lifted herself from the pallet, holding her belly in both arms. "Ngala!"

"Ogbu," he said, coming forward with his weapons. He stopped at the edge of where he and his wife slept, looking at the clothes, the weapons, and loot out in the open. "What are you doing?"

"Just playing with Zaki," she said, her tone defensive. "Where are you going?"

"Black Lizard is going raiding. He wants me to take command of his raiders." Ngala shifted his hunter's eyes in Zaki's direction again. "I have to..."

"Go," said Mama, one hand off her belly to clap her husband's broad shoulder, which bore scars Zaki found ugly. "This is your only way out of the hold and off the bench."

He kept checking between the mother and child. "Who can I send to watch you? What about you and Zaki?"

"We'll be fine," Mama said.

"What about Zaki?" Ngala asked, peering past his wife to give his child a smile one did not expect from a hard man.

Mama's voice changed, and her tone put an ease in Zaki. "Zaki will take care of me."

Like the passing of the tide, Ogbu died, her heart giving out in a sigh as her infant son screamed his first breath into the world.

And like that infant son, unnamed and a stranger, Zaki was left alone.

The void her leaving created in the world made a home inside of her child's heart. The smiling, happy face of a goddess, her joyous laugh, the warmth she brought with the sun, and her nestled sense of safety became more and more haunting. Every day began, continued, and ended with the baby crying, and Zaki crying, for the one person who could never come and soothe those miseries.

Weeks passed. Zaki woke to scream-shattered mornings every day when he would carry the little baby down to the edge of the beach, plop down where the sea reached the squalling creature's filthy bottom and wash it clean. Zaki would pat his little bottom with pieces of cloth lent to him by the salt-wives who suckled his little brother while the salt-husbands, mates to those women who like his mother had braved blood and sea-swells, instructed him on things too complex for a toddler himself to understand.

They burnt his mother's body out on the beach beyond the cove's great, yawning cavern.

Her smoke sent black tendrils toward a sky brightening from navy to a blue-gray Zaki never forgot. The way the body lay on the heaped pyre, shrouded in the bloody blanket she died upon, seemed wrong to a child raised by beliefs of the sea, in the freedom of it, but for Ogbu's child, no words were there to say those things. Cinders crackled and danced as the flames ate the remains.

A horn blasted from one of the lookouts. The blow of it startled Zaki, who almost dropped the baby he labored to hold on to as the writhing thing wept and wailed, drawing hard looks from everyone older around him, as if it had been Zaki who had wanted to break Mama's final peace. Those same eyes quickly went to sea, where a trireme's dark red sail caught in the sunlight like a fleck of blood on the Mirror Sea.

"Black Lizard rides," called one amongst the crowd, and immediately they ceased to mourn.

The slip of the tide, a turn of breeze, and the sun began to shine on Stone Cove as it always had.

Zaki did not leave the beach until the last orange lick died on his Mama's charred skull.

Struggling to bear the baby back to the rooms they still claimed, Zaki found an intruder had entered. The strange man searched the empty apartment for something, or someone, who was not there. He carried an iron sword, finer than anything Zaki recalled from Mama's hoard. He turned in the dimness, his piercing eyes fixing on Zaki immediately.

"Zaki?" the figure called in a grim, hoarse voice. A voice the child knew.

The baby screeched in Zaki's ear, so loud it drew tears.

Fighting to make sure he did not drop the little monster, Zaki fell hard to both knees and screamed as well.

Ngala came rushing from the shadows, darkness banished from his hard face. Shock—utter, cold shock—held his expression as he gathered both children up in his corded arms, grasping them tight to the hard leather of his armor. The dark giant held them and heaved, weeping like a storm-torn sky.

When he spoke, the words came broken, edged in dire questions.

"Where's your mother?"

"What happened, Zaki?"

"Where is she?"

And Zaki cried, unable to answer.

"You think yourselves worthy of your freedom despite your gross, horrid irresponsibility," mocked Clermiel, his black outline cut by the sunlight drifting through the open doorway to the bedroom. "And you apes want self-determination?" he asked with a rasping breath.

Ngala rocked back and forth like the tide, until Zaki lowered his head to the corsair's and fell in rhythm with his sobs. They settled into their sorrows while the smallest of the trio wailed himself to sleep before Ngala carried them back into their chambers. He slumped down with them in his lap, his back to the wall. He started at the empty entrance while the baby lay against his chest and snoozed.

Fallen in the crook of his arm, Zaki dazed in the dark.

"I'll never let you go alone again, Zaki," Ngala whispered. "Never, ever again."

At some point the baby woke again, crying like it always did.

Cradling the child on his thighs, Ngala gazed down at the little boy with a tear and a half-smile, too trapped by his torments to hide them before Zaki. The oldest child watched as his father took stock of the nameless infant.

"Tausi," Ngala said. "She wanted to name him Tausi."

CHAPTER 4
SPIRALING

She shook in her bonds, all the tendons from shoulder to wrist straining against the spongy coral. It cracked a third time, a breaking sound Zaki cherished to repeat, a hope she had found a way in the dark to cause a change to it.

Anything to shift the endless space she had been left to hang in.

A hard pebble, smaller than a broken piece of shell, dusted and tumbled onto her shoulder.

Zaki snorted hard, sobbing for a second before taking a mighty breath. Loosening her arm to let some blood in before the next attempt, she closed her eyes and imagined a sunny cove or the gleam off the new boards on the deck of her boat.

Clermiel had not spoken for a long time. Wondering if she was asleep or awake, Zaki spent those gaps in the void trying to distinguish between her breath while awake and her breath in the unreal, the places where the devil ripped her into the mind. What purpose or reason he had seemed distant and unknowable.

She wondered at his intent.

She tried not to think about Ngala, or Tausi, or Agwe.

Did Agwe live? Did she need to worry? What did she worry about in that question?

She worried about who he might be. But why?

A grunt broke the droning words she had asked no one. Out went every thought of everyone she knew until there was only her, alone, again in nothingness. She tightened her numb fists, each finger squeezed shut as she readied. Setting her shoulder back as far as she could, Zaki threw her right elbow forward and jerked down.

The coral shattered into large chunks. Spongy pieces struck her bare right leg. Before she could celebrate her victory, the other bonds withdrew, protrusions molding back into the walls of the cell. Her limbs suddenly free, Zaki tumbled head over heels out of the holding space, into a larger chamber. The soft ground, a rubbery surface, softened her half-roll.

The floors thrummed like a thousand hearts.

From the twitching floor, Zaki slowly rose upon hands and knees, padding the soft spaces she could touch before daring to place bare feet on the ground. Both knees wobbled and every muscle awoke as she stood, still swaddled in the ether but grounded, firm upon a plane hard enough to let her gain her senses. The first few steps forward revealed no barriers, nothing to block her path as she groped with tingling hands. The surface she stood on breathed beneath her, shifting to meet every footfall.

An incline met her march. Tapping her way up its slope with her toes, a breath of cool air bathed her face. To the right, she turned in its direction and paused when she caught light in the distance.

A ray of sunlight.

Zaki angled her body until she was sure which way she faced, putting the point to where it never left her field of view. She started forward again, hands held out, daring without fear. At any time, she knew an Ulmo could reach from the constant night and snuff her life out like a torch in the gale winds. She bumped her bare feet into the fibrous corner of a barrier, and padding her way around it with her hands, she found sure footing on a path to the right, curving for what seemed like forever before her direction returned toward the beam.

Closer than before, clarity yielded the sunlight of a dying day. She could see the pink-bronze sky beyond.

A breeze from the ocean wove its way through the immense conch, stronger than before.

Chilled by the rush, Zaki trod in its direction, thankful for the beam of sunset warming the way ahead. Into a narrow, warped channel where the ceiling disappeared in an unknowable expanse, her bare feet found a harder, smoother floor in a series of twisting rises.

The daylight had gone by the time she ascended to the murky heights of wherever the channel led, leaving her again to the black.

She traveled along another sightless passage when she realized she could see outside if she looked to her left.

There, laying outside the ribs of a horned protrusion, the sky sparkled in a thousand points aglow.

Zaki pressed her back against the nearest wall to her right, mouth shut tight so a gasp did not escape her. Fighting the urge to dash for the open air, she paused, listening for any sound.

Only her breath.

Zaki heard no other sound, no movement, nothing but the heart pounding in her chest as she lurched forward.

She leapt clear of the open vent in the conch's twisted point. Landing hard on one of its horned protrusions, she seethed as the crust skinned her palms. One quick glance back at the now-visible window of some strange deck, she crawled down the side, in search of a better vantage point.

The sudden exertion reminded her quickly how long she had gone without food or water. The dryness in her mouth and difficulty swallowing halted her as she slid down to a natural balcony shaped over the conch's yawning aperture. The sea wind, salted and warm, carried its nighttime chill. Knees tucked under her chin, Zaki pressed her hands against her chest and rubbed against the gnawing hunger and urge to fall asleep. The meager warmth, enough to keep her heart beating, soothed her calloused hands.

Between waking and dozing, the sky turned from navy to orange-fire. Dawn battered the exhaustion clawing at her eyes.

When the morning warmed her aching limbs, she crept from the shade of the hollow she had fallen into and peeked over its edge.

Below, a small tide flooded the channel leading into the conch's depths. A few Ulmos, too far away to crane their bulk upward and spot her, scuttled from the placid surf into their grisly home. A blue sky, empty of any clouds, lay above her.

Desperate for the sun again, Zaki climbed the horn.

At the top, she straddled one of the wider growths of mottled-blue shell, its rough skin chaffing the inside of her thighs. Able to see far and wide, Zaki discovered the conch still rested on the bar the corsairs had happened upon, surrounded by the sparkling Mirror Sea as it muted from gold to its smoky color. Resting at an angle so she could not look west or northward to check on the fleet, she climbed higher as the sun beamed down until the first bout of hunger scrunched her gut.

The climb to the highest point on the vessel took enough time that the sun had reached its midpoint between dawn and noon when she crested the edge. Laying on her side in the heat for long minutes while she regained her strength for the next push, Zaki stared down the long smooth back of the conch shell where it fell northward, into the froth. Light-headed, she considered a slide and tumble along the smooth curve before the better sense of how painfully the fall would kill her prevailed. She chuckled past dry lips and scooted to some shade the sun had thrown around the natural crenellations the shell formed. The coolness lessened the burden of her weakness, and she considered making time to sleep again.

She opened her eyes when the air choked in a dry heat. Her feet burned in the sun where they lay past shadows. The bright orb towered at its apex; hours had drained away by her slightest moment of relaxation. Zaki snarled at herself and scooted into a ball. She watched from the tight spot and tried to take time of the sea at the bottom of the conch's steep end.

Did the water come gently, or did it slam into the hard-shell wall? Would she be able to break past the tide-swell? Would she survive the plunge? How far could she swim on an empty stomach and no real sleep?

What if it wasn't deep at all, and she broke both her legs on the sandbar? Or struck headfirst?

"Stop," Zaki whispered.

She watched the water and waited.

And she thought of Ogbu.

It had been so long, but never long enough. Bright-faced, like her, Zaki counted the breakers as best she could from her high position. Beyond her wonderful face, how much did she remember? How much of it was Ogbu, and not Cleona, the dreaded pirate-aunt her father had failed to stop from influencing her?

How much of Zaki was the mother she never knew?

When the sun pitched past noon and the shade diminished, she started down the hot back of the massive conch, hoping to find her kin before the end. Whether any of them remained alive or dead, defiant in the face of ancient horrors, remained unknown. It didn't matter next to the real risk ahead: Where would Zaki go? How far could she swim? Would it matter, with the sea choked in Ulmos?

The ink-blue skin of the shell burned hot where the daylight gleamed on its glass-smooth surface before a roughness returned, secret layers of thin, sharp chitin. Tearing at her heels and back of her legs as she slid down on her bottom, the steepening decline forced her to scoot sideways, close to a ridge where she could rest in the sun.

Zaki braced her legs apart and let her entire weight rest on her bare back. Rough shell brushed against the long, thick scar slashed across the slabs of muscle, a grim reminder of what waited in the water.

"Zaki?"

She tried to flatten herself tight against where she rested, hoping she had moved far enough down the angle of the conch to obscure her location. Air ran in and out of her nose, her lips sealed in terror. Zaki waited for the call again, straining to hear over the gentle roar of the ocean, the wind, and the sky.

No one spoke.

Starting the descent again, the sloped ridge of the shell plunged, its swollen hull thinning to the next density for what seemed like hundreds of feet below her. Zaki rolled forward on her palms and knees and tried to crawl back up as far as she could before the threat of gravity pulled her weight down. When she reached the invisible point where the shell leveled off, she laid down on her bare chest and stomach. The sun baked her scarred back as she looked along the conch's horizon. Lacking a better choice, she set a lateral trajectory, continuing along the easier planes in hopes of finding a gentler exit to the water.

Luck provided when she discovered a shallower decline on the north-western side of the conch's shoulder. Able to scoot on her bottom along its length, Zaki came to its end before sliding down a sheer groove where she landed in the natural shade the conch's unnatural angles created. Exhausted, hungered beyond thought, she sank into the hard cradle and let nature sap her last strength.

A groaning, gurgling stomach chewed on acid and emptiness when she revived. Thirst drained her throat, her muscles, leaving her lifeless where she rested. After orienting her eyes to focus on the water, she found it now within reach if she mustered it. The white breakers, thin and foamy, flooded instead of crashed where the sea met her prison.

"Zaki? Zaki, where are you?"

She knew his voice.

Agwe yelled her name again. "Zaki? Zaki, call to me if you can hear!"

Zaki did not move a single muscle.

The voice grew nearer. "Zaki?"

It came from behind. Craning her head, the back of her skull scuffed on the rough shell while she spied everything south-east of her when she accounted for the sun. No one appeared.

"Zaki?"

No steps echoed. She expected her love to wear his war sandals, to hear the clack of the hobnails a blacksmith she had known since she was a child fixed to the soles and the rich, soft bindings. She had a pair of those same sandals made before they had been lost.

There should have been a clack. He would have known about the clack—they had joked about it so many times.

"Zaki?"

No clacks.

There would have been more than just him, if he had come at all. Agwe would have made himself known.

Zaki fought the urge to sit up, to rise from her hiding spot and truly see if he had come.

Night came, another uncounted day's end. Between the sun's sinking and the stars emergence, she crawled weakly from the hollow she hid within. The thirst made the scum-gray and green swirls against the shell swim in her eyes, folding within themselves before exploding back into their rough, scrapping patches. When her knees hurt too much, she willed herself to her feet, shuffling down the incline.

She could not see the water in the dark, but Zaki heard it in her ears, in her heart, calling her forward.

The roar of its crash, the whisper of its retreat, the endless churning of the Mirror she loved as much as she could love...

"Zaki."

She made the mistake of looking up, expecting to see him there.

An Ulmo stood before her. Beyond, just a short jog beyond, lay the water and its white froth.

The monster towered over her, blotting out the screaming stars as he raised a heavy claw to strike.

CHAPTER 5
THE LAST IN LINE

Radiance struck Zaki's eyes from where he leaned on the bench, and a sudden jolt of fear righted him before the first coarse word escaped the timekeeper. He bolted right up, the heavy handle of the hardwood oar sliding off his lap and the lap of the man next to him. The carved beam banged on their feet, drawing a pained yelp from the other man.

"Up, you dogs," screamed Nkuku from his drum stand near the stern. "Food's on the beach and Captain wants us ready in two hours! Off your benches!"

Before Zaki even moved, the man next to him, Kalu, swatted him hard on the top of his woolen head. A blinding pain drew tears to his eyes in an instant, and he crumpled into a knot on the bench.

"You fucking did it again, whelp," the older rower said. On the cusp of manhood, unlike his bench mate, Kalu seethed down at him. He pressed a hard finger into Zaki's shoulder. "Drop that oar one more time and I'll beat you to death with it, you motherless little shit."

"A reverent culture," mocked Clermiel from the ceiling where he crept in its eaves.

Zaki did not move from where he sat until the looming shadow stalked toward the wooden stair at *The Gamka's* stern. Uncovering his

260

arms from around his head, he did his best not to look at those who had watched the same scene replay more than once on the trip, too shamed to bear another day of their callous expressions. It mattered little, for in the dimness of the long, narrow hold of the trireme there was no place to avoid a glance of judgment, a sorry head shake of dismissal. Real or imagined, they followed Zaki up the aisle between the two staggered halves of the ship and up the back stair into the daylight.

Morning blinded Zaki as he fell into the line of rowers milling for the boat's starboard, where the gangplanks had been laid out on an empty beach. The heat, already high and roasting, coated him in a light sweat in his armpits and between his legs. Sticky in places he'd rather not be, he kept his hands pinned at his sides to show no discomfort like the other men.

The rowers, like they always did, followed each other toward the tree line. Beneath the breeze-touched fronds, they found the raiders already at their meal, seated behind the large fire they had built in a sandpit. The sweet-savory musk of roasted fish and drying rice cloyed the shady den, and beyond the steaming pot of stew, rested at the pit's hot edge, was the command crew of *The Gamka*. Her raiders spread out on the soft ground behind them.

At the small round table dragged off the boat sat Nkuku, the heavy-set timekeeper, his thick beaters laid alongside his equally stocky legs that he crossed at the ankles and propped on the table's surface. Wedged between him and Commander Mtumbwe, a broad-faced man who smiled often and laughed louder at larceny, Captain Ngala watched the other half of his crew wander from the beach to the camp they had made. His bowl of fish stew half-eaten, he peeked his head in search before his golden eyes fell on Zaki.

"Was his the worst gaze of all?" Clermiel goaded, standing behind the captain.

Not hesitating, Zaki broke ahead for the table, out of line with fellow rowers. Shorter than most of them by a full-head, and still in the body of a boy, he approached his father's table. The three men paused their small talk and paid some exhausted attention.

"Good morning, Zaki," Ngala offered in a strained voice.

Nkuku cleared his throat. He nudged his captain and nodded his scarred, bald head toward the son left under his supervision. "Strong back on him still, Ngala, and eager. Up before the rest of the men."

Mtumbwe made an affirming grunt.

Zaki noticed his father's gaze train off him and to the rowers passing by the table, studying each of them with a keen sincerity and offering a nod of acknowledgment. "I'm sure."

Alone before the table when the last rower fell into the shade after filing past the pot to have their doll of fish and rice, Zaki stood there, waiting for Ngala to say something.

"Go eat," the Captain said.

Nkuku sighed loudly as Zaki rounded the table, left alone to find his bowl. The timekeeper swept his feet off the table and leaned toward Ngala to say something Zaki tried his best to hear but worry of the rower's eyes and the grumble in his empty stomach left him with little will to stand there and try to piece it out. The ship's cook—whose name Zaki still hadn't learned since they left Stone Cove—scrapped some fried bits of rice and burnt corners of a whitefish into a wooden bowl. Slinking off into the circles of men sitting where the sun did not burn so harshly, Zaki plopped down beside one of the outer rings and chewed the gruel.

The unappetizing lump the stew left in his stomach swelled when the rowers and raiders broke rest to return to the ship. The raiders, as always, went into the hold first to pull the loot they had reaped from a Gypian settlement only a few days east and northeast of Stone Cove's hidden fortress. A quick, violent raid in the night had left the storages under the rower's benches packed tight with treasures taken from western imperial hands, which they laid out on the sands for all to see.

Every bauble, every bag, every good considered of worth was presented for inspection by the captain.

Zaki dreaded this moment. Even as a boy, he had heard from the older ones strong enough to work on the benches of what happened to those last in filling their raider's loot bag. Beatings, marooned on the first shore the ship beached, obscene humiliations before the crew—the expectations of punishment ran deep, hard, and mortal every time one of the older boys answered the dreaded question.

Worse, Ngala refused to answer if those stories were true or not.

And Zaki had carried his father's loot bag.

He remembered little of what had happened when they attacked the village. A few times he lost Ngala in the smoke where the corsair and his ceaseless sword struck down shadows as they ran to and fro. He remembered how the smoke stank, the look on the faces of the dead men, and the crazed calm he felt when the man who held him after his mother died marched beyond the bodies he had left in his wake. A silent order to steal whatever they had in their possession, wherever they fell, the boy tried to recall everything he had grabbed.

Nkuku ordered the rowers back to the trireme while Mtumbwe and his warriors picked the spoils. Setting them to work on the rigging, they spent hours on the busy tasks required of a ship in need of constant attention before it was turned on its side for the night to dry the wooden hull of the seawater weighing the soaked beams and planks.

When a crewman discovered a rip in *The Gamka's* dark green sail, the timekeeper summoned Zaki and two more of the youngest rowers.

"Not pissed yourselves yet?" he said, openly checking their loincloths with his nonchalant gaze.

Zaki tried not to squirm. He had heard rougher things said—many of them to him—but the timekeeper's rude nod at his genitals bothered him for more than his pride. He'd rather no one looked at them or that they weren't there at all.

"You two pin the cloth down while Zaki and I mend the tear," he told the two other boys.

They spread the sail across the middeck after the boards were swept. While their crewmates went around its perimeter, pulling it flat and weighing its borders with whatever weights they found, Zaki and Nkuku gently stepped on its oiled canvas in search of the rip. They found it near its center, a hole large enough a seagull could fly through.

"A seagull indeed," Nkuku said, his fleshy finger running the rough edges of the rent. Kneeling down, he pulled a ball of hemp twine and a long, hooked needle made of copper from a small leather bag on the side of his sword belt. "You can tell by the little bits near the hole. Poor little bastard probably ran into it last night and had a time getting out."

Not knowing what to say, Zaki nodded. "Yes, sir."

Lowering his girth down on both knees, he tore a length of cord from the ball. He threaded an end around the needle's twisted eye. "Hold the wound together while I mend it, Zaki."

"Yes, sir." Zaki squatted and pressed the cloth to the boards. The warmth of the sun-bleached wood wormed into his palms as he held the tear together.

Nkuku stabbed through both sides of the rent at the other end. "You know you don't have to be up first."

"Sir?"

He gave Zaki a knowing look. "This morning, boy. When you woke Kalu. Again."

Frozen on the spot, an ache flooded Zaki's arms. No longer fixed on the mending of the sail, he fretted for an excuse.

"You don't have to say anything," Nkuku continued. "I remember what it was like when I sat on the bench, and I was never the son of a captain. And that's not to mention Ngala." His fingers, for their size and thickness, moved with a knitter's dexterity as he slowly zipped the tear shut in fine knots. "It's scary, isn't it?"

Exposed, Zaki nodded a few times.

Reaching halfway, the timekeeper shook his head and grunted. "Tough shit, kid."

"What do you mean?" he asked, wishing his voice was not so high and light when he asked the question.

"Your daddy can't help you, Zaki," said Nkuku. He stopped sewing to meet the boy's stare. No malice resided in his honey-brown eyes. "You mess up with Kalu again and he will beat you to death. Nobody will stop him; nobody will talk him down. Not even your daddy. A corsair has to defend themselves if they are to have any worth, and they can't suffer fools."

"But I didn't mean—"

"Even if the fool is a captain's son." Nkuku picked the needle back up and returned to the sailcloth.

Unable, or unwilling to argue, Zaki fought to contain the trickle of fear pricking the central line of his back. Pain throbbed in both wrists as he put his full weight on the cloth. His hands slid apart.

"Keep it together, boy," Nkuku said. "Don't need these stitches stretched before the wind gets to them."

"What do I do, Mr. Nkuku?" he asked, trying to keep the panic out.

The timekeeper half-scoffed at the question as he healed the wound between them. "You really want to know?"

The horn sounded from the beach a few hours later, signaling the call to make camp. The rowers left the trireme at the edge of the sea, ready for departure after the final business had concluded.

To their relief, they found the entire horde of raiders in a merry mood, Captain Ngala most among them. The treasure hung heavy over the shoulders of the fighting men who split their shares into the sacks they carried. Both sides broke without order when the rowers all made it to the golden sands, three or four rowers to every raider. Meetings were held, goods reviewed, arguments had, or agreements remade, and the shares were dolled between the small teams.

By tradition, the captain only claimed one rower for himself, and of course, he had chosen Zaki.

Father and child fell behind the last grouping of men to walk off for their dealings, trailing behind Commander Mtumbwe and his rowers as they squabbled over trades.

"You did well," Ngala said, weathered eyes to the shade.

Zaki smiled, pleased beyond compare. There had been no finger-pointing, no shaming. The sand beneath his feet, cooled by the setting of the sun in a draining sky, eased him enough to let his mind wander.

"Zaki?"

He popped back to attention, raising his gaze to his father. "Yes, sir?"

"What are you thinking about?"

Zaki wondered how he might answer. Did he ask his father about Kalu, and the things had Nkuku told him to do? Did he hide it, and not shame himself anymore? Swallowing as they traipsed into the green-tinted shadows, he acknowledged his questions aloud. "How do you see through the smoke?"

Ngala's laughter met him, containing not a bit of harm. "I didn't stand in the fires."

An orange sun rose on a blushing sky, the stray and shredded clouds arrayed from gray to purple before the dusk seemed to banish them away, leaving the morning clean and clear.

Zaki had made sure to find his bench on the starboard side long before Kalu boarded. He had tried his best to sleep during the night, but the churning knot of worry in his stomach hardened into a stone. The club he had laid on his bench, hidden behind his right knee, felt heavier as it kept rolling to lean against the joint.

The rowers huddled their way into *The Gamka's* hold, no worse for wear after a night beside their fires and no drink to muddy their brains. Perhaps the lack of it made some of them more alert to what went on around them. Some noticed Zaki already at his post. Uncharacteristic for one who was often the last in line, the veterans took their benches with curious looks.

Zaki did not move to store his loot bag beneath the board he sat on, or ready the oar on his lap.

Out of the shuffling line of rowers emerged Kalu, stripped to his loincloth in preparation for the day's heat. The brawny man paused when he spotted Zaki crammed onto place, his heavy face dulled with a passing curiosity. Tossing his sack on the piece of floor before his side of the bench, he side-stepped and sat down, the wood creaking under his weight.

"Lift the oar up, boy," he said in his grumbling tone while he stowed his things.

Zaki stared ahead. "You lift it."

Some of the surrounding men stopped.

Kalu twisted toward him. "What did you say to me?"

Zaki tightened his grip on the club. "You pick it up, Kalu. I don't have to do it for you."

The older rower hacked his mean, cruel laugh. "Pick it up, boy."

Zaki remained still.

The man's shove came without warning, his palm striking the middle of Zaki's arm in bruising force. Startled and panicked, but ready, Zaki let himself be moved from his spot as he stood up in the small space. Screaming out in terror, he brought the club down on Kalu's brow. The flesh above the rower's eye, already scarred by an older mishap at sea, fountained in a gush of red. The darkened hold awoke.

Everyone faced the scene in unison by the time Zaki drew back and struck a second time at the wound.

Kalu fell off the bench and into the aisle, onto his knees, and clamored back up in a rage.

Pressed against the inside of *The Gamka's* starboard, Zaki raised his meager weapon at the ready.

"Bean him again," someone called out of the cacophony of roars, cheers, and laughter.

Kalu's hard, blistered hands reached in first as he dove at Zaki. He grabbed hold of his knee, but failing a firm grip, tried to probe his other hand for the boy's throat.

Zaki dodged Kalu's groping fingers that clawed at his cheeks and eyes, bashing the bully again and again and again. On the fifth blow, the same hand at his neck receded to cover the gory wound. Yanking his leg free, he threw one more stabbing strike at Kalu, shattering his teeth as he forced the wooden club's swollen end into his mouth.

Kalu collapsed backward.

Zaki flew off the bench, his weapon raised for a final blow.

"Enough," Nkuku said, rushing in with a grace and quickness belying his frame. He snatched Zaki's club in the meat of his paw, stopping the swing. At the sudden appearance of the timekeeper, every word and everyone halted.

Save for Zaki.

Fighting to keep the tears from his eyes, he fought the grip before the battle-rush left. One foot on the bench where he rowed, another on Kalu's chest, he glared down at the man in angry despair. Those same hands that had reached for him in harm now reached up, pleading for a mercy he had never given. Blood oozed from the ruined eye.

Whatever happened next, Kalu had lost his eye.

Zaki did not resist Nkuku when the timekeeper pulled the club away.

"Is everything right, Mr. Nkuku?"

Posted behind the drum like a summoned spirit of judgment, Ngala surveyed the scene with cold intensity.

Rowers stood at attention, their fists on their chest. They looked dead upon their captain, mouths shut and waiting.

Save for Nkuku. Pushing Zaki off Kalu, he juggled the club he had taken from the boy. He gave Ngala a warm smile after a few seconds. "Just a needed discussion among the rowers, sir. We might have one less on a bench today, though."

Ngala shook his head. His hard stare fell on Zaki. "Get the poor fellow up on deck. Mtumbwe's surgeon can check his eye."

"Might not have an eye, sir," Nkuku said.

A small chuckle spread amongst the men, dark and mean.

Zaki felt the world close in, his father's gaze everywhere no matter how much he tried to hide from it.

"Then whomever is on the bench will do the work of both. Savvy, Mr. Nkuku?" asked Ngala.

Something passed between the captain and the timekeeper, and Zaki noticed. An exhaustion in Nkuku's heavy-lidded eyes, the stoniness of Ngala's passive, unyielding glower he paid to him, the rowers...

His own child.

Zaki realized the two men did not agree on everything.

"Savvy, sir," replied the timekeeper, his smile now forced.

Ngala ascended the galley stair.

Every rower at attention eased their salutes and went back to stowing their goods for the journey to Stone Cove. Picked off the floor by a few men chosen by Nkuku, half-blind Kalu was carried away. The trail of red leaking from his face was the last thing Zaki remembered about the man.

Nobody paid him any more attention, yet neither did they look away. A different character exuded throughout the cramped, tight space. The sinking in his stomach, a pang not made by hunger, settled with the hard realization that Zaki felt more like them.

And there, after what he had done to one of their own, Zaki did not feel like anything.

Certain to meet orders, he took the bench alone when the raiders pushed the trireme back into the Mirror Sea. Left alone with the oar, all Zaki could do was hold on for dear life while its long, hard length wrestled like a shark hooked on the line. Torn from his grasp many times, those around him abandoned him again to long, annoyed glances, offering no support as he threw himself into the beat Nkuku made from his drum stand. Desperate to stay there, to stay worthy, Zaki fought all the way home.

"Did you learn anything worthy of you? Of them?" Clermiel asked after every stroke Zaki struggled to make as the miles, the darkness, and the child's emptiness echoed. "Were you ever really worth anything at all?"

CHAPTER 6

DEMONSTRATION

L ight seeped past her shut eyes first, waking her from the stagnant dream. Face down on the pulsing, breathing floor that smelled of brine and uncooked cruster-fish, the buzz in her fingers and toes woke her further as she moved from where she lay.

"You may arise when ready," called Clermiel in his high, warbling tone.

Palms first, Zaki got her knees under her, the numbness working out of her back as she rested there. The thirst she had remembered, if the day happened at all, was replaced by the fullness of a good meal. The floor glowed in her face, a blue light beyond beating walls of blood and tissue. Invigorated by a will beyond hers, Zaki stood slowly, hands at her sides.

The room was the same one she had found when she escaped—a long galley sitting high up in the conch's leaning orientation, near the spiraling horn serving at its bow. The sun shone brightly beyond the empty window-like openings. The breeze roared past, smelling of the salt and sweet of the waters. The entire chamber twitched, the pinkish walls and ceiling part of the larger, weird muscle of whatever beast the devil employed to inhabit this shell. Rhythmic spasms, timed with the breathing of the floor, tied her stomach in a knot.

"You will get used to it if you do not focus on the movement. Fall in with the measure of the sea."

"Where are you?" Zaki asked, alone in the galley.

"Was I there, on the decks of *The Gamka* and *The Ube*? Was I there when my devoted found you?" The words reflected dispassion. "Where am I, beyond everywhere you see, everywhere you hear?"

Zaki threw her elbow back in a wheeling strike, hoping villains remained true to the clichés. The point of her sinewy crook sliced the air.

"Everywhere you touch, you see," whispered Clermiel in her ears, heavy with a cruel mirth. "I am there."

Heaving in anger, Zaki pressed her mouth into a tight line and relaxed. "Was it you calling me outside?"

"Does it matter?" The devil gurgled an inhuman noise that translated as laughter. "Do you need the hope he is still alive? That he is actually coming? That he cares? That anyone cares?"

Zaki smirked where she stood, despite her terror. "You don't know my father."

"I've seen enough to know you. To know him. The ones you love." Clermiel's voice thinned. "If it can be said of mortals. Yours is a rutting lot."

"Bitter about being put down by us...what did you call us?" She dared some mockery of her own. "Apes?"

"You think your kind put me down?"

"Agwe told me of you devils. We sent many in search of everything we could find out about you." Fear ripped away by defiance, Zaki stood tall. "Azinza told us even more."

"I'm sure she did."

The wind blustered past the windows, roaring like the waters far out of sight. The room twitched in a quiet, even rhythm while the fibers and sinew glistened like melted rubies and glossy oil.

Zaki waited, ready for the devil's rebuttal.

None came.

A weird squishing and pulling sound, like a sexual noise ground together in dry, rough stone, warped the wall behind her. A sudden orifice opened in a gaping yawn. Out of the darkness emerged the hulking, sharp shape of an Ulmo. His clicking mandibles perfectly still as the black, beady eyes leveled upon Zaki, he stood at complete attention.

"Let me guess what she said," Clermiel said from behind the monster, somewhere in the gyre beyond the beast. His glowing black eyes, pinprick stars upon an ether, shone in the deep fog. "We, powerful devils sent by the Ashed One, tamed the seas and built the greatest empires ever seen upon the face of the Dovhain's brilliant blue jewel. She probably told you we built it on the backs of slaves."

"Nations of them. And the things done to them were worse than anything the Latians or the Gypians ever did to my father's parents," said Zaki, leaning to the right so she could look past the Ulmo. She stared back at those two points of abyss, unflinching despite the cold in her chest. "And those devils still died on the sword."

"Then why am I still here after all those swords?" he asked from the darkness.

She blinked at the question.

The Ulmo disappeared as her lids closed, and when they opened again, Agwe stood before her. Her breath caught, a slip of her facade. From the top of his shaven head to the silver-gold embroidery on one of the many colorful robes he wore well on his swimmer's frame, none of his finery or appearance equaled the silver scales pierced and scared into the flesh of his face. The seahorse design brightened the copper in his eyes. Those full but firm lips made her hunger for the taste of his salt.

The devil's laugh caught her before she caught herself.

"Did he tell you everything?" Clermiel questioned from his veil of shadows. "Or did he lie to you too?"

Her focus broken, Zaki seethed through her wide nose, at war with the heaving in her chest.

"Do you really think apes with copper swords stopped us? Do you really think it would have been so simple?"

Agwe's apparition started forward from the spasming hole, his gait smooth on the rippling floor.

"None of your kind was ever given anything without the gods. It was the gods who made you, shells of worthless dust, spirited by whims and natures too savage for such simple vessels. You are tools, as you were always meant to be."

The sorcerer's apparition advanced on Zaki. Unsure of what she saw, she backed away as he closed in, her hands up in a defensive posture. Agwe took one staggered step toward her and swung his arm in a solid backhand to her forearms.

"We are more than some simpering gods."

A blast of bone-numbing pain lost itself in the horrid rush of air against her back as if she had become weightless. Her body slammed against one of the nearby walls; the impact stole the air in her lungs. Black and white lights flashed. The brief daze ended in time for Zaki to see the floor race up to meet her. The crash ended in a second round of lights.

"You won one temple, barely survived its twisted shade, and only with the help of a lying, scheming whore did any of you make it back to the miserable rock you squabble over."

Clermiel's gurgling tone edged with a droning whine in Zaki's ears. Her head aching in endless stabbing pain, she curled herself in a ball, screaming in sheer agony.

"You are nothing." The devil's voice pierced the horrid ringing. "You were born nothing, made to do nothing of great import and die as you are. The only reason you and your brood are confused is because of what you were told."

Gripping her head between her hands, Zaki willed herself up, rising on her knees so she could at least see where Agwe was. Light feathered at the edge of her vision as she scanned the room through squinted eyes, lost in the pulsing pink flesh and the bellowing sea wind outside. A sudden trickle down her face, the smell of iron and blood flecking into her nose, made her snort at the wrong time. Coughing, she tried to steady herself. She curled up, sucking the salt air into her gaping mouth.

She opened her aching eyes to see Agwe walking toward her.

"He is not nothing," said Clermiel. "He is not born of nothing. What he does is of great import to me, if I'm allowed to consider it to the fullest. He, unlike you, will simply not die."

Zaki whimpered as she focused on the light shimmering off her lover's scaled face. The whine somehow resided in her eyes, backed by the dull grinding intensifying with every step he took.

"He is not confused at all of this place. He knows where to be when he wants."

Agwe stopped a few feet from her. His starlight gaze fixed upon her coldly, faraway and alien.

Mouth quivering, Zaki looked up at him, pleading against his stone expression. "Agwe..."

"Who is he? Where did he come from?" Clermiel asked, more to himself than her. "Why would a god bother with an abomination like you?"

"What?" Zaki asked the apparition.

Agwe raised his hand back and belted her across the mouth. Amazed none of her teeth knocked loose, Zaki collapsed on her side in a heap to sob before survival overrode emotion. She kicked away. Wet blood congealed in the back of her throat, making her wheeze every time she moved.

"What's his name?"

"Who is he?"

"Tell me."

"Tell me."

"Tell me."

"Tell me."

She banged the back of her head against the curve of a wall, its twitching muscle iron hard. The jolt caused her to go limp.

"Tell me," Clermiel whispered, right in front of her face.

Zaki opened her eyes so she could sneer at the devil, but she found only black and white, a constant screech-whine. Agwe marched upon her. His footsteps boomed. "I don't know who he is," she whispered through swollen, busted lips. She considered the truth of it, of everything the devil put in her head, the blood from Kalu's eye, the last smile of her mother...

She knew nothing. She knew nothing about the man she loved, or who her mother was, or who she was anymore. Did it matter? Had all the boats outside sank to the ocean's floor, lost to the goddess' everlasting night?

Was anyone coming for her?

"Yes..." Clermiel ran through her thoughts like a spiny eel, slithering from under the dark stones. "This sorcerer who is no mere mutterer. Out for themselves, justified by whatever little shallow reason they have for doing the things they do. He is no better than you and would tempt you to believe you are equal to him for the sake of your mortals. He lies."

The shape of her lover stood over Zaki, cut from the ambient sunlight seeping into the conch's galley. A glistening idol of ebony, shell, and silk, his silver eyes paid her no emotion.

"Tell me who he is."

"I don't know," Zaki said. She tried to shrink into the wall, bury herself in the viscera of her hell. Perhaps it was a trick of the pain, or a lapse from her senses, but she thought the devil sighed.

The apparition of Agwe shot his foot out, nailing her square in the groin. Her breath stolen, the pain bent her body in half, a cascade of numbness she thought would never, ever end.

Until his next kick found her chest.

The air driven out of her again, Zaki hoped death had stopped her heart until a small wheeze escaped her throat. Barely able to draw the scantest breath, she somehow wrenched herself up in time to see Agwe rear back for his last blow. The Ulmo, his true form revealed, stood in the apparition's place. He raised his claw high once more.

She hid her smile as the creature smashed her consciousness apart.

CHAPTER 7
DIFFERENCES OF INTERPRETATION

W hat awoke her first she did not know, but the pleasant release of nothingness made Zaki sit up.

The floor she had fallen unconscious upon thrummed at its slow, steady pace, like a gentle heartbeat coaxed by restful sleep. Morning lit the conch's galley ports. Overlooking the shining azure sea, a cool western wind carried the scent of charcoal.

"Do dragons still roost in this world?"

Jolted to her feet by the sudden intrusion of the devil's voice, Zaki staked herself on the spot in a battle stance. Rested, somehow healed, she refused to be tricked again so simply like the last time. She held her right hand low at her side, as if she would find a knife there.

"Would this help?"

The solid feel of a hilt in her hand, the weight of the broad iron dirk surprised her to the point she almost yelped. Zaki tossed the blade down by her feet instantly.

"I'd rather die clawing and kicking," she shouted.

"Why? Why continue to enslave yourself to those who do not value you at all?"

"You know nothing."

"How so?" asked a gentle voice behind her.

Zaki turned to find she no longer stood alone in the galley.

A tall, slender man dressed in the brightest coat of gold coins over a robe made of the whitest silk she had ever seen stood at one of the windows. His long silken hair hung down to his square shoulders, the black tresses strung with fine lapis and gold beads. The bangles, all of brass and gold, gathered in thick layers as if to form guards for his strong, wiry arms.

He had the most handsome face, so much so Zaki knew immediately it could not be real. Those eyes were too cruel, the smile on his firm yet supple lips too smirking to be sincere. The sword hanging from a series of carefully tanned and inscribed belts around his waist had an evil air to it, its black handle and red garnet pommel mismatched with the rest of the illusion, and yet in some ways was the most honest part.

"You can't fool me a second time," said Zaki.

Clermiel's new husk grinned. "I would not dare at this juncture," he said, this time without a drowning man's gurgle. He paced toward her on his sandaled feet, the mechanics of his movement impossibly smooth from the hips down. "It would be dishonorable."

"What does a devil care for honor?"

"For mine and my own alone, as every creature does," he rebutted as he stopped before her and turned toward the galley's views, his nebula eyes seeking the rising sun outside. The gold disk cast the sky red, revealing all the wisps of cloud still hidden on the horizon. Deep iridescence faded to orange and yellow before dissipating into the blue of the sky.

Clermiel watched the sun with fascination for a time, saying nothing or even acknowledging Zaki's presence. The ligaments and tissue of the room gleamed a velvet luster.

"You've not tried to kill me," said Clermiel.

"I've not the means," said Zaki, gaze set toward daybreak, so she avoided him. "Not yet."

"Why?"

"Why what?"

"Why fight?" The devil turned her way, hair falling perfectly along an armored shoulder. He folded his strong, smooth hands on his lap, offering no sign of obvious threat. "I destroyed your fleet."

Her vile host let the point hang between them as the sun climbed.

"You've said that before," said Zaki. "You've said many things."

"Look at me, Zaki."

"No."

"I destroyed your fleet," he said, unceasing. "Your father is dead, your brother food for the sharks. Every single person you know, loved, respected, and called to you is gone. I have won. Now, look at me."

"If you had won, then you wouldn't need me alive," she said, daring a laugh. Not contented by quiet, she dared some more. "You wouldn't have spent time beating me up, healing me, beating me up again, and healing me some more just to do it. I'm an ape, an insect, so very, very far beneath you..."

The devil said nothing.

"Stop it," said Zaki. "You're staring."

And he laughed aloud. "Well, I guess you are right," he admitted. "None of them are dead. Not yet, anyway."

A breath seized in Zaki's chest. "That might be a lie too."

"Entirely possible."

Infuriated by his glamour, Zaki strode forward toward the bay-like openings. At the threshold where the seam of gristle adhered flesh to the conch's massive shell, she halted and worked to hide her seething.

"No fight you could give me would be worthwhile," said Clermiel, answering an unasked question. "It'd be rather boring."

Zaki roared around, charging the devil.

Skidding to a halt immediately, she almost collided with a long, upright oval of water. Her feet somehow found purchase on the gross ground, and she teetered back a few steps on her tall frame. Hands flat in front of her to defend against whatever came at her, the transfixing play of water and silver before her narrowed all attention. The oblong length swirled, mingling flecks of gold and white. Its edges, rounded yet sharply defined by a constant flow, held its borders together by the same ineffable forces. Its surface firmed, mercury and molten smoothing into a shining, shimmering mirror.

"Go to it," the devil beckoned.

Zaki held her ground. A quick smile broke across her strong features. "You gave me a knife, how about a..."

A rock appeared in her hand. She squeezed its solidity, trying to break it. The veins rose on her arms before her knuckles ached too much.

"Walk up and destroy it," said Clermiel, his tone placid. His comely form stepped from behind the mirror, his moon-bright gaze catching hers like a lover dropping one final hint in hopes the other might follow. He passed on the other side a breath later, his coat of gold coins catching the sunlight anew like fresh fire. "Do you need a sword? A hammer?"

Not allowing him more mockery, Zaki came forward with the rock cocked back in her hand. The mirror, freed of gravity, drifted toward her to close the distance.

She threw her full weight behind the rock. It splashed through the watery sheet that rippled a few gentle rings before returning to its original perfection.

Unable to stop its advance, she started to back away when she caught her reflection in the mirror.

The goddess she beheld in its reflection startled her. Tall, with a firm set of shoulders, the muscles of her broad hips and full thighs where rounded, not compact and defined by a soldier's work. She went dressed in a sparkling mail of silver accentuating a full, feminine form, and arrayed along her arms were worked vambraces of wrought iron and platinum textured into half-clamshells.

Her lips, her eyes, her cheeks, the way she stood, the confidence— Zaki saw everything she wished she was and more.

In one hand, she held a sword of golden light, hilted by a black handle matched to the one protruding from Clermiel's own sash, and in the other, a shield bore the glyph of an azure conch.

She saw the queen who reigned in her deepest dreams, cast in the light of a champion.

"I will give you this," he said, invisible compared to the glowing manifestation he presented. The points of his needle-like teeth edged his lips every time he spoke. A shadow across his face, one that should not have been there, drained the morning light.

"What?" she asked, too transfixed to care.

"I'll make you the person you wish to be—that you've always wanted to be. I can make her real. I can make you her."

Beyond the cruelty in Clermiel's voice, she heard truth. The woman before her, the person she yearned to be seen as...

She noticed the azure conch on the heater her reflection carried.

"And what would you get?" she whispered.

The devil seized the opening by the mirror's side. "Look at me, Zaki."

She tore her eyes away from her mirrored self.

His eyes burned a bluish-purple color. The twisting walls of tissue past beyond his outline in swirled and knotted. "I would simply get the fruits of your desires. I would make you a queen, a goddess, and upon the world we would ride towering waves of glory not seen since the days when this planet still cooled. There would be no Latia. No Latians," he said, almost in a sing-song. "The world would kneel at your feet."

Beyond the murkiness of her defined, perfected vision, the world beyond Zaki's future revealed itself.

The Mirror Sea laid out before her: every league and great coast was captured in a broad, shimmering flank overlooking every coastal city, town, village, and even the smallest shanties where crippled old fishermen wasted their dying days. Every single life across the world, such numbers her head swam at their lights, were revealed at their grandest and most depraved. She saw from the glittering heights of Laconia—the high capital of war-bound Latia—to the bronzed towers in Gypus where kings and priests sacrificed thralls to chthonic gods to bring down Latia. Wars of arms and magic that raged across Juut's western plains for centuries fell silent. Like she rode upon some eagle's back to be lifted across the earth, the scene ripped across the whole of the continent and beyond, to lands, people, and places she had never seen before, yet yearned to know and reach.

And at the head of the journey, the harbinger of a great fleet, was *The Ulmo.*

"All shall come to be," Clermiel said.

Adhered to the vision, Zaki let those words infuse her mind, fueling hopes she had kept from so many.

Save her dearest.

Those thoughts were not the kind found in the devil's illusion.

"At what cost?" she willed herself to say aloud.

The illusion beyond her manifest destiny hazed, as if someone had taken a brush and coated the mirror in varnish, until only her image remained visible, the startling transformation from who she had always been to the radiant divinity faded. The beauty, the wealth of silver on her limbs, an entire future of safety and certainty, disappeared until only she remained as she was.

The devil peeked from behind the mirror. "You wouldn't be alive to know, Zaki."

"So, you, the master. Me, the slave."

"As it was always meant to be."

"I'll cut out your heart first."

Those burning points of purple turned the walls a sickly pink, disturbing the hidden dust in the air until it swirled like kicked-up milkweed. Clermiel emerged from his translucent shield, stood up to his full height. Almost two heads taller than Zaki, he glowered down at her.

"I will only give you a few more chances."

She did not shrink. "Might as well give me none."

He straightened and shook out his jeweled mane as if none of it had mattered. "As you will."

White light flared behind the devil's armored shoulder. Blinded by the strobing effect, Zaki wheeled back on her feet, her equilibrium stolen. In the depths, the flashing shapes took form. Large and nebulous, they sharpened into the hulking outlines of three Ulmos.

She never saw the blows of the second beating.

CHAPTER 8
ONE OF THE BOYS

Z aki smiled like a madman, euphoric as he glared at the flaming shore ahead.

The raiders flanked his sides and stood behind him in an arrow-shaped wedge. They pounded the bottoms of their hide shields into *The Gamka's* planks, urging the rowers to stir the black sea harder beneath them. They sang salt songs, old battle hymns and charms they had learned from their first day on a boat in the moment that could be their very last. Entranced by the beat, Zaki pressed his helmed forehead against the trireme's rail and let her hum throughout his entire body, every rough bump over the chop a blessing from the goddess herself.

"Archers on the beach," one of the lookouts near the starboard called.

He raised his head, high enough to where he could see under the edge of his Gypian helm, a prize claimed years ago on his first raid and had to grow into. Zaki spied the bonfires laid out upon the sands. Lines of men buzzed about the points of light, small and indistinct. Flames roared brightly at their backs, casting smoke to obscure whatever lay past.

Zaki did not have to see the full extent of their numbers to know they had more soldiers than *The Gamka* did.

His raiders had to make it past those flames.

No matter what.

He rose from his supine position, a short iron spear in one hand and his shield in the other. "Screen!"

The raiders rose in perfect unison, set on one knee as they slid into a new shape, layering their shields atop the other. The arrow point swelled into a hammerhead, the fighting men and women on the deck making a narrow spine toward the back, minimizing their exposure.

Dozens of shafts fell from the smoking skies. An iron point burst through the stretched cowhide Zaki carried but was caught by the tanned leather. More struck the other side of the wall the raiders crowded behind, the sweat-smoke smell of his comrades heavy with the heat of their breaths.

The arrow fall died a second later as the trireme charged the currents.

"My lions! My lions!" Zaki used what time he had before the next volley. "Clear the beach for the rowers! Do not let a single one of those worthless bastards live!"

The raiders shouted their adoration, banging the boards beneath them with the butts of their spear shafts.

"You! You! With me, and I shall be with you!" Zaki screamed as the next wave of arrowheads rained on the deck. "My lions!"

"Hah," Clermiel said, standing before the corsair's defense. "Master and slaves, indeed."

The cheers of the maddened warriors inflamed Zaki. A field of feathered flowers sprouted, bright and upright in the waxing dark, and spread between them and the bow. The second volley died, and before he could push his shield aside to look, someone appeared at his side armed only with a club.

Then his father's voice boomed throughout the night, clear and distinct above the sloshing current ripping at *The Gamka's* flanks. "To Port! Archer volley to far starboard and astern!"

"Go," Zaki roared on the order, altering strategy at his father's command.

The trireme suddenly cut hard to the left, the force of the sea and its inertia causing it to bank. All possessing worthy sea legs, the raiders broke from their shield wall and took up their bows. In a chorus of twanging bowstrings, each of the fighters lifted their aim skyward and blindly loosed.

Zaki, hands moving as they had tens of thousands of times before, focused on making sure every shaft flew behind his shoulder, not over it, where the arrow would catch on the night winds and fall lifelessly into the surf. He imagined each one finding its home in a stupid man's heart, or his skull, or whatever flesh the arrow bit.

"Starboard for the beach," Ngala shouted.

"Yes, Captain," Zaki shouted back. "To the rail, my lions! Take the sands and dig!"

The few shovels tied to the rails were freed, taken by raiders who leapt over the sides with their spears and sword in one hand, shield, bow, and whatever arrows they had left in the other. Without waiting, they dropped into the shallowing sea below.

"Commander Zaki."

His weapons in his hands, Zaki spun about to find Captain Ngala standing with him at middeck, near starboard. Both clad in light vests of mail and lamellar, the ridge of his father's Latian helm, more of a harder wedge at the front than the elegant Gypian design his son wore, caught a scant bit of the stars in the sky.

"Oar locked?" Zaki asked.

The captain nodded, withdrawn. "I, Mtumbwe, and Nkuku will bring the rowers ashore," he said, grumbling lower than the tides. "They'll take cover in the woods. Make your picket in the sand. They'll come in on the enemy's flank. We'll push them into the sea from there and kill them."

Delivered lightly as if they were dinner plans, Zaki accepted it equally. "Make sure you don't lose Tausi," he said before he vaulted over the ship's rail. He slipped into the goddess' warm, churning embrace. Lost, he sank in the last fleeting comfort he'd feel before work tore it away.

Zaki kicked with the tide, his shield tight against his arm to keep it from dragging against the current. He broke the surface and gaped for one solid breath before he swam ahead, salt-stung eyes already finding where the white breakers crashed. Letting the up and down pull of the ocean's rhythm set his approach, he emerged from the waters with all his armaments still with him.

The Gamka bore upon the land, her rostrum rutting the wet sands as it beached. His fellow raiders' dark bodies emerged from the water and closed on Zaki while others appeared farther down the shore.

His order came quick as they converged. "I want a dry trench that dies in the water. Bow men keep a weather-eye for torches. Not one spark makes it past us."

Those with shovels went to work, digging as far and as deep as the sand allowed. The other raiders stabbed the pointed frames of their shields into the sand, set their arrows, and crouched into a line stretching from surf to the nearest tree line, where the shrub forest started. They toiled silently in the dark, eyes always trained to the far-off points of flame. The smoke of the enemy bonfires, now small points miles to the southeast, blossomed large columns of smoke drifting landward beneath an empty heaven. The distant smell of their cinders caught in Zaki's nose as he watched them burn.

The first red torches came in ones and twos, then three or four, and then finally it halted at a total of a dozen.

Zaki harrumphed at the enemy's confidence. He plucked the arrow from where it stood by his feet and set it on the string. The first of eight shafts he had left, he stood tall, measuring the winds against his body. He waited on the first foreign voice to reach his ears before lifting his weapon.

The torches drifted closer, and beneath their ruddy lights, so did the faces of the men who carried them.

Zaki took aim, the arms of his bow creaking as the fletching brushed his ear. He spied the first face, fully formed.

Out went his breath, away went the arrow.

The torch dropped in the sand, flowering the enemy formation into chaos. Those carrying torches ran toward the downed point of red light caught in the dry sand, crowding together.

More corsair arrows flew.

Two more torches were snuffed in the earth as the screeches and cries of wounded men echoed across the crashing waves.

How many died, Zaki could not tell from his place in the gloom, but the sudden advance slowed to jerking halts. Conserving his shots, he left himself two more arrows until his father called on the horn.

A second blast, farther to the corsair's line in the wood, echoed a ghostly note, a signal the rowers had departed *The Gamka*.

Zaki fired one arrow high for one of the torches still marching forward and the second straight ahead, hoping to slow the enemy's forward guard. He retreated until he spotted the spear blade one of his men flashed against the oncoming torchlights. Discarding his bow, he shook the shaft of his short spear, finding its balance as he hopped the three-foot deep trench the raiders had dug in the sand.

"Sing," he said at normal volume to the two men beside him.

Someone struck up a song:

"Doom to thee,
Doom to thee,
Dance on my dusty line!
Doom to thee,
Doom to thee,
Hang the dead up high!"

Simple but effective, corsair men and women howled like hyenas in laughter. Doom rang along the beaches, in the fall of the waves, and rode in the roiling canopies of the forest beyond where the wind struck hard.

The torches illuminated hundreds of armed men marching head-long toward them.

The rower's droning horns sounded in the thickets, and an unexpected cry went up from the defenders. Torches fell to the sand.

Raiders still holding a few arrows fired them off into the scattering mass.

A third blast of the rower's horn called the charge; from the dark woods rose a line of corsairs whipping slings above their heads. Bullets rained on the village men, who fell injured or dead from errant shots. At the rower's head charged the one raider that had been left behind, sprinting yards ahead of the closest rower behind him, a small boy who struggled to keep up.

"The great hero," Clermiel cawed, cackling aloud.

"Bastard!" Zaki rose past the trench's ledge in a bound, focus fixed on his younger brother Tausi. "Red sands, my lions!"

Those raiders, left between Zaki's order and their captain, fell in behind without hesitance. No masks were needed to betray the evil on their faces—they squeezed it into the handles of their weapons. Their advance, coming first as a measured, straight walk, quickly turned into a death race. Corsairs screamed the names of their old gods, to Agwe the Sailor, Oya of the Seas, the stars where their greatest ancestors lived, and the spirits beneath their feet.

Faster than the rest, Zaki lowered his shoulder and set his spear when the first man carrying a sword appeared. His tanned olive skin starkly different from Zaki's umber hue, he started too late to stop the spear's cruel point from destroying his abdomen.

Blades clashed. Edges blunted on shields and bone.

Too surprised to recover, the town's defenders fell almost in an instant. Killing every fool who challenged him, Zaki slowing waded forward, leading the way while his spear struck like a sand-snake. Dyed in fresh blood each time he pulled it back, he did not shout in the face of those he had slain, nor did any of the raiders closing on their perimeter. Mauled by the rowers to their right, slaughtered by the raiders before them, the fighters of another Gypian settlement wilted beneath the push and stumbled into the ocean's grinding surf. When their numbers hollowed, the entire body of corsairs swung around and smashed the bodies against the oncoming waves, laying the last man down beneath the moonless sky.

The corsairs divided again, and a portion of the rowers returned to *The Gamka* while those paired to raiders gathered, marching on the bonfires and the settlement beyond. Zaki searched among those young souls who manned the benches as they mixed with the fighters until he found Ngala and a skinny, scrawny boy heaving the last of his guts into the sand.

"Is he alright?" Zaki asked, incredulous.

"Aye," said Ngala with a proud, fearless smirk. Blood glistened across his face and chest, none of it his own. "Boy made his first kill."

"Oh," said Zaki, forcing a grin—one to trick his father and to ease his little brother. "Get him good, Tausi?"

"Get on, you two," Ngala said, catching eyes with someone.

Bosun Mtumbwe emerged from the raiders, decked in his old armor, sword, and a loot bag. A strong, scarred man, he nodded to all three as he joined their circle. "He all right?" he said, giving one more nod to Tausi.

"He's fine," said Zaki, worried now at how many eyes might look his brother's way. "I got him."

"Good," said Ngala. He shouldered forward, his sword low. "Let's put them to pace, Mtumbwe."

The bosun chuckled and followed his captain.

Left alone, Tausi switched his shield to his main hand and used the freed left to rub his brother's back. "Take your time."

Tausi swallowed bile and coughed a few more times before he straightened, his heavy club hanging from the strap on his wrist. Tears flowed from his wide, scared eyes.

Zaki put his arm around his brother and towed him down the beach, toward the raid. "C'mon. I know. I know."

"I didn't even feel the hit...and then he was just..."

"I know, I know Tausi. You did what you had to do. We all had to."

Dragging Tausi along, Zaki let him set their pace, arriving last to the bonfires after the corsairs had cut the throats of the sentries. Past the hazing cinders, a path appeared in the trees, dividing the ancient palms and blooming fruit trees lining the road to a ridge. At the apex of the rise, overlooking a wide valley set between two verdant slopes, they took in the darkened village below. People ran to and fro in the dark, gathering what things they could as quickly as possible. The oldest men, left behind while their sons and grandsons had gone to fight, made a meager line to defend themselves.

Ensconced in shadow, the corsairs watched, pleased by the terror on the old men's faces.

Zaki and Tausi found their father at the front of the war band, hands held aloft in a quiet signal. Looking over his shoulder to nod to Zaki, he smiled. Both hands waved forward.

"Have at them, my lions."

"Yes," cried Clermiel, his mirth high on the wind. "Have at them, you masterful apes!"

An hour before dawn, Zaki and Ngala sat before a small fire in the alley between two clay houses, the light off the twigs and dry leaves white-red against the bleeding, cindered skies. No words exchanged between captain and commander, father and son had even less to say while the meager smoke from their light joined the cloud that blanketed the village. Roofs bloomed smoke off the molten thatch, creating the columns of a corsair's temple to murder, lust, and larceny. The screams, which had lessened with the coming daylight, pierced the roar of the devouring flames alongside haughty laughs. Salt songs, varied and broken by bloodthirst, chorused in the places where the dead lay.

Men, women, and children.

Zaki balanced his bloody sword between his hands, the point dancing in the dirt while he rolled the blade's stained flats across his rough palms. The way the vicious fluid danced against fire's horrid leaping, the ease at which the tip pierced the dirt as it had flesh and bone...

Men, women, and children.

He snatched the hilt in his left hand, pressing down on the end of his sword. Tausi had gone out again hours before, more confident after both he and Ngala—more Ngala—prodded him to leave, to go claim his own spoils from the rich feast laid before them. The image of his brother's tears after he heaved on the beach and the way the light played on his soiled weapon caught Zaki. He craved a moment to feel.

But not before his father.

He checked on the man sitting to his right.

Ngala watched their little fire, lost somewhere in his thoughts.

Zaki cleared his throat. "Captain."

"We're not in front of men," Ngala replied in his usual gruff manner.

Zaki blinked twice before he tried again. "Father, I think we need to keep Tausi home on the next raid. Or put him on a different boat."

"He's on our boat. Black Lizard put him on our boat." Ngala shifted his gaze toward Zaki, a predator staring at his lesser. "Unless you want him on your boat."

"I'm not here to talk about that again," said Zaki. "You can ask one of your captains to take him. One of the younger ones."

"No. He's either here or he's with you. Which do you want, Zaki?"

"Father."

"Zaki."

They glared at each other, faces half-sheathed in dawn. The alley seemed to darken, matching the ichor between the two proud adventurers.

"He's too wrapped up in trying to be like us," Zaki said, firmly, slowly, making sure every word was heard. "He can't do it. I couldn't."

"Then you take care of it," Ngala said, not breaking the ire in his eyes. "You're old enough now, and he's old enough to be on a boat. I can't help he's the captain's son, no more than I could with you. But I either need you both on *The Gamka*, with me, or on the ship next to mine. You best remember."

"Remember what?" Zaki said, snapping back.

His father's voice did not waver. "You're captain's sons. There are no boats for you other than those you build or steal for yourself. Or the ones I give you."

"Says the man gifted—"

Someone coughed behind them.

Zaki bolted up first while Ngala remained where he sat, lingering on the fire.

Nkuku, fleshy with age as his jowls deepened like the lines of his face, stood in the mouth of the alley created by the two emptied homes. A bloody club in one hand, his girth took up most of the space, leaving Tausi with scant room beside the timekeeper. Zaki froze at his little brother's searching, seeking eyes. The tears on his cheeks had long dried, and the mask of anxiety had faded into something harder, harsher, than Zaki would have liked.

"You two need a minute or can we get this done?" Nkuku said, bouncing on his bare feet. Agitation creased his freckled forehead. "We got all them lined up."

"Perfect," said Ngala, popping to his feet. Leaving behind the fire to wither and die, he led them from the alley into the hot streets. They passed scores of dead lying in their blood, the fire having consumed those too damned to escape the immolated homes quicker than the rest. Blackened char soaked the stale air.

Zaki swallowed through the stench, trying to catch up so he was the extra body between Ngala and Tausi, wedging himself between Nkuku and his father. The timekeeper made the room, lifting one of his heavy arms to drape across the youngest boy's shoulder at the far end of their line.

"Good run, today," Nkuku commented to Tausi as they neared the center of town. "Going to have to run the keel after that turn."

"I didn't give the order," Zaki whispered back.

"I did," said Ngala.

"And a fine order it was, sir," said Nkuku, striking a jovial tone. He jostled Tausi in his arm. "Had real fun clinging to our benches, huh boy?"

Tausi chuckled. "We almost went all the way sideways."

"That we did," said Nkuku, laughing at the response.

Zaki rolled out the tension in his neck and shoulders. Falling into an easier pace, he entered the town's square first where the corsairs had herded their captives. The children, forced into a corner of the limestone square, shivered under the gazes of their devils while their mothers, sisters, and friends were lined up like cattle before the stone fountains. Leading the flesh market, Mtumbwe watched over the proceedings with a dark glamour, saying nothing while female raiders beat the defiant women into place. Rowers picked over the loot they had gathered, heaped in a great pile.

Greed drew Zaki's eyes to the loot.

Boxes of spices in their many hues shone beside twinkling pieces of iron and silver wrought into wondrous shapes and fine tools. There were coins atop old Gypian armors atop more plunder. Many of them would never think twice about again once bartered, squandered, and spent away. Zaki glanced to Tausi, cautious to make sure his younger brother's path was diverted toward the mound. Thankful for Nkuku's forethought when the timekeeper shooed him over with the other rowers, he steeled himself as they started for the line of women.

"Fifty of them left," said Mtumbwe, thumbing the edge of his thick lips as he looked over the first one, a comely lass just into her teens. "Couple of them might fetch a good price in Butcher's Bay. Probably a few good salt-wives in here, too."

"Might be," said Ngala, staring at the first. He shook his head quickly at the quivering, shuddering mess. "Not this one."

As quickly as she was rejected, a raider appeared, hauling her off to be gutted. Zaki shuddered himself when the screams died and was replaced by the captive women's lingering silence as she realized the futility of it.

Down the line they went, Ngala deciding who would be thrown into enslavement or simply killed for the sake of an implicit message: Stone Cove decided their fates as much as the sea did.

Halfway down the line, Ngala paused, turning on his heels to study the girl forced on her knees. Unlike the rest of the Gypians, this one had the dark velvet skin of the plain's folk—the same folk the corsairs had arisen from when the empires of the West were sundered by their irresponsible magics.

"Are you slave?" Ngala asked her.

Her bright eyes, large in her head, moved from the tile and up at Ngala. She nodded.

"What's your name?"

She looked between Ngala, Zaki, and the bloody sword Mtumbwe held. Quick to understand, she fixed on Ngala with a more pleasant expression. "Anaya."

As if by some damnable angle of the light, the way the fires glistened off his father's smirk filled Zaki with abject terror. "How would you like to live past today? To bear children to captains?"

Her words were worse than a simple no—savannah-woman or Gypian servant, she knew enough about the old ways to understand the salt laws. Her gaze went right to Zaki, taking in what was being offered.

"Aye, Captain," she said. "I'll be any man's salt-wife you tell me to be."

Clermiel whispered as dead girls bled out around his ankles. "And yet I'm the devil?"

CHAPTER 9
AN EVENING OF MEASURES

A
t first, Anaya acted like any hostage salt-wife—meek, quiet, and slavish to please her new husband.

At first.

No words passed between Zaki and Ngala the day she stepped onto the beaches of Stone Cove, where the denizens of the cutthroat hideaway welcomed *The Gamka* and their fierce captain home. Many greeted the news of Zaki's new marriage with an unexpected, performed joy, welcoming the new member of their new community with lukewarm embraces. The treasure was divided; the tithes were paid to Black Lizard, who in his withering vigor rewarded the daring and well-liked Ngala with more than his fair share of the loot they collected. Heaps and praises were given, ribald feasts held, and joy bled into the preparation for the next raid.

Much like how he did not have anything to say to his father, Zaki had less to say to Anaya. Long days of her lounging about the same chambers his mother died in went by in silence. She wore the finest silks his father afforded her from Zaki's share while she supped on the spoils from the silver dishes their servants served his meals on.

What joy there was to be found, he did so in raising Tausi while his father stoked fury among Stone Cove's corsairs. Zaki had little appetite for incitement and focused on the things that actually won the day.

The will. The mind.

Swordplay.

"Keep your guard up," Zaki scolded, bringing his club down on his little brother's head.

Tausi raised his guard, which bent when the carved, crow-turned heads of their clubs cracked together. He held under the force of his older brother's strike.

Zaki sprang back a few steps, relenting as he easily dodged clumsy stabs.

Huffing, Tausi let the distance open between them, using the space to catch his breath.

"Don't always follow your defense with an advance," Zaki said in a clear, cautioned tone. "You'll waste energy and spend yourself out if caught on the defense."

The club in his brother's hand snaked at the advice. "I know."

Smiling his broad smile, Zaki raised his club and came at Tausi again. "Then make room!"

Tausi refused as he always did.

The two met in the middle of the sandy beach, alone along the thin shoreline. The slim border between the cove's hilly forests and the shimmering expanse played theater to the sibling's training as the calm breeze carried the screams and sharp clacks of their mock war. Wood bit into wood, muscles and tendons strained while breaths were cut and carried in every move, every attack.

Advancing on Zaki at first through sheer ferocity, Tausi spun and slashed, ducked and stabbed for every opening he tried to create by his blows. Ever nimble, always calm, Zaki held off his brother's onslaught. Leaning back to goad Tausi into a more aggressive attack, he waited for his brother to come forward.

"You're too pretty when you smile like that," Tausi said in the wide circle they had created in the softer part of the sand. "Stop smiling like that."

"Too distracting?" Zaki teased. He backed toward the hard-packed ground where the tides had smoothed them overnight. "You like pretty things, don't you? Look at Tausi, with all his pretty little things!"

A strange wrath crossed Tausi's smooth, sweating brow. Lips twisted in a wounded snarl. He charged. "Stop!"

Unsettled by the outburst, Zaki danced away from his brother's glancing swings. He planted his feet down when he felt the sun on his neck and back, turning for his riposte. Grunting every time, he came forward against the daylight in his eyes, and Tausi threw himself into basic attacks—head, head, then to the leg, then to the head again before the other side. On the switch to the other side, Zaki darted in, knocking aside Tausi's club while shouldering him hard in the chest. The air rushed from Tausi in a hollow gasp and was cut short when he struck the sand, flat on his back.

Zaki kept his laughter to himself, letting the waves hold the silence as Tausi heaved on the ground. He went and retrieved his brother's club, holding both in his sword hand.

"I'm sorry," he said as Tausi stared at the sky. "I shouldn't've roughed you so hard."

Pained and embarrassed, Tausi sat up with more darkness in his eyes than sunlight hid. He stood stiffly and dusted off the back of his legs, silent to his brother's gaze.

"I said I'm sorry," Zaki said.

"I heard you."

"Then why are you being sore about it?"

Tausi hesitated too long on the question before he turned away.

"Fine," said Zaki, throwing his hand up. "Be like that."

Tausi turned back, his stance square and firm. "You need to get rid of Anaya."

The life left Zaki when her name slipped from his brother's mouth. "You know I can't. He'll make me take a boat."

"Take a boat and drop her in the sea. You have to."

"That will be letting him see me flinch."

"Then flinch," said Tausi. "Whatever reason isn't worth her."

"Blind little fool," Clermiel whispered over Zaki's shoulder. "Did they ever pay any real attention to you?"

Zaki paused on his brother's words, leaning forward where he stood. "What did you see?"

Tausi put his eyes to the earth, mouth shut in a hard, fraught line.

"Tausi."

"She's your salt-wife, Zaki. Those bonds are not made forever."

"She's..."

"She is whether you wanted her or not. Your captain—"

"What did you see, Tausi?"

"I can't say."

"Why can't you?"

Zaki almost started at him when his little brother raised his dark eyes to meet his.

"She's your salt-wife, Zaki," he said. "Just remember that."

Zaki stormed through the doorway of his chambers, the same ones he and his brother had crossed throughout their entire lives. It was where his mother had perished and where his father's presence now left a cold ghost. The first of two rooms and the balcony overlooking Stone Cove's east-facing beaches lay empty, the small iron hearth in the center of the packed sand floor...

And the two pairs of sandals beside the entryway to the bedroom, the ties wrapped around the hilts of their scabbarded swords.

His blade belted to his waist, Zaki drew it free, the rasp of iron against the wooden throat of its holder waking a rage.

Anaya's first panting cries reached his ears before he ripped the curtain open. Yanking the beaded length of emerald Gypian silk, he beheld the three sweat-slicked bodies writhing upon the mats he rarely shared with her, grinding in enjoined passion. Oblivious to the new eyes upon them, their screams of ecstasy tore raw words from Zaki's throat.

"Shame upon my very bed," he shouted.

The two men sandwiching Anaya, one of whom he recognized from another raider crew loyal to Black Lizard, unsheathed themselves and leapt from the bedding. Panicked, they dropped at the sides of the pallet when they saw his sword.

"Please, commander," they shouted, hands clasped together to beg.

Anaya screamed as Zaki met the nearest, a man who shrank under the threat of his upraised edge. Pulling his cut as it came down, Zaki beat the man off his knees with the flat of the blade, bludgeoning him back onto the bed. Blood leaked from his face as he groaned, covering up to spare himself the next attack. The second raider tried to run, only to be stopped when Zaki's point blocked his path.

"Move and there will not be a place for any of you to run," Zaki said.

The three froze, perspiration gleaming on their naked bodies.

"You should kill them," said Clermiel. "Teach them the truth of their ways."

Teeth gritted, Zaki shifted the point between the two men until his ire focused on Anaya. Backed against the wall, she stared at him, open-mouthed as her wide eyes revealed her terror. A red bead dripped off the sharp point of Zaki's sword, spotting the blankets she had piled for her lovemaking.

"It doesn't matter where you run," Zaki said to both men, fixed on his salt-wife. He whipped the stained iron toward the bedroom's exit. "I'll find you both anyway."

Understanding his dire promise, the two men who made him a cuckold collected their sandals and swords and ran without a word of apology.

Weighed by a promise his honor required him to complete later on, Zaki let them pass into the night. He dropped his sword to his side. "You'll be gone in the morning," he said, rage smothered by exhaustion. "I don't care what you do, where you go, or what happens to you afterward. But you'll not come before me again."

Anaya remained quiet. Her glare switched between his sword, speckled with the blood of her lovers, and Zaki's face. Then a smirk, deep and wicked, crept across her own.

"No, I won't." She replied with a simple confidence to match his. "I'm not going anywhere."

Zaki raised his head, a lion looking upon his next meal.

Peeling her nude body from the wall, she stood on the bed. "I'm not going anywhere, you gutless wretch."

The righteousness flagged in Zaki. He raised his point at her again, lips peeled in a snarl. "Then you'll—"

Anaya barked in light, girlish laughter. "I'll do nothing! And neither will you." The eager woman Ngala had plucked from death to punish Zaki revealed herself, envenomed as much as she was voluptuous; she had a form men slaughtered other men over—but not him.

She had figured it out.

Reaching up to hook her hands behind her neck, her toned forearms covered her breasts in a pleasing fashion, a mocking pose she perfected

297

by the slight tilt of her full hips. "This doesn't stir you. In fact, no woman stirs you, and I've made sure to watch. Every time I press my skin against you, every breath I let you hear when I try to entice you...and nothing. Why is that when I've stirred more than one man in this hellish place?"

"Some are warier of snakes," Zaki retorted, disturbed by her wantonness.

Anaya noticed. The smirk blunted into a frown. "Or more than one person in this room hungers for a man's touch."

"Not a man here will believe you."

"But what about their women? What about the women you've loved? The ones you've touched?" she asked. "Are there any?"

The question went unanswered.

The sword he held aloft against her weighed more than a mainmast.

Anaya stepped off the bed. She walked past his sword and stopped inches from where the small round end of her nose leveled at his throat.

And his sword-arm failed.

Her smirk returned, vicious and mean. Her eyes smote Zaki with malice. "If you want to keep your peace, you will let things go on the way they are," Anaya whispered, jutting out her chin. "You say a word about the men I bring to bed, I'll tell your father. You harm one inch of flesh on my lovers, I'll have the ones you haven't seen say how they made you a cuckold. And if you harm an inch on me, Zaki..."

"You've made your point."

"No," she said, her teeth close to his face. "If you ever think about harming me, I'll tell about the clothes you're keeping for yourself."

He made a slight sound, a weak noise.

Anaya chortled at his response, relishing it.

A voice called from the entrance to their chambers. "Zaki?" Tausi shouted. "Zaki, are you there?"

"Go answer him," said Anaya. "And say nothing about this."

One last surge of defiance welled within Zaki. He stood tall before her.

"Now," she said, unimpressed by his bravado. "Or I'll let him know first."

Zaki slunk from the bedroom, broken by the order. Following a trail of blood spotting the floor past the curtain, he found Tausi in the next room, a club upraised as he traced the crimson path to its origin.

Tausi saw his brother's sword immediately. "What happened? Where's—"

"It's fine, Tausi," Zaki said, quick and pointed. "I ran them off."

"And her? Is she...?"

"What are you here for?" he asked, interrupting.

Tausi started at the bark in Zaki's voice. Shrinking back, he did not lower the club he held and waited to see what his brother did next.

Zaki dulled the edge in his voice. "Tausi."

"Father...I mean, Captain Ngala sent this." He produced a scrap of the papyrus the corsairs produced on the island: bamboo, honey, and water mashed into a writable medium they used to save the vellum for their sea charts. Zaki crossed the rest of the room and took the offered note from Tausi's hand.

Written in his father's quick, rough script, the instructions remained short:

BL's vodunis sense a sorcerer. South shores.

You and Tausi search him out.

Be back quickly before tomorrow's sunset. I have more orders for you.

-N

"When did he give this to you?" Zaki asked.

"Just now." Tausi leaned to look past Zaki, his eyes still tracking the points of blood.

"Is he still out there, Zaki?" Anaya shouted from the bedroom.

"Let's go," Zaki said.

Shaking his head, Tausi started to point at the stains on the floor.

"Let's go," Zaki said again, turning Tausi about and pushing him toward the exit.

They left before Anaya called a second time.

He rode the horse hard, squeezing his hips to her flanks. Low in the saddle, head pressed near her pounding shoulders, Zaki tried his best to drive the mare farther and faster than Tausi could go before the tears took him. The ache in his heart, its heaviness, added cracks with every pound of the hoof. The sun tipped over its apex as they raced the far beaches where no one would be save mad hermits and a few solitary fishermen plying the waters.

"You should have killed her," Clermiel said, standing alone in the surf as Zaki whipped by on his horse.

"Zaki!" Tausi's screamed echoed behind him. "Zaki! Zaki!"

The mare exhausted, the shape he hated aching from head to toe, Zaki slumped in the saddle and let the horse slow to her pace. She dashed for the water, unguided, right to where the waves etched a soft line in the sand. His brother's shouting heightened in the distance behind him, Zaki watched his pursuer ride to him.

"What the fuck is wrong with you?" Tausi roared, his voice deeper than it should be at his age. A commander's voice.

Zaki sat up in the saddle and stroked the mare's neck.

"Zaki!"

He looked from the mare to his brother, his expression forlorn. "Go back home, Tausi. Go sleep in Father's chambers from now on."

"Zaki, why did Anaya—"

"Do not argue with me," he shouted. No longer rested in the saddle, Zaki realized he had lurched at his little brother, the same little brother he beheld the day he lost his mother. Every day he had to conceal the self-loathing gathered in the pit of his stomach, the bile of it forming a volatile brew.

"Zaki, I just..."

"I don't need you, Tausi!"

The poison, now on Zaki's tongue, worked its ichor.

Tausi's expression transformed from one of concern to a dead one, withheld of its love. He wheeled his horse around and rode back toward Stone Cove. Nothing deterred his exit, and with no last glance given, Zaki let his little brother fade into the distance. The despair in his heart steeped with the shrinking outline.

Zaki righted his mare southward along the beach and carried on toward what cruel encounters the world had left him to resolve.

The sunset lit the waves gold and silver as they scraped the land, melded with the wind in his ears. Letting his mare walk the sands at her own pace and trusting her animal sense, Zaki brooded in the waning light as he slumped in the saddle. Glancing askance at the water, hoping by some weird miracle it would offer up a solution, he laughed coldly at the mad idea of running into the surf, past the breakers, and into its depths.

The embrace of the sea, the warm tides, might offer comfort. His mirth died as he imagined the blanket of darkness washing over him, and then nothing more.

"I would suggest you don't do that."

Whipping his head hard to the right, Zaki froze when he realized the mare had stopped dead in her tracks.

Someone stood in front of her, his long-fingered hands stroking her dappled neck.

"By the goddess," Zaki shouted, almost falling from the saddle in surprise. Drawing his sword, Zaki posted on his free hand and shoved himself backward, sliding off the mare's rump to land on both feet. Trained to dash forward and away at the slap of her flank, she instead stayed where she was, her attention still ahead.

He came around, point held forward—

At no one.

The mare turned her head, stared at Zaki, and snorted.

"I hope that is not for me, my dear."

Zaki spun on the balls of his feet, turning low into a half-crouch, blade extended toward the new voice.

Standing on the dry sand, a tall man of a thin frame—but with the shoulders of a powerful swimmer—gazed back, his silver eyes so bright they made the ebon luster of his skin all the darker. Wrapped in a loose robe of shimmering red silk, the rippling coat lay open to reveal a body carved in honed muscle and graceful sinews. Across a handsome, bare face shone dozens upon dozens of silver scales, pierced and healed within the flesh, creating a visage of a seahorse crowned by the sun's dying fire.

The smile on his perfect, supple lips set Zaki's heart aflame. Failing to find words, he simply gaped back, dumbfounded to silence.

301

The stranger looked past the sword's point. "Are you going to attack me?"

Somehow Zaki found his voice. "Who are you?"

He smiled, his teeth the color of new, polished ivory. "You can put that down if you'd like."

Zaki slowly rose from his crouch, sword still aloft. "Who are you?" he asked a second time, with much less force.

"A constant question, it seems, for you and I," said the stranger. Perfect in his stillness, his silver eyes went to the sea beyond them, where the waves broke on the land in white, foamy mantles. "I guess you may call me Agwe."

"I may?"

Those eyes settled on Zaki a second time, seizing the corsair's breath in his chest. "Well, what would you like to call me?"

The playfulness in the stranger's rich baritone, the way his eyes glinted when he said "my dear," Zaki let his sword fall, easing his stance as he recognized this man offered him no threat.

It made him even more terrifying in some way.

Yet Agwe did not terrify him.

"And what's your name?" the stranger asked.

Zaki paused at the question. "Zaki."

Agwe's smile heated the silver in his eyes, those rings of moonlight. "Zaki. I'm absolutely enchanted to meet you."

CHAPTER 10
A MIDNIGHT SUNRISE

H*o, man, to the left, to the left!"*

The oars of *The Gamka* beat up on the sea as Zaki clung to the port rail, the sea spraying in his ocher and coal-painted face. He had kept his bow when his father lurched the boat to port, tilting the deck. Many clung for dear life, desperate to stay aboard. Beneath his feet, the board reverberated inside the maelstrom of the rower's den, their song ingrained in the creaking hull itself.

"Ho, man, to the left, to the left!"

The Gamka's hard turn smoothed into a breaking, driving calm. The deck buzzed in a sudden fury of raiders dashing to reclaim the weapons they had dropped.

Ngala's call pierced their noise. "Bows, port to bow!"

Reaching into the quiver strapped to his belt, Zaki's joy did not muster when his hand fell upon a fletching. Drawing the shaft, he aimed high and to his left. Loosing, he drew two more arrows and fired them before scattering along the deck to find what arrows he could recover before the next call.

Ngala did not leave his raiders much time. "Retract oars! Brace!"

"Ho, man, to the death, to the death!"

"These songs aren't getting any better," murmured Clermiel in his typical dispassion, perched atop the mainmast.

303

The heartbeat of the ship found in the rowers's strokes boomed like thunder when *The Gamka* surged forth. Lifting up a sword and a small bronze buckler, Zaki faced the bow in time to see the starboard of the approaching Latian vessel. He threw himself forward to the mainmast, joining the other raiders grabbing what bits of rigging they could. The swells battering *The Gamka's* sides sloshed one final shower, wetting every fighter to the flesh before the rostrum. The bronze ram cutting the waves just beneath the water slammed through the side of the Latians.

Snapping planks splintered inward as the water rushed into the hold. Hundreds of men screamed, their mass writhing in the darkness as they started to drown.

His father screamed louder. "To your feet, men! Oil!"

The mere mention of the corsair's greatest terror resounded in Zaki's nerves. On graceful instinct, he bounded forward until he stood amongst his own raiders, all of them lifting the buckets of thick, dark pitch.

Ngala appeared before them. Face slashed with flecking bits of blue and white, his blazing eyes filled Zaki with a strange power of terror and pride. The monster who had born him offered a burning torch, a point of ghostly red light in the gray daylight.

He took the brand from Ngala and charged ahead. Raiders rallied before Zaki reached the bow. Faces he had known for years, some for months, some for only days when they came aboard, all known by their violent visages, raged beside him.

The first few at his sides broke ahead of the order, slinging their buckets from their deck to the next before they joined the climb for the enemy position.

"Blood and fire," Zaki screamed before he leapt onto the Latian deck.

The echoes of the cry thundered around him as he alighted on the opposing side, immediately torn into the storm of iron and death. Oil spilled from thrown buckets, painting the gratings running the westerner's center deck, which served as the ventilation and ceiling for the open hold where all their rowers sat. Rained upon by the reeking substance, tan western slaves and dark-skinned Juutans rioted on their benches.

Zaki slayed every armored Latian who approached, striking down hoplites too heavy for the corsair's mobility. Shoving the flaming end of his torch into the face of a helmeted marine, he kicked the writhing body away and charged to the edge the rower's pit. Finding a large enough hole in the grate, he upturned the torch. The heat licking his forearm, he forced the end through the shrieking faces. They started stomping where the seawater did not swirl around them, though the flame spread there too.

Turning from the flesh-rending smoke, Zaki caught a spear thrust on the edge of his buckler in time. He glared at the Latian who struck him and peered back with equal hatred.

Zaki hacked at the wooden shaft, severing it in two. The armored marine reeled back, his compact form carrying his iron cuirass and crested helm well through the motion. He found his feet and drew his sword in time to meet Zaki's follow-up attack.

They dueled, stabbing and parrying upon each other until Ngala's voice rose again:

"Retreat to *The Gamka!* Impact off the starboard prow."

Zaki met the marine by the rail when the Latian ship heaved to port under an impact from the opposite direction. Knocked from his balance, Zaki and the Latian fighter pitched the same direction, the weight of the heavier marine turning him over the edge and into the sea.

Ribs smarting from the impact, Zaki staggered off of his knees. Smoke choked the way, the roar of the hold billowing black cinders out of its hellish depths. The sea breeze whipped the cloud in all directions. Beyond the flames consuming the Latian trireme, the last of *The Gamka's* raiders leapt from the side and caught onto the bow. A few slipped, plunging into the tide between the boats. The Latians able to tread water immediately swarmed them, dragging both deeper.

"Zaki!"

A hand latched on his shoulder and tore him about. It belonged to a broad-faced woman in her late forties with skin thickened by years at a ship's rigging. Her glare struck him still, enough for her to hook her strong left hand on the back of his neck and nearly bowl him toward the starboard. Thrown off balance, he caught himself before he crashed face first into the rail.

Captain Cleona, queen of Tip Town and captain of *The Immammou,* ascended to the bow of her ship in two steps and a leap of fluid motion, turning when she reached the most forward point of her ship to offer a hand. Already the rowers of the gallant trireme, made of a much darker wood than Zaki had ever seen, had appeared to push the boat free with long poles.

"Are you going to gape and die?" she yelled.

Stepping upon the rail, Zaki caught Cleona's outstretched hand. She hauled him aboard as her raiders, streaked in splatters of dark purple and ash-gray, stabbed the Latians clinging to the rostrum or climbing the sides of *The Immammou*. The last fool fell, bleeding chum for whatever creature claimed them, and the corsairs of Tip Town started southward at a long, hurried pace.

They set sail when the moon loomed, nestled amongst the stars. The oars were retracted as *The Immammou* followed *The Gamka* on the winds toward the coast Cleona and Ngala had agreed they would meet after their daring adventure. Given leave to rest, the raiders fixed their high shields to the rail and tended the rigging while the rowers below deck tended to their cooking fires. The wind filled their sail, spreading their savory scents amid the growing, deepening, star-speckled darkness.

Tip Town, a plunderer's stronghold easterly of where they set to meet, cultured a far different realm than the ships Zaki had grown up on. The raiding crew, made up of far more women than his father would ever abide, buzzed in quiet activity. The meal was served quick, fish and gruel like the kind served on *The Gamka*, but came with a warmth in the spices not expected on his father's boat. Small oil lamps were raised up to illuminate the corners of the top deck where they remained out of sight of any watcher looking from afar. Raiders and rowers gathered together, tossing dice and trading stories to whittle away time.

And Cleona was nothing like Ngala.

While they shared a clear courage and fierce presence, the differences between the two were stark.

Whereas Ngala placed his men's discipline in the upkeep of the boat, a constant grind of adjustment and measure, Cleona chose the upkeep of crew. Rowers were given freedom to leave the hold and stray far from their benches, a shock Ngala would have beaten a man close to death for. Food was shared instead of doled out in individual portions accorded, with raiders eating from the same bowls and plates as their rower brethren. Much to his surprise, there was no furor of how the treasures they had taken from the Latian convoy would be divided.

All of these things were reversed on *The Gamka*.

"Are you going to stay there and gawk, Commander, or are you going to come eat with me?" Cleona asked as she shoved the locking pin into the steering oar, letting the sail carry them on the currents. Standing upright on a sturdy frame honed by the fair balances of seafaring and killing, something about her face caught him.

He straightened like he would in front of his father and nodded. "Aye, sir."

Cleona gave him an odd look as she motioned over to the pallet a few of her bosuns prepared—she had more than one, and all of them young men. The pallet was constructed out of old calfskin pillows and a few blankets, they circled around a platter of steaming barley beside a flame-crusted fish, its delectable juices on a stone plate. A few bottles of dzan, the heavy brown liquor made from the green-crowned sugar grown along much of Juut's southern coasts, were nestled in one of the finer blankets Cleona took for herself.

The bosuns, all of them fawning over their captain, hurried to prepare their plates as Zaki claimed the mound of pillows opposite hers. "I owe you my life, Captain Cleona," he said as he watched her toys busy over her. "I hope in time I will find some way to repay it."

"She died, alone in a bed," said Clermiel in Zaki's ear in a pleased tone. "Can anything ever be repaid?"

"There's no need for that," she said in her plain, to-the-point fashion. "You are Ngala's son. What would it have been if I simply left his son to die when I could have saved him?"

The frankness of her question pierced Zaki, ripping open something he held up within.

Within herself.

"Frankly, Captain..." Zaki swallowed all hesitations. "I think he'd expect it, even from an ally. He's never been one to seek trust in those outside of his crew. He owes his allegiance to Black Lizard, *The Gamka*, and himself."

"That's not entirely true." She reached forward and tore a piece of meat and skin from the cooked fish between them, the yellow-gold juices flowing around where her strong fingers dug the flesh. Cleona mashed the white tissue into the barley heaped on her plate that she seasoned with dashes of salt from a small bowl beside it. Staring at Zaki with those familiar, striking eyes, she chewed the first bite of her meal.

"What do you mean, Captain?" Zaki found the words to say.

Cleona smiled while she swallowed before seeking the bottle of dzan on her blanket. "I know your father well. Quite intimately, for a time," she said as one of her handsome bosuns quickly plucked the bottle up and drew his dagger. Her cat-like smile appeared when the cork popped free after he cut the beeswax seal. "He married my sister. Your mother."

"That means you're my aunt," Zaki reasoned immediately. Teetering on the sinking feeling of how much was kept from him seemed clearer than ever before, certifying his own words about his father. "Why wasn't I told?"

"Ngala became a different person after your mother died in the way many women do. He still, perhaps, bears a grudge against me for accepting what happened simply as what happened. Women's truths are often too harsh for men to accept for themselves."

"He's never been—"

"Yes, he has," she said. "I can take one look at you and see it." She glanced down at the plate in front of him. "Aren't you going to eat? We have a long time ahead before we reach shore. I'm already certain he will be ornery about how the loot is split."

"Now, that is also him." A small pang of hunger seized him. Zaki tore a handful of fish away from the bones, heaping it on his plate. Beside the barley, a quick dash of salt initiated his slow, guarded meal.

Cleona smiled. "You eat like him."

"Would you like me to give back a portion?" Zaki asked.

The Immammou's captain studied the questioner as much as she pondered the question. "No, I made them catch a big enough fish for the both of us. Does he ask for a portion back?"

"No. He tries to make sure everyone gets their fair share."

Cleona's expression softened. "Have you gotten yours, Zaki?"

"What do you mean, Captain?"

Her bosuns served them clay cups of dzan, the bottle placed on the platter between them.

She sipped her liquor before she answered. "Call it an auntie's intuition. You know what old vodunis say—a mother knows her child like no other. Sometimes the gods take a mother from her children, but the spirits of the sea are kinder than your father makes them out to be. They understand responsibility is needed, and they are thankful when they find kindred. I feel like I know you like you were my own."

"I have a brother," Zaki blurted, unable to process the emotion risen in response to her words. "His name's Tausi."

"I know," said Cleona as she set down her cup. "I will most likely never meet him."

"But—"

"We're corsairs, Zaki. We are family through salt—the salt in our blood and the salt in our seas. You might have more than one brother or sister you're not aware of in Tip Town, where your father used to frequent when he went off on his days of mad quest."

Zaki lifted the bottom-heavy vessel the crewmen had granted, the sweet, burning syrup slipping like honey into the throat. Warmth carried down and spread around his heart. "I remember those. He left me to raise Tausi by myself until we were ship-worthy."

Her brow furrowed—in anger, or in sorrow? Zaki did not know.

"Of course, he would," she said. "One nudge toward being an adult, and one giant shit on the boards trying to do it. That's Ngala, too."

"He gave me a life," Zaki said.

"A life where you're terrified," Cleona said back, as sharp as a honed blade cutting bone. "I know who your brother is. I hear he is as daring a warrior as your father, battle-mad and eager like all of Black Lizard's folk. But I also know his brother is held in greater regard. Zaki the Shining, growing heir to a great captain who is destined for greater things still. And a cuckold."

Zaki sighed, almost on reflex.

In the pair of years since Ngala had bound him to Anaya in a salt marriage, rumor had been widespread and piercing. Like the whispers of why he spent so much time at sea, commanding shock assaults on

Latian triremes on patrol in well-traveled waters, nothing dimmed the questions they had against his salt-wife's flagrant, disdainful actions. No matter how many times he outdid his father reaping the shores in fury, no matter how many ships he sank for himself, no matter the numerous victories or loot counted, word persisted.

No matter the glory, Zaki the Shining was a cuckold.

Cleona started eating again, taking to her meal with a gusto befit of one who spent the day raiding.

"What was my mother like?" Zaki asked. He reached for the bottle of dzan, drawing raised brows from her fawning bosuns. Ignoring them, he filled the cup to the brim and took a hearty sip. The taste of vanilla, sugar, and maybe flowers burned his tongue. Zaki firmed himself as he had done many times in the recent years, expecting the alcohol's comfort to bring its punishments as well.

"Nothing is gained in self-sacrifice," Clermiel said. "Only in exacting action. Only in power."

"She was braver than brave, and the best sailor I had ever seen. A captain before your father was, and the only reason he became captain is because your younger brother's birth complicated things." Cleona let out an amused snort through her fine nose. "But I keep my suspicions of Black Lizard to myself."

Something about her nose and cheeks, the wideness of her face and the glow it seemed to capture, tugged at things longed buried in Zaki. Her voice felt like he had heard it before, but never realized until now.

The captain continued, not noticing his breaking expression. "You look more like her than you do your father. Very much so, in many ways."

"I'll take it as a compliment."

"You better," she responded with a winking sort of laugh.

What if he told her? What if Zaki told her everything?

What if she wouldn't be alone anymore?

The tension broke when Cleona laughed louder. She ripped away the final guard, seeking the paths to the soul's depth.

A hunger grew in his stomach with a sudden strength. "Captain Cleona," he asked, still not taking to his food. "What do I do about my father?"

"I have no fucking idea what is to be done about Patros Ngala," she said, almost with equal humor. "What fate has in store for your father is what fate has in store. I believe that which is why I don't think your mother's death halted him."

"He had us," Zaki said.

"But what do you have, Zaki?"

Another question laid Zaki bare. "I met someone," he said. "He's very different from everything else I've ever come across."

"What's his name?"

"Agwe," said Zaki. "I even lie to my father about him."

Cleona's laughter rang out through the night, high and happy and short. Joined by a few of her bosuns also enchanted by the delivery, she scooted close to the table and held her hand out for the bottle of dzan. "And what does this mister Agwe do? A rower? Raider?"

"A voduni," he answered as he leaned toward her.

She caught at the bottle, a building cry of laughter bunched in her full cheeks. "Zaki—a voduni?"

Zaki shrugged. "You asked, Auntie Cleona."

Cackling with a joyous glee, all the words came out. Tales of the past —of his mother, Ogbu, and Tausi, of how Ngala was before the death of a finer captain and how he was afterward—spiraled and danced like the flames of the oil lamps on the breeze-swept deck. Paired together at long last, like they had never been lost at all, they talked until the next day's glow warmed in the east.

"What do you think your father will say? What about your crew?" asked Cleona.

The freedom she felt beside this captain withered at the obvious answers. "I don't know," Zaki said, slurring. "I don't know what to do about Anaya, and the truth may set me against the men on *The Gamka*. We aren't as open in Stone Cove as you seem to be in Tip Town."

"Then why don't you come to Tip Town?"

The question caused a gurgle in Zaki's gut. They exchanged drunken glances.

"My father would forbid me."

"Are you Zaki, the future captain of *The Gamka*? Or of your own boat one day?"

"I would like to think so. But it wouldn't happen if I left, even for a little."

"How do you know?" she asked. "How do you know it isn't exactly what you both need?"

Head alight from the claws the dzan had dug into Zaki's skull, some questions left her with more uncertainty than ever before.

"Wake up," whispered Agwe.

CHAPTER 11

HOLY DIVER

A gull cried at the edge of darkness between the rise of the sun and the sudden return of the night.

Zaki raised her head. Every inch of her body felt like it had been torn some place. Beaten, and squeezed, sawed, sliced, and rawed until she questioned whether she had escaped the sightless dream. Curled in the corner of wherever she lay, not a hint of light revealed the difference between reality and what lay in the depths of her mind.

Clermiel had not spoken for hours. Or had it been minutes?

The squawk sounded again in the depths.

She stared into nothing. Waiting.

A breath of air bathed her bruised face, making her blink at the blood crusting the corners of her eyes. Zaki tried to keep herself from crying yet wanted those tears so badly to clean out the rust. She let them sting as they ran, blinking every awful blink just so she felt something there, something other than the expanse of breath, sound, and darkness.

Ears opened and questing, she tried to pick out a sound, wondering if it had indeed been a gull.

What if it was a trick?

Zaki tried to open her eyes more, to widen them when a gnawing, wretched pain flamed around her brow and cheeks.

Her eyes had nearly swollen shut. Delirious, nauseated by the sudden reminder of her corporeal sense, she gurgled something out of her throat—a hunger-belch of bile and blood. Zaki fought the need to blink her eyes again, and her belly was full of the gross gore she had swallowed over the many hours she had slept.

The gull cried again.

Keeping her eyes shut as tightly as she could, Zaki sobbed at the sound. The nerves throughout her body kicked, fraying her consciousness with the agony of every ounce of life remaining in her limbs. The muscles in her torso hugged against broken ribs, staggering her breath as she heaved.

The gull cried, closer this time.

"Go away," she mumbled through chapped, bleeding lips. Snot dripped from her nose, on the upper edge of her lip, salty and sharp in the wounds. "Go away."

The darkness brightened a shade behind her battered eyelids. Her sight reddened by a bright light, Zaki clenched her entire body against the torn ache of her flesh, the violation and punishment the Ulmos had etched on every inch of her with their sharp, sawing claws. Like the ragdoll of blood and bones they had tossed aside when done, she lay like a mound of misshaped clay, unable to defend or reject whatever sculpted her next.

A wind blew through the open galley, gentle and mild with the smell of the sea.

The ground thrummed under her, and she knew she still lay in the conch's galley, high above the bar it rested on. Or did it? The devil could have moved his impossible, improbable fortress. They could be far away from where she had fallen into the Mirror Sea, maybe some place where the cry she'd heard were not even gulls at all. Salt was salt, but where had she ended up?

Then he spoke.

"Zaki?" Agwe called. "Is that you?"

She froze at this voice that drove hope and despair against each other, two tides meeting. She chose not to move, to stay where she curled against one of the shallow alcoves made in the conch's muscled chamber. If she did not move, nobody could find her. She should not have moved when she had made it outside. She should have stayed there and died of thirst.

"Zaki."

The honesty in Agwe's voice drew a whimper out of her when he touched her wounded arms.

Gathering her up, he held her to his chest and shook her gently.

"Please awake," he whispered, sounding so human. "Please, my love."

She waited for the change, the trick, whatever the devil had concocted to punish her for something she didn't know to be real.

He laid his soft, tender lips on Zaki's forehead.

Before the healing of her wounds by his magic commenced, her arms had wrapped around Agwe, clinging to a truth she knew through feel alone. Power, at once cool and easing, oozed in her cuts and mended the breaks beneath the skin. Zaki hung in her lover's arms, letting out the first comforted breath she had failed to release since she came to as Clermiel's captive.

"He said they're all dead," she whispered into him. "He made the Ulmos look like you. He keeps looking inside me, trying to find you."

"I know," he responded, filled with far more sadness than she had ever heard.

Zaki clutched to Agwe out of love, then out of terror, too cognizant and aware of everything. Her eyes healed back to their normal size, she gazed into the rich silk of his blue-and-white-checkered robe.

Silence carried where it should not have.

Agwe broke it first. "He has not sensed me. Not yet. It's all going like we planned."

"I know what we planned," said Zaki, still whispering. "What I need to know is if he's telling the truth."

Silence continued its reign longer than it should have.

Zaki spoke, her strength regained. "Agwe."

They moved together, first up and away from each other, the ability to stand on her own restored. The roomed seemed too bright to her long-blinded eyes, and even worse so for the silver helm on his head. Sleek in perfect, minimal lines, yet designed for the rigors of battle, the glare of it did not sting her eyes as much as made her look away. Every inch of her sorcerer-lover, from the helm to his perfectly clean robes to the luster of his skin, almost repelled her.

Zaki did not know this person.

"What did he ask?" he finally dared to question.

"Don't you know?" Zaki asked. "Couldn't you just read my mind, if you wanted?"

Biting the inside of his cheek, Agwe nodded to himself. "Do you remember what you asked of me the night we came together?"

Zaki blinked, slinking back until her shoulders touched the leathery, pulsating walls.

"Do you?"

She bobbed her head, confusion and frustration and the simple joy of him being there whipping storms within her.

"And do you remember what I promised you?"

"That when asked, you would never keep anything from me."

"Zaki, my love...I am the spirit of the sea, and sailors, the fish, and the coasts. I am the one who makes the tides turn and churn beneath the storms of my brothers and sisters as we serve our mothers and those who serve them. I am older than I—"

"Stop," Zaki said, breathless.

He did. Without hesitance, surprise, or scorn, Agwe stopped.

It was almost too perfect, how he stopped. The subtle, impossible way his mouth shut on the word when demanded entrapped Zaki. A flood of memories struck, recollections of every time she thought his form too perfect, without blemish, or how no place on his body seemed asymmetric or uneven like every mortal body should be. The way he smiled, without a shred of anxiety or fear.

The things they had made for *The Ulmo*.

"Is all this," she asked, motioning to the twitching space, the massive, living palace of their enemy. "Is this all just part of some grand plan? Is this all some scheme? Am I just a—"

"Never, in my many paths, have I ever," Agwe interrupted, the deep words booming throughout the chamber.

Zaki shushed him and turned into a wretch by the mere notion the devil might hear them. "Shhh, shhh," she shushed, a strong finger held against her lips. "Shhhh!"

Agwe shook his head, the ambient sunlight outside of the gross galley glinting every time he moved. "He's bigger problems to worry about."

"How?"

"The fleet landed on his dune and built the flotilla," he said. "Clermiel won't move, and we've taken the lower chambers of the conch."

"You have?" Zaki asked, almost in disbelief.

"Tausi and Oya are leading the siege now to the sealed tunnel the devil disappeared within. We are coming, Zaki."

Agwe's admission, the news of her brother and allies and the notion fate had not stolen all hope from her yet, trapped Zaki in one place with too many routes to follow. Standing off the fibrous tissue she leaned against, she stood crooked.

"You need to go, Agwe," she said. "You need to go help Tausi."

"Zaki, I—"

"Clermiel knows you're here, Agwe. He's still not sure, but he knows, and he knows you are here. He has to."

"Then we should leave." He held his hand out to her.

"No," she replied, fighting the urge to shrink from him again. "You have to leave me here."

Agwe grabbed at her hand. "I cannot!"

On instinct, Zaki tried to bat him away, as she had tried to bat away the mottled claws as they clubbed her near the point of death. Zaki half-gasped in shame, in release, as she stepped back from him a full foot, farther than she thought she would ever dare. "I can't. If he comes back and sees I'm gone he'll know, and he'll move. He's not moving because he thinks he wins. No matter what happens, Clermiel wins."

"You don't think that."

"No, and that's why you need to leave," she said, sobbing the words. "You need to be at my father's side. At Tausi's. They need you more than I do right now."

"That's not true, that's not—"

"Agwe, no."

The spirit of the sea silenced on the word.

"It doesn't matter if we don't beat him here," Zaki said, voice sinking to a whisper. "He'll move the conch and crush everyone in its path."

"But we're close, Zaki! We'll have him in a day!"

"And he'll turn the tide of the battle in a moment when no longer distracted by his plaything."

"So, you would just have me leave you here?"

Hugging her arms to her body, Zaki staked herself there, unwilling to back away anymore. A surge deep inside her, a need to know she still stood, fought against every shred of anxiety telling her this was not real. She looked at the gleam off his silver helmet. "You need to wipe this from my memory. You need to leave me in the dark."

Agwe shook his head. The silver scales set in his helm glistened in the ambient sunlight in the galley. "I won't."

"You will," Zaki replied, brooking no argument.

The silver in his eyes flashed as he searched the hard stare she gave back. A slight pause in his breath, so immediate one could not help but notice, made this creature of divinity and magic seem mortal, if only for a pause. He tried for some words, thought on them, and tried again.

"You'll forget about me," he said. "About what happened here."

"After how I found out, I don't know if I could trust you if I remembered."

The words stung, wounding his expression. Jaw tensed; he opened his hand. "All right, Zaki."

"Come get me when he's ready." She turned from him, searching the wall where she thought she had fallen before she awoke. She took a few steps toward that pulsing, beating narrow, almost too eager.

"I won't put you back in your wounded state," he said to her back.

The idea of fresh pain, the sting and suffer of what the devil might inflict later on weighed itself against her lover's small, desperate kindness. Zaki glanced over her shoulder at him, despairing at how different he was now that she knew everything. She tried a slight, comforting smile, but no life resided in it. "Just don't let me know that," she said, trying to halt the tears.

She dropped to her knees and crawled against the wall, laying against it as she balled her body up into a fetal position.

Agwe came over, his footfalls silent on the leathery floor. He knelt down on both knees, in front of her face.

The warmth of his palm pressed onto her bald scalp.

"Tell me the truth if you get the chance again. Tell me yourself," she whispered, forcing past her terror.

Oblivion wiped her vision.

CHAPTER 12
A HARD DAY'S NIGHT

"So have you thought on her offer?" Ngala asked, his facial expression as dead as the day's breeze.

The rowers beneath the deck groaned together, rowing through their strokes against a chopping sea that twisted its currents every time they tried farther west. The outline of Stone Cove's coast was within sight.

With the smell of brine and the creak of his solid weight on the boards under him, Zaki took it all in as he looked back, putting the sun off his face.

He enjoyed the unease Cleona had drawn from his father. "I still think on it," he said, giving the seasoned corsair an up-down with his detached gaze. "Do you wish to speak on my business, Captain?"

Danger flashed in Ngala's eyes, as hard as his mouth. An amused snort ground through his wide nose; the quick turn of his head brushed away the onus of the question. He cocked both shoulders in a quick shrug. "You are able to go and do what you need to go and do, Zaki. And bear the consequences for it."

"Tausi can have the boat. I'll capture myself a few Latians and build something better than this."

His father did not share in the amusement Zaki made of his tone.

The silence was punctuated by the grunts of the rowers beneath them. Striding to middeck and the mainmast, they scanned the silver coast and the dark green forests beyond the sun-bright beaches. The steady but labored chop of the water, the slow pace of the rowers chewing against it, fell into a steady rhythm that coaxed Zaki's mind far from where he stood, back to the shadowed grottoes not far from where the corsairs called home.

"You can send her away now," Ngala said.

"What?"

"Anaya." Ngala did not look at his son. "You can get rid of her, if you want. None would fault you."

Zaki turned on him. "Now that I'm leaving, you want to dangle something in front of me."

"That's not it," said Ngala.

"Liar," said Clermiel. "You are both liars."

"Then what is it?" Zaki prodded his father.

"Not here."

"Why?" asked Zaki, louder for the rest of the raiders on deck to hear. "Is it too late to not make me the cuckold of Stone Cove?"

Ngala reared like a viper, mouth bared like a beast. He did not shout or threaten, nor place his hand near his sword as his commander had, a habit too familiar to the crew of *The Gamka* over the intervening years since they daringly took the first Latian outposts. No matter how high Ngala had risen in the world of pirates and smugglers, never mind the grand fame Zaki had gathered for himself at his side, the fact of what Zaki was, despite every accolade, every golden word, remained.

And the crew had sat there through the years, hiding their faces while the two fought aloud about it.

Until that day.

Grown almost as tall as his father and as wide as Zaki, Tausi stormed over from where he had rested with his hide shield and weapons.

"Stop it," he said, his deepening voice curt. "You swore to me and Nkuku."

Ngala leveled a finger in Zaki's direction. "He's..." He snarled himself quiet when he realized the weary eyes upon them.

The tension on the deck, hot and heavy as the day on the windless sea, put the raiders at ill ease as they attended the rigging. Hard men bit their tongues, hard pressed not to remind the finest among them the sworn oaths both had taken to keep peace, or to chide Zaki for speaking to their hearts things he did not know about. Not a single man spoke of their commander as a cuckold, but neither did a single one of *The Gamka's* crew speak against her captain.

Nor did their captain speak after his growling.

He stared off at the nearing coastline, weather eyes fixed onward.

And Zaki let Ngala stare, walking off to the stern and the steering oar.

The Gamka rowed into Stone Cove's port. Tense after the spat between Ngala and Zaki, the rowers and raiders together hauled the trireme into its dry berth along the pier covered beaches that extended well past the breakers. Leaving her tilted on her portside, they emptied her of all the loot they had gained in their recent ravaging of the Latian trade routes. *The Gamka* was stocked well in both weapons and finer goods like spices and silks, and more than one clay vase weighing heavy in silvers made the boards creak as corsairs hauled them down to the sand. The shares already apportioned and split before they arrived, many of the raiders and rowers disappeared before command gathered their own things.

Of the final four, Tausi departed with Nkuku first. The timekeeper promised the boy the perfect place for them to drink dzan on the beach with the nicest salt-wives he knew. Without a word to neither Zaki nor Ngala, another constant in a proud family, Tausi departed with the only one they counted as their fourth.

Ngala and Zaki remained, the pair walking from stern to rostrum and back while the noon sun bathed the entire hull in light. Finding no work for Black Lizard's shipwrights to repair, they trudged up the sands to the low catwalks leading deeper into the cove's hidden fortress. Silent to the men who stepped out their way in respect, the two plodded deep into the stronghold of their powerful master. Going deep, where the tunnels had been carved from the stone itself, they came to the final passage to the throne room.

"Wait," said Ngala.

"Now is not the time for us to wait," said Zaki, but he stopped anyway. "Is there something we haven't accounted for?"

"Do you truly hate me so much you wish to leave?"

"Could you consider perhaps not all things are about you, Captain?"

"All things are in the mind of a father," hissed Clermiel. "The first failed god."

"Then what is it about?" Ngala asked.

Hands on his hips, Zaki, looked down at his feet. He shrugged. "Maybe it's about wanting more."

A subtle insult to Ngala's nature, or the way of anyone who sought higher things than they were born to, deadened his father to a mask of deep, abiding anger. He edged his head forward in Zaki's direction and took a step.

"You leave my side, you leave my favor, Zaki," said Ngala, "for whatever reason you give it."

"I stopped being scared of you a long time ago." Zaki checked his father's hand, which found its way to the hilt of his sword. "Careful. I brought one, too."

Then, to his shock, his father surrendered.

A look came over Ngala's face, revealing the hard lines the years at sea and bloodshed had etched. Zaki almost did not recognize him, until without any great warning someone he had not seen since the day Ngala realized he was a widower appeared. He found failure everywhere he looked on his father's features, a brokenness foreign to everything he knew of the man.

"Was it so foreign?" Clermiel asked.

Ngala pulled away first. They marched the last half of the hall in silence.

A pair of corsairs, heavily armored in Gypian helms and breastplates, opened the double-wicker doors into the palatial den of Black Lizard, lord of Stone Cove and a corsair-lord of the highest acclaim. Oil lamps guttered and glowed on sandstone shelves carved from the rock, illuminating rich purple tapestries hung to cover every wall while flames glittered piles of silver and jewels. A great throne of old sun-bleached wood stood erect, overseeing the glowing heaps of wealth, covered in the old standards of the murderers who had sat upon the chair before its current occupant.

A sixth flag, a white piece of sail stitched with a simple black lizard, lay spread across the others.

The rightful owner of the throne was nestled in that cloth, long legs up on a footstool made of stacked furs, and his hands rubbed by two comely lasses in garb more inviting than comely. Swaddled in a simple loincloth, he trusted to the blades strapped to the sword belts at their bare sides.

Those fierce companions checked over their shoulders first before he did, his head leaned to the side as he snoozed. Black Lizard started when one of his lovers squeezed his hand, calling him to immediate attention.

"Ah, Ngala," he called in his high, strong voice. The exhaustion left his aged face in an instant, and he sat upright. Scarred feet firm on the cool silver carpet beneath them, the corsair-lord's fixed gaze shifted toward Zaki, as did his grin, which took an unusual bent. "Commander Zaki. I see you two have returned from your accords with Captain Cleona. Did that she-devil from Tip Town live up to her half-sworn promises?"

"Fully and then some." Ngala brought his hand to his armored chest and bowed his head, a salute to his overlord. Zaki matched the movement and its reverence on cue.

"Is this the case, Commander?" Black Lizard asked.

Zaki raised his head in surprise. To his further amazement, he caught his father doing the same thing in time to catch Black Lizard's growing mirth. "Aye, Black Lizard. I would be half-sworn to the truth if I did not mention she saved my life."

"Did she now?" Black Lizard looked to both his salt-wives and pulled his hands away. Not troubled by his interruption, they turned in perfect unison and leaned against the corsair-lord's long legs. He rested a hand on one of his wives' heads, his hard fingers massaging the dark copper flesh. She rubbed the back of her head against his touch, a cat's smile on her full lips.

"Aye sir," said Zaki. He checked with Ngala, who stood at ease. Lowering his hand, he eased his own stance.

Black Lizard nodded in his chair like an expectant listener. "And did you offer her your life, as the salt laws demand of a corsair heart?"

"She refused it when offered and rescued me out of her own sense of duty." Zaki did not try hide to his smile. "She has even offered me a place on *The Immammou*."

"It seems Captain Cleona thought well of your ventures, too, my lad." He threw a knowing smile and a pop of his thin brow Ngala's way for teasing effect. Black Lizard adjusted on his throne, legs open like a reptile sunning his belly. "It seems after a life given and given back you would have a hard decision."

Ngala spoke. "My son is—"

"Zaki can speak," Black Lizard said, his joyful expression unmoved by the hard words he had spoken. He did not take his amber eyes off Zaki. "What decision did you make, Commander?"

"I have not made one yet, sir."

"You have not?" The corsair-lord's voice raised in concern. He lifted his hand from one of his lovers' heads and motioned at Ngala. "Patros?"

"My father has nothing to do with my lack of decision," Zaki said. "I have waited."

Black Lizard no longer rested on the back of his bare wooden throne but leaned up and toward the two leaders of *The Gamka's* crew. He switched back and forth between Ngala and Zaki, his bare jaw tensed. "Well? Why?"

Zaki watched his father shudder at their liege-lord's tone. Knowing the sly figure before them decided their fates upon his answer, he picked his words well. "Because if I sail under Cleona, I sail under Tip Town. My heart is not in Tip Town, my lord—it is here, in Stone Cove. To leave here is to leave my heart, no matter how much my yearning soul would yield to that same heart. And I would not have my loyalty come to question if our two companies were to meet at the end of ire. Not with my heart where it is."

The corsair-lord's warmth returned to his pleasant face, and he lay back into his chair nodding. He snapped his fingers, and one of the salt-wives turned on her naked bottom and lifted a wooden slate from behind a mound of silver. A stacked set of cups and a carafe of dzan rested on it. She set the tray in front of her salt-husband's scarred feet.

Black Lizard waved Zaki and Ngala in while his most favored pleasure-partners prepared drinks for all five of them. "A fine, fine answer from a grand salt," he said in his booming joviality. Resting to one side on an elbow, he bobbed a finger in Ngala's direction. "I've always thought you raised good children, Ngala. I value that in my folk."

Ngala swallowed hard. "As do I, Black Lizard."

"I think you should go, Commander," Black Lizard continued. His most favored put down her pitcher, picked her cup up first, and served the other salt-wife who accepted it with a warm smile. "Better relations between Stone Cove and Tip Town would help us consolidate accords with Butcher Bay against the Land Dogs, and I have fair views of Cleona as a captain." He took a cup when one of his salt-wives presented it. "Don't you, Ngala?"

"Aye, Black Lizard," he said, no emotion to his answer.

"Ah, so there it is," the lord of Stone Cove replied as his queens served Ngala and Zaki their sugar liquor. He raised his cup high. "Commander Zaki, I bless you with fortunes and fast currents ahead, wherever they lead. I'm eager to hear your choice."

Unable to comprehend what passed between Ngala and Black Lizard, Zaki watched the corsair-lord's attention leave him completely to fix his father with an amused, knowing smile. He raised his cup in unison with the rest, never daring not to meet his lord's toast.

Nor whatever weight it carried.

Zaki rode as hard and as fast from Stone Cove as he could when the sun set, leaving behind the cloying burn of sugar and cinnamon and the machinations he had heard while his father and Black Lizard conspired. Infused by the noise of the waves, the stars sparking like the silver heaped around Black Lizard's throne, all worries about the choices ahead disappeared in the joy of his freeing heart. Escape tore away the need for decisions. Passing through sandy glens of low hung trees and over grassy dunes over the moon-fired Mirror, he made for one of the peninsulas jutting into the waters.

Directing the stallion to the southernmost point, Zaki charged through ankle-deep puddles of brine mirroring a night sky dusted in diamonds. They wove the canyon between two mounds of white-ribbed pink sandstone, then beneath a natural tunnel made by the sea. The air seemed to still there, despite the constant warmth of the late summer, and splashing through a final straight of shallows the tides failed to wash out, mount and rider pressed into a great sea cave.

A bay refilled by a swirling pool at its center every day, the green-blue waters glowed with a phosphorescence when Zaki neared. He halted his stallion at the rounded edge and dismounted, holding a moment to let the light bathe his face. The moonlight glared off the sea outside, and he spied a wooden shack at the other end of the cave, near where the waves and currents washed out.

"I know this power," Clermiel whispered. "But not this specific one. So, who? Who is he?"

The waters murmured.

Stillness bled into the pores of Zaki's dark skin. "You were right," he said, calling aloud. "It all happened as you said it would. My rescue. Her offer." He searched the pool again. "And you were right about Black Lizard. He did exactly as you would and blessed my leaving."

"You sound surprised about him most of all," Agwe said, somewhere close.

Zaki turned his shoulder in the direction of the voduni's voice, or at least where he thought it came from. The stallion he held by the end of his reins tugged in protest, drawing back his attention.

"Let him go. I can call him back."

Zaki dropped the reins, and the ashen horse darted off into the night, his hooves clopping the stone before he found the water. Listening to the beast splash and play, he waited in the half-glow until the noise died off.

"Do you want to come swim?"

"My bones ache," said Zaki. "I've been on a ship all day, and I don't think I offer much."

"Then it is a perfect reason to come in," said Agwe, deep in the mists. "The salt will soothe you."

Zaki reached up and unbuckled the leather harness strapped to his hard torso. He smiled, if a tired smile, at his easy surrender, letting the armor fall where he stood. The war dress and sandals were peeled away with every other bit of cloth.

Naked in the soft, salt air and night's shroud, he slid down into the pool. Enveloped in a warm current, Zaki crawled toward the pool's luminous center. The water leeched exhaustion from his tight limbs, and the ache in his back fluttered away with every small kick he made to keep where he treaded. Laying on his back, he looked up.

The cavern's open roof displayed every star in perfect clarity, despite the hazy glow.

The water moved at Zaki's side.

"So will you go?" Agwe asked.

"You've already seen my answer, haven't you?" Zaki let his feet drop in the water until he treaded upright again.

Agwe lay against one of the pool's sides, his hands clung to the pink sandstone, so the tide did not pull him away. His silver eyes smoldered, burning a luster overwhelming the bright scales set into the flesh of his face. Perfect and naked, his flesh made his limbs seem like dark oil as he braced there, glistening in magic's light.

A yearning stirred in Zaki. "Haven't you?"

The smile on Agwe's lips said enough. He reached out with a wet, beckoning hand.

Zaki shared the same smile as he reached forth, secure in where the winds were about to take him.

CHAPTER 13

THE RIGHT SHADE OF ROUGE

Z aki sat in front of the three mirrored panels rested against the stairs leading up to *The Immammou's* deck. She almost did not recognize her face beneath the wire-held mane of the black wig she wore. Its silver-shod droplets of pure glass, threaded into the dark horsehair locks, caught the scant morning light leaking through the deck above them. The inner lining slightly padded and shaped to her skull, she turned her head back and forth, awed by the reflection and how well it sat.

"Captain," she said. "I don't know what to say."

"Just don't lose it in one raid," Cleona said, appearing over her shoulder. A warm smile creased all the happy lines in her aunt's face, sharing something deeper. She thought she might cry along with the woman she had come to think her captain as much as Ngala.

"Now, don't," said Cleona. She reached around and caught the first tear on a rough finger. "You don't want to ruin your eyeliner before the rain does."

Zaki laughed aloud, wrapped in her aunt's arms. The rowers worked hard behind them, grunting in unison with the strokes the timekeeper lashed on his drum. They held each other firm against the beat for what might be their last moment together. Sliding the mirrored panels beneath the stair, they ascended to the deck where *The Immammou's* raiders readied under thundering storm clouds. The trireme, wider and heavier than the ships Zaki had grown up around, held strong against the waves battering the trireme's dark sides. The deck gleamed, already wet from a brief shower.

"Bosun," Cleona nodded to Zaki, signaling to the stern and the steerage. Without another pause to see her order executed, the captain strode forward, her voice calling high over the flashing, booming sky. Drops fell from the twisting gray clouds above them. "Archers at the ready! You all should be fucking ready now!"

Zaki felt the rain strike her bare shoulders and arms, at first a drizzle while she pulled the pegs and unlocked the steering oar. Taking the length of fire-polished oak, the force of the sea cutting against the rudder woke in her hands. Cleona emerged out of the mass of moving warriors, carrying her short spear and a shield painted purple with Tip Town's gallant seagull on it. Laying her weapons to the side, she nodded to Zaki for the oar, who gave it up without question.

"Full beat to the rowers and tell Obinna to have them ready to pull oars. If we're hit, we'll be struck at stern on the portside," Cleona said, full of passion, but in full control. She set her eyes ahead, squinting through the mustering rain.

Again, wordless to the order, Zaki jogged for the hold's stairs, stumbling at the top for the weight of the light leather and chain she had armored herself in. Keeping her balance as she pounded down the steps, she found her feet when she reached the floor and dashed to the time-keeper's side.

Obinna stood at his full height, nine-heads tall of wiry, snapping muscle. Beating the goat-hide, he quickly caught sight of Zaki on approach. He cocked an ear her way.

She grabbed hold of his arm, which did not cease or alter the beat his hands carried. "Full beat until we draw oars. Watch for your portside if things go south."

"Blood and fate, Miss Zaki," he said, his voice like thunder itself. An unceasing statue of motion, he surveyed his rowers, accepting the grim but simple duty Cleona left them. "Tell her I said that if you can."

Water leaked through the boards over the heads of those in the hold, which she always remembered as she left. Zaki retreated above deck in time to catch the edge of the portal and brace when the sea knocked against the trireme's starboard. A wave of saltwater splashed over the rail, dousing the fighters clinging to the side. Flowing across the deck, it flooded the heels of those who had made it to the mainmast while some poor sod rolled on the wood, on his way to the portside. Caught by the corsairs braced on the other side, they righted him as the ship steadied beneath a blinding crack of lightning.

Crawling on, Zaki found her aunt still posted at the oar, tugging hard on the rudder to keep the ship level against the chopping ocean.

"Archers at the ready! Volley from bow to port!" she screamed, a siren's call in the storm-song.

Zaki echoed the order, shouting as loudly as she could. "Volley! Bow to port!"

The raiders answered the call, springing from their places with arrows rested on the string. Drawing back on the deck's slick surface, some knelt as they loosed in the directions Cleona indicated. The spread of shafts vanished in the downpour.

"Second volley!"

The raiders responded on cue, another mass of arrows firing forward and to the left as lightning blinded them.

Dragging her own weapons to where Cleona had left her gear, Zaki scooted back to position beside the straining captain. She searched about one of the small bins beside the oar, unable to find the oilcloth she might use as a shield to—

"Ramming," shouted Cleona. "Brace!"

Startled by the sudden announcement, Zaki fumbled for her sword and shield as *The Immammou's* bow slammed into the starboard of a Latian trireme. The rostrum splintered boards, which cracked louder than the thunder. The vibration shook her from the top of her head to the soles of her feet at once, a sickening endurance against too many forces. As immediate as the crash came, the entire boat settled before a crush of waves shifted the hull, moving the rostrum inside the Latian's shattered side. *The Immammou's* raiders gathered at the front of the ship and had already levered the gangplanks onto their ends and over, making a hanging ramp between them and their foes.

Cleona worked furiously to secure the steering oar, so it did not alter her ship or snap against the sea's current. No warning given, she dropped to both knees and hugged the housing the handle fed into. "Impact!"

The prow ship of a merchant sloop slammed into *The Immammou's* left side, crashing against her stern. Employed by the coastal towns and hamlets run by petty lords sworn to too many western kingdoms, these wide-bottomed boats featured fewer warriors and no rowers, and none carried a rostrum. A groan followed by another loud crack that was neither thunder nor lightning. Constructed to break from the ship and leave her sail-worthy in battle, *The Immammou's* ram gave with a terrible sound.

Paying little damage to the trireme, the jolt sent corsairs flying.

Nearly all the raiders were dumped to their knees or worse, tossed into the gray waters where even their light armor blanketed them into the goddess's embrace. Many fought, and those staying afloat were mashed between the boats, torn asunder by behemoth forces pulping their bones. Long moments passed in the whipping rain and wind while the three boats, joined together by their bridges, endured minutes of battering waves that claimed a scattering of lives.

When the rain lightened, Zaki picked herself off the ground, her left elbow cut open during her tumble. The hot sting of it ran down to her hand, but she snarled past it, rising in an instant with shield and spear. She rapped the shaft against the wooden frame stretched in animal hide. "Up, my hearties! Up before you feed the goddess more of her banquet!"

The raiders struggled to their feet as gangplanks from both ships wedging *The Immammou* banged loudly when they struck the rails. Sailors from the merchant ship and hoplites from the Latian trireme mounted an offensive. The Latians came in better armor than their cohorts on the other ship, shod in bronze while the others made do with wicker and hide.

"On the prow, on the stern! Hold your ground!" shouted a bloody-nosed Cleona, having recovered herself. Her swords flashed as bright as her gaze. The captain of the corsairs advanced from her steerage toward the merchant's gangplank. "Rowers, to deck!"

Zaki remembered her duty as bosun, turning where she stood for the hold. Navigating the unbalanced crowds of her own folk as a wave crashed over the starboard to soak her again, she descended its slippery steps. To no surprise, she found Obinna braced at one of the ship's sides, armed with his carved hardwood beater and a small iron buckler. The other rowers had risen with their chief, armed with their stout clubs. The boat rocked and heaved upon the sea, but here in the darkness, these men had waited, steadfast to the order.

"To red days," she cried with a sword thrust toward the outside.

The beating heart of the ship surged in unison up the stair, joining the surging battle. The rowers, almost double the count of *The Immammou's* raiders, crowded behind the warriors in the midst of their blood-letting, rescuing the fighters holding back the enemy tide. Though they had made quick work in halving the merchant's numbers, the constant pecking distractions of the braggarts allowed the Latian dominance of the gangplanks, a fool's position on the gorging sea, but a foothold, nonetheless. The corsairs rallied under the influence of fresh, dry men, who quickly overpowered the merchants.

Zaki fought at their head, hacking down any man who stood in Cleona's way to the merchant's sloop. Stabbing away each parry, any misdirection, she pressed her shield into any spot open to harm her aunt. They slew half a dozen men together before Zaki ascended the gangplank to the merchant vessel. Her nape, back, and arms goose-fleshed against the rain, adrenaline fueling her as she dispatched two men at once.

A Latian horn, used to signal the advance, blew in the distance as the rain abated.

Left to waves and gales, the battle upon the waves lay bare its awful truth. Beneath the blackened skies, the three-ship fleet from Tip Town had engaged the two Latian escorts that had accompanied the three merchant vessels joined together in a convoy. One sloop had fallen to *The Sobo* while *The Pwen* attacked the second Latian alone, like *The Immammou* had the other. The other merchant had overturned in the churn, sinking with its cargo and crew. Taken quick and forgotten as quickly by the survivors, the battles raged far apart from each other, with little hope of either sister-ship coming to Cleona's rescue.

Never to ask for it, Cleona called out from behind Zaki. "Back on my ship, bosun! Rowers to the bow! Slay the Latians to the last!"

Pulled by the sword belt under her aunt's strength, her spear was torn from Zaki's hand when it caught in the ribs of her latest victim.

Releasing it, she fell backward in a panic. Cleona and another raider caught her, setting her right as another merchant struck.

A wave broke between the trireme and the sloop, knocking out the gangplank connecting them together. Untethered, the merchants aboard decided against further fighting, choosing the storm instead to contend with.

The Latians held no such thoughts. Committed to the end, grappling hooks flew through the spray, hooking *The Immammou's* rail. The zealot slaves that manned the benches for the hoplites hauled the two boats together with all their strength. Any who failed to exhaustion or exposure suffered a stab in the back, only to be replaced by the western or Juutan slave who had been ordered to knife them. More gangplanks lurched up, the fresh hoplites behind them ready for a turn at death.

The gangplank at the bow fell away when the edge of the storm rolled through, broken in half by a sudden shift in the Mirror's sloshing surface. Latians drowned in gray-green depths, their armor inescapable anchors. Another wave rolled through, knocking the two foes together in a sudden collision. Men in horse-crested helms looked across from their deck at the corsairs, any fear banished by pure, focused hatred. Some flung their spears, killing one rower while the rest missed or dropped in the fresh chasm created when the sea split them apart again. The grappling hooks kept both ships in distance.

After another enveloping wave drenched half of *The Immammou's* deck and a quarter of the Latian's, the gangplanks came down.

Someone from the corsair's side shouted. "They're taking on water!"

True to the word, the sea flooded into the wound the torn rostrum had made of the Latian's starboard. The enemy's ferocity took stark clarity, their focus now geared to pure survival. Many of them dared heroic leaps from their deck, some of them landing atop raiders and rowers, killing one or two before they were dragged down. The others plunged into the ocean.

Hoplites sprang over in teams of four and five, armed with only their swords and a willingness to sacrifice themselves. Blood reddened the deck, sliming the saltwater to make every step a sucking one.

Yet Cleona held.

Unrelenting with her sword work, she laid low every bastard daring for the middeck of her ship, her life, where no difference lay between. At her side through it all stood Zaki, hewing their foes down until she ascended one of the gangplanks. Roaring like a creature not bound to water, but to sand and soil, she chopped and stabbed hoplites, dashing their corpses in the red foam. The cheers, the goading of the corsairs behind her, drove her forth.

"The Lioness lives!"

Her black and silver tresses whipping about her rain-washed face, Zaki dropped her shield and reached forward, yanking the sword out of the hand of the hoplite in front of her. The Latian, stunned by the feat, hesitated too long before his head left his body. She sprang forward, again and again, her feet finding the right place and the right time to tear them asunder.

Cleona stormed in behind her, rebuffing another charge while a contingent of rowers and raiders at bow made enough room for their own leap across. The Latians, forced to two fronts, thinned their line to slay those brave salts before two of the gangplanks slipped off the Latian's rails, taking the six men boarded upon it.

An explosion of water sprouted from the Latian's hold. Rowers by the dozens attempted to escape the sudden intrusion of the sea, their bodies crowding the stair before terror claimed their senses and they clawed over whomever lay before them.

This time, Zaki pulled her aunt back in time, leaping for their deck as the enemy trireme capsized on its stern, throwing every hand aboard in the water. Quick to foot, many of the raiders and a few rowers fit enough grabbed what bows and fallen arrows they could, shooting down survivors who attempted the swim. Many hoplites sank, gone in an instant, while some fought toward the portside. Those who made the climb had their hands cut apart by sword and wedge.

Not a single Latian lived to tell of what happened when they met *The Immammou.*

Zaki stood alone at the mast, watching the setting sun yellow the graying sky. Her entire body had been washed clean in every nook and corner beneath her armor. The headdress she wore gleamed like fire at the dying light. Her blood-crusted sword still in her hand, she stood on the empty deck, transfixed by the next shift on its way.

The bodies had been cleared, the merchant sloops looted and drowned with all hands aboard. Cleona detested slavery like Ngala did —but the red stink of gory iron haunted the boards.

Zaki thought of the men she had slain, the looks on their faces, the cheers at her back, the serene knowledge she had finally been set free. The sword had felt different, more alive to her than ever before, as had each step taken, knowing full well if she died, she died as who she was, as she meant to be.

An exhale of the sea escaped her, carrying away every day of old her life so she could start anew.

CHAPTER 14

TIK TOK

Zaki held the first breath she took as she descended *The Immammou's* gangplank, her head shaved bare and face naked of the makeup she had grown accustomed to in the nine months spent with Cleona in the eastern waters of southern Juut, where the seas stretched before golden wheat coasts and the waves carried ships from places none in Stone Cove had ever dreamed.

Again she was Zaki, child of a captain who did not know her, of a people she did not trust.

Those feelings were not captured in her departure from her aunt's ship. Crowned in her locks, painted like a goddess, she had stood before them while they sang old salt songs meant to bless their families. Tears were shed in the dawn light upon the deck. Rower and raider, they thanked her for her service in the furthering of Tip Town, in the defense of their lives, pledging by the salt in their flesh to serve her in time of need. Left to the last, Cleona and Zaki departed the trireme in Stone Cove's bay together, where they met a large welcoming party gathered for their native child's return. Flutes weaved and glided over bounding drumbeats. Netted shells cascaded on dark, polished rattles as deep horns blew in a battle hymn of victory. The musicians Black Lizard had corralled, loud to the point of abrasive, trumpeted their coming.

Their line, cheering and dancing, enveloped Zaki and Cleona.

As expected, the tall, spindly, graceful Black Lizard sashayed forward in his fine black robes, the lapels fringed the head-feathers of the ferocious sea-serpents of the deeper seas, the sleeves flaring in ridge-lion fur. He opened his arms for a sweeping embrace.

"Captain Cleona of Tip Town," he declared. "Too long have my eyes gone without seeing you."

"Lizard," Cleona responded in a withered tone. She did not step forward. "You haven't changed."

"And why would I need to go and change here, in my home of Stone Cove?" he cried in response to a hundred automatic cheers. "Now come now, woman, let's get to drinking!"

And beside Black Lizard, standing a more staid vigil, Ngala stared at Zaki. They beheld each other, parent and child, at a loss for anything to say while the lords of the sea began their diplomatic carousing.

"Captain," said Zaki with a firm nod.

Ngala matched it. "Commander. I hope your voyage with Captain Cleona went well."

"Yes," she said, squaring with the man before her. "I learned much to bring back to *The Gamka*."

He hesitated, his mouth open to speak before he shut it and nodded to Zaki. "We will speak of that when the time comes."

From there they parted, Ngala to his table where he and a fellow crewman from *The Gamka* supped, while Zaki went to where Black Lizard and Cleona sat for the evening's feast to be served. Stews smoking of tomatoes and peppers bubbled next to platters heaped with fried fish spiced in thyme served on beds of hot rice cooked in palm oil. Honey wine and millet ales flowed from stone pitchers into clay cups, fresh and heady. Onions and garlic hung in the air with the incense of old herbs fired in bowls, blown about while salt-wives sang, clapped, and danced to the beats of the musicians always at the edge of the festivities.

Hungered after her long voyage from Tip Town, Zaki ate well of her meal and conversed with Black Lizard when the corsair-lord deigned to speak to her, often asking for affirmation or support to something Cleona said in passing. His enthusiasm a wall between her and Ngala, she let the wild, wonderful leader of Stone Cove play court however he wanted. She laughed at the jokes, answered the questions, and ate her food, but she was always searching for someone amiss.

Tausi had not appeared for the feast.

She spent the rest of the night spying on every table for her younger brother. When she failed to find him, Zaki excused herself from the banquet to rest from the long journey. Saying nothing to her father, who paid her no mind other than to nod along with Black Lizard and Cleona when they gave their leave. Working her way between the tables packed with drinking corsairs laughing and singing old songs, she left the beach for her home's inner halls.

Through torch-lit passages and sand-gardens that opened to the yawning holes in the cavern that nestled the fortress, she traced down the old ways she remembered best, slinking to the same drinking dens and smoke dens she tried as a teen. Recognized by some of the red-eyed dwellers who were current crewmen on *The Gamka*, they shared with her that Tausi did not often frequent their dice games and dzan-circles, choosing instead the solitude of the stables near the gates. Recalling the last time she had spoken with her brother, when life seemed the most crowded and choking, Zaki felt a pang in her chest as she returned to the path she had come.

"He doesn't matter," Clermiel grumbled from the corners of the musty chambers. "Where is the spirit?"

The sky had coppered when Zaki reached the stables outside of the fortress gates. The few years replayed upon every step she took, guilt and shame of his abandonment ringing every thought. The anger she had felt at Ngala, at herself, at Anaya for never claiming what she wanted boiled inside her—of all the people to pay the cost, Tausi should have carried none of it. The smell of the hay, the manure, filled her nose as she checked the stalls, the dark cells left open so the horses could graze when needed, all of them trained from yearlings to answer the stable masters' calls.

One after the other, she passed to the end of the row and thought to—

"I didn't expect you to run off."

She jerked to a halt at the second to last stall.

There on a squat stool in an empty corner sat Tausi. Elbows on his knees, he hunched forward like a beast, eyes trained on Zaki like a predator to prey. A sword, its blade nicked and burred along the iron edge, leaned against the inside of his thigh, not far from reach. He cradled the bottom of a green glass dzan bottle in the other, the sugar liquor already slacking his features to reveal the angry, wounded child before her.

Jaw tight, he said nothing from his meager throne, stinking of drink and sweat.

She stepped to one of the stall's supports, leaning her shoulder against the wind-smoothed wood. Unarmed, she paid his weapon no attention and put on an easy smile. "I was wondering where you were. You did not come to the welcoming feast for Cleona."

"I am a commander and raider aboard one ship, among many commanders and raiders aboard many ships. More important men attended."

"None are more important to me than you."

"Was I that when you rode away?" The wound bared in his shaking voice, Tausi snorted hard to hide the tears in his eyes. He laid the bottle of dzan on his knee and tried to shake the emotion off his face, failing to do so.

Zaki straightened on both feet and drew an uneasy breath. "I know what I did."

"And it was done."

She stepped into the stall. "I did not know what to do. Ngala foisted this devil upon me and—"

"Don't call her that. If she is, we are the dread sorcerers who summoned her," said Tausi. "We're as much to blame for her as she is. She's become a lady of ill repute upon Stone Cove, its most sought-after, and also its most venomous. Men pay her salt to do things respectable salt-wives won't, and she has started to turn many of them to her practices as well. She speaks of Gypian gods and curses the sea, and for all the people that have disowned her, she has even more adherents. She has become criminal among criminals—but one for us to deal with. And her salt-husband was nowhere around to do it."

"Where was Ngala, daring corsair-captain? What of ferocious Tausi?"

"Don't you fucking dare," Tausi said, rearing up from his seat. His sword and bottle came with him. "We kept trying to live past the stain while you ignored it, and then you ran from it. No matter what is done now, that stain is there. She is still a blight upon us, our reputation, our good name. Your name."

"I don't care about my name to those that cling to her."

"She is still your wife."

"We don't own people, Tausi. Ngala acts like he owns everyone, but he doesn't. He doesn't own me, and he doesn't—"

"Stop fucking patronizing me," his brother said. "You think I don't know that?"

Zaki stopped, raising her hand in a gesture of peace. "Tausi…"

"She's in our mother's bedroom, you awful—" The tears flowed, helpless rage breaking his expression. "That was our home."

She struggled for the words needed to soothe the sneering, sniffling man she had left behind, abandoned like all of them had abandoned each other. She furrowed her brow and shut her eyes. Zaki stood there, defeated before she had even started.

Until she decided otherwise. The truth could wound like a surgeon's pin lancing the infection to drain it out.

"I shouldn't have kept the truth from you," Zaki said. "I shouldn't have run. Not from you."

"Well good that you know that now," shouted Tausi, slamming his bottle of dzan against the packed dirt between them.

The shattering riled the horses a few stalls away, whining before they calmed, but not the beast that stood before Zaki. He heaved, eye clenched shut to stop tears that would not cease, bathing his dark cheeks until beads dripped from his chin. He sobbed and sobbed.

She crossed the distance, fearing every second that he might skewer her. Zaki threw her arms around Tausi, who dropped the blade and buried his face in the hollow of her neck, his whole weight dead in her embrace. Zaki held her brother up and let him fall apart.

Zaki and Tausi marched, swords bared for all to see as they strode the passageway to their rooms. None of the corsairs and their salt-kins hid in their cells but acknowledged the two with heavy nods as they passed. In the few hours after midnight, Stone Cove reeled in strains of music amongst the pleasure dens. Incense stinking of beech wood and honey-blossoms congealed with the spilled dzan and ale that frothed in puddles where it gathered. Flutes and drums ceased when the glint of steel caught the player's eye but quickly resumed, charged with a deeper, airer, faster tune.

The lions of Ngala stalked their haunt.

Years of shame fell from every face that turned her way, every recognized glance that followed her movement. Zaki felt naked to those eyes, perhaps truly naked for the first time in the way that mattered—the pride lost, the taunts they had whispered, and not a single thing said replayed itself. Tight to the hilt of her sword, she kept lockstep with her brother. On the final bend before they turned onto the breezeway that led to their lost home, she caught his visage.

Tausi did not look at her or look away—only ahead. No life, no passion, a killer's mien had formed in the months that she had gone away with their aunt. She wondered how much of that killer had become her brother.

Two men, sharing a bottle of liquor and girded only in their loin-cloths, posted outside of the entrance to their rooms. The first man nursing the dzan dropped it when he made eye contact with Zaki. He turned and ran, giving no warning to his friend who looked and followed him down the breezeway a second later.

"Not a man alive if they rise against us," Tausi said.

Zaki did not have time to respond as her younger sibling took point, crashing through the red silk curtains. Keeping to Tausi's rear, she came up on his left side.

The entire room hushed when they entered. Men and women, the later a few of the salt-wives convened to service Anaya's needs, spread out on the floor in naked, sweating piles, carafes were overturned, and broken shards of empty liquor bottles littered the places where human bodies did not lay in startled panic many of them caught in the middle of carnal deeds. None had swept in the floor in as many years since Zaki had last seen them, and many of the old pieces of wicker-furniture had been frayed from thoughtless use. Graffiti, some of it directed at her and declarations of who had made her a cuckold and when, were scrawled across the plaster.

Men rose to their feet in an instant, some running for the balcony outside while others dug through their garbage in search for their blades.

"Leave them where they lay and you'll have one last chance at life," Zaki warned. "I'll not say it again."

Most of them understood immediately, taking the last reprieve to depart the large sitting room.

Three remained behind. One of them, a raider Zaki recognized from somewhere in the past, drew his sword and tossed the scabbard to the floor. The other two matched, with one sliding to the right to square himself against Tausi.

All set upon each other instantly. Zaki batted aside her first attacker's thrust and scored his throat, which sent the man sprawling in time to let her parry the second man's chop to her bare head. Twisting his blade, she freed from the bind and sliced apart his wrist. He screamed in agony before she opened his neck with a cut, ending it.

Tausi smacked aside his attacker's feeble lunge and drove his sword deep into the third man's chest. Roaring into the dying corsair's face before he pushed the corpse off of his blade, he retrieved his victim's weapon and checked on her.

Zaki nodded to him, her face speckled in a warm gore.

"What the devil is goin—"

Anaya gasped from the doorway to the bedchamber, her curvaceous form wrapped in a blanket. Dark circles crushed her reddened eyes, which widened in terror when she saw Zaki as if she saw her death and was certain of it. She backed into the bedroom.

"Ejifo! Ndukala!" she shouted. "They've come! Ngala's children have come!"

Zaki and Tausi burst past the curtain of the bedchamber to find Anaya crouched in the corner, guarded by two raiders both of them knew.

The first, a tall warrior with a swimmer's build and spring-tight thews, Ejifo set his strong eyes on the two intruders to his current dominion, a homestead he had scared from others that thought they had claimed or beaten out of Anaya for permission. A killer on one of the other boats in Black Lizard's wide employ, he regarded neither Ngala nor his children with any sense of loyalty. He waited, as naked as the sword he held.

The second raider, Ndukala, had dropped to his knees in shock. A raider on *The Gamka*, he held his hands out in surrender, begging as he jabbered. "Commander Zaki, I knew I lay with her when I served, but I—"

Tausi did not waste words. Driving his blade into Ndukala's chest, he bored the raider's body onto the floor where it leaked on the packed dirt from his piercing. He wrestled his sword free of the gory chasm he made.

Anaya's screams welcomed the geyser of red.

Ejifo darted toward Zaki. She met him, lithe grace and precision against the quick attack and athleticism behind his muscular frame.

Zaki let the skilled but overeager raider wear against her guards, diverting his stabs and follow-up attacks as Ejifo drove her out of the room. Backed into the previous room where they had found the orgy, the two dueled until she tricked him into a false counter, raising his sword every time she blocked his downward blows.

Feinting on the third exchange, Ejifo pulled back suddenly in expectation Zaki would follow, slashing wide where she would be.

Smart to the plan, she lunged after the intentioned cut, the tip of her sword parting the skin and slipping between the spaces of his dot-scarred ribs. The point fixed his heart. Rearing back for one last strike, Ejifo glowered at her with his wide-set eyes, the life in them fighting until they dimmed.

Zaki had had a few moments of quiet to catch her breath when Tausi forced Anaya into the room, robbed of her blanket and left bare. A few months pregnant, her skin had become dull and limp by her days of excess, and parts of her that had once held firm and supple had distended from the lewd play she had made of her body. Tears slicked her wide cheeks. She coughed through her sobs as she fell onto both knees before Zaki, one hand to her belly while the other reached out, held up to beg for mercy.

Tausi stood over her, the front of her bare body streaked in the same life that coated his sword. He looked down his nose at the human heap.

"You brought me here," Anaya seethed through sobs. "You and your damnable father. It's not my fault you're a freak, a farce playing something he isn't, something nobody would ever want. Nobody wanted you anyway," she said, talking faster to stay the rising terror in her voice.

The tears ran free with the venom. "I'll tell. I'll tell everyone everything, Zaki. I'll tell them how you're off fucking other men. I'll tell them about who you think you are—the lies you want to live. I'll tell them."

"Not unless we kill you," said Tausi.

Zaki saw Anaya's hand tighten on her swollen belly. The soaked blade she held felt heavy as she measured the poor thing before her. Her focus flicked toward Tausi. "We're not going to kill you, Anaya. You're going to get up and leave."

Tausi's passion returned. "What?" he said, almost choking on the word.

Heaving, Anaya gaped at Zaki, unsure of what to do.

"Tell them," said Zaki, looking down at her horrid salt-wife. "Tell them that Queen of the Silver Coast and her brother have reclaimed what you took, and that for the grace of their better souls they spared you what you were owed. Go do what you want, Anaya, say what you want, but you'll no longer do it here or in my name. We never traded salt anyway."

"You can't simply throw me out," she said. "Ngala said I could have these rooms. Ngala made me your salt-wife. He has to pay me my sum."

"And I'll make him do that," Zaki replied. "But you're not here anymore."

Anaya sputtered, unable to form words.

Zaki nodded at her womb. "You're not the one getting this chance, if you can think beyond yourself."

The bluster broken from her expression, Anaya let the weight of the warning ease her sobs before she knelt there, naked and shivering. "Can I at least have some clothes?"

"Of course," said Zaki. "You can take a blanket too."

The long embarrassment of Zaki's salt-wife ended more quickly than any had expected. Minutes later she was gone, disappearing into the dens and bowels of Stone Cove, where whatever fate waited. Left alone in their home for the first time in what felt longer than a few years, the siblings basked in the quiet.

"What now?" Tausi asked to their emptiness, once again.

"Now we'll get ready."

CHAPTER 15
ROUND WHATEVER

S he woke in the gentle warmth of the galley, sunlight flooding the twitching red hall to glisten upon muscle and sinew. The blue sky outside the wide openings overlooking the sea was startling in its bare beauty, and she wondered if she still lived in the devil's dream. The answer came when the door near the rear of the chamber slid open with a gross, slimy sound.

Two Ulmos entered, their hulking, chittering masses posted side by side. Their baleful black orbs watched Zaki in her corner of the weird room, but they did not move to take her from where she sat.

"You will tell me who he is. Now."

Clermiel's voice echoed throughout the galley, with no point of origin.

"I'm tired of digging through your primitive mind. You are as low and as corrupt as your blood, and even worse for the falsehood you would make others of your ilk bear. You are lowly, and this fight has come to an end."

"So, I've run out of chances," Zaki said to nothing and him. Unmarred, hungry yet fit, she slowly got up to her feet and took a few tentative steps forward. The light in her eyes fuzzed the way ahead. She mused at the thought with some perverse pleasure, knowing it would be harder to see them when they came for her.

"You never had one."

The certainty in the devil's voice changed her mind. Zaki reached up and rubbed her eyes out until they cleared and settled her focus on the Ulmos. The armored terrors had yet to move.

"I don't know who you want him to be," said Zaki to their blank, antenna-ed faces splotched in green. "You can—"

"You know his true name. He told you it," said Clermiel, each word rising in anger. "Tell me."

Zaki laughed at him and turned away from her guards.

A blow to the back of her head knocked her forward against the rubbery muscle of the floor. Stunned, Zaki tried to crawl onto her hands and knees, unwilling to face the Ulmos unprepared. Her attempt failed when an invisible force caved in her chest, driving the air out of her lungs as she broke on her side.

"Tell me," Clermiel screamed, his voice blaring loud and sharp.

Whimpering at the agony in her inner ears, she curled into a ball and tried to block out the deafening tone.

The formless devil beat her again with his magic, knocking her in the temple and the stomach.

"Tell me," he said, drawn to a whisper.

She tried to push herself from where she lay, bare heels digging into the weird flesh beneath her. Hugging her arms to her chest, as if she could shield herself from what would follow, Zaki crawled on her knees, fighting to get both feet under her.

"Tell me," he screamed again, making her cover her ears.

Sharp stabs from every direction struck her neck, back, thighs—everywhere. Under the battering, she mustered the will to keep dragging herself away and toward the light. The sea lay that way.

"Tell me," he said, this time flat, as if he stood in front of her.

Zaki looked up.

The devil in the flesh of the dead Captain Popobawa stood before her, with his wormy smile and yellowed eyes. He carried a silver sword, long and sharp, waving it over the crown of her head.

"I could cut your skull open and figure out why you're an abomination," he said, as if it was a kind offer. "See why you think you can be...you. At the cost of so much."

"You..." Zaki hacked out a mouthful of blood from the back of her throat. "You just don't like me."

"No," Clermiel said. "But yet this god is plagued with fascination for his mortal toys."

Zaki heaved through her open mouth, unable to snort through a broken nose. "You're no god."

The dead captain's apparition smacked Zaki in the side of her head with its free hand, the devil's unnatural strength flinging her into the air. By some cruel miracle, she landed on her shoulders first instead of her head, tumbling before her body could right itself, and flopped onto her stomach. The sear of a separated right shoulder fused her eyes shut. She tried to wiggle her fingers on the injured arm.

"What is his name, Zaki?"

She struggled to breathe through her nose, the blood thick in her mouth. Her guts rebelled, stomach gurgling threats of bile.

"What is Agwe's true name?"

The air seemed to congeal around her right wrist, tighter than a rope, and yanked her straight off the floor. Zaki lost sight and hearing in the pain.

"I don't know," she screamed as she hung from the tatters of her shoulder, the sensation of its tearing away forcing every bit of the truth into her words. "I don't know! I don't know! I don't know!"

Clermiel stood before her, seemingly staring past her with his rotted eyes. Slack of any expression, he turned to the Ulmos at the galley's door. He leaned his husk on his sword, the point sunk deep into the floor. Blood welled around the wound and ran, but the room thrummed as if nothing had changed.

"I could have them kill you, here and now," the devil said, facing her again. "The only reason we keep doing this is because I'm curious. It's always been my weakness. How the broken break things, and yet we all sit around and smile about it." The white face crinkled in bitterness, his purple lips puckering in hate. As quick as the evil revealed itself it, it was gone, a slack expression left in its wake. "But I like your brother. I hope to convince him to serve me, like I would have you, but he is a far finer gem. None of the slag."

Zaki gritted her teeth, tightening her jaw past the flame ripping her arm from her body.

"I need a voyager to guide me," he said, almost distantly. "I need someone to herald my rule."

"You'll never get him." She raised her head and glared right into the eyes of the sorcerous demon, that ancient filth of a forgotten era. Grunting, Zaki chuckled through her teeth and made a smile. "Just like you never got me."

He said nothing, gazing at her with no emotion.

Maddened by her injury, Zaki pressed, caring for her life as much as he did. "You, you and your bastard-kind fell because you wanted too much. Do you know what wanting too much is? Having things you can't have."

The shackle of air around her right wrist pulled her higher off the floor before dropping her back down half a foot in a sudden jerk. The torn shoulder, now a fever, re-awakened in a blinding cascade. Her screams escaped her no matter how much she struggled to keep them in; she accepted it in small hiccups of laughter.

"You'll never get him because you could never get me," she heaved between gasps. "You could never get me!"

He lifted his sword from the flesh-floor, the tip against the hollow of her throat.

"Do it," she said, goading the devil. "Tausi will spend his days running you down!"

"I will break him on more than your little life," Clermiel replied. He peered at her, half-lidded, and turned his wrist.

The point shed blood from her throat. A red, warm drop trickled and mixed with the sweat on her neck. "Find out."

In sudden, liquid smoothness, Clermiel tore the blade away and snatched Zaki by the throat with his free hand. The binding on her wrist loosened. His gross strength on full display. he raised her higher, as if examining a fish he had caught.

"And what do you think I'll find?" he asked as he squeezed tighter to her neck.

Zaki made to say something biting and pithy. Fighting for a breath, the darkness closed her vision, shrinking to a pinhole of vanishing light.

CHAPTER 16

EDGE OF GLORY

"L et me bring it out," said Agwe.

He disappeared into the small shack in the corner of his private lagoon, where Zaki and Tausi sat on the natural ledge, their feet dipped in the swirling pool. Her brother had remained tight-lipped the entire trip down to the voduni's domain and was curt once she introduced Agwe and explained exactly, in the fullest detail, who he was and why they had come here.

Tausi only stayed silent for the few minutes they were alone before impatience claimed him. "So, you've been coming down here to be with your salt-husband."

"In every sense of the word," Zaki said over the gentle breakers splashing on her shins.

"I know his name," Clermiel whispered from beneath the water's surface, glaring up at them. "I have to know his name. It is the only way to stop him."

Tausi made a sound in his throat when he swallowed, bobbing his head as he stewed on the information. The noon sun shone on the green pool before them, its foamy surface swirling gently.

Zaki waited, wondering if something had changed. She wondered how deep his worry would run when it came to Ngala. "Tausi," she whispered.

"It's not that I can't accept it, or that I disagree with it. I don't completely understand it, yet," he said, not taking his carnelian eyes from the water. "I always knew you didn't feel right the way you were, as if you were carrying on something you didn't like every day. I thought it was just what came with the boats. If this is you, then this is you, and I love you."

The declaration, simple in its delivery, stunned her to a new quiet. Caught between wanting to embrace her brother and leave him be, to accept this for what it was, warred in her before Agwe interrupted.

"Here," the silk-robed sorcerer said as he exited his beach-wood hut. He carried a medium-sized wooden box in his long, smooth hands, which he placed behind where they sat. Lifting the lid before he straightened, he dipped into the container and drew from it a gleaming gown of spun silver. A waterfall of sparkling wind and salt, it hung in Agwe's fingers like strands of realized grace gathered together by some spell of his making.

He presented to Zaki, who held her breath in astonishment.

She looked between it and Tausi, both of them awed by a treasure so wonderful, so amazing to two corsairs who had already stolen many of the finer things the world had to offer. The mere presence of the gown destroyed such notions they had of worth. So priceless, the garment was seemingly spun from the stars themselves.

"It will do what it needs to do when you need it done," Agwe said.

"What do you mean?" Rubbing her calloused thumbs against its woven rings, Zaki marveled at how soft the metal felt, so smooth and cottony, yet as strong as iron.

"You'll see," he said, appraising her and his gift with a proud smile. "Now, it's time for us to leave."

"A faker. A fool," the devil said from behind the voduni. "And yet a wonder-maker. There are only so many of those. It could be among the twelve of you."

"Where do you venture, sorcerer?" Tausi asked, his attention torn from the treasure.

"Homeward, little brother," said Agwe, putting his back to the warrior and an edge in his voice. "To Stone Cove."

As the voduni returned to his hut to gather his things, Tausi drew close to his sister.

"What are you planning?" he asked, whispering. "What is that for?"

She stared at Tausi; her expression blank before the immediacy of the question set in. "Did you mean what you said? That you accept me as I am?"

The questioned stiffened Tausi, his expression wounded. "I gave you my word, Zaki."

Desperate to balm it, she grasped his shoulder, the silver dress balled in her right hand. "Then trust me. I won't be alone in what I'll do, but when it happens, you will have to make a choice."

"What choice?"

"Which one of us you will stand with," she said.

"You'd—" Shrugging off her hand, Tausi took a step back. He gaped at her, unable to make the words he wanted.

Then he found the worst ones.

"He's going to give you a ship, and that will come with the assent of the other captains. Some of them are not going to be open to this. At all."

Speechless, Zaki blinked at her brother in astonishment. Her hand drifted to her mouth, but the sickness she expected to gather in her gut never arrived, nor did endless, perplexing anxiety. She stepped back, wordless still.

"Zaki," Tausi said. "Say something!"

"What is she to say?" The voduni asked from the entryway to his hut.

Never shirking a challenge from another, Tausi stepped toward Agwe, his left hand clutching the throat of his sword's scabbard. "We have a duty, sorcerer. Not everything can be done on whims and want. We are at constant war with the Land Dogs, while at the same time racing against what western invader who would rape our leagues and coasts for themselves, and there are more every season."

"And the point of this speech?" Agwe asked in a droll monotone.

"See how he lorded over you, and yet did not reveal his truth?" Clermiel asked. "Why do you trust this? Why not give up in spite of him?"

Zaki stepped between her lover and her brother before the latter drew his weapon. "Tausi."

"You will be better than him, Zaki," said Tausi. "Wait. Wait until he is dead. We will rule Stone Cove by then. Then you can—"

"I will not wait on me," she said to his face, silencing him.

Her answer transformed the man into the baby she remembered writhing in her arms, hungry for food they did not have before their father came back. Already a killer, a reaver, and not knowing how to be those things and still be himself, Tausi broke into the tears that came. A trembling fear ran over his face at the idea that Zaki, and Zaki alone, might stand against their father highlighted a terror she recognized in herself too well for her comfort.

"Why do you persist?" Clermiel questioned, almost whispering the question. "What drives you to defy?"

The hall wobbled in the cascading sounds of long reed flutes and rattling steel drums that seemed to shake the air through the smoky chamber reeking in incense set to pyre. Salt-wives danced languidly to the beats before the leering, lustful eyes of raiders and rowers packed from wall to wall, corner to corner.

At the back, dead center of the celebration, Black Lizard commanded from his highchair. His many wives arrayed themselves to his left and right, and a special seat had been made out for Cleona.

The corsair queen of Tip Town came in her finest adornment, a grand gown of silk that cut down the center to her navel in sequined purple that outshone the purple banners set up as posts to her chair. Armored in square pauldrons made of gold and jewels capping her shoulders, a matching diadem that draped strands of pearl and silk on her full cheeks rested elegantly upon her head. Little impressed by the debauchery and drunkenness splayed before her by the corsairs of Stone Cove, she sat idly by and paid small, if insincere smiles to her gaudy host whenever Black Lizard looked her way; he sat stitched in a complete bodysuit of gold cloth that covered everything but his face, hands, and feet on which he wore bright red slippers Zaki was sure were meant for a woman's foot.

"How could a god bless this debauchery?" Clermiel asked from a bench between two men already keeled over. "Perhaps it is that whore-goddess. It could always be her. That narrows down the possibilities."

And there, not far from Black Lizard and Cleona's view, sat the captains of Stone Cove in their armor. As much as their lord was flamboyant, bright, and exuberant, these men were the opposite. Many of them were drunkard-murderers who kept their seats through the brutality of their larceny, not a one showed a sliver of depth beyond the simple lusts they looked to sate, save Ngala, who watched the proceedings with equal amounts of mirth, interest, and caution. Dressed in his full armor, save his helm, he nursed his wine cup in one hand while thumbing the pommel of his iron sword with the other, eyes always keen to every new detail that caught his attention.

Zaki watched him from the doorway to the smoky party rooms of the pirate-lords, where even more crews were herded around small, squat tables heaped in roasted meats, rice, and what fruits, spices, and bits there were to claim.

And there was plenty of dzan.

Barrel after barrel made its way down the aisle set up between the entrance to Black Lizard's sanctum and the outside, which basked in a dry night. The stinking sugar grog went down by the mouthful and came up by the gut, but by the hour more of it went down.

Amongst the den of thieves, cutthroats, and murderers, the lord of the evening leapt upon his long galley table and thrust his wine cup high. The raucous crowd of corsairs followed him along in bawdy songs full of plunder and repine. Battle-scarred women, fresh from raids north along the coasts, beat their naked breasts alongside men worked lean by the oars. The salt songs carried over the hours, repeated many times and in the many versions, some chorus dueling, until they were broken up by servants bringing in fresh trays of food and jugs of heady ale that tasted of lemons and thyme.

"Ho, my hearties," Black Lizard boomed above the din. "Ho-yo-ho-ho-ho!"

"Ho-yo-ho-ho-ho!" chorused the crowd, lifting their cups of wood, horn, and clay.

"Terrible singing," remarked Clermiel. His voice wavered, hard and heavy, as if he had lost breath. "I will find you, in the end."

"A night unlike any other," the lord of Stone Cove shouted over the merrymaking. "For many generations, we have rowed against foes both western and at home, clashed swords with hoplites as well as heroes, and through that bloodshed, we have endured! We have endured the tides! We are lords of the Goddess's grand seas!"

The cheer reverberated through the hall. The captains of Stone Cove toasted their lord-host's cry, their shoulders more scarred than others for the toil all had endured.

"It is even a rarer occasion to celebrate peace before spoil," he added, taking a sip of his cup to applause and laughter. Swallowing with dramatic flourish, he paced down the long table, his slippered feet careful around the wooden platters of hot food. "We must welcome with our open hearts and open arms Captain Cleona of Tip Town and her crews! Long has she been a fierce wind upon on the waves, dashing Gypian boats to the depths while pillaging Latians like a lady should!"

More than Cleona's table cheered for the famed queen, who rose and toasted the welcome. She gave Black Lizard an doff of her cup before promptly reassuming her seat. Casting her gaze askance at Ngala, on the other side of her host, they shared an intense stare.

"But more, my hearties, we are here to grow. Is that not what free folk do? Grow their families, their homes, their wealth? Do we not all share in that? Not a salt-man or salt-woman sits here tonight that is not drinking the finest dzan across the breadth of our mother's southern shores, but so does the lowest man outside, far-flung in the galley on some ship. No one sits lower than the rower, so why should he not sup on the finest?"

A reverent quiet held Black Lizard, who in turn held his crowd. "Tonight," he continued, "we shall give many the chance to sit in those dark holds in far-flung galleys. Tonight, we shall berth a new beast upon the waves! Tonight, of all nights, we shall give rise to a spirit of Stone Cove!"

The call of a new ship, a new crew, and a new captain stoked a larger resounding. For many, it was more than the ascension of another cutthroat, but also an opportunity to place themselves forward for the gamble of the salt spray, the violence of the raid, and all the red rewards that fed the lucky and ambitious. Many saw their way to the best life on the bench, then atop the deck, and in the dreams of the wildest, cagiest among them, at steering the oar of their own ship given to them on a night like this one.

"And yet again, it is a rare night, for its captain is beloved among us.

Child of Lord Patros Ngala, the lion of the deeps, tonight we crown Zaki as a lord in making! Will this captain come forth to claim their right?"

"I will."

Zaki appeared. Not to cheers, or gasps, or shock.

But to awe.

The lights of the room gleamed off the infinite strands of her silver dress, like comets fallen to the earth and trapped by the hand of an impossible weaver's divine hand. The paint on her flesh, purple and green and red in the design of a snarling lioness patterned like Ogbu wore when she terrorized the seas, clung to her face and chest like another layer of skin. These strands ran down her shoulders in shifting murals that revealed the swirling, crushing churn of the waves. Belted to her firm hips, a shining sword with a matching cross and pommel polished to a mirror shine caught the lamplight and brightened the room.

Upon her bald head rested a silver crown complete with plaits of spun gold, which fell in wire-waterfalls like locks of the finest blond.

Parting the sea of people, Zaki marched through the feast of eyes upon her. She stared into the eyes of everyone that dared to look, finding too many emotions to measure at once while her heartbeat like Nkuku's drum. Somewhere in the sea of faces she thought she saw him, his smiling jowls, but in the flash of an instant, or the flare of her skirt, she found herself before Black Lizard's table, one war-sandaled foot on the first step to his stage.

The hard silence broke at the corsair-lord's wild laughter. Black Lizard stood on his grand table.

"What is this?" he called to Zaki. He turned quickly to Cleona; his expression enchanted. "Where exactly were you raiding?"

"I come to claim what is my right," said Zaki, keeping her voice even. She dared not look at Ngala—not yet. "And I come to claim it as I am and will be."

Black Lizard made an odd sound. "How would you mean, Zaki?"

"All my life I have lived as someone else, Black Lizard, since as long as I can remember." Zaki raised her head in Ngala's direction. "Since before I took an oar. Before I was on any crew."

Nothing registered on his face. No ticks of emotion, no reaction, simply the cold face Ngala always wore. The men around him gripped at the hilts of their swords, their own expression filling with confused rage.

"I'm of a different spirit," Zaki said, hand drifting closer to her weapon. "One that finds herself—"

"Not for a moment," one of the captains from the galley shouted, a man she knew as Captain Ikemba of *The Egbe*. One of Black Lizard's senior captains, and of equal voice to her father, he drew his sword from his scabbard and laid it on the table. A clear challenge to violence, he glowered at Zaki. "No woman captains a ship in our navy, Black Lizard, as it was set down by your predecessor, and his predecessor before him in our salt law! And to think you would have...*him*...among us at this table? Ngala, how could you allow such an abhorrent thing to happen?"

"Of course, the goddess," said Clermiel. "Only she would let this madness reach such peaks."

"I'm no spawn of your tired loin, Ikemba, and better as one woman than each of them to the man," shouted Zaki, drawing her sword in reply. The blade scraped the chap of her scabbard, ringing like a clear bell. Leveling the point at him she rose to the dais, right in front of where Black Lizard stood on his table. Not daring to brandish her sword his way, she made her intent clear to see. "And I will dare one of you curs to come and take what is mine!"

"Ngala, tame your freak," another one of the captains shouted in her father's ear, his sword laid in front of the captain in warning.

The rest of the crowd had broken into chaos, some of them shouting down others who rose in Zaki's defense—many of them among *The Gamka*—while others took up their meat knives, turning over tables and shouting at each other.

Bristling through the entire scene, Cleona leapt upon the table, standing alongside Black Lizard who yelped in surprise at her sudden ascendance. A sword in each hand, she signaled her commanders while, at the same time, her raiders and rowers seated among Stone Cove's folk stood together, revealing the iron daggers hidden in their clothes. Organized, they rushed to Tip Town's queen, flipping two tables along the way and dragging them to make a wall between them and the other rabble.

"You rotten bastards!" Cleona screamed at the top of her lungs, kicking aside a plate of roasted fish and oozy fruit. "Only Stone Cove, full to the brim in its backward scallywags and grub-suckers, fall so low in your filth! No matter the deed, no matter the feat, you care only for your will and the way of your errant seed! You dare throw your daughter to their blades, Ngala? Death to your mongrel-dogs! Death to you!"

"Wait, wait, wait..." Black Lizard said, blocking her way with his waving arms. "Ngala, get your ass up here!"

"Don't you dare move," Ikemba shouted, his sword immediately at Ngala's throat. "This madness will not stand while I draw breath!"

In a blur of movement, Ngala grabbed Ikemba's iron and wrenched it out of his fellow captain's hand. He flipped the blade over in a deft trick of his wrist and impaled the original wielder throat-first on its point. Shoving the dying fool against the half dozen men behind them, Ngala vaulted the table in the space he had created, landing on his feet on the other side. He faced them, his own sword out in an instant.

"Stay your hands," he shouted, his voice booming above all the others. The room's chaos crashed into sudden, disheveled order, everyone lurching in the midst of the riot. "Your lord called you to stay your hands or be found in mutiny!"

The captains waved their blades, shouting and thrusting in the air at both Ngala and Black Lizard.

Stunned by her father's quick, cold killing, Zaki backed toward her aunt Cleona's line of the room when, from the back, came a fresh clatter of furniture, bodies, and blood. One man fell down, gashed open at the neck and shoulder. Tausi, his sword reddened by his work against a mutinous raider, strode forward with Nkuku at his side. The time-keeper, armed with a sword in one hand and one of his beaters in the other, led a troop of club-wielding rowers and fighters from the raiders. The sight of the blood, the dead man, incited the captain's loyal followers.

Shouting calls to commence mutiny, the storm of bloodshed gathered anew.

The bolt of Black Lizard's voice broken like thunder on the sea boomed in that storm. "Every soul hold fast or I shall take yours."

One of his wives, waiting on him behind his throne, passed him a sword from the many they carried. He swept forward armed to fight, lifting Zaki's sword-point away from the captains. Flowing past her and down to the stage, he stepped beside Ngala and placed a hand on his man's sword arm. "This will not stand in my hall! Down! Down, all of you, or I will make my vodunis curse your children this night!"

The fear of their lord, the power of his presence, cowed the entire room. Even Cleona halted.

His searing gaze a scoring wave, he softened his sneer when he finally settled on Zaki, letting down her sword with his own. A fine sweat on his neck and face, Black Lizard blinked a few times and stepped close enough to whisper. "I knew," he said. "You're braver than I, who will never be how they wished to be. But these are men, Zaki, and not the good kind. To keep them at bay, to keep their peace, you may have to lose. Your father and brother may have to lose."

Already past the point where his pronouncement mattered, she nodded. "I'll suffer at them first. Take from me if I live, Black Lizard, but only if I live."

"You look like her." The corsair-lord swallowed a sad sound at the back of his throat. "I loved your mama. She loved your daddy more," he said in his lowest, hoarsest whisper. "He knows I hate him for it. Yet I love him. And you."

Stepping back, Black Lizard marched in front of his warring captains, glaring at them until they lowered their swords. "Nothing will be given today besides the drink in your belly and the food you supped," he announced. He turned back to face Zaki, Ngala, and the crowd. "You all are kin by salt, sweat, and blood. Never raise your arms in my presence again, or I will take them from you, at the shoulder, one by one. Now go, but not the captains, and not their commands. Not you, Cleona, my lovely guest. And definitely not you three," he said to Zaki, Ngala, and Tausi, still seething over the man he had slain.

The audience of salt-kin, raiders, rowers, and anyone smart enough to know when to exit did, filing out quietly in an orderly fashion. Cleona descended from the table, standing guard with her command behind their belly-high wall, though she sent many of her crew home as well.

"We are made as we are made," called one of the rebel captains. "Our traditions reflect the Goddess's nature, not aspirations to it. There are natural ways of things, and the salts of Stone Cove followed that, Black Lizard."

"Cutthroats and thieves don't follow anything, Captain Kachiside, and our ways change as the tide chews a new edge for the land," Black

Lizard shot back. "Remember when we used to kill crewmen for simply laying together? Still have crews today, and nobody is unaware of who lays with whom."

Kachiside, a short but robust raider who had risen to fame on his deeds, raised his rounded chin. "So, what are we to do? Let women command boats and risk the real wealth of our future? Zaki is not even—"

"I dare you," Zaki growled from the center of the room.

"Times change," said Black Lizard. "The waves chew the edge of the land, shaping things with every brush."

"The nature of the wave does not change," Kachiside countered.

"Will you mutiny if I give her a boat?"

"We will," the rebel corsair said, the captains behind him silent but solid in their support. "We will stand for the rights of Man. We will stand for the salt laws of Stone Cove."

Black Lizard glared at them before a sedate disappointment flattened his face.

The captains of Stone Cove, not cowed by the warning, unsheathed their swords. Most of them did not remove their hateful focus from Zaki, who bared hatred back at them, shaking on the spot to withhold her attack.

At long last, they knew.

"What?" Clermiel asked. He sounded so far away now. "What did you know?"

A weird mix of relief, pride, and anxiety broke inside her, and for the first time, she knew what the world held for her. "When the laws of men have no honor, to hell with them and their salt."

The captains came across the table, screaming obscenities and curses while the edges of their sword raked the wood.

A flash beside Zaki whitened the room with the sound of a thousand rattling beads scattering like a rainstorm. Stunned by the light, the captains found themselves off balance and shocked. Agwe's strong shape appeared out of the haze left behind by his spell, red-robed and face glistening like it was masked in a rain of silver. Armed with an ornate sword, its narrow blade long and pointed, the golden hilt swept around his dark hand. Ensconced in a clean aura of illumination, he grinned fiercely at the shocked corsairs around them.

"Who in the hell is that?" someone cried from behind them.

"Good question," Agwe replied. The sorcerous voduni, graceful in his movement, stepped around Zaki to stand right in front of her, face to face. "Ready?"

"Every day," she replied.

Agwe kissed her hard on the lips, which she accepted like a serving of honey and cream.

"By the gods," Ngala cried.

Breaking off the kiss, Zaki parted from Agwe, putting a small amount of distance between them.

"Now you know," she said to Ngala. "Where do you stand, Father?"

A strange feeling of satisfaction mixed with sheer terror came the moment the question left her mouth. The man that defined her life as much as she fought to define it herself looked back in confusion, anger, and to her surprise, a tenderness she had never seen. His chest heaving under the pressure of her stare, the captains' expectations, and the sincere possibility they might all die anyway, his jaw firmed. Resolve conquered the emotions on his face.

Ngala turned and lifted his sword at the mutinous captains. "I stand to defend my child."

The room erupted in clashing iron and death.

CHAPTER 17
AIN'T NO GRAVE

S
he woke to the sounds of clashing blades, screams, and the sick, wet sound of slicing flesh. Broken from head to toe by the last beating the Ulmos had given her, Zaki breathed out of her gaping mouth and one crusted nostril, coughing herself awake when the ache of it set. Laying still, she knew the game now, and let whatever was coming come.

Nothing changed.

Content with that fact, the torture of it, she rested her battered face back on the warm, twitching floors, letting their pulse lull her to what sleep might find between those snatches of terror.

"Zaki," Tausi shouted.

She awoke again.

Mouth raw, she moved her mouth to repeat his name, or at least the thought of it. Somehow her legs started moving, and she posted on both knees. Willing the strength to put her hands beneath her, life flooded her in a piercing flow of pain. Her foot would not move on her order. Her ankle would turn, but she could not wiggle her toes.

They had broken her foot.

Holding herself through the feel of the pulped, shattered bones moving in her foot, Zaki fought to remain where she was, neither rising nor falling, until mustering for the next attempt. A long, low, wet ripping sound, following by a wetter sucking, came from over her shoulder.

"Zaki," Tausi shouted.

"This is it, this the room!" Agwe called. "Zaki, answer me!"

Blades sunk into tendon and snapped them apart. Zaki forced herself to rise slowly, to not be tricked by the devil's possible illusions. She had fallen unconscious on the upper level of a galley, far from where she thought they had left her broken corpse near the door leading into the depths of *The Tide's* inner chambers. Her focus trained on that door, she stumbled toward it when the iron bill of an ax burst through, spitting a jet of blood.

"Zaki," more voices called from the other side of the portal. More wedges and swords pierced and poked, rending the flesh.

She said nothing, standing there in complete shock. What if it was another one of his tricks?

"Move," a familiar voice shouted beyond the membranes of viscera. The volume of the rabble died as the keen point of Agwe's sword slipped through a new channel in the door. It sparked with a loud electric snap. Like pieces of paper pulled apart across a flat surface, the flesh-made doors slid open.

Clean to the hems of his silken, bright red robes, Agwe let his rapier lead him inside the galley, looking about until he found her. In an instant, he swept her up in his arms, faster than the breath she took. He carried her back at a quicker stride, his silver helm a beacon of hope.

"Tausi, her armor," he shouted. "Block the door!"

"I have it," Tausi said. "Hurry! Azinza has coaxed the last Ulmos asleep, but we can only hold the devil in his hole before he decides to come out. We need her on her feet."

"Of course," said Agwe brightly. "Aren't you ready to stand up, Zaki?"

Cradled in his arms, a sudden jolt of brightness coursed in Zaki's every nerve. She closed her eyes to harsh, numbing cold and opened them to tender, healing warmth. Agwe smirked down at her with his glittering silver face and golden eyes before he deposited her on both feet. The broken bones had been knit together like they had never fractured, never cracked.

She marched shoulder to shoulder with her lover. "Is it time?" she asked, desperate to know. "Did it work? Did I keep him?"

Tausi appeared before her. Streaked in the yellowish gore of dead shell-beasts, he carried the silver-spun dress, gathered in his hands like a net. He broke ahead when he saw Zaki walking toward him, and they ran into each other's arms where they held for long, long seconds.

"We have to go," he whispered into her cheek, his tears hot. "Put this on."

She stood there and started to put her feet into the gown's cavity when the moment caught her. Zaki searched between Agwe and Tausi, then to the door. Scores of corsairs, rowers and raiders, put their backs to her, torches held high to light the cavernous channel they traversed to reach her. Screwing her face in honest relief, Zaki worked her arms into the straps before her lover, the sorcerous voduni, turned her toward him.

"Here," he said, handing her his golden-hilted sword. The blade felt like a feather in her hand, long but balanced. He raised the silver helm off his head, turned it, and laid it atop hers.

Zaki brought the sword's flat, near the point, toward the crown. The iron touched the silver.

A small flash issued.

The bodice of her dress, now a cuirass shaped to accentuate a feminine form, gleamed mirror-bright against her restored ebon shoulders. A pair of iron-worked bracers appeared on her wrists to match the greaves strapped to her shins, the latter part of an integrated war-sandal. The silver locks hung down from Zaki's war crown, the mane of a war goddess brought to light.

"Where is Ngala?" she asked.

"No time," said Tausi, pulling her along toward *The Tide's* hall. "We have to reach him."

For all the celebration of her rescue, none of their folk in the channel cheered or greeted her as she was folded into their numbers. Instead, focused, they moved along as one herd toward the next point in their run. The mechanical, fluid determination of the raiders and rowers around her, some of them swarthy Latians from the Illus's Land Dogs, went at a practiced, steady pace, never dropping their shield wall to the side or lowering their swords.

Agwe shouldered his way to her side and marched most of the way through the hall with her before they entered another cavity, a room that seemed more a sitting area that previewed several chambers lit in stranger weir-light. A notion of familiarity brought her attention to one of those pod-like alcoves when the voduni finally spoke.

"We broke through about a day ago," he said. "The flotilla is mostly intact, and we only lost five more ships in the siege through the spiral-stairs that led up to this level. We slaughtered most of his Ulmos when Azinza discovered one of their sleeping chambers and learned the song that keeps the beasts at rest. After that, slaughtering them was easy until he appeared."

"How long have I been—" she dared to ask.

"It has been a day since we last saw each other," Agwe said. He did his best not to look at her as they marched to a central ramp that spiraled upward toward the unknown.

Small fires had been set on the downslope, and in the ruddy light, she watched as corsairs stabbed into the heads of dead Ulmos set on their sides, carapaces hacked apart to certify the monsters were done. Hustled to the right by the herd, she saw they headed up again.

"After the Ulmos fell, we battled him back to the chamber we're coming up on, Zaki," said Agwe, pointing ahead to make sure she looked. "He's hidden somewhere in there, waiting. And we waited for you."

"Right," she said, and it clicked—the answer brought something back to her mind, a set of facts and ideas she had buried deep beneath the devil's searching for his perverse satisfactions. This had been planned, and somewhere in the morass, all the details appeared in grim, gray certainty, tasteless compared to the bitter torture she had endured. A swelling rage in her breast set, and her choppy, running steps evened into a marching gait.

Zaki remembered the sword in her hand. She remembered the things the devil had said.

"Out of the way," she called to the backs of those in front of her. The herd halted on the order, disciplined to the word. Zaki took the lead in the approach to the yawning, open doorway that led to whatever hell the devil made at the top of his bizarre sanctum.

"Agwe, Tausi," she called at the threshold. The voduni and her brother rose at her sides. "Where is Azinza?"

"Still below," said Tausi, staring hard into the darkness ahead. He had brought a spear and shield.

Agwe brought nothing. "Leave her be. She found the acoustic chamber where the devil had sung his spell to wake his troops, and there she needs to be until the last Ulmo dies. We will slay the devil."

"Do you..." Zaki started to ask when his voice came from the abyss.

"Zaki?" Clermiel asked, long, slithering, and wet. "Is that you out there?"

She froze.

His laughter warbled, chilling her to the skin. "How wonderful! Everyone came to the party."

"And quite a feast we'll be having, dear," she shouted back at him. "Lobster bisque!"

Clermiel's laughter rose, hard and chittering like a thousand snapping claws. "Well," the devil said, "come on up. I would not keep the sharks waiting."

Agwe stepped forward and raised his hand. Whispering a slinking, sinking chant that ended with a click of his tongue, a radiant light engulfed his fingers in a bright, white flame. He went forward first, his silver scales a death mask against the illumination. Zaki followed next, then Tausi, who hid his head behind his shield to keep the magical blaze out of his eyes. They ascended the last rise and reached the top, where the voduni's torch threw back layers of the groaning void. The uppermost chamber flashed bright to match Agwe's spell, panes of translucent shell glowing ghostly against the midday sun beyond them. Narrow and conical, the shadows left few eaves for their prey to hide in.

Not that the devil wanted to hide.

Clermiel stood in the center of the light.

Shorter than Zaki expected, the pale creature before them still loomed. The devil's face, a gross collection of inhumane features beneath a set of purple coral horns, gazed into her with his opaque blue stare, like he had when she awoke at the beginning of their long, long journey. An instant delight of recognition wriggled a wormy smile from his lip-less mouth. Naked and slick, he spoke from a tight, fanged mouth.

"You have to pardon my state of dress," he said in his drowning voice. "You seemed to have finally caught me, plain to see."

"I could say likewise," Zaki responded.

The devil flicked his head to the side, considering her. "No. No, I'd say not." His fish-eyed gaze twitched toward Agwe. "You ran your confidence game, Sailor, but now you have to actually gamble. Are you ready to meet your end?"

"Ends are inevitable, and the world is still full the next day," Agwe said. "I'm surprised you honestly did not see this coming. I've dealt with far better than you, I'm afraid."

"Careful." Clermiel leaned his smooth body in Agwe's direction, his hand turning outward to reveal the sword he had wielded in front of Zaki before, a shining brand with its dragon-clawed quillions and polished pommel made of gold. "I am prepared."

"As we knew you would be." Zaki went forward. "Did you ever find what you were looking for? Or were you too busy playing to type? 'Certain to cruelty, quick to shine,' as they say about your kind. Could you not stand how I shined brighter than you?"

Agwe closed his hand and snuffed the silver light.

Clermiel chuckled before lunging forward.

Zaki raised her sword, catching the point on her flat. She battled back at him, trading blows to his blade before she stepped to the left and backed away. She came forward again, up at his face, then his knee, which he parried with ease.

Tausi entered from the right, aimed at the devil's belly with his spear. Turning his upper body on lithe hips without stepping from his spot, Clermiel dodged the thrust perfectly. He did not even move to address the second attack as Tausi stumbled by, more focused on grinning his needle-fanged grin at Zaki. Without offering a beat, she stabbed at the monster's head and throat, cutting for his forearm every time Clermiel spun his blade up to defend. The single edge of his sword seared sunlight as it came down, defeating whatever thought she had of a real attack.

Tausi tried a second time, sweeping the long blade of his iron spear for Clermiel's shins. The devil stepped over the iron like he had jumped rope, thrusting his sword forward to score on the captain of *The Ube's* shoulder, near the neck. Losing his footing, Tausi crashed against the wall and struggled to find his legs again.

"Was this the plan?" the devil asked as Zaki broke away, seeking to put distance between them. He followed, his sword leading limply in front of him. "Distract me with your meaningless pain while you all took everything from me? My army? My focus? Is that what you thought would happen?"

Recovered, Zaki sallied into an upward cut, then down for his elbow, before traversing away again when he negated her attempts. She struggled to keep space between them, ducking behind the natural columns of the chamber's structure that held up the translucent ceiling. Like an eel, he matched every duck and reversal she tried, throwing out lazy stabs that always seemed too close for how lazy they were.

"What happens when I kill you, Zaki?" Clermiel asked, everywhere at once. "What happens when I kill your brother? And everyone outside? What happens when I track down each and every person you love and make them mine?"

His left arm covered in blood, Tausi lumbered forward to harry at the devil, swiping first with the barbed end of his hide shield. He brought his spear forward in a thrust meant to skewer Clermiel in the heart, but he was passed by like a bull, though one smart enough this time to keep his head down. Avoiding the devil's quick cut to the nape of his neck, he reversed course and threw his spear low.

Zaki came up behind Clermiel as he smacked the weapon from the air and slashed the devil across the back. The wound leaked black-blue blood as he staggered forward a few steps before he righted, the gully she had made sealed together in a fading line.

"Do you think you proved some point?" he asked. "So, they stood with you. You stood for yourself. I'll still kill you."

She gave one note of laughter at that before she advanced. Moving him through the beats of her blade, neither probing for a strike nor offering any defense, she fought on a hunch.

He matched her, move for move, one second ahead of everything she did.

But he waited.

He always waited because he knew the attack she would make. He knew when Tausi would try again, this time closer with his sword and near enough that any mistake would be the final one.

Zaki led him through the simple back and forth, beating away his beats before she stepped back.

The devil didn't follow.

"Prideful, aren't you?" Zaki said, gathering her next wind. "You can't help but preen."

"Spare me," Clermiel retorted before he turned to meet Tausi.

Flinging his shield at Clermiel, Tausi charged with a heavy cut at the devil's head as the fiend ducked the frame. Zaki dodged out of the way of it and set herself forward as well, falling on his flank. Tausi ducked their foe's swipe and went for his legs as she did, forcing him to raise one leg up while parrying Zaki's blow.

Throwing himself forward, Tausi tackled Clermiel. The devil wrestled against him. He raised his sword to bring it down on Tausi's back.

Zaki struck off Clermiel's hand at the wrist.

Keening an inhuman sound, Clermiel wrapped his remaining arm around the bullish Tausi's torso, picked him up, and flung him to the side. Frenzied, the devil faced Zaki and took two lunging steps when another terrified, pained screech issued from his maw.

The entire conch shell, his sanctum made of his spirit and flesh, quaked as he dropped to a knee to cradle his leaking stump.

Zaki rushed forward and cut him across his smooth, fleshy brow. Stabbing and slicing as he flailed away from her, she chased Clermiel to the other side of the room. Faster than a shark, he fled from her nicking slices, his long tail scored and chewed by her iron. Splotches of blue-black blood dropped and ran where he crawled. Bleeding from many places, he finally tripped on his webbed feet, scrambling and squirming. Wounded stump to his chest, he held out a clawed hand in a gesture for mercy.

She stabbed through his palm. Screeching, he withdrew, curling into a ball at her feet that she raised her sword high against.

Zaki paused.

The devil trembled beneath her.

"You talked too much," she said. "You gods and devils are so certain about your infallibility because you think nobody truly has the will to stand against you. You wanted to break me, but I was always made for sterner stuff than you hatched from."

Clermiel shuddered, silent and defeated.

"That's why your age ended," Zaki said. "It ends again, Clermiel. Here and now."

Agwe appeared, a red spirit walking forward with silver hands. The devil screamed like a man when those fingers touched his pale marble flesh. Melted away in flakes of black fire, the essence of Clermiel whined, begged, whimpered before he was snuffed from eternity.

The corsairs at the door watched in complete silence to the battle's end, thinking well to themselves what worst thing they may have inflicted on their longtime enemy. Gathered back to his feet, Tausi was brought to where his sister stood over the charred husk. Agwe, robes soaked to the skin in his sweat, broke apart the leftover pieces with his human hands.

"We did it," Zaki said in absolute surprise. Her battle lust slipped away. She looked about the chamber where she stood, at the surrounding faces, searching, *needing,* for a specific one that should have been there.

"Where's Captain Ngala?" she asked to silence.

Squatted over the devil's remains, Agwe spoke first. "Our strategy worked, Zaki. We followed it to the letter and won."

"What does that have to do with my question?" she asked. "Where is Ngala?"

More than two dozen corsairs stood before her, faces cast to the floor. None of them met her searching gaze.

One failed to keep tears from speckling their eyes.

Not a single one of them made a sound.

Tausi laid a hand on her shoulder. "Zaki, I need you to listen."

"Tausi, where is he?"

His mouth opened to answer, but he stammered a noise first, trying to shape the words.

Agwe stepped in, removing Tausi's hand from her shoulder, moving her about to face him. "I need you to listen, Zaki. I need you to listen."

Without thinking, she grabbed his elbows, her grip hard on the joints. "Agwe, where is he?"

"He fell," said Agwe. "He's taken a blow to the head."

CHAPTER 18
WITH A WONDER AND WILD DESIRE

They sat somewhere south of Stone Cove, bathed in total sunlight without a cloud in the sky to worry their quiet.

A child's laughter broke atop the hoarse whisper of the waves. In the shifting shallows, a toddler ran in the water, his toothy smile wide and happy as his feet left dimples in the saturated sand. He ran down the shore, squealing as a pair of gulls took to the air, pumping their bright wings as they fled.

"I'll get him," Agwe said, rising from his seat to march in the toddler's direction. The shoulders of his robe pulled to the sides to expose his shoulders and chest, his sparkling face blazed bright as he jogged after the child. "Achebe! Achebe, slow down!"

Zaki watched in wonder as the spirit of the sea chased her nephew, startled at the ease she accepted that despite his divinity, he would be more humane to that baby than most mortals ever could be. Blinking through the salt of her tears, she measured herself a grin through the sorrow. She gripped the hand in her left, feeling the strong fingers squeeze back.

Ngala slouched in his chair, the left side of his body limp. A deep scar crossed his shaven pate, and the loss of so much more by one errant blow, slouched his features. The sting of fate, of a brave adventurer taken by a simple accident, caused more than enough heartbreak to share. Stationed on his right, Zaki sat in a small chair, dressed in a gown of cotton striped in sailcloth, patterned cream and white.

She had left behind her helms, her dresses, her swords, and her armor.

She had brought nothing but herself, as she had come into the world.

Alone.

The grip she held on her father's hand could not have been firmer, in her mind. Every breath threatened sobs and tears—the last things she wanted now when she had to accept something she desperately did not want to.

On the other side of Ngala sat Azinza, the sorceress-queen of Song City. Her eyes closed, she whispered low incantations, her thumb pressed hard into the bones of Ngala's old, sea-worn hand. Robed in bright white silks, her blue-green mane fluttered in the breeze. Tausi stood behind her, arms crossed as he kept watch of the horizon, lacking all emotion. Not breaking her silent recitation of the final spell she prepared, her immortal youth created a sense of calm in the sadness.

Zaki could not stop thinking about how old Ngala looked. They had kept him this long thanks to Azinza's healing magics and a few slight miracles she begged from the spirit of the sea. Both the former brine-singer and the embodied divinity had given Ngala as many days as he could to make peace, but the ravaging of a failing body demanded its due at last.

A failure completed there on that sunny beach.

Azinza opened her bright eyes and smiled. Tears came, but she held as she rose. Bending at the waist, she pressed her full lips onto Ngala's head, the drops from her eyes running on his dark umber head.

"Thank you for saving me, pirate," she whispered.

"Wasn't the plan," Ngala said. "Thank you. For being good to my children. To me."

Azinza nodded while dabbing away the tears. "You two have about five minutes," she said to Zaki and Tausi before she turned away, walking with purpose toward Agwe and her son playing in the surf. Sinking into helplessness when she realized there would be no running, Zaki readied as Tausi sat on the other side.

"This is not the life we expect," said Ngala, without warning or preamble. He reached out to his sides with both hands, which his children took without pause. "My father came here from a place that burnt to the ground. A place where we were slaves. Neither of you were born slaves, and for that alone, I was born blessed."

Zaki felt Ngala's grip tighten on her hands.

"I'm sorry I could not give you the love a mother could, but I tried what I knew. I'm sorry if any of it hurt you along the way. I never wanted to hurt you."

From there she did not remember much, lost in her sobs as she pressed her face into Ngala's old, strong hand. The waves crashed in her ears. Zaki snorted a wad of mucus at the back of her nose. Her hearing returned.

"You are a king where I was a chieftain, my son," Ngala said to Tausi, leaning to his left in the direction of the weeping warrior. "You care for our people in ways I only came to because of how much I cared for you and your sister. Never forget how much you care about these things in life. It was my honor to care so deeply for you."

"I only wanted to be brave," Tausi said, forming his words from despair. "I only wanted to make you happy."

Ngala tore his hands away from Zaki as Tausi buried his face in his father's shoulder. The old captain, the Old Bones, held his son for the last time. He whispered into his ear promises of how things righted themselves in time, how much more wonder the world had in store for him. Finally, per the custom of a corsair-lord, he sent his son away.

"Go make them happy," Ngala said in the clearest farewell to Tausi.

Watching as the broad-shouldered buccaneer marched, heaving and hissing to keep his wail within, Ngala struggled to scrub his face with the back of his hand, rasping loudly as he did so.

"Father," said Zaki.

"I have no need to say things to you," Ngala whispered, panting as he collapsed into his chair. "...that you won't find out for yourself on the morrow when you rule these beaches. You know these people, our people, as well as you know any other. What you do with them is yours, as it was mine, as it was Black Lizard's."

"As they will be for the one that comes after me," she recited, completing the final rite. From that breath onward, alongside or against any wish she had made in the bloody, burdensome past, Zaki now ruled Stone Cove as her queen.

None of it mattered or mattered more in the coming years than the last moment she had with Patros Ngala in the sea's quiet peace. The breakers ground against the hard-packed sand of the shore, leaving new ripples of salt and shell, the only law truly known within the land and the water. Like breaths of the breeze, they huddled together against the chill in the air, Zaki holding her father in her arms.

"I feel like the day I came home after your mother died." He shivered. "I'm sorry for everything I did. Every time I didn't see, or every time I failed to love you. I'm sorry for every order, or any time I asked you to keep yourself secret."

She shushed him. Zaki rocked them back and forth as she watched the Mirror sparkle. "Things were made clear. We don't need to waste time on that."

"All things?" he said, squeezing her hard limbs as tightly as he could.

Zaki kissed him on the top of his head, lips quivering as she nodded. "And I will take on more. I don't forget, Father. I won't forget Laconia."

"I'll be there," he said, now a ghost of a voice. "Me and old Nkuku. Me and your mother..."

"Even Aunt Cleona?"

He snickered. "Even her."

The sob that escaped Zaki rattled her ribcage as the salt in her tears blinded sight.

"I'll be ready to defend you, Zaki," Ngala said. "I'm ready now."

There was no time left for more goodbyes.

The cheek guards of her war crown were warm against her face, warm like the sea against *The Ulmo's* smooth gray sides. Striding forward across the deck, Zaki passed by her raiders as they buzzed about, their sparkling vests of leather and mail bright in the approaching dawn. Fitted with new iron spears forged in the foundries of every corsair hold across the Mirror, she searched as many faces as she could on her way to the bow. Those not busy with securing the last of their armaments before the time came saluted their queen when she moved among them, fists to their chests.

She offered what smiles she could before their destination loomed, drawing all of their attentions. Past the bow's sharp nose, the sea ran ahead, blue and bright before the horizon ended in land. For as far as the eye could see, the coast of Latia laid in the dim, the white walls of Laconia still pink by the great braziers guttering in the gentle wind.

There it lay, the city of their age-old enslavers. Everything Ngala had wanted for her and every corsair.

No horn sounded yet.

She was not surprised no watch on the coast had seen the fleet of two hundred ships behind her, their sails still rolled to the swing arms before the order came. The wonder of it, the closeness between her and an actual empire, prime among the many who had enslaved her ancestors in places like Tolivius and Brynthia, stoked a dangerous understanding that she was the first captain close enough to spit in their faces. No treasures were to be taken that day, no loot savaged from the terrified.

Only death. Red, red death so that the world understood.

She studied the high towers, burning silver and bright with a misting sheen. Situated in the middle of the metropolis, she surmised that was where the best hostages were to be found, if they reached it. Breathing deep through her nose, Zaki turned back for the stern. When focused, she could feel the oars cutting the waves behind the boat, born forth by rowers who let the crystal-shod handles row for themselves to save their strength.

She placed the myriad sensations to the side and kept on, her eye fixed on the helmsman guiding the sorcerous trireme. Garbed in a leather cuirass over his blue robes of silver and gold, a hide-and-mail cap framed Agwe's pierced face. Mouth set to a grim line, the spirit controlled the steering oar with one hand, the other hooked to his sword belt by his thumb.

"How did you do that?" she asked, trying not to sound breath-taken by his beauty.

"Illusions are small things, my captain," Agwe said. "Imagine how the Latians will feel."

"How much time do we have?"

"Until the sun rises. And then they will know."

"They will know," Zaki said in a solid, sincere declaration. "Mani!"

From the ranks of the raiders came her commander. The scars of where an Ulmo had grabbed him in a mortal struggle marked one of his arms.

He raised his fist to his chest. "My queen."

"Sound of the first horn and ready the fleet," Zaki ordered, holding the throat of her sword's scabbard where it hung at her belt. "Then get your lions ready. We will not tarry here or there for long."

"Aye, my queen," said Mani, lowering his fist. Going for the signal horn at his belt, he hesitated before giving Agwe a cautionary glance.

"If they can't see us, I won't let them hear us," said the spirit. "But those behind us will."

Nodding his thanks, the commander put his lips to the horn and blew a loud, long note, followed by two short, stuttered blasts. Hundreds of horns, almost too many to hear, answered in a cacophony that startled Zaki even though she had heard it dozens of times on the journey west around Juut's broad breast, then northward to where the western kingdom of Latia based their great port of Laconia.

A nerve center for the entire continent's flesh trade.

When the noise died, she dismissed Mani with a nod and a salute. Zaki breathed deep of the sea air and checked to the east again. Light crested where the night had laid claim, swelling at the edge.

Any moment now.

"I'll take the oar while you go get the rowers on the benches," she said. "Tell Ibekwe to be ready to go full beat if—"

"I'll have him ready for a full beat, Captain," said Agwe kindly as he moved for the square opening of the hold, down to where the time-keeper and his crew waited for a charge they had dreamed their entire lives of making. "Take the time while we have it, Zaki."

Her supernatural lover descended the steps into the blue-glow dark below, off to find *The Ulmo's* heart before...

She checked to make sure she was not in the devil's dream. Pinching her thigh, biting the inside of her cheek, the pain stole her focus from her. The trireme's weird, bleeding sense flooded in, stacking upon her physical sense with notions of feeling that were not human, nor thinking, but conscious of themselves. The current carried them closer to the shore, beyond the main fortress where the third wave planned to break upon when signaled, tasked to burning the naval ships. Tausi's second wave would keep north to the smaller, richer coastal towns while she made the main strike with her forces, the first wave, driving into the heart of the harbor. Thanks to her love's magic, the Latians would see them too late to respond.

And yet she wondered if she remained in the illusion.

The devil had not spoken for many, many months. Not since she watched him burn.

Her thigh smarting, her mouth tasting of red and iron, Zaki still wondered until she felt the steering oar come alive in her hand, alive in her mind.

Holding fast, Zaki looked past the stern to the fleet arrayed behind her.

Their sails were not up yet, but she wished deeply that she would be able to see them at least one more time in the morning. Many had come: captains who had given up their flags, bringing only their sails, their swords, and souls to bear. The colors, ranging from the darkest blues to bright, shimmering yellows and greens, would light the sea aflame when the call arrived. Most Latians had heard of the treacherous corsairs to the south, but few knew them.

Sighting *The Ube* not far from her, the outline of her brother's boat in the gloom heartened her.

"They will know," she repeated.

Hundreds of hands beneath her feet laid palms to the oars on the banks, a revelation in contact that she hoped added one more smidgen of truth that she was still awake. Aware of the simmering vibration on their benches, the tightening of the bodies in anticipation of the call, the way they all braced their feet against the boards, Zaki took the steering oar in both hands like she had done a thousand times. She braced her feet apart like she once saw Ngala do before he sailed them into the reefs of Shallow Bay. Trying hard to put his memory to the side, the want of him there, she blinked through mournful tears, set her shoulders, and breathed one more time to settle her thoughts into order.

Agwe rose from the hold, nodding to her to confirm the timekeeper's acceptance. One hand to the rapier on his belt, he came to stand on the other side of the steerage, at her right. "They're running silent until the assault starts, then they'll sing," he said before he searched the dawn. "And we have a minute."

Zaki followed the direction of his eyes. As Agwe said, the sun's red edge broke over the earth, casting sheets of light on the ocean. Entranced by the cadence of wind and water, she tried to etch its beauty in her mind's eye. "Mani! Sound for the third wave, then the first, then the second. Raise sails."

Her commander drew the horn from his belt again.

A wicked smile crossed her face. Certain that she was awake, alive, Zaki laughed high on the ocean wind. Agwe, without wait or order, began to sing long, low words, the language too far away to be placed beyond the fact the crew knew, somewhere in them, they had heard it before.

The breeze, once a warm murmur in the ear, growled in thundering strength.

The horn blew, then a hundred horns, then two hundred horns, a chaos of orders given and accepted.

The sun rose, banishing the distant stars by its unyielding light.

The corsair raiders of *The Ulmo* raised her bright blue sail, which caught in the forceful gale. Pulled forward by the force of the unnatural wind, the echoing laughter of the Silver Queen joined many others when they saw how quickly they would reach land and glory, waking Latia to a sacking none forgot after it ended.

THE END

ACKNOWLEDGMENTS

Nothing I do is possible without the love and support of my wife Margo, my son Ben, my parents, and so many more. This series wouldn't have happened without John Hartness, Melissa McArthur, and Erin Penn at Falstaff Books believing in it. I must acknowledge Aaron Toliver, Jose Yamil Camacho, Linden Shroyer, Eden Royce, Michelle Drew, Darryl Mansel of Poprika, Les Boyd of NerdTalk and the lands he allowed me to cover in shadow, Nathanael Fosaen, and Samuel Montgomery-Blinn for holding me up through many down-years.

Finally, I want to thank all of the authors, artists, researchers, and people I was able to read about, learn from, or interview in the process of creating these stories. This saga of piracy, empire, love, family, identity, freedom, and the pursuit of them all is the journey of many, not just Ngala, Tausi, or Zaki's. We are all seeking to discover our quiet places.

Safe journey in finding yours.

ABOUT THE AUTHOR

Risen from the hills of North Carolina, Jay Requard is an award-winning author of Epic Fantasy and Sword & Sorcery living in New York City. When not pursuing his interests in hiking, fencing, and reading every-thing he can make time for, he enjoys cooking, homebrew, and melodic death metal. His family included a mystical shadow cat named Mona Underfoot.

FRIENDS OF FALSTAFF

Thank You to All our Falstaff Books Patrons, who get extra digital content each month! To be featured here and see what other great rewards we offer, go to www.patreon.com/falstaffbooks.

PATRONS

Dino Hicks
John Hooks
John Kilgallon
Larissa Lichty
Travis & Casey Schilling
Staci-Leigh Santore
Sheryl R. Hayes
Scott Norris
Samuel Montgomery-Blinn
Junkle

www.ingramcontent.com/pod-product-compliance
Lightning Source LLC
Chambersburg PA
CBHW050613110726
47899CB00001B/90